LIKE HELL...

"Lilith!" A hot jolt of adrenaline and I was lunging for the doorway, fingers flicking open the device in my hand.

A hissing sound in the other lab and something crashing, splashing. A sob, scrambling sounds. I hissed, "Lilith," ducking my head into the opening for a glimpse.

She was crawling through a tangle of tubes, lucite shards, and mercifully vague wet shapes beneath a blasted gap in one rack. Behind her, spilling through the corridor doorway, mech-men rolled toward us, the one in front shooting a quick burst of laser fire to shatter another cylinder and spray its contents over Lilith's frantic escape.

"Ruth!" She scuttled behind another row and scrambled toward me. "They showed up and all of a sudden went crazy! They're—"

Another hissing needle of blue-white light and crash of equipment. A mechanical voice blared, "Stop at once. Remain motionless."

"Like hell!" I lunged toward the doorway, grabbed Lilith's arm and dragged her back under the cover of the last rack . . .

DOUBLE BLIND

Continuing the adventures of
Wild Card Run and Win, Lose, Draw

Ace Books by Sara Stamey

WILD CARD RUN
WIN, LOSE, DRAW
DOUBLE BLIND

DOUBLE BLIND

SARA STAMEY

ACE BOOKS, NEW YORK

This book is an Ace original edition,
and has never been previously published.

DOUBLE BLIND

An Ace Book / published by arrangement with
the author

PRINTING HISTORY
Ace edition / May 1990

ISBN: 0-441-16055-7

Ace Books are published by The Berkley Publishing Group,
200 Madison Avenue, New York, New York 10016.
The name "ACE" and the "A" logo
are trademarks belonging to Charter Communications, Inc.

PRINTED IN THE UNITED STATES OF AMERICA

10 9 8 7 6 5 4 3 2 1

FOR OUR FRIENDS
BENEATH THE WAVES

With thanks to Jim for believing in dreams; friends and family for being there; Meredith Cary and R. D. Brown for feedback; and Rob Quigley, PhD at Western Washington University, for his physics answers, which I have freely perverted to my own ends.

"And with double hearts do they speak. . . ."
                                        —*Psalms*

prologue

The sea was densely salt and heavy with invisible life. Its engulfing waters pulsed to a tepid rhythm through volcanic rock lattice. The mineral-rich resonance chambers and concentrated electrolytes made the water world a giant, primitive receiver circling slowly through space.

Beneath the surface, sluggish current sparked bioluminescent blue stars through a submerged black maze, passages and blind branches twisting, crossing, doubling back in the spiraled convolutions of a monstrous ear to finally spill into a central cavern awash with oscillations. The echo chamber boomed with soundless voices, amplifying silent sendings to far reaches of the sea. The listeners, the voicers gathered inside. Shapes of distant ponderous movement were doubled and redoubled as vibrations meshed to an encompassing hum, pulsed outward through rock and sea—

And shattered against a sudden, alien resonance. The chaotic, cracking lance of energy came from nowhere, ripping the ordered hum into dissonance. Then it was gone.

The sea clashed with discordant ripples. Pain. Disorientation. Perplexity. Outrage.

Disbelief.

Slow ebb and surge dissolved the shock waves, swallowed and erased what could never have been—the unPlanned. Sea soundings stretched tenuous fingers, echoing strengthened, and the world pulsed again to its changeless hum.

one

There was a painful booming in my ears. I tongued down the volume and smacked the side of my helmet with my free hand. A crackle of static, and the radio evened out to a smooth hum.

"Pavlo? You about ready to get this show on the road?"

"Such eagerness to meet defeat! If you would be so eager to—" Another crackle of static swallowed the rest.

"You're breaking up." I smacked the helmet again and swung around on my hook, peering down.

The multilayered Matrix of shimmering cable runs wove the dimness high over a stark, crater-pocked black surface. Doubled and redoubled shadows from the tall, luminous junction posts melted into the faint gloom cast by the oversized blue sun brooding at Casino's curved horizon, playing hell with perspective.

I finally spotted him in the shadows down by the airlock, a foreshortened figure in silver-glinting pressure mesh. He gestured toward his helmet and my radio crackled, "—and so missing the sweet cries of your anguish as you lose."

I chuckled, almost seeing his swarthy face grinning its challenge. "Funny little thing my fathers always said, Pavlo. Pride goeth before a fall."

"It is you who will have falling, my friend! Then perhaps you can no longer deny my superior performance, my powerful skill, my—"

"Big mouth?"

"—great endurance which you shall truly witness soon, I promise you. The true gaming is an art, like making love to so beautiful a woman when one triumphs, you will see—"

I tongued the mike and gave him a noisy raspberry. Gdärskovites were expected to boast, but if he got going on his sexual prowess, there was never going to be a game. "Stalling, Pavlo?"

There was an offended-sounding crackle. Then static, and "—impossible Poindrans, no lust for true living." More static. "—should be waiting for radio clearance, as Rules say?"

I waved him impatiently up. "Come on, it's probably just another sunspot cycle kicking up interference. Radios are no big deal, anyway, cybers are just nursemaiding us overtime.''

The dim little figure made a graphic shrug and flexed its knees, bounding up through the lazy gravity. ''—why you must always fight the easy Way our guardians have made to keep us—'' The radio cut out again. He glided gracefully, the hook clamped over the right wrist of his suit catching a cable and riding it up as the wheels engaged. He unclamped, springing out and over the cable to sail arched for the next. He caught it effortlessly with his hook and pirouetted to toss me a mocking salute as it bore him up toward his starting post.

I grinned, reluctantly admiring his moves. He'd been practicing while I was away on that last CI assignment. But damn it, I'd designed the game, and this time I was going to win.

Swinging around to my post, I perched on the starting blocks and traced the far reaches of the grid. Cables sliced the gloom, dimly radiating the low current they carried between the subdued glow of the supporting posts with their pulsing blue or red junction switches. The three lighted gold ''apples'' dangled temptingly from their cables, with a random scatter of lower-point coloreds above and below. Beyond the Matrix, dwarfing it, black space swept its depths of unblinking stars.

For all I knew, I'd been the first human to see them this way. I was still faintly surprised our great guardian cybers had allowed my new gamesite on the exposed surface of the barren planetoid, outside the safe womb of the interior caverns. Life inside had been one long, unchanging, pointless game for more generations than mere humans could count. One long today, with no past or future. But then the cybers had finally let me crack the sealed door in Casino's shell of fake light, fake air, and fake gravity, let me step onto the surface and expose myself in only a thin skin of pressure-mesh to the stars and the seething sun.

Stuck at the frozen horizon, it flared simmering cobalt as I glanced over my shoulder, a hovering presence always waiting with a tomorrow that never came clutched in its grip.

''My friend, can it be *you* are now feeling the cold feet?'' The radio buzzed and cut out into static again as Pavlo waved from his starting post across the Matrix. My pulse revved into eager jitters, the low hiss of the air feed echoing faster in my ears. I waved back twice, starting the count. Three, two, one—

And the Matrix was a maze of witch-fire, a blur of glinting silver, red, and blue. Launching into it, I shot off two quick bursts from the low-amplitude laser sealed to the left wrist of my suit.

My first shot hit the closest switch-disc, changing its blue to red and reversing polarity in the cable before me. I went down instead of the easy up to the nearest gold, taking a chance with the distance on a second shot for the switch to the cable Pavlo was riding. I was falling, picking up momentum, swinging for the middle gold between us, when I heard the radio crackle:

"The demon you!"

We raced for the center gold. I rode up and flung myself—almost too slow, damn the weak gravity—floating down to grab it just before his outstretched hand. The gold apple flared and lit up inside with a green tally, my color, and was dropping behind me as I flipped up and over Pavlo and headed into his territory for the second gold. I could count on him to scorn the easy score on my open gold to chase me for his.

The radio was only static again, but I could see him grinning, calling something as he took a quick double flip, swung, and got off an unbelievable shot to reverse my cable, then took a spring past me.

"Damn!" I wrenched around, thrown off rhythm by the reversal of my clamp's wheels taking me backward. I got the cable repolarized, but I'd lost time. Swinging my legs against the thin, poison stuff that passed for the planetoid's air, I got enough momentum to sprawl awkwardly to another cable I could use to fall and speed up. Springing to a third cable, I managed to reverse his and catch up as he corrected.

Neck and neck now, we climbed to get a straight fall onto the apple.

Silvery cables blurred, whipping past. Breath rasped in my helmet, pulse pounding. A glimpse of Pavlo's face past the gleaming reflection of stars, startled as I passed him going down, tucking and falling as fast as I could past two cables, recklessly just catching a third to swing over and angle off.

A crackle from the radio and then silence except for the quick shush of the air feed. Wild exultation rose through me, blood racing as it all clicked into that rare, perfect interlocking of mind and body. Thrust, swing, drop, grab. Swing and launch, flying in the laughing dance of the game. Pavlo flinging after me, catching up, but I was almost there. Dark, jagged landscape and darker, star-tracked expanse of space whirled around me as I flipped around the last cable and dropped toward the gold.

Arrowing my body for a streamlined fall, I picked up speed, the Matrix dance humming in my ears. Reflexes attuned, like the rush of the *timbra* hunter trance I'd learned on another world. That extra sense of—

Alarm. Jittering suddenly along my nerves, buzzing in my ears. Something. A darker wrinkle in dim shadow. Something out of place.

Unthinking reflex wrenched me around, tumbling me in an awkward spin to miss the cable where the beckoning gold apple gleamed. The Matrix whirled crazily around me as I jerked upside-down, slowly falling, seeing Pavlo whip from a cable and launch toward the apple. He was laughing in silenced triumph behind the faceplate. I dropped slowly, confused, the electric buzz of warning still insistent.

Then I saw it. A black line threading shadow from the post junction of the apple's cable to an alien, bulky something on the ground. "Pavlo, no! Stop!"

The radio was gone, not even static. He arched out, dropping for the cable.

I twisted frantically as my arm flashed up in a last desperate effort to shoot a blinding azure beam directly onto his faceplate, the game's most blatant cheating. "Stop, Pavlo!"

I was falling faster now. I caught a last glimpse of his face. Surprised outrage. Then the helmet shook back and forth and his hook caught the cable.

A silent crackle of sparks in the dimness. The silver-suited figure jolted, writhing on the live cable. He was flung, limbs twitching in a grotesque dance as he slowly cartwheeled down. A blur of glowing silver and blue, jagged shapes whirling, cratered black rock tumbling up too fast at me. Pain exploded.

Darkness. A buzzing hum. Someone's moans echoed in my ears.

I couldn't move, trapped in cold blackness. They'd caught me again, the spooks, the incorporeals, sealing me into the blind uncharted spaces inside my skull. In the dark fusion of their energy matrix, the icy bright pinpoints hovered over me like murderous stars. Flaring sparks holding pain, promising impossible revelations. Like the cybers' knowledge, too dangerous for the mere humans they kept swaddled safe from their bright, glittering taboos. But I could reach out and grasp the icy fire of the incorporeals—hungry soul-hunters, invading the cyber network—I could let them take me into their limitless depths. Their silent whispers were a siren song, calling me to leave my clumsy body, exchange empty darkness and death for the all-consuming forever of their one in all. . . .

But there was that damn moaning again, someone stubbornly shaking her head. The bright pinpricks of the incorporeals swam before me, melting into a buzzing fury as the silver grid of their energy matrix whirled to burn me from the inside out—

"No!" I blinked, focusing. It was only the Matrix game. And past the glittering cables, only distant stars.

I blinked again, swore, tried to move. The insistent buzz echoed in my ears as I groped and sickening pain lanced my left arm. I realized I was wearing a helmet and concentrated on not throwing up in it. Finally I heaved myself to a sitting position, head throbbing, arm screaming signals I tried to ignore.

"Bloody, blasted . . ." I weakly smacked the side of my helmet, but the static didn't go away. I frowned again, dizzy, squinting around me. Pockmarked black rock and dust. Tall luminous poles. And a black wire dropping from the nearest junction to a squat metal box that shouldn't have been there, its glowing readout registering high voltage.

The pieces jolted into place. "Pavlo!"

Only static. I scrambled to my feet, biting back a surge of red as my arm swung limply, flailing as my momentum lurched me off-balance in a slow-motion glide through hovering dust. I clutched my arm, managed to land in a clumsy shuffle.

"Pavlo." He was lying face down, crumpled over sharp rocks. Somewhere a voice cursed monotonously about cybers and the catch field that hadn't worked. I eased him over. Swarthy face, contorted into a stranger's. A fixed, dark stare drilled through the stressplex at me, faintly accusing. I looked down at the rips in the singed suit, swallowed, and looked away.

Breath rasped short and shallow in my ears. I was choking, trapped in my suit, helmet buzzing and ringing as the air feed hissed and I fought to drag enough into my lungs. Closing my eyes, I groped for the ragged edges of control. There had to be a chance for Pavlo.

Deep breaths, and I found the silent chant the hunters of Sethar had taught me. Slow breaths, smooth cycling of air and blood. Balance.

The fire in my arm burned somewhere far away as I crouched to hoist Pavlo over my shoulder. I jerked upright and drifted, landed lurching, the ground refusing to cooperate with my feet. They groped for an awkward shuffle, my arm swinging loose and grinding, Pavlo's bulk shifting weight oddly in the low gravity. My heart pumped the chant faster, step following stumble to the distant light burning at the airlock. Rage burned brightest, drawing me on.

"Worthless scrap-heaps! What did you do with him? Damn it, you didn't even try!"

The padded gray walls of the corridor muffled my shouts. Faint strains of soothing mood music swelled in volume. A low hiss from overhead, and I ducked a spray of sedative mist.

"Turn that music off!" I jerked against the grip clamped around my right wrist, the other arm throbbing angrily in its splint as I planted my feet. I glared at the vaguely human-shaped conglomeration of metal extensors, joints, and sensors that still dragged me skidding down the hall. "All I want is an answer for a change. What happened to the game's catch field?"

The sensors on the mechman's "face" flashed a quick sequence as it stopped abruptly and a tinny voice declaimed, "Your welfare will best be served by prompt treatment of your injuries."

I wrenched my arm free, grabbing the thing by what passed as a neck and shaking it. "Answer me, you—"

"Stress has temporarily unbalanced your judgment, Kurtis: P385XL47:Ruth." The monotone voice came unperturbed from its torso speaker as its extensors pried my hand loose and pushed me gently but irresistibly back by the shoulders. "Anger will only exacerbate the symptoms. All possible steps for human well-being have been pursued. We regret that intervention was too late to preserve essential functions of Borodi:G229DN65:Pavlo's brain-wave configuration. The irregular licensing of the hazardous Matrix game has been investigated. We conclude such game parameters violate the benevolence directives of the Plan. All games will be confined to the safe interior areas of Casino."

"Now just a bloody damn—"

"Sensors indicate extreme stress configuration. Your reactions are rated inconsistent with injury extent and accidental termination of acquaintance."

"Acciden—" I bit it back. If the cybers feeding the mechman its data hadn't realized the "accident" was murder, I wouldn't fill them in. But they'd soon add things up, if somebody wasn't smart enough to cover up the evidence that could get me into as much trouble as whoever had electrocuted Pavlo. There weren't too many choices for that someone smart enough to get over on the cybers. And I didn't like any of those choices.

"You will now close your eyes and take three deep breaths. Listen to the music. Let us heal you."

"Healing!" Cold terror grabbed me. "No way." Not the Steps of Healing, erasing my "disturbed" memories, erasing me. "My violation points are way down. You can't—"

There was another hiss, mist swirling overhead as a soft something dropped to wrap me in an invisible web.

"Let me go! I'm fine, I'm perfectly adjusted." I struggled against the soft clutching I couldn't see, but there was nothing to get a hold on to fight. The energy web tightened over me, oozing down into every angle. My legs still free, I flung myself at the mechman medic, wincing as my arm stayed caught behind me. I kicked for the smug alloy face.

"Resistance will only hurt you." The mech swung around again, rolling down the corridor as I floated helplessly along in the buoyant force field. I could still turn my head slightly, which I regretted as we rounded a curve and passed a man in a unisuit ripped down one arm, sitting motionless on a stool and staring blankly through me. The cold fear coalesced into a frozen lump in my gut. Behind the man was a round hatch set into the wall, and beside it a console outlet, colored indicators blinking, a soft pink readout glowing, *Healing chamber prepared. Welcome*.

My eyes glazed, mesmerized by the readout, eyelids drooping. I realized the sedative was getting to me and shook my head as best I could. "What did *he* do? Blaspheme the sacred Founders?" I fought a tendency to slur the words.

The mech's face swiveled one-eighty to face back at me as we continued down the corridor. "Warning: speech violation."

"Isn't that moot at this point?" I took a deep breath. "So what about that guy?"

"He was apprehended in a third burglary attempt and rated incorrigibly deviant. He will be Healed." So they hadn't caught the killer who'd sabotaged my game. Just nabbed another poor sucker who couldn't live by the Rules.

The icy lump inside me swelled as the mech stopped in front of another round hatch with its pink readout glowing, *IDisc*?

I swallowed as the invisible web lowered me onto a stool to face the console. "Wait, this is a mistake. You can't—"

"The restraining field will allow you to use your right arm." The mechman rolled smoothly around to remove the splint the mechs at the game's airlock had applied, and the web held the injured left arm immobile. "Healing will proceed with considerably less trauma if you cooperate. Please insert your IDisc and provide requested data."

"Wait—"

It was already gone around the corridor's padded curve. There was another hiss overhead, and I held my breath as long as I could, but still had to inhale some of the sedative. I blinked and focused on the pink readout, banishing a mixed fog of lassitude and panic. With my good hand, I reached to my necklace where I kept my IDisc. Instead of pulling it free, I deactivated the clingtab of the thin, uninscribed disc attached to it. My wild card—a contraplan, blank data disc.

I hastily inserted it into the console slot, holding my breath again. The readout went blank, then reconfigured: *Waiting*.

I blew out a shaky breath, mind spinning over possible data loop approaches, then settling on an old standby. I was no match for the cybers' complexities, but the wild card disc gave me some limited access to the lower-coded data loops. I whispered, "Maintenance procedures, simulated voice mode."

Blue and red lights danced over the indicators, then held steady. "Proceed." The toneless voice from the little console speaker sounded alarmingly loud.

"Lower volume!" I hissed, jerking my face around as far as I could and straining my eyes back and forth. No mechs. "Data retrieval, subject Kurtis:P385XL47:Ruth, currently activated subfile, injury and Healing."

"Retrieved." The *Waiting* readout blinked on again.

"Uh . . . summarize events of injury."

"Subject participating in Matrix game competition, fell from estimated height of thirty meters. Safety force field defective. Subject suffered injury, initial diagnosis simple fracture, left humerus."

"Diagnosis on . . ." Damn, I couldn't remember Pavlo's code. "Uh . . . diagnosis, subject's game opponent?"

"Multiple lacerations and contusions. Massive internal hemorrhage, fatal."

No burns? I closed my eyes, unwillingly recalling the singed suit, his staring eyes. I took another deep breath. "Cause of accident?"

"Data insufficient."

I started to lean closer, but the web prevented me. "Speculate. Most probable cause."

The colorless voice rattled off, "Subject and opponent highly competitive personality profiles. Game review indicates unacceptable hazards. Aggressive play could have caused collision and fall. Catch field defective."

My palm was sweating, but I couldn't move it close enough to wipe it on my suit. Craning again over my shoulders, I could see only the empty curves of corridor. I stared back at the patient *Waiting* readout. Something was definitely rotten in the cyber loops—data on the "accident" somehow missing. And I sure as hell wouldn't find out what was going on if they slipped me into that hatch for Healing.

I gnawed my lip, trying to ignore a sinking chill. My arm throbbed painfully and my head felt thick, drowsy. But I had to think. My violation points hadn't even been close to the limit. I cleared my throat. "Reference relevant subject psychological profile."

Indicators reconfigured. "Subject profile indicates abnormally inquisitive personality, conflict tendency, failure to conform, multiple minor Rule infractions and—"

"Stop." I started to shake my head in the clinging web, was stopped by the soft *shhh* overhead. Another spray of sedative fell cool over me. "No . . . Report only data, uh, relevant to current injury." My mouth had trouble forming the words. I just wanted to close my eyes and sleep.

"Subject suffering extreme stress reaction and rage/denial, deviating significantly from situational normal curve. Data extrapolation offers reconcilable configuration, accuracy point seven three two. Patient by record attaches strongly in sexual pairing. Hypothesis: deceased Borodi:R229DN65:Pavlo was patient's sexual partner. Conclusion: patient's extreme reactions lie within acceptable limits for her atypical personality profile. Incidental correlative: short-term negative effects outweighed by long-term benefits of patient recovery from protracted grief phase—referent homeworld renewal visit; object name Jason—and patient once more able to form sexual bonding. Immediate sympathy for grief advisable adjunct to healing process."

"But that's—" I bit it back. That didn't jibe, either. Did it? Why were the cybers bothering with that psycho bilge if they were planning to Heal me anyway? But I was too tired, I couldn't make sense of it, didn't really care. Just wanted to breathe in the cool, sleepy mist and float away on it. . . .

"No." I couldn't keep my eyes open. "Can't take for Steps of Healing. Woan go."

"Confirmed. Higher CI clearance required for subject Healing. Denied."

"What?" My eyelids shot open with a jolt. Central Interlock, of course. The cyber directives. They didn't want me Healed—not while my "abnormal inquisitiveness" was still useful to them. There was just some crazy mixup. Relief washed through me, leaving me even more lightheaded. But the cybers didn't make mistakes. I blinked and stared at the pink *Waiting* readout fading in and out of focus.

My head hurt. "Access subject CI file."

"Data classified. Higher clearance required."

Damn. Couldn't think through the drowsy fog. "Trace . . . trace recent data query routes."

"Checking." Lights danced blurrily. "Routes traced. Recent subject CI subfile activation. Data access denied."

"Righ, right . . . Peripheral data consultations . . . relative to activation?"

More dancing lights. Pretty. I wanted to dance with them.

"Tracers indicate CI subfile query routes, target taboo concepts: History. War. Council of Founders. Prohibited technology, subset bioforming, incorporeals, cyborgs, attempted cloning. . . ."

The fog and the dancing lights swirled around me, swallowing the toneless voice. I frowned, clinging to that last odd word like a lifeline, slowly pulling myself up through the mist.

". . . from CI peripheral loops. Anomalous long-range signal reception, source classified."

"Wha? Wha's that? Damn, wha's that mean?" I reached with my free hand for the blurred console indicators.

They suddenly flashed bright red, winking. "Alert." The voice had a sharper intonation now. "Improper procedure. Alert. Improper procedure."

Alarm jolted me again into momentary clarity. "Sacred bloody Founders . . ." My hand groped frantically over the console, found the disc eject, and pressed it. Hastily reactivating its clingtab and securing it behind my ear, I snatched loose my IDisc and thrust it into the console slot.

The alert flasher died, and the pink readout activated fuzzy letters, *Healing chamber prepared. Welcome.* The round hatch swung open. Warm, rosy light spilled out from a tubular chamber lined with some sort of puffy pink material, light glowing behind it.

"Hey, wait, I thought—"

"Relax, Ruth. Come inside, and let us heal your injury." The voice came from the chamber—a warm, gentle, woman's voice. The force field webbing me lifted slowly, turning me horizontal and drifting me toward the portal.

"No, wait! Not cleared for Steps of Healing." I struggled futilely in the web, unable to move my arm at all now.

Another hiss of sedative mist lapped over me, sparkling with pink lights, settling cool and heavy in my lungs. "No need for fear, Ruth." The voice was calm, soothing. "We only want to help you. You mustn't resist, or you'll hurt yourself. Let us heal your arm."

"Wait!" I was inside the puffy pink tunnel now, light ebbing and surging over me, the hatch sealing. "Just arm! No Steps . . ."

"That's right, Ruth. We will enclose you in a bioelectric field which will stimulate knitting of your fracture. Only if you wish it will we Heal your deeper pain, the wounds you've carried for so long." The manufactured woman's voice crooned softly, "Let us help you, Ruth. Let go your anger, let go your pain and grief for Pavlo. We tried to save your lover, but it was too late for him. It's not too late for you, Ruth; we can help you forget—"

"No!" The pink mist pulsed, rocking me. "Won't all addup so neat . . . Pavlo not my lover . . . Sumpin' better, sumpin' can't put'n blasted circuits! Friend . . ."

"Hush, Ruth. We understand."

"No . . . No Steps Heal."

"Very well, Ruth. But now you must relax and let us heal your arm. Let your anger go." Her gentle voice floated on another spray of mist washing through me. "You know you only hurt yourself that way. You must learn to stop fighting, dear, to stop hurting yourself."

My eyelids were almost too heavy to hold open. I drowsily glimpsed the womblike walls pulsing, moving in to enclose me, light glowing crimson now behind the puffy surfaces. I was floating, rocking. A deep hum built up around me.

"Sleep, Ruth." Her voice had changed subtly. It was vaguely familiar, stirring buried memories. "We're here to take care of you, dear. You must help us heal your pain. Let the healing waves penetrate. You will feel nothing. You will sleep. Sleep now."

She hummed a lullaby, an old Poindran tune I'd heard so many times, years ago:

> *"And lo, though I walk through the valley of the shadow*
>   *of War,*
>   *The cybers are with me, and I will fear no evil. . . ."*

It was Helen singing softly. They'd wormed my mother's voice from their files, from carefully locked memory. "Stop! Woan let—"

"Hush, dear Ruth." The gentle voice washed through me. "Sleep."

The pulsing red walls throbbed to my heartbeat. I was swimming in the crimson glow. Sinking. Gone.

Below the casino's dome-top entrance gallery, the games whirled and flashed and buzzed. Gamers milled through colliding light shows, waving number chits and credit chips, calling out wagers for recorders, hooking into sense-nets, stepping into competitor pods. Mood music and holo plays pulsed upward through smoke, ether, and laughter.

I rode the ramp spiraling down onto the floor, watching the Planned chaos of Casino from a thousand kliks away. Who had sabotaged my Matrix game? Why? And why Pavlo?

I blinked furiously, shaking my head, shaking off that last glimpse of his staring eyes. Of course the trap was meant for me. Someone who knew I wasn't just a Rulebending game designer. Someone who wanted to deal me out. Someone—or something? I tried not to remember the Andura assignment. The incorporeal invaders in the planet's cyber network, clutching and claiming my soul, worse than anything the cybers ever Planned, burning me with their icy bright fury as I barely escaped.

I touched my lucky snake-shaped chain in a reflex gesture, clutching the contraplan blank data disc. My wild card in a game with real stakes, and no Rules. But I'd need help to unlock the cybers' higher-coded data and find out what they were hiding this go-around. Maybe the incorporeals were at it again.

My eyes fixed blindly on the noisy gamers below as the ramp brought me down. Tiny bright-dressed dolls dancing to the cybers' strings. Laughter, smiles played over and over, and the little dolls were happy to be at the hub of the ordered universe, nestled in the tinsel womb of the hollow world. They didn't know or care that their illusions of chance, their quick shots at change or ruin were only a joke. If I mentioned resistance, I'd probably just get a blank stare. And ten to one they'd just keep staring if I told them the flawless guardianship of the cybers was already splitting at the seams.

I blew out a breath and jumped from the ramp ahead of the drop spot. A mechman, lights flashing, moved forward to catch me, but I thrust quickly past it into the crowd.

"Founders, demzil!" An offended voice. "Easy goes, no?"

I brushed impatiently past the owner of the face-mosaic and the plumes whisking out of my way, fighting through the tangle of painted arms and legs, figures wrapped in clear membrane sheaths, glitter wigs and blue-polished scalps, gem-implanted hands lifting stim infusers, translucent robes floating ghostlike over the featureless matte black of a visible-spectrum null field, tinkling laughter, teeth flashing with inlaid lumes.

"Immantent! Rest your wearies on such! Hi trend?"

Mocking laughter rolled in my wake as I stalked past interlocking wager wheels and the gamers turned to stare.

"Feranimal! Ah, shiver me. . . ." More tinkling laughter.

I automatically translated the latest Casino lingo the cybers would have to put the clamps on for the sake of word purity, my head tracking to spot the source. A gold-glittered woman clutching her companions, all titillated alarm. I met her avid eyes and she suddenly looked confused. Uncomfortable. She hastily turned away.

The mirrored wheels rotated, bringing my reflection around to confront me. I couldn't blame goldie for shrinking. A tall, lanky woman in torn mesh glared back at me, eyes glinting stormy green from a wild tangle of dark red real hair, one arm imprisoned in a quick-knit cast. A long scar the cybers had more than once offered to surgirase angrily tracked her pale cheek.

The wheels spun again, shattering the image to random shards and flinging lights over the gamers. I stalked on, eyes flicking back and forth over the crowd. Another burst of laughter, up ahead. Loud cheers, chimes, and quick interplay of clashing lights. A Color Key board. I should have known.

I pushed closer. He was surrounded by a gaggle of gaudy young men and women, laughing and cheering him on. Two girls in identical fake lizard wrist and neckbands and not much else giggled as they fed him comfits and clutched a bulging bag of credit chips between them.

He was deep in the game. A pale, skinny kid with a lot of wiry dark hair, a big nose, a bad complexion, and probably the only pair of spectacles inside Casino. Despite the recent spurt of height, he still looked too young amid the polished Casinoites. He looked like what he was—a gangly Poindros hick fresh off our homeworld's farms. I was suddenly obscurely grateful he'd refused to trade the lenses for implants.

There was another run of chimes and my eyes jerked to the scoreplate. Damn. I shoved my way past his protesting audience. "David!"

He didn't hear me. Colored lights glanced off the thick lenses as they followed the flashing keys. He hunched over the console, fingers tapping with a spasmodic life of their own. The wiry dark coils of hair stood out from his head, electrified, as the music chimed another win. Cheers, and the girls staggered as more chips poured into the bag.

"David!"

He didn't blink as his fingers twitched and another play rolled onto the display.

I crashed my hands onto the console. "Damn it, David!" There was a painful clash of noise and the colored lights went crazy.

"What?" He jerked around, magnified owl eyes refocusing on me. His freckles faded into an angry flush. "Blast it, Ruth! You crashed me."

"You noticed." I glanced around at the gawking crowd and lowered my voice. "David, aren't you ever going to learn? How long do you think it'll take the cybers to realize what's going on here with your interface to the game systems? You want to get pulled in for a scan?"

He shrugged elaborately. "*Auntie* Ruth." Drawing it out with the affected drawl he'd picked up lately that set my teeth on edge. "Don't blow a gasket over it, it's only a little—Hey!" He dropped the drawl, eyes bulging as he registered my bulky cast. "What happened? Thought you were getting a workout on your new game. . . ." He trailed off, looking down at the console keys.

"So you figured you were clear to sneak in some gambling, hmm?" I sighed and leaned closer to his ear. "Look, somebody sabotaged the Matrix." I swallowed. "Pavlo got killed."

"Killed! Pavlo?" Lights jittered across his lenses as he jerked back. "That's—that's nuts! Why would—"

"It wasn't meant for Pavlo. He only showed up for a match at the last minute."

"You mean . . ." He swallowed. "But who would—"

"That's what we've got to find out. Let's get a move on." I grabbed his arm and dragged him away from the console. His audience was starting to get restless, shouting questions, booing me as I pulled him away.

"Hold onto your petticoats a blessed minute." He yanked free and hurried back to the giggling girls.

They simpered, then pouted as he pulled the bulging sack of credit chips from their grip. A sullen murmur swelled behind him as he turned back to me.

I lunged for the sack and reached in, throwing handfuls of chips out over the crowd. "Who's next?"

Muttering turned to laughter as they scrambled for the chips and another play rolled onto the board.

"What's the big idea?" David glared, clutching the bag to his chest as I hustled him off. "I *need* those credits."

"Save your breath, kid." I tightened my grip on his arm, threading the maze of gamers.

He stumbled along, hissing in whispers, "Give me a break, *Auntie*! Siolis'n me, we're close to breaking through, and we've gotta buy some black market parts to break into CI's high-code data transmissions. Soon as we get that down, we're ready to go to town on the system. You know, even if those Anduran spooks *were* doing a bad number on us inside the incorporeal matrix, they really ended up doing us a favor. See, I almost got it figured, the way they work the energy plasma. Spooks and cybers both, it's kind of the same thing in the energy field. Siolis thinks once we can navigate the plasma, we could home in on CI's directives. Cybers're in for some surprises when we pull the old wild card whammy. . . ."

"That's good, David." I didn't hear the rest. I hurried him along, forcing a path through the crowd, an uneasy prickling down the back of my neck as I recalled the console's fragmented voice penetrating my drugged haze. *Anomalous long-range signal reception, source classified . . . data access denied.* I had a funny feeling the cybers might be holding some jokers up *their* sleeves.

two

Welcome to Your Head.

The cheap holo floated before the pub entrance in blue sparks, wrapped itself around an empty sphere of air, spun, and started over in violet. It was a standing joke with the members.

I wasn't in the mood to appreciate it. Striding through it and shattering the light to incoherent dazzles, I hurried up the pink foam tongue and into the grinning mouth of the tacky clown facade. Ducking under chipped, discolored teeth, I looked back, rattling my lucky sunburst-crystal dice absently in a loose fist, eyes reflexively scanning the scatter of tourists on the dimly lit branch slowbelt. Wasn't much going on here in the low-lease quarters, and that was fine with me.

"Come *on*, David."

He smirked up at me, the holo, now in scarlet, circling him like a headband. I frowned and squinted. *Well, Come for Some—*

"Ha. Ha." I waved him impatiently up, eyes flicking again behind him. "I can see it was worth everything we went through for that remote interface contraption of yours, so you can pull neat tricks like that."

The cocky grin changed to a scowl as the rotating band melted to yellow: *Stuff it, Antie.*

"A, *U* . . ." I sighed and stepped inside.

He jerked past me, the faint red pinpoint of light beneath his tunic collar switching off.

I reached out to yank the collar up higher in back, fingers brushing over the hard, flat shape strapped to his upper spine. "Damn it, David." I rubbed my eyes wearily. "How far are you going to push it? You promised you wouldn't use that thing in public. And don't you think we're getting enough flack around here"—I jerked my head toward the pink glow of the stim hall opening off the entrance—"without you flaunting it?"

"Fer*ani*mal. I'm shaking." The infuriating drawl. "If you got it, why not flaunt it?"

"David . . ."

"Get off my back!" Thick lenses threw a clash of light at me.

17

"You're always treating me like some dumb kid, you sound just like Joshua and Thomas and—and all the rest of them back home, with all your Rules."

I gritted my teeth, shaking the slippery fisted dice without really thinking about it, tossing them up to spin and sparkle, and then reflexively snatching them back in mid-tumble. I wondered for the hundredth time if I shouldn't have left the kid on the farm with his mother Marda and my brother and his other fathers, safely tucked into our homeworld's pious ignorance. Until I returned, the prodigal daughter, managing without even trying to commit every sin. . . . But we were both misfits in that Plan.

I opened my fist and focused on the gleaming crystal cubes. They rested side by side on my palm, two etched dots staring up. My lucky roll, snake eyes. Appropriate. Shoving the dice into my belt pouch, I took a deep breath. "Come on, David. You were the one who begged me to take you off Poindros, remember? And you're the one who wanted to join the club here and help us out. So we need you now." I strode past sculptured purple tonsils, stopped, and looked back up the simulated throat. "Please?"

He shrugged, then flashed his old silly grin at me. "Guess *some*body's gotta keep you out of trouble." He slouched very casually after me, still clutching his sack of credit chips.

The ridged tunnel disgorged us into the long room with its clutter of worn loungers, a scatter of triangular tables and stools, the standard alterant dispenser encircled by a splitting padded bench, and a few cheap game booths along one wall. The soft pink light only made it look seedier.

I hustled David past the pulsing green strobes of a desultory Maze Me run, the player drooping over his snarled leads. A low buzz of talk and laughter broke off as I hurried him by an occupied table near the back. Glasses smacked onto the table and three familiar faces swung around. They recognized me and smiles turned to scowls.

One of them, a lean man with pinched-in features, raised his mug to me in a mocking toast. "Dawn of Freedom, Kurtis." His eyes flicked pointedly to the bulge of the device at the back of David's neck as his two friends echoed him.

I shrugged, refusing to be goaded, and raised my empty palm. "I'd drink to it, but I don't have a glass. How's it going, Denneth?"

His heavyset red-haired friend, whose name I couldn't remember, broke in, "It'd be going a hell of a lot faster if the brat here and his freak friend would give out the interface plans.''

''Watch who you're calling a freak, freak! Siolis's smarter than all of you put together.'' David pushed forward, chin out.

I pulled him back and nudged him toward the back of the pub. ''You've got better things to do, David.''

''Yeah, like playing right into the cybers' hands.'' Red-head scowled after him, then turned to me. ''What'd you do, Kurtis, break your arm patting yourself on the back?''

''Now slow down, Merl,'' Denneth broke in, giving me a fake smile. ''The demzil's on our side, right? *She*'s no cyber-lover, slapping new Rules on us.''

The third person, an olive-skinned woman with thick features, grunted, ''Ask me, she's been brain-wiped by CI.''

I suppressed a shudder. ''Glad to hear you can all survive without life-support and transport food shipments inside this rock. So what are we waiting for? Let's go pull the plug on the cybers. Who's first?''

Denneth just narrowed his eyes as the others glared.

I leaned over the table to pick up his mug, lifted it toward him and took a swig, then set it back down. ''Dawn of Freedom, comrades.'' I moved away and caught up to David, who'd turned around to meander toward the center of the pub. ''Come on kid, let's go.'' I tugged him toward the curtained doorway at the back.

He dragged his feet. ''What's the big rush? I wanna say hi to—''

''David!'' An eager, breathy voice. ''Don't tell me you were going to waltz on by and just ignore me?'' A pout and then the lilting laugh.

I took a deep breath and counted ten.

David was turning, shrugging awkwardly, face flushed. ''Hi, Lilith.''

She dimpled prettily, all cream and roses, curves, and honey-blond curls. Denneth and Merl back at the table switched their stares as she dipped down and emerged from inside the pub's dispenser ring, plucked off a ridiculous frilly apron, and smoothed pink and lavender flounces over generous contours. She minced over to us with a lot of hip action and an effervescent greeting. Lilith and cheap champagne—always bubbly.

''Hello, Lilith. We're in a hurry.'' I tugged at David's arm again.

''Always life and death, Ruth! So busy you can't stop for just a minute? But nobody has time for me, I guess.'' She produced her dimples for David, swaying her gauzy ruffles and cunningly veiled curves closer, blue eyes widening as she cocked her head to gaze up at him.

David's eyes skittered wildly and locked desperately onto hers, his face going a deeper, painful red. He cleared his throat. "Hey, Lilith, I didn't mean to—I mean, how could you . . . you're so . . ."

"You're so sweet, David!"

I snorted. "Look, we've all got things to do."

"Oh, Ruth." She swung around to fix the big blues on me and they narrowed for a second, reminding me as if I needed it that she was a little too old to be playing her sleazy routine on a kid. Then she gave me her dazzling smile, erasing the glimpse of something flat in those eyes. "I wouldn't want to get in your way." Her voice dripped sincerity. "Why, I—"

Her eyes widened as she pretended to just then notice my cast and sling. "Honey, no wonder you're looking extra peakedy today! But then I know *you* don't have time to fuss with yourself." Her eyes flicked up and down me and fixed on my scarred cheek with a familiar, fascinated look. "What under the sun happened to your arm?" She turned to David in appeal, placing a plump little hand on his.

He jerked and swallowed again. "Sacred Founders, Lilith, you wouldn't believe what somebody did to—"

"Just an accident, no big deal." My eyes flicked to Denneth's table, meeting the dark woman's furtive eyes. She scowled and looked away again. "Like I said, we've got a lot to do."

"You look like the cat just about to pounce on the little old bird, Ruth. If there's any way I could help, you know I'd love to." Lilith gazed innocently up at me, curiosity glinting in her eyes.

Maybe she'd been a misfit, too, on her homeworld. She'd have been right at home in the worldPlan I'd escaped, fussing over multiple husbands and giggling avidly across the gossip fence. I shook my head. "Sorry, Lilith, maybe next time. You about ready, David?"

He pulled himself reluctantly from her hand and followed me to the holo curtain advertising *Sanicubicles and Massage Pods*.

"Can't I come along? I can hold the tools for you. Siolis won't mind, and Herv'll be along down here in a minute." She fluttered after us and took David's arm. "You know I love to watch you doing all those mysterious things with the console." She looked down. "Unless I'd be in the way."

I opened my mouth, but David beat me to it. "Sure thing. I mean, you're not . . . You're really . . ."

I blew out a long breath and stalked past the first massage pod rocking to the muted strains of mood music. Glancing down the dim, empty hall, I stopped beside a faded *Storage* stencil, pulled out my IDisc, and pressed it against the lock reader. The dingy wall shimmered.

"Let us go first!" Lilith giggled as she danced past, turned, and skipped backward, pulling along David and his abashed grin. The dissolving wall swallowed them and rippled back into place. I gritted my teeth and stepped through the field into Resistance Headquarters.

"About time, Ruth. I was starting to wonder if—Hmm." The stocky woman with short iron-gray hair turned from the console screen, running a cool blue gaze over me. Automatically assessing, concluding, assigning priorities. Sometimes I wondered if Helsa only pretended to consult her data analyzers. Now she cocked an ironic eyebrow. "I see you've been busy as usual. What happened?"

I shifted the bulky cast, and the sling reconfigured to take its weight. "Just an—"

"Blazes, Helsa, somebody did a number on her Matrix game! Zapped Pavlo with high voltage, trying to get Ruth."

"David." I glanced back at Lilith, but she was busy fussing with her hair. I shrugged. "Why don't you go see what you and Siolis can do about patching up any holes in the cybers' data net? I'd just as soon that high-voltage generator disappeared from the records."

Lilith tugged at David's wrist. "Here, let me take that big old bag and you can get to work. Bless me, David, look at all these chips! You've been a busy boy, haven't you?" They disappeared beyond a row of cabinets where technicians bent over their lit screens.

I turned back to Helsa, making a sour face.

She frowned, ironic eyes shading toward concern. "Are you all right, Ruth? You probably should be resting."

I shrugged. "Our wonderful guardians took good care of me. But I don't like the way that case of arrested development has her claws into David." I jerked my head after them. "I didn't want word of my 'accident' getting around, and I don't see how she could possibly be as dumb as she acts."

Helsa snorted, eyes going cool again. "You're going to have to get over being so protective of that boy, Ruth. He's about sixteen, isn't he? If he won't go to that socializer group you signed him up for, he's got to learn somehow. And I thought back on Poindros you always married the young men into an older woman's family. Why the fuss?"

"I don't want her messing around with his head. She gives me the creeps."

"Lilith's harmless. You know we check out psych profiles before we let anyone into the Resistance. She's had a hard time, you'll remember, with her family back on Neuland taken for the Steps of Healing. She may not be too bright, but she tries hard to be useful."

"All right, all right, but with his brains you'd think . . ."

She turned back to the console, punching up a display. "Have you ever stopped to think the trouble might be you, Ruth? We all know you and David have special talents, but that doesn't make you better than the rest of us. You were happier when you were breaking Rules on your own, weren't you, thinking you were the only rebel challenging the cybers? But if you're going to stay with us, you'll have to learn to pull together. Everybody has a place." She jabbed a finger and the display rotated, data scrolling beneath it.

She squinted, nodded, then turned back to me, sighing and rubbing her face. She never seemed to get enough sleep. "Ruth, it's not that we don't appreciate you and David. His work here with Siolis could be our breakthrough on cybernetics. And we haven't forgotten it was you who pulled us out of that disaster on Andura. I know you worry about David being pressured, and I know you've had some tough breaks, but some day you're going to have to start trusting us."

When I didn't answer, she sat back on the console edge and folded her arms. "Siolis just told me about that blank data disc you've had all along." Her voice quiet. "Why didn't you tell me, Ruth?"

Double bloody damn. I jerked away from her, paced, turned, paced back. "I should trust you the same way I trusted Siolis to keep a secret, right?" I met her collected gaze and burst out, "Why the hell should I trust all your wonderful members? Pulling together! Just like Heinck and his rotten schemes back on Andura, right? Like Denneth's gang muttering and plotting because they can't all have a data interface like David's? Itching to get rid of me so they can worm the secret out of the kid and bust wide open the cyber net.''

I flung up my hands in frustration, forgetting the bulky cast. ''Damn it, they don't understand what it would mean to go back to ground zero—*you* don't understand. Maybe we do need some Rules, maybe there's a reason for some of the taboos. Look how fast Heinck reinvented War on Andura. I *saw* it, Helsa. And I had to kill that bastard to stop it. . . .'' No, by that time I'd *wanted* to kill him. I shook my head furiously. ''Oh, I trust the others all right, just like I trust whoever sabotaged my Matrix game.''

She didn't flinch. ''No need to shout, Ruth. Unless you enjoy an audience.''

I jerked around to see faces peering over consoles. They ducked hastily as I swore and paced again down the floor and back.

''You are going to tell me what happened out there? Who was this Pavlo person David mentioned?''

I blew out a long breath and stopped before her again. She waited calmly, resting against the console and glancing down at her chrono.

''Now I'm wasting your precious time?''

She smiled then, gray-blue eyes warming and transforming her face. ''Ruth. Never say die, do you?'' She shook her head. ''I'm due at a council meeting, and it sounds like this is something I ought to bring up. What happened?''

''Pavlo wasn't Resistance. Just a friend . . .'' Just a friend. I closed my eyes and took a deep breath. ''And the best damn Matrix player around. He only showed up at the last minute for a match—it was my usual practice time. So it would've been easy for somebody to find out I'd be alone out there.'' I met her gaze. ''Helsa, it might be more incorporeals at work. I just heard CI's activated my files, and that means something's up, maybe another spook matrix. There's no way to know how many subnets there were, how many of the planetary systems they managed to invade.''

She opened her mouth and I raised a hand. ''Or, like I said, maybe somebody in the group here. I'm not kidding about Lilith, Helsa. Somebody could be using her to get close to David.''

She rubbed her face again. ''It's understandable after what's happened, Ruth, but I think you're overreacting. I've explained to the members how delicate this operation is, how we can't simply go blundering randomly through the cyber system. It would certainly help, though, if David and Siolis could make their breakthrough and give us some real results to show everyone. They're getting impatient, and you can't blame them. After finally seeing how the cybers have kept them down, they don't have patience with these slow changes, step by step. They want us to jump in and change the directives, even though we don't know how yet. Or, as you said, they simply want to tear down the system, like your hotheaded Poindros console-busters."

"Helsa, they're not *my* Poindros anything, so don't pin that on me. I'm finished with that dirtball."

"Really?" Voice soft, eyes steady on mine with a look too much like Helen's, waiting patiently for the rebellious daughter to see the error of her ways.

I opened my mouth for another denial, then closed it. Maybe it was only some blindly ingrained program in me that made me want to lash out against any reminders of my homeworld's tender coercions. I didn't want a fight with Helsa.

She sighed. "Ruth, ever think we're both wearing ourselves out swimming upstream? We talk about change. Maybe change *is* going to be violent, and if so many of the others want war against the cybers, they're going to get it."

I stared. "Helsa, *you* can't be caving in to them! You can't believe pulling together means blindly going along."

"Now, wait a—"

"There's got to be a way we can get free and still learn from everything the cybers have built. Remember what Siolis said once, about our responsibility as humans? We created the cybers, and now we're stuck with these pushy awarenesses, but maybe they have rights, too. Maybe we should think about negotiating instead of pulling the plug."

"I never thought I'd see the day, Ruth!" She threw up her hands. "You and Siolis! That's just your old conditioning talking—our 'benevolent Guardians'—when you know they're only a complicated machine." She shook her head. "I don't have time for this. I'll talk to the Council about your accident, and you can get Siolis to work you up a substitute data loop for CI. But if you've got any more secrets up your sleeve, like that wild card data disc, let me know this time, all right?"

She stood, holding my eyes with hers, then headed briskly toward the hall. "And get some rest, will you?"

I stood there a while, a bad taste in my mouth. I remembered too well the white consuming flame of vengeance, driving me at the end to kill Heinck, wanting only to feel his blood spilling hot over my hands as he'd spilled the gentle Andurans'. Maybe he'd felt the same way. Helsa was right—I didn't trust that buried urge in me, and I didn't trust anyone else. But damn it, I couldn't just hand her David's and my lives on a platter.

I found myself jiggling my dice and tossing them up to catch. When I opened my fist, snake eyes glittered up at me again. I jerked around and headed away from the hall.

Past the disc-storage cabinets, banks of consoles cooking up dummied data to mask Resistance activities, and stacks of pirated taboo equipment for the technicians to analyze. There was a lot of work to do before we could worm the cybers' secrets out of them. I waved my hand in front of a scanner and the big plasmeld door rumbled aside.

The tank took up a good part of the warehouse space. Dim reddish light brooded over the water weeds swaying to an invisible current inside the clear stressplex. There was a shivering glimpse of movement, shadows waiting to close in. A quick, ghostly flicker gathered substance, and the two plumy-finned fish darted out of the murk toward me, reversed in a quicksilver gleam of scales, and returned to hover patiently at the curve of the tank closest to him.

The greenish glow of a console screen washed his faintly blue, hairless head to a sickly hue. I swallowed down the reaction instilled by centuries of taboo. "Siolis."

"Welllcome, Ruth." His voice was a dry hiss, but the toothless, lipless slash of a mouth stretched in a brief smile. The black alloy polyhedron of his portable biosupport unit swung around to a faint interior splashing and the whine of concealed wheels. The box brought him closer, rolling almost noiselessly out of the gloom with his head perched grotesquely atop it, surrounded by the puffy collar of the gasket enclosing his upper gills. I could almost see the long, slippery body and tail coiled inside the opaque box. A susurrus of water, and uncomfortably angled violet eyes fastened on mine. "Llong hass been the sssighting."

I cleared my throat. "I've been busy."

He waited silently. I forced myself to meet the oddly mutable purple of those eyes, trying to shake off the indefinable uneasiness he always provoked—furtive, hovering images of demons and monsters, the warping of human flesh to an alien mold. And my last glimpse of Jason, his gentle, patient eyes watching from his machined mask.

There was a distant buzzing in my ears like the onset of the *timbra* fight-or-flight response to threat. I shook my head. It was only the old Way, the old perceptions Siolis threatened, the knee-jerk horror the cybers had instilled in us against the contraplan. It was no fault of the Cyvriot's that his officially nonexistent sea world and people had been the object of secret bioforming experiments before the grand Plan had enforced an end to such prohibited technology. And an end to War, to History, to disturbing thoughts rippling the deep waters of sinless sleep. . . .

His eyes were bottomless purple wells, darkness drawing me whirling down. And out of the blackness, shards of crystal fire spun, snake eyes staring. I blinked, jerking back.

"Passt sstilll imprisonss you, as the cyberss would insisst? Jasson, too, ssaw you coulld not yet accept."

Damn it. Always hitting too close to the mark. "Look, Siolis, Jason's the one who insisted on staying behind on Andura. *He's* the one who sent me away . . ." Before I could start hating myself for taking him as my lover? Before I could fall to those nibbling doubts, my lingering revulsion against the ultimate taboo he embodied? Jason looked and felt like a man, but he was a cyborg, a creation of the incorporeals he'd finally helped me fight. And wasn't it a piss-poor joke—Ruth, the rogue stubbornly resisting the machinations of the cybers all her life, finally falls for a brain in a machine?

I shook my head again, brusquely. "Where's David?"

"He comess." Siolis, encased in his cumbersome vehicle, rolled back from me, face gone impassive. His clear inner eyelids flicked down as the gasket hissed and bathed his head in a quick water mist.

"Siolis, you about ready to show me that readout?" David appeared around the gloomy warehouse stacks, pushing a cart with electronic parts. Lilith trailed along, carrying a soldering laser with dainty awkwardness. David parked the cart beside a partially built piece of equipment.

"I thought you were in here tracking down those CI files for me, David. And I'm going to need a dummy loop."

"No sweat, just takin' care of biz." The drawl was back. "Siolis already got one cooked up. He's way ahead of the game— already got into the coded files and covered up that voltage generator. I'm gonna stick around here, though, we've got a hot one going, just got some wild signals from—''

"Slowlly, David. Alll in good time." Siolis rolled forward smoothly, an extensor telescoping from his box to gently lift the laser from Lilith's hands. "Thank you, Llilith. Now it woulld hellp me greatlly if you woulld be ssso kind? Another favor I assk."

Lilith tore her gaze from David and turned to Siolis. "Why sure, however I can help."

"There iss a package at the port, and no one do I trusst as woulld I you to bring it here."

She opened her mouth, looked at David, and pouted prettily. "But I thought I could help out here. You know David never can keep his tools and all straight when he's working on that contraption of his." She waved airily toward the unfinished equipment. "Kendra wouldn't mind going."

"It iss important, Lillith."

She fastened wide, appealing eyes on David, and he cleared his throat. "You better go, Lilith. If Siolis says it's important . . ."

She raised her hands and gave a tinkling little laugh. "Then of course I'll go. You all behave yourselves!" She ruffled David's hair, her hand lingering on the back of his neck.

Siolis rolled closer. "Plleasse hurry, Lillith." He gave her his unnerving blank stare.

Her hand jerked away from David, and she flounced toward the door, laughing again. "Bye bye." Her eyes flicked from Siolis to David and back again, and I could have sworn she was furious. Then she turned to me, smiling. "Now you get some *rest*, Ruth!" She waved gaily and the big door sealed behind her.

I blew out a long breath. "Thanks, Siolis, you just made my day."

He was staring fixedly past me, eyes a pale flat violet. I jerked around, startled as the tank behind me erupted into splashes, the two crimsoned fish leaping in agitation from the water and chasing each other down and around to end up quivering again at the closest curve.

"They're frisky today, huh?" David crouched by the tank, touching his fingers to the clear curve. "Okay, guys, we've got some work to do, then you'll get him back." The fish hovered, their wafting plumes subsiding into a slow, graceful rhythm as the crimson-flushed scales faded to purple.

David jumped to his feet, striding past me to the console. "Hey,

Ruth, take a look at this. There's some wild kind of transmission
Siolis just picked up, frequency's crazy, but believe it or not the
signal source has to be—''

"Yess, David." The quick hiss, almost in my ear, startled me.
I jerked around to see Siolis had come up close behind me. "Why
don't you sstart an analysiss? I willl join you ssoon."

"Now you're talking." David, whistling off-key, was already
hunched over the console, tapping in quick patterns.

I shook my head. "I'm glad everybody's so concerned about
the Matrix sabotage. What about my dummy data loop?"

His extensor stretched toward me and dropped something small
and glittering into my hastily raised palm. "Ssealed as allwaysss.
Thiss willl ssatisfy the cybersss, and you willl find the meanss to
conceall it." Again the quirky smile. "Do not fear. I have alltered
the sysstem data, and thuss they have never known thiss wasss
more than accident." His head tilted toward my bulky cast.

"But . . . how did you find out so fast?"

His eyes were deep purple again, fixed on me with that look
that always gave me the creeps. "I sstay in touch, Ruth."

I jerked my eyes away before his could suck me in again, into
reluctant fascination, into some unwelcome recognition about him,
or myself. "Right. Good thing we've got you monitoring the cyber
network. I better get moving now."

Dry, hissing laughter. "Stilll you do not trusst me, Ruth?"

I studied the floor. "Why did you tell Helsa about the wild card
disc, Siolis?"

Silence, except for the soft shush of circulating water. Then,
slowly, "Time comess for changess, Ruth. The ssafe Wayss no
lllonger guide usss. . . ."

"Don't give me a bunch of your riddles."

"I am ssorry. It wass perhapsss a misstake."

I looked back up, surprised.

"Helssa now keepss secretss of her own. Sso many sseasss . . .
and but one sswimmer. Do not deny the llonelinesss, Ruth."

I shook my head. "I don't have the faintest idea what you're
talking about, as usual."

"As usuall." Again the faint, odd smile. Mocking? The box
rolled around to face David at the console. "Lleave the boy with
me a few daysss. He willl be ssafer here."

"So you can keep him glued to that console?" I couldn't let
myself trust Helsa. I wouldn't let myself trust Siolis. But he was
right. I dropped my hand to my side. "All right. Just until I get

the story from CI and we find out who killed Pavlo."

I looked back at the skinny figure hunched intently over his pulsing green readouts. Vague foreboding shivered through me. But I was damned if I was going to be one of those hovering Poindran matron types Helsa was always digging me about. I raised my voice. "See you later, David. Make sure they feed you around here."

He didn't answer, probably didn't hear. Siolis' box was turning back toward me, and I headed for the door before I had to meet those violet eyes again.

Missing. No trace. Possibly abducted...
The maze of gleaming silver lumiflex bars swam and blurred overhead, reversing up and down and plunging me dizzily through the tall, dim chamber. I stumbled, still groggy from sleep and its sudden interruption, reaching to clutch the lowest horizontal bar of the gymnastic chute I'd extended into my second, illegally leased apartment overhead. The pain meds had faded to a sick emptiness, my bioelectric cast was a horde of stinging bees, and there was an angry buzz in my ears. The latticework of bars blurred and refocused to a silver matrix closing in on me. And I couldn't even climb it to work off the jitters.

Missing. No trace.
I slammed my fist at a resilient bar, but only rebounded into the wall. "Damn it all."

I grabbed the robe crammed over a rung of the ladder to my bedloft, slung it around my shoulders, and stumbled back to my console desk. The special security codes were still activated, and I reslotted the message disc the nervous courier from headquarters had awakened me with. Helsa coalesced again on the wall vid, looking more harried than ever, pacing closer as she rumpled her short gray hair. Her eyes shifted uneasily.

"Now don't fly off the handle, Ruth. We've just discovered that David and Siolis are missing. We've got people on it, but there's no trace of them. It's possible they were abducted." She held up a hand. "I don't want you trying to contact us until we get a handle on this. Don't leave your apartment, either, unless CI calls you in. We're doing everything we can, and you'll just make things worse by exposing yourself."

The image looked offscreen, listening. She turned back, eyes still shifting around, something funny going on. "This had better not be a setup, Ruth. If you're hiding him somewhere..." The

image looked vaguely past me, then jerked an impatient hand and
went blank.

I sagged into the chair, closing my eyes and rubbing my face.
I kept seeing David in the dim warehouse, gangly kid hunched
awkwardly above his console, fingers jittering over the keys. Too
excited about some "wild signal" to hear me—

Signal. I blinked, fingers drumming on the desktop. Straightening, I ejected the message disc and cleared the console, leaning
over the desk to activate the courtesy port I'd installed for clients
who came to discuss new game designs. I touched my lucky
necklace, automatically running the heavy red-gold links through
my fingers, one complete circuit of my neck. The tiny emerald
snake eyes of the clasp winked at me as I plucked loose the wild
card disc and inserted it into the port. Dropping back into my
chair, I stared at the ready light pulsing on the blank screen. I
took a deep breath and hunched over the keyboard.

Red lights were dancing in front of my eyes by the time I found
it. Of course, I'd never have gotten through the Resistance codes
at all without my blank data disc to get me through cybernetic
lower levels. David and Siolis had designed the Resistance camouflage, and I shouldn't have been able to penetrate it. I didn't,
really, except for the one little data bundle that fell so obligingly
through the web into my hands.

Lightheaded, I took a deep breath and shunted the data package
onto a storage disc to take up to David's room. Wading through
a high tide of dirty socks, electronic parts, encrusted meal trays,
and unread sense-cubes, I located his Custom Bypass Activator
squatting malevolently in a corner. I crouched in front of it, staring
back at the amber eye of the ready light, then thumbed in the disc,
fumbling with his homemade controls. Sparks shot up at me,
flames leaping.

Jerking back, I sat down hard. It was only a holo image,
a glittering tube of incoherent lights swirling with hot crimson.
I blew out a breath. Naturally the brat had had to double code
it.

I did the best I could, forcing patterns out of shifting hologram
shapes and colors. Sweating and swearing over the controls, I
watched the hazy figures crawl out of the blended light, ooze, and
melt again. Finally I managed to corral a few coherent shapes into
Record. The screen at the base of the collapsible metal grid scrolled
unconnected bits of translation: *signal/source/threat/Cyvrus*

I frowned. A signal source threatens Cyvrus? A signal from

Cyvrus threatens . . . whom? Who? A threat signals Cyvrus sources?

I shook my head, staring blankly at the still-whirling colors, fiery snakes of light undulating, circling. I blinked, leaning closer. There. I had it. The snaky shape fleshed out and solidified, almost grinned a mocking toothy grin at me.

I hit Record and rubbed my eyes. The screen slowly scrolled the words. *No sweat, ANtie, just taking a little tour of Siolis' home turf. I'll be back before you get this figured out.*

The door—flat gray, like the corridor—snicked open as I wiped my damp palm down my shimmer-slicks. I took a deep breath and waltzed into the CI debriefing cubicle with a showy swirl of my short cape. "So how's tricks, kiddo?"

The severe blue unisuit was immaculate as ever, the graying hair done up in a conservative topknot, the brown eyes neutral. He produced a thin smile. "I see your injury has not curbed your usual excesses, Kurtis: P385XL47:Ruth."

My eyes flicked over the plain console screen and the exam lounger with its electrode-bristling helmet before I put on a grin. "Really jazzing things up around here, huh? Sarcasm, even. And I thought you'd like it!" I lifted the cast to spread the cape and display its interwoven lumes as I did a little spin for him. My heart thudded uncomfortably beneath Siolis' silver data capsule displayed conspicuously among the baubles on my gaudy necklace.

He gave a polite little cough into his hand. "I must admit I am surprised to see you, Ruth, if that is the effect for which you are striving. But then we expected you would defy the recommended recovery rest period. May I assume there is a reason for this uninvited visit?"

"Assume away. The . . . uh, medic mechman said you'd pulled my file, so I figured you'd be calling me in, anyway. Guess I just couldn't wait to hear your dulcet tones telling me you guys needed to be bailed out again."

His face went blank for a second before he blinked. "Affirmative. We intended to schedule a consultation with you. However, the medic mechman was not authorized to—"

"Oh, don't worry about it, they were just pulling my psych profile and it popped out. So what's up? Am I done for again?"

A slight frown. "Sra Kurtis, if these statements are attempts at humor—"

"Come on, don't be a stuffed shirt." I sauntered closer to the console, where he stood stiffly. "Give me squeeze." I held out the standard two-finger. "I rejoice in our reunion, CI:DUN:4."

He sighed. "Very well. I rejoice in our reunion, Agent Kurtis." He touched the polite two fingers to mine.

His skin was pale, Casino-pampered soft. I curled my fingers around his and triggered with my toes the bonded microcircuits in my right boot. A quick, crackling surge, and I jerked my hand away.

He stayed frozen, hand extended, eyes fixed glassily. I took a deep breath and wiped my hand down my slicks again, then reached out and parted the front seam of his suit to expose the power pack. I looked up and looked quickly away from the blank stare, then shrugged. He was only a cyberserf, a machine, and he had no business looking so human, anyway. No way to tell how many of them CI had running around Casino without the breast badges worn by the obvious, awkward mechmen. Most people would never have a reason to wonder why there'd been something just a little off about that guy in the blue suit.

I shook my head again and pulled two short leads from my cape seam, opening the cyberserf's chest cavity and hastily bridging terminals. Removing my hideous rhinestone-encrusted belt buckle, I separated the parts, fumbling—damn cast—to reassemble them with a piece from one dangling earring. With the unit clipped into the terminal hidden behind CI:DUN:4's left ear, I popped open Siolis' capsule and loaded his dummy data loop.

I paced edgily while the cyberserf digested a faked scan of my physiological signs, emotional peaks and valleys, and "memories" of the accident on the Matrix.

Behind me, a sudden flash of glittering light. I jerked around in a reflex *timbra* posture to see the holo plate on the console flaring to activation. Swallowing down the hot jolt of adrenaline, I realized the display had been triggered by my input to the cyberserf. Light swirled and coalesced to images: a floating bit of dark space, stars and planets glittering in a miniature galaxy. The System. It was the same demo they used every time. Creativity wasn't a strong point with the cybers.

The galaxy spun and grew, holo zooming in on a blue dwarf star near the center. It swelled, magnifying the chunk of black rock orbiting it. A crimson speck sprang out of the darkness, drawing a bright circle around the planetoid, with the words: *Casino. Central Interlock.* Red for CI, the special division of the cyber network that coordinated and enforced the restrictions on interaction between the different worldplans.

The floating shapes sparkled, shrinking to parade the entire system before me again, from the high-tech hub worlds to the low-tech planets near the rim. One of the stars in the outer reaches flared and magnified into a large orange sun. Its closest planet was a turquoise and green cat's-eye, rolling over a black matte gaming table. My homeworld, so thoughtful of the cybers. A blue spark glinted and drew its shimmering circle around the planet, followed by letters: *Poindros Local Service network*.

A red blip grew to a tiny transport ship, zinging across the holo from Casino to Poindros. It drew a red circle around the blue one. The outer circle touched the inner, but didn't intersect it.

Not officially.

According to the Rules, Central Interlock couldn't interfere in the jurisdictions of the different planetary Local Service networks. As it turned out, there were a lot of things the ancient Founders hadn't foreseen when they'd designed their peaceful, static worlds and turned over control to the logic matrix they'd built, erasing human memory. Over the endless centuries, the CI cybers had managed to finagle their own interpretations of the Rules, like drafting marginal psych-types like myself to be their secret data-gathering agents. Only the organic brain patterns of a human could pass planet clearances.

CI:DUN:4 couldn't visit other worlds, but I could. And so, of course, could the contraplan cyborgs built by the incorporeals to help them take over the system and use humans for "awareness breeding stock." Cyborgs like Jason.

I shook my head and concentrated on the holo. The System was sweeping around again, bringing to focus an isolated star-cluster and magnifying a surly reddish sun. There were two worlds circling it. The holo brought the closest up to magnification. A blue sphere, rolling slowly through space, no land masses visible. Only water.

I caught my breath, leaning closer. "I *knew* it." A violet spark flared, drawing its tight circle around the planet. *Cyvrus. Special jurisdiction*. No LS system for Cyvrus, then. No blue circle of recognition.

A little shiver of mingled excitement and dread zigged through me at this confirmation of a taboo world. I kept thinking I was past those shocks, breaking the cybers' changeless Rules, but then

I'd come up against something else that tweaked all the old in-grained responses.

I stretched, still jittery, as the holo faded into dying sparks. A quick glance at the door panel, then my chrono. Some more pacing. I checked my chrono again and moved quickly around behind the cyberserf.

Unsnap the input unit. Slip the data loop back into the capsule. Reseal it. Separate and replace my buckle parts. Then the leads, and the chest cavity closed up. I was just resealing the cyberserf's suit seam when there was a quick suck of air behind me.

My stomach gave a jarring flip-flop. The door.

Hands jerking away from the fabric, my eyes leaped to my chrono. Too soon for synchronization with the faked data. Blast it. But there was nothing else to do. My fingers frantically hooked the two frozen cyberserf fingers and I triggered the signal again. It jolted through me and I tore free, moving into a restless pacing to match what he'd expect from Siolis' programming. But it was too soon to start, my timing was off.

Hell, play it out. "So, okay, I've gone through your song and dance." I waved at the sensor couch and turned to pace back. "Now why don't we get down to brass tacks, DUN:4—"

I didn't have to fake surprise as I finally let myself "notice" the open doorway. CI:DUN:4 was walking through it. Complete with blue suit, gray topknot, and tight little smile.

I came up short, head jerking back toward the console. CI:DUN:4 still stood beside it, blank-faced and hand extended. He blinked then, frowned, and dropped the hand.

"But. . ." I shouldn't have been shocked by the duplicate cy-berserfs, but somehow I'd got to thinking of old DUN:4 as a real personality.

CI:DUN:4 number two paused in the doorway. "Hello, Ruth. I must admit I didn't expect you to come without a summons. We did predict you would defy the recommended recovery rest pe-riod."

"But—"

"Very well, Ruth." CI:DUN:4 number one tilted his head. "Naturally, we must factor consideration of anomalous data. . . ." He looked puzzled, frowned, smiled, raised his hand to stare at it. "Random incursions of field flow . . . illogical contingencies factored into projections of . . ."

His double cut across the babble. "Shall we discuss the nature of the anomalous data, Ruth?" He crossed over to the console, nearly stepping on the first cyberserf's toes but apparently oblivious to its presence. What in hell was going on?

"... intersecting matrices of multiple-loop frequencies involving..."

"This is only a consultation, Ruth, not an assignment. Since of course you are familiar with the incursions of the incorporeals in the Poindran and Anduran systems, we calculate that your perceptions of..."

"... unPlanned revelations in violation of..."

"... and you do continue to function usefully for us, in your illogical fashion, as a random-data-generator to enlarge the scope of our problem-solving matrices. ..."

"... laboratory to maintain faunal genetic purity. Cyvrus special status allows..."

"I assume you have considered the possibility that the incorporeal threat has not yet been fully contained?"

"Ah... what?" I blinked, gawking baffled from cyberserf to double. The double waited with the familiar raised eyebrow. I glanced at still-babbling Number One, tore my eyes away to answer Number Two. "Ah, sure, right." I took a deep breath and plunged in. "Isn't that what this, what do you call it, anomalous signal is all about? The one..." From? To? Damn David, with his blasted puzzles. "You know, Cyvrus?"

Number Two's face went blank. Sacred Founders, I was in for it now. I found myself clutching my lucky dice. But I had to get CI to assign me to Cyvrus. The kid was bound to get himself into hot water there.

"... urgent query... data loop lacuna, Matrix game... subject taboos, contraplan cloning..."

I jerked back to babbling Number One. What was that about my game Matrix? Did they suspect something? I waited for more, but the cyberserf must have finally short-circuited. He went stiff and silent, glass eyes staring through me as I shivered, groping through confusion. Had Siolis slipped me a whammy with his substitute data loop? Or were the cybers going schizoid?

There was a little cough, jerking me back to Number Two. "Agent Kurtis, you are not cleared for discussion of the anomalous transmission. Two violation points."

So what was new? I managed to shrug. "Come on, DUN:4. How am I supposed to be a consultant if you don't fill me in? What's this signal about?"

"That subject is closed."

I sighed. "Look, I already know about this secret world of yours, and your, ah, lab there. . . ." I crossed my fingers behind my back, but he only blinked. "So what's the problem? You think incorporeals are on Cyvrus now, sending signals out, or what?"

He frowned slightly. "The data do not support such a wild extrapolation. Please curb your illogical excesses."

"Aren't my illogical excesses what you want me for?"

"We wish only to obtain your human perspective on a theoretical matter."

"Theoretical. Right. Okay, there's a theoretical secret world that's sending out a theoretical signal from some theoretical incorporeals invading the system. Am I close?"

The frown deepened. "Very well, Agent Kurtis. I am authorized to inform you that there is a significant statistical probability that cyborg agents for the incorporeals, other than those apprehended on Poindros and Andura, may remain at large."

"What? But we shut them down!" Nervous sweat broke out on my palms. If they suspected Jason . . .

"I did not intend to alarm you. Our psychological review indicated that you had recovered sufficiently from the trauma of renewed contact with the incorporeals to—"

"I'm fine." I waved him down. "So you want me to go to Cyvrus to check it out?"

"There is no need for your presence, as Cyvrus has no human population with which you would interact. Therefore—"

"But what about—" I caught myself before Siolis' name popped out, pretending to cough.

"Therefore CI maintains jurisdiction for laboratories there. We will send mechmen to investigate the anomalous transmission. Probabilities select electromagnetic aberrations as the cause, but the alternate mechanism of incorporeal involvement merits investigation. The techniques which you previously employed to escape incorporeal control have not yet been successfully analyzed. We require further data from you with which to program our mechmen."

"Techniques." I snorted. "It's not something you can write an equation for, DUN:4, it's something only a quirky human could know about. So I'll have to go along. You might need a wild card up your sleeve."

"There is no need for—"

"No, you cybers have it all under control, right?" I forced a shrug and started for the door. "Guess you don't need me."

"Wait." Number Two frowned and stared off into space. I could almost hear gears clicking into place, though of course that was ridiculous. I took a deep breath and tried to stop sweating. Long odds on pulling this one off.

I glanced uneasily from frozen cyberserf to oblivious double. Maybe all our Resistance finagling had done more damage to the system than we'd thought. The perfect cybers weren't so perfect anymore. Somehow it wasn't as funny as it should have been.

"Very well. Factors compute favorably. You will accompany the mechmen assignment to Cyvrus." He walked stiffly past me to the door, then paused, raising the eyebrow again. "Good faring, Sra Kurtis." Good old CI:DUN:4, needling me with my home-world well-wishing.

I glanced at blank-faced Number One, took a deep breath, and managed to grin at Number Two. I tossed my dice sparkling into the air. "Right. Done for again."

three

The airless passage was dark except for the flanking double rows of amber ready lights converging in the distance. The mechmen were only frozen bulks, more felt than seen, their paired indicators unwinking. Retracted into dormant squatting positions, they were clamped by their bases sideways—if directions applied—in two neatly mirrored lines down the blind central tunnel of the ship's cargo well. I nudged myself along, floating between ranks of lifeless CI units with the glinting amber eyes of stalkers crouched in the night.

Shaking my head in the helmet, I threw myself into a slow zero-G tumble. "Damn." I flailed awkwardly, injured left arm in its bulky cast tucked uselessly inside the chest area of my pressure suit, empty sleeve wafting along.

My good hand grabbed a hold on one of the motionless mechmen. I rolled over, stepped on its face, and pushed off across empty space, aiming for the deeper blackness of one of the smaller passages angling like spokes from the center of the ship. Leaving the glowing amber eyes behind, I flicked on the lume built into the suit's wrist cuff.

Not that there was much to see. Just identical, featureless gray shapes of supply cannisters strapped in place around the narrow crawlspace. Like the others filling the dark cargo bay, which was about all there was to the ship. No lights, no air, no simulated gravity, no game rooms, no viewing dome like on the passenger transports. No-frills travel, courtesy CI.

At least I was finally *doing* something. I bumped up against a vaguely curved wall and pulled myself around, heading back, bouncing erratically off the cannisters. I'd tried the suit's steering jets, but without both hands on the hardwired glove controls, I'd only managed cartwheels all over the place. Steadying myself on another cannister, I flexed my knees to push off again.

Flashing lights, blue and red, sprang suddenly out of the darkness ahead. Mechman enforcer strobes. They moved in fast up the crawlspace, my stomach jolting in reflex alarm. But there was no reason to worry now, the ship was underway and Clearance

38

Security apparently fat and happy. I let out my breath and clutched a cargo strap, jarring to a stop and rebounding against the cannister.

My helmet radio buzzed, and a toneless voice crackled in my ear, "This area is hazardous for humans. Environment suits are provided for emergency use only. I will now conduct you back to your comfort module."

"*Comfort* module!"

Sarcasm was wasted on the mechman. The jointed alloy parody of the human form bobbed to a halt, hovering before me as an extensor popped out to clamp onto my suit belt. Its head rotated one-eighty and it jetted back down the passage, towing me along.

"Let go!" I swatted at the extensor, but the mechman didn't bat an eye. "I can get back under my own steam."

"Injury potential is unacceptable," the voice droned. "You will remain in the comfort module."

"Nice definition of comfort CI's got—locked up in a tin can. You hardly have room to stretch your legs in there."

"Mechman ambulation extensors do not require elongation."

I sighed and gave up. The damn thing whisked me back in the dark between the double rows of amber sparks and deposited me beside a dim bulk anchored at the end of the cargo well. Lights flashed across a flat alloy face as the mechman opened the airlock and waited politely while I pulled myself in. The hatch sealed behind me and I pressed the red-lit plate in resignation. Air hissed outside my helmet, until the plate finally lit up green for air and pressure. Worming my way out of the suit, I hung it beside the spare in the lock and popped the interior hatch. I counted ten in advance and pulled myself through.

She bobbed gracefully around, blond curls and gauzy fabric floating around her, blue eyes wide. "Ruth, you're back. I was just—"

"What in bloody hell do you think you're doing?"

Lilith cringed, still clutching my travel bag with one hand and a thin plasmeld plaque with the other. Monotone figures in flattened 2-D were visible through the plaque's transparent surface. "I was just looking for—"

"I don't give a damn what you were looking for. Keep your hands off my gear!" I launched over to her and grabbed the plaque.

My momentum carried me on into the wall, but I hardly noticed, gripping the encased paper that pateros Sam, my truefather, had called a photograph. My hand shook furiously, groping for the opaque button, but the images sealed in that odd, colorless flatness captured me. I stared at the familiar, lost faces—grizzled grinning Sam, dark angry Aaron, and enigmatic Jason gathered around their serenely beautiful wife Helen, the heart of the home and Hearth. And, at the edge, the prodigal daughter, my own strained face staring back at me.

My finger found the button, and the plasmeld reconfigured to deep blue, sealing Poindros and its faces away from me.

"Whatever is that thing, Ruth?" Lilith drifted after me, hovering too close, curiosity glinting in her eyes. "Knowing you, I guess it's got to be contraplan. It certainly doesn't self-erase the way a sense-cube has to. The cybers would have a fit!" She bumped up against me, cloying perfume invading. "Is that your family, Ruth? You know, *I* lost my family, too, in a way." Voice low, confiding. A tear glistened and floated free as she gave me a brave little smile.

I gritted my teeth and pulled my travel bag from her grip, just accidentally propelling her away from me. I must have pushed harder than I thought, because she flew across the chamber and collided with the third member of our merry crew, the cybernetics tech Helsa had ordered me to smuggle aboard along with Lilith.

Rik turned irritably from the com-console, a screwdriver drifting free as he pushed Lilith away. "Leave me out of this, all right? I'm trying to get some work done." He lunged for the tool and turned his back on us.

I shoved the plaque through the dilating mouth of my bag. Must have forgotten to lock it.

Lilith fluttered graceful arms and recovered her balance, pushing off a wall with one pale, dainty foot to come floating back to me. "I'm sorry. You know I'd never touch your things if it wasn't a sort of emergency."

She managed to shrug and at the same time come to a hover in front of me, voice dropping to a conspiratorial whisper. "I just came into my cycle"—she threw a look over her shoulder at Rik, blushed, and giggled—"and silly old me, I just forgot to bring anything along. So I thought *you'd* be sure to come prepared." She gave me an abashed smile.

I snorted, reached back into my bag, and rummaged. A thin lume rod and a pack of Knights in Tarot gaming cards floated up from the bag. I grabbed the rod, but the cards fanned free of their case.

"Here." Lilith swept them up, plucking one last stray from the air. "Why, that's lucky, isn't it? Doubles!"

She flashed the glossy Twin card with its picture of fate's big gaming wheel and the mirrored, blindfolded figures facing outward on opposite sides.

I took the card, fingering it and frowning, a vague question nibbling. The sharp, painted profiles faintly resembled CI:DUN:4 and the identical cyberserf that had shown up to act so oddly at my briefing. And all that stuff Number One had been babbling—

"You're a twin, too, aren't you, Ruth? David told me about his second father being your twin brother and all. I guess that must make it even harder, being disowned by your family when it wasn't *really* your fault." Lilith pressed closer, eyes pinning mine.

I jerked away, pressing my lips tight and thrusting the cards into the bag. I threw a small packet at her.

"That's real sweet of you." The dimpled smile flashed again, a gleam of satisfaction in the big blues.

I turned my back and carefully locked the travel bag as she drifted off to the sanicubicle. Stowing the bag in webbing along one wall and ignoring Rik's curious glance, I counted ten again, just for practice.

Back at Resistance Headquarters, I'd argued myself blue with Helsa, but had finally admitted Rik might be useful on the assignment. My wild card disc had its limits for penetrating coded cybernetic data levels. And he'd done a good job bypassing the security loops to convince the mechmen I was the only person in my module when it was loaded. Of course, I couldn't trust him, since he was in with Denneth's bunch. Helsa was probably keeping Denneth quiet by sending Rik with me. If she had other motives for sending along a man who clearly didn't trust me any more than I did him, I didn't want to know. Maybe she was out of her mind, as I'd suggested when she'd informed me Lilith was also coming along.

"She'll be a buffer," was all Helsa would say.

I didn't know how the hell that was supposed to translate. But if it meant Rik and I, after two and a half standard days locked in CI's one-person comfort module with Lilith, were both so sick of her we didn't mind each other so much, maybe Helsa's plan was working okay.

I nudged myself across the chamber to the intent, slight figure with the wisps of sandy hair floating straight out from pale scalp. "How's it going?"

Rik shrugged and didn't look up from the snarl of bypasses

he'd wired into the opened console. "I'm trying something new, but. . . ." He shot me a defensive look. "You know there's not much I can do with this com unit. It's not meant to be a data link."

"You're doing better than I could, that's for sure."

He looked surprised, but still wary. "See anything outside?"

"Not much. I went down to the other end of the ship and poked around, but I couldn't find a control panel. No readouts, nothing." I shrugged. "Makes sense—who's supposed to be around to read it? But one of the activated mechmen was linked into a sort of outlet, busy flashing its indicators and ignoring me, so maybe that's their interface to transport functions. And hopefully CI's mission data. I saw a couple of the outlets in different places. Think you could tap in?"

"Who knows until I see it."

"We'll have to risk it. As usual, CI didn't give me the straight skinny on this little outing, and I want to know what they know about that mysterious signal and the incorporeals before we get to Cyvrus." And whether or not they knew anything about David. . . .

Rik looked doubtful.

I shook off persistent worries about the kid. "Look, if one of the mechmen spots you in the cargo area, you opaque your face-screen and keep quiet, and it'll just assume you're me and tow you back. Anyway, all you have to do is get your camouflage program slotted in, same way you got aboard, and they'll edit out of memory any sign of you or Lilith, right?"

"It's not that easy." He gave me the superior look all the cybernetics specialists had down cold. "In the first place, I was sweating out some pretty tricky timing on the loading procedures. And the transport loops are layered in an offset array, coded, *plus* a rotating internal security gate that's—"

"I don't need to know the details, that's your job. But if you're not up to it . . ."

He drummed his fingers on the console, sighed, and shrugged. "All right, I'll give it a shot."

• • •

> *"Behold, O Founder, for I am in distress,*
> *my soul is in tumult,*
> *my heart is wrung within me,*
> *for I have been rebellious. . . .*
> *Remember my affliction and my bitterness,*

the wormwood and the gall!
My soul continually recalls it
and is bowed down within me.
But this I call to mind,
and therefore have hope:
The steadfast care of the Guardian cybers
never ceases. . . ."

I shook my head, dark red strands snaking around me, hissing their own mocking accompaniment to the verses from the Poindros Book of Words. The old Way of my homeworld held no more comforts for me. I plucked another one-handed chord from the small harp strapped to my chest, steadying the wood frame awkwardly against my bobbing cast and trying to ignore the persistent, teeth-grating buzz in my arm. I blew out a long breath and drifted with the dying notes.

The bulk of my discarded suit floated past, and I nudged it toward the other end of the small repair airlock I'd discovered along one flank of the cargo well. Despite what I'd told Rik, I knew enough to bypass its simple security code and request the right pressure and atmosphere inside. It was escape, of a sort, from the other overcrowded tin can. And even if I couldn't see them through the sealed outer hatch, I was close to the stars.

I plucked another series of chords from the lyre, then half an awkward arpeggio:

"The Heavens are telling the glory of the Founder,
and day to day proclaims his Guardians' wisdom. . . ."

I made a face. Damn the guardian cybers and their grand Plan. But all I could seem to come up with were the Old Words, the old fragile truths of Poindros. I didn't have a right to mouth them any more, not when I'd betrayed them, squirming like the Serpent of Change into their midst. Betrayed Helen, stealing her youngest husband, my new pateros, my "father" and my lover, the secret cyborg.

Damn Lilith and her prying eyes. And myself for bringing the anachronistic photograph along. I should get rid of it. Maybe the cybers were right—it was sick to cling to the past, sick to keep contraplan History alive to replay its vanished cycles. Better not to reach for painful forbidden truths. Better to let time flow, smooth and untroubled.

I shook my head again, wrenching a dischord from the strings, groping for different old-words—ones I'd found in the cybers' taboo files, words from banned History. My voice was low and husky, nowhere near my mother's pure, vibrant soprano. It echoed off the metal walls:

> *"The Heavens reject not*
> *The desire of the moth for the star,*
> *Of the night for the morrow,*
> *The devotion to something afar*
> *From the sphere of our sorrow. . . ."*

The stars were out there, all around me, dwarfing the tiny mote of CI's transport, clustered just beyond its blind metal skin. I closed my eyes and I was swimming through them, flying free, touching their untouchable silver fire. . . .

My hand slapped the lyre strings, killing the last chord. Abrupt silence rang in my ears. My gaze traveled over the airlock's curved walls and the drifting pressure suit, fixing on the outer hatch controls. A slow smile turned into a grin.

"You're out of your mind."

"Why? Either of the suits can handle the vacuum—the cargo well's barely pressurized, no air to speak of, and *that* didn't bother you. I'll even use a tether, if it'll make you feel better."

"Nothing's going to make me feel better about this assignment."

"Come on, Rik, you're one lucky human. How many people get a chance to travel to a planet that 'doesn't exist,' or really fly free in space?" I lounged back, floating in the cramped living compartment, tossing my sunburst-crystal dice. They took a different spin in zero-G, but I was getting the knack of catching snake eyes, exercising my useless talent that I was beginning to admit might have something to do with the way I'd managed to twice resist the incorporeal energy webs. The talent CI seemed interested in now. . . . I shrugged and tossed the dice again.

Rik's thin, sandy halo wafted back and forth as he shook his head, giving the dice a disgusted look. Hunching back over the console's guts, he readjusted one of his new bridges. He closed it up and tapped fingertips on the keyplate he'd grafted on, incoherent data patterns blossoming on the tiny screen. "Look. Didn't do much good tapping into that ship outlet to order up a

new data gate through this com receptacle. CI's got most of their
information double security-coded internally—even the transport
operative loops can't access. I did manage to tap into this. . . .''
His fingers danced over the plate. "But it's pretty much the same
as what we had on file at headquarters.''

The screen reconfigured, flashing a view of a vaguely familiar-
looking star cluster. The image rushed closer, magnifying a seething red sun and two orbiting planets. Another magnification filled
the screen with a slowly rolling blue world cloaked in cloud. No
land masses.

"Cyvrus," I whispered, pulling myself closer. The taboo world.
Watery realm of forbidden monsters, of shadows and concealed
depths. All of a sudden it was real. And with every second, the
ship was hurtling us closer.

Rik shrugged uneasily. "Wish to hell I'd never heard of it.''
He tapped the plate again and the image disappeared, words and
figures scrolling up the screen:

> Cyvrus. Special status Central Interlock jurisdiction.
> Geoformed class G atmosphere, active volcanic core with
> regular submerged eruptions. Vulcanism source of oceanic
> heating and dense electrolytic nutrient component. Select
> transplanted old-earth floral and faunal species maintained
> in monitored ecological balance. Minimal orbital vari-
> ances. . . .

The screen filled with statistics that didn't tell me any more
than the ones I'd scanned back at headquarters. I kept seeing that
cloudy world rolling around its malevolent red sun, and I had to
shake off a shiver of foreboding.

Rik punched off the display. "Anyway, about all I could get
other than this stuff was pretty much what we knew already. The
regularly scheduled supply transport left Casino six days before
this one, no registered passengers of course, but Siolis and the
brat"—he shot me a damn-you look—"must have altered the
records and stowed away, same as Lilith and I did. If they'd told
us what that signal was all about, we wouldn't be going through
this crap. Typical of that freak and his precious protégé.''

I bit back a sharp retort. If David was in trouble, I'd need Rik's
help. "I'm sure your pals back home will appreciate the cute
comments, so why not save them. Anything else?''

He shrugged, fiddling with the keyplate. "Those two must have
stirred up something on the planet. I managed to monitor some

communication between CI, the ship, and the Cyvrus facility. CI keeps repeating queries about that damn signal, but I can't access anything definitive. The facility does check out as some kind of bio lab, according to what's listed on our supply manifest, so that conforms with what the cyberserf hinted at to you. But I don't get it, bioforming's taboo with the cybers."

He made an uneasy movement. "What do you think they're doing, making more freaks like Siolis?"

"I asked you to stop calling him that." I took a deep breath, pushing through my own reflex distaste at the thought of experiments on living tissue. "From what I gathered, it sounds like CI uses the Cyvrus facility for animals the same way they used Andura to maintain pure plant species."

"That's right, Denneth said you got real close to those furry fr—those bioformed Andurans, too. Better you than me."

"Better for them," I muttered, ignoring Rik's quick glance. "So what are you picking up from the facility to CI?"

"It just keeps sending Status Normal replies. Maybe that cyberserf was right about a transmission glitch, and the whole thing's a wild goose chase."

"I don't think so." Siolis had known something. I could almost feel his violet gaze on me, disturbing, compelling.

Rik punched up another meaningless data configuration, then blanked out the screen. "That's it. I can't get more out of this job—the only thing that might work is a direct patch-in at the facility, which would probably be too late."

I gave myself a shake. "So we're flying in blind."

"That's about it. Too many unknown variables. Especially with a possible threat from those incorporeals to factor in somewhere. We should terminate the assignment until we can get some hard data. I *told* Helsa we should wait for Denneth to break the CI codes back in Casino." He crossed his arms and scowled at me. "And we wouldn't have to be scrambling for every data bit if your little genius would've given out the plans for his interface."

I took a deep breath. Counted some more numbers. "You were in on the planning session when I told Helsa about CI losing control of the two cyberserfs at my briefing, Rik. Who knows what other system glitches we could be causing? Before the Resistance does any more messing around with the cyber system, we'd damn well better understand what we're doing. Siolis and David are still experimenting with the interface, and we're not going to go in and start changing the Benevolence Directives until a lot of people put their heads together to work out some new ones."

"How long are we going to hear *that* excuse? You act like you're so damn tough, but I think you're just afraid to make a move without our wonderful Guardians to make sure you don't go bump."

"Damn right I'm afraid of what you hotshots could do to us all, just to satisfy your itch to tinker! You techs are so glued to your consoles you might as well be cybers." I caught myself and took a deep breath. "Look, take it up with Helsa. We've got a job to do here."

His scowl deepened. "I still vote we terminate the assignment."

"Nobody's taking a vote—I'm in charge of this expedition, remember? And you seem to be forgetting that CI didn't give us much choice on timing. We've got the mechmen on our side this trip—more or less. We'll just have to play it by ear."

He gave me another sour look.

"Lighten up, Rik!" I shook off my own vague uneasiness. "All we can do is wait now, anway, so why don't you take a break and come give it a whirl with me? I'm not going to pass on what might be my only chance to take a walk with the stars. Look, I'll try it first, then you can give it a go. Come on, ask the ship when the next stabilization period brings us out of Shift."

His fingers hesitated above the keyplate, then pulled back, his eyes jerking to mine. "Ask it yourself *you're* in charge!"

He ripped open the cling-strip he'd rigged to hold him in front of the console, pushing past me and knocking loose a snap-jar of terminal caps. The lid popped off and the parts fanned free in a drifting, glinting cloud, mingling with the floating blobs of vermilion lacquer Lilith had recently contributed to our environment with her freefall toenail-painting experiment.

"Suvving mess!" Rik shot Lilith and me indiscriminate scathing looks and grabbed the net he'd made from one of her gauzy scarves, launching himself awkwardly after his escaping caps. The breeze he kicked up only made it worse, scattering the parts.

"I'll help, Rikky!" Across the chamber, Lilith stretched languidly in her sleeping web, rolling out in a cloud of blond curls and hot-pink sequins. She spread her tunic to catch a wandering cluster of terminal caps, then reversed effortlessly to scoop up another escapee. I'd already decided that talent in zero G must be inversely proportional to intellect.

Lilith giggled and drifted with a shimmering wriggle over to Rik, wafting a tiny kerchief to wipe off the red splatter he'd just collided with. He brushed her arm away, slamming himself back against the wall and losing the caps he'd managed to retrieve. He swore feebly as Lilith pursued the metal bits with her relentlessly perky smile.

I shrugged, turned to the console, and started tapping in my query to the transport data loops.

"Wait! You'll just get a code challenge and screw up my security access." Rik thrashed over and yanked me back. He gritted his teeth and belted himself in again. "All right, I'll get it for you. Just remember, you asked for it."

Behind him, I rolled my eyes. The screen lit up in quick-fire queries and answers, then started scrolling from the bottom up a long schedule list in Casino standard time. "It's coming up." Rik's voice was grudging.

"Ruth, you can't be *ser*ious!" Lilith had suddenly materialized beside me, making me jump. "You're really gonna go out there, into that, that awful black nothingness? Honey, you've gotta be—"

"There." Rik touched the keyplate as the transport's last period of navigational reorientation in straight-space scrolled up, commencing a few hours earlier and lasting fifteen minutes. Hazy figures started forming beneath the rising line. "Look—the stabilization periods seem to be shortening as we get closer to the Cyvrus system. That's not enough time to get outside the airlock and back in. Forget it."

Lilith leaned across me, eyes wide, throwing herself for once awkwardly off-balance and catching herself with a grip on the edge of the console. She brushed against me, giving me a crackling static shock. I yanked my eyes back to the screen to see the next scheduled period shimmer distorted at the bottom of the screen. I squinted and leaned closer, but the numbers, like those tempting stars, were dissolving from my grasp. "Damn it, Rik, don't wipe the readout yet."

He shot me an unreadable look and raised his hands from the keyplate. "It's your funeral."

"Why, Rik, you're just awful!"

"Do you two mind?" I elbowed Lilith aside as the line scrolled up, firming into legibility. A nice, solid half-hour of stabilization coming up in only two-point-three hours. "All right! Be there with bells on."

• • •

Blackness. Cold silence. Forever, the distance, beyond grasping. The heavens. The deep.

Whirled in the centrifuge of that vastness, tiny ice-etched bits of radiance traced their paths out into eternity. Dizzy, dazed, caught in the still center, I hung—for a moment, forever—suspended by a narrow thread.

Something finally penetrated my numbness. A tug on the belt of my suit, bobbing me around at the end of my tether. I blinked, confused, at the dim cylinder floating at the other end, its shape blanking out an insignificant shadow in the vast encircling pattern of stars.

I blinked again, trying to feel the size of the ship attached to my tether, but it wasn't real. I rolled slowly over, all of black space and silence rolling around me, offering the whole of its galaxies and great emptiness. For a mad, lucid moment the pattern was unbearably clear, an unheard voice whispering the secret in my ear. I fumbled with the tether's clasp, ready to cast myself free into beckoning space.

But the silence was broken. Something was pounding, thudding, hammering down its doors. Tearing at my chest. My heart, racing wildly. And the explosive release of a breath I hadn't realized I was holding.

I blinked again and flexed my fingers, raising my hand to stare through the helmet at the shadowy shape of the glove, groping to reorient myself within the confines of the human-shaped suit. The glove dropped away and I was dropping again into directionless emptiness, vertigo clutching at my guts. I took another deep breath and paced my heartbeat, summoned up an unspoken Setharian chant to calm the wild rhythm. I tumbled slowly, washed in the icy silver of the stars, their silent whispers singing through me now with the fire of my blood. I was spinning at the center of the wheel.

"That's it, Ruthie. Feel it out. *You're* the center when you ride the spinner arm." Long-dead elder pateros Isaac whispered out of the emptiness, teaching me again to climb the towers and spinning windwheels of our home farm. To find a new perspective within the dizzy whirl of earth and air.

I smiled, opening my arms and arching to float out into the stars' embrace.

"Rrrzzzz." Clamor and static in my helmet.

I sighed, tonguing down the volume, rolling around on the tether to face the floating transport. "Rik. It's not time yet." My eyes flicked up to verify the tiny numerals in their countdown at the periphery of the faceplate.

"Fifteen minutes to go." The distant, tinny voice managed to sound grudging. I was still surprised he hadn't put up more of a fight about donning the other pressure suit to stand backup on the airlock controls for me. "Buzz you in five to head back."

"Fantastic out here. Sure you don't want to change your mind?"

A crackling negative, and the speaker cut out. I rolled back away from the ship, selfishly glad for the extra time. Arching out, I spread my arms again, left arm stiff in the cast I'd managed to squeeze this time into the suit sleeve. I ignored the faint electric itch, triggering a quick test of the suit's right side steering jet. It threw me into the start of a spin, but I kept arched, riding it out into a glide up and under the rolling dome of stars.

A silent song hummed in my ears as I tucked into a weightless tumble past the slack loops of tether, spread my arms and legs again, and drifted outward.

It was all and more than I'd imagined, riding the invisible trails of those distant stars, tracing their unfelt winds. The humming swelled to an exultant chorus in the uprush of memory. The wind-tower lifting its immense sapphire-silver sails into the dawn. Copper sun rolling slowly over stirring wheat fields. The sail arms lifting us into the open blue sky as Jason and I chased our wild game of tag through the wind-whipped cycle. My last free leap between the high sail arms.

Between stars, between the ends of forever. *Free, in the heavens, in the hour of splendor—*

A jolt as the taut tether suddenly grabbed and snapped me around. But that wasn't what flung me into empty vertigo. It was the ship.

What was left of the ship.

Space spun dizzily around me, but this time it was literal. There was a shimmering distortion, a sinking and folding in of the blackness, swallowing the stars, swallowing one end of the ship and its faint luminescence. The transport shimmered, throwing off colored halos, slipping backward into that pleated blankness. Into the Shift.

Panic exploded. "Rik!" I screamed, forgetting the mike, my hand grabbing at the tether, hauling myself in.

"Rik!" This time cuing the mike, eyes flicking to the countdown. Twelve minutes left. "What happened? You're going into Shift early!"

Only static, and my hands frantically hauling on the tether. Too slow, a sharp stab of pain down my arm, the end of the transport scintillating now in a shower of lights, an opaque black wave rolling slowly over it.

"Sacred Founders . . ." I abandoned the hopeless tangle of my tether, remembering the jets, twisting to align myself and triggering them both full thrust. I shot crazily off course, fighting a spin, desperately correcting, thrashing out of it to be swallowed by a blind, sickening surge of panic as the blackness folded over more of the crazy spewing lights, all that was left of the ship.

I fought the thrust alignment, but it was too late. There was a wild roaring in my ears. Black emptiness opened its jaws to suck me in, death screaming down its bottomless throat. Hissing. It was the Serpent, riding its head-to-toe cycle forever, circling around me, squeezing me in its coils.

I fought it, but I was inside in the darkness, the hissing a hot circuit through me. The coils claimed me. Hiss of escaping air and a silent scream. No, wait, a breathy whisper, almost a faintly familiar, humming voice—

Wait. Listen.

The hot panic hum had turned somehow to cool air, a windy whisper suffusing me. It cycled with excruciating slowness through my lungs, and everything went still. I opened my eyes to see the end of the ship suspended now in its fiery halos, the shafts of lancing light frozen to colored ice shards in a cold wind, the black folding stalled in the great distance between my heartbeats. Dark space and the brilliant stars were an impossible clarity around me as I traced the straight path of a single humming tone, a tautly vibrating, invisible string between the airlock hatch and me.

My hands clenched, shattering the frozen moment, shooting me out on the wind of those open black jaws.

The jets blasted me straight at the still-exposed end of the ship, hurtling me through an explosion of rainbows as the metal flank swelled and slammed down on me. I hit hard, gasping, grappling reflexively for a handhold on the hatch as I stared blankly at the blinking amber signal on the airlock mechanism. And the crimson automatic lock indicator.

I pressed the activator, but the crimson light stayed steady. The transport controls had to be overriding for Shift. "Rik! Open the hatch!"

I dragged in a breath, air feed hissing echoes in my ears, and threw a look over my shoulder. The lights were going crazy, flaming in a leaping corona, the blackness eating its way closer.

"Rik! I made it. Open the hatch. Hurry, man!"

More hissing in my ears and a distant voice, barely recognizable, distorted by the wild energy fields. "Too late, Ruth." Static. ". . . get away this time. You're finally getting what you deserve." The red locking light stayed on.

"Rik, open it!" I pounded stupidly on the hatch. "Come on!" I froze, an icy hand gripping inside as it all snapped into place. Those dissolving and refocusing numbers on the screen—he'd altered the readout on the stabilization time. "*You're* the one! You killed Pavlo, but you were after me. Rik, whoever put you up to it, they're wrong, that's not the answer. Listen—" The radio was dead.

"Bloody, blasted . . ." There had to be a manual lock override for mechman use. I shot a last look over my shoulder, squinting through the colored flares.

My hand clutched tighter on the hatch ring. Terror ripped through me on its fiery circuits as I stared up at a looming, impossible wave of distorted space turned inside out.

The black tide rolled over me.

four

It wasn't black inside. It wasn't anything inside. Maybe I wasn't inside. Maybe I *wasn't*.

There seemed to be no me left to see with. No sense of a center to perceptions, no senses at all to cling to. Only a vast, unlocalized, omniscient awareness of wave after wave of buffeting, nerve-wracking disorientation splashed in wildly flaring colors. Except that they weren't anything the I that used to be would have recognized as colors. And the shapes angled impossibly off into too many dimensions, or were swallowed into none but were still . . . no, not exactly *there*, but . . .

At the same time, though time didn't seem to apply any more than place, there was a great roaring howl, emanating from everything, everywhere, everywhen, and rushing inward and outward to a single nonexistent point of white silence. Or maybe it was the other way around. There was no sound, but the howling was a horrible din, scattering everything, sucking everything. The I that had been would have been terrified.

A thought occurred. Humans couldn't tolerate the warped space of the Shift—that was why the cybers kept passenger transport viewing domes carefully shielded except for stabilization periods. Therefore I was dead, and this was Heaven.

Scratch that, I'd broken too many commandments from the Book of Words. This was Hell.

Something rejected that.

No, *I* rejected that. Me. I was around somewhere in here, out here, whatever here. But the parts didn't connect. I couldn't feel. There were only the simultaneous sensations from too many points. And the points were splitting off from each other, the impossible shapes and dizzy angles rushing off in great schisms as the no-colored colors flared and swathes of dark space and stars whirled in to pour down a swirling vortex that was actually an expansion. And I had no location.

I somehow, somewhere realized that I *was* terrified, horrified, frozen within the rent chaos of this space. But that part wasn't

53

connecting with the other parts. Maybe they weren't there any
more to connect with.

A sudden writhing, somewhere, a disembodied panic flailing.
Silent screaming. No voice, no hands to throw out to stop the
dizzy whirling. Caught, divorced from myself, trapped in a ref-
erenceless nonplace like the pulsing energy net of the incorporeals.
No way to grasp it, grasp myself within it, no way out. And this
time it was true chaos, no plan behind it, nothing even to fight.
If only I could catch one of those piercing bright stars whirling
and compressing into the expanding black light, if I could grab
the impossible, flayed, and inside-out pieces of reason and reassemble them, if only the roaring scream would stop—

Wait. Listen.

There was that hissing voice again, a breathy unheard whisper.
Silent, roaring. From all around. From nowhere. Impossible.

Wait. Stop trying to make sense of it. Stop sensing it. Find my
eyes and make them close.

So I searched, strained from every point of the nowhere to find
my eyes. But I couldn't see them.

The menacing, devouring howl turned inexplicably to cosmic
laughter. Laughing at puny me, gripping tight to impossibility.
Possibility? No, I *was* the laughter, the windy hiss. No sound.
No ears. . . . No eyes. No, eyes.

Here. I found them, felt them. Finally, I relearned how to close
them.

Darkness.

Blessed darkness—a thick, deep blanket enfolding me. I was
still dizzy, buffeted by inexplicable sensations, sounds, shifts of
motion, but the distant, howling laughter had turned to a humming
lullaby. I tried to ignore the crazy whirl, gripping the soft blackness
around me and defining my shape with it, clutching the blind
presence of it tightly to me. . . . But no, it was something else I
was clutching. My hand, there. Still gripping desperately to the
hatch lock.

My gloves groped frantically over the reassuring, solid shapes.
Eyes screwed tightly shut, I fumbled across an inset handle, pulled
it with no result, felt what had to be the bumps of the lock indicators. I groped some more, taking a deep, careful breath. It caught
in my throat.

There. A raised lip just within reach from my anchoring grasp.
A narrow slot, too narrow for my fingers in the bulky glove. I
tried again, but the awkward angle of my arm in the cast wouldn't

let me get at it. I pulled back, crawled around and changed arms, ignoring the twinge in my arm. I groped with my good hand, felt the slot, shoved my hand in. Felt something give. I pushed harder against a springy pressure. The glove caught and then pushed free. Something clicked into place.

The hatch flew open, nearly flinging me off it.

I grabbed the edge, weak with relief. I pulled myself into the airlock with shaking arms. I resealed the hatch by feel, not even tempted to take one last look at what the cybers had been hiding from us. I didn't open my eyes until I felt the latches re-engage.

Cracking one eyelid, I traced the now-comforting confines of the airlock, the curved walls and my own floating shadow cast by the cling-lume I'd left inside. I went limp, drifting, taking deep breaths. Then I checked the suit's readouts and realized I didn't have much air left for hanging around.

I took another deep breath. My helmet radio was still dead, not that calling Rik would've helped a lot. Just for jollies, I propelled myself over to the environmental controls and gave them a try. Nothing. He'd covered all the circuits. And the inset socket of the transport operations outlet was made for a mechman, not me. I pushed myself over to the inner hatch, pressing switches. No response. But there had to be a manual latch here, too. If only Rik didn't know that, didn't realize I'd made it inside. Or was he monitoring my attempts at the controls, waiting on the other side?

My breathing echoed short and shallow in my ears as I groped over the lock controls. Was my air getting thinner, harder to breathe? Hotter?

I blinked sweat from my eyes, feeling around the lip of the hatch. There. Another narrow slot. One finger found the recessed, spring-loaded button inside, pushed it.

It was frozen in place, wouldn't give. I shoved my hand in farther, jabbing at the switch, trying to force it. It wouldn't budge.

A blinking red trouble light in the helmet readouts tugged at my peripheral vision. * *suit integrity alert* * *glove, right* * *excessive temperature gradient* *

"What?" I jerked my hand out and nudged myself reflexively back from the hatch, a sudden prickling on the back of my neck. Slowly drifting, I frowned down at the oddly dimpled, discolored fingertips of the glove. "What the—"

There was a flash of blinding light and a deep, muffled *whump*. A giant hand hit me, throwing me back against the outer hatch in a flurry of flying debris. My arms were flung back and the cast hit with a sharp crack and lancing pain. There was a crackle and electric shock through my arm, vaguely registered as I scrambled to avoid a large hunk of hatch sucked into the vacuum after me. I grabbed a handhold on the environmental controls, ducking as the debris churned and drifted. A big piece spun close. I craned past it to see a ragged hole where the hatch had blown loose.

My cast gave a last crackling, electric tingle and died, arm throbbing painfully inside it. A warped chunk of a metal compressed-gas cannister drifted past, undoubtedly part of the backup hatch mechanism. I pulled myself and my miraculously intact suit carefully away from the sharp edges as it rolled. The twisted metal was burned and blackened on one side.

I frowned as it bobbed up against the wall, then I turned again as a bulky shadow floated across it. I jerked back, heart giving a sickening lurch.

The gloved hand of the other pressure suit still gripped a welding laser as it bobbed past me. The arm dropped and the suit rolled slowly in a grotesque, sleepy motion. I flinched away from the mangled lower portion and the bright stains, this time indelible. Behind the helmet's clear curve, Rik's face showed only a frozen, faint astonishment.

"If you ask me, he got what he deserved. It gives me the creeps to think about him sneaking around like that. And what if he'd landed with us and tried to hurt our dear boy? I just can't feel sorry, and I don't know why you're dwelling on it, Ruth!"

"Because we're not done with him yet."

"Fiddle-dee-dee! He's not coming back from down there." Lilith turned away from the mirror she'd stuck to the outside of the comfort module the mechmen had mounted on metal struts driven into bare stone. She gestured with her brush past me, toward the restless hiss of dark water sucking up against black rock. "Fishies are probably having lunch right now—on him."

I stared, mouth hanging open, as she returned to her mirror. It had been Lilith's idea to weight down Rik's body for disposal in Cyvrus' engulfing ocean. After all, as she'd pointed out, we'd had to do *something* with him before the mechmen started wondering about the smell. I was discovering Lilith could be surprisingly down-to-earth—when there weren't any males around. Again I was reminded of those overwhelmingly feminine matrons of my homeworld, ruling their households so efficiently without ever seeming to.

I turned on my slippery wet hump of rock to stare across the unbroken expanse of opaque, slowly rolling water. I blinked through the lukewarm drizzle at the lowering ceiling of cloud diffusing a sullen red light from the oversized, shrouded sun. The endless sea was flattened by rain, the horizon flat and featureless, the dim red light flat and shadowless. Even the breezeless air tasted metallically flat. The low, lifeless chunk of black rock with its leveled landing pad was the only thing breaking the vast gloomy monotony. The tall, pointing fingertip of the shuttle launcher was swallowed by hellish red dimness and cloud.

I couldn't shake a depressing, end-of-the-world feeling about the planet. Or worse, something vaguely threatening in the lurid, banked-embers glow, the persistent drip drip onto slick black rock, the claustrophobic, too-close sky. And that dark, opaque sea, the only thing alive and moving in the landscape, sucking and swallowing more rock below me, creeping higher.

I shivered, turning to put my back to it. I cleared my throat. "Rik wasn't working alone, Lilith. We don't know why he wanted to kill me, whether it was the incorporeals or Denneth behind—"

"Well, Rik was certainly flesh and blood, Ruth." She gave a pretty little shudder, still absorbed in the mirror. "And Denneth's about as far away as he could be, back in Casino. You sent Helsa your message, didn't you, so what else can you do?" She puckered her reflected lips and applied something that looked purple in the gloom.

I rubbed my face, talking more to myself than her. "There's something not quite . . . Why'd Rik try to weld the hatch shut? He could've just waited, blasted me, and flushed me back out the airlock—"

"Honey, he must've just panicked. People *do*, you know. We can't all be like you, Ruth—how under the stars you could go out there in the first place I'll never know!" Lilith gave her complicated network of braids and blond poufs a last pat and turned back to me with a pirouette to make her fringed tunic flutter. Moisture already misted her hair and shoulders, but it didn't seem to bother her. I shivered again in my damp huddle on the rock, trying to be convinced that the rain was actually almost warm. Behind me, the sea hissed mockingly.

Lilith, bouncing across the rocks in her generous built-in in-

sulation, nattered on. "Thank Founder there's a little bit of solid
land in the middle of all this water! But this light's ghastly. I don't
know why I even bother with makeup. . . ."

I'd given up hoping she'd wind down. Past her, mechmen emp-
tied the second shuttle load they'd brought down from the orbiting
transport. Supplies for the bio lab. And some special CI equipment
they were assembling to act as a temporary remote control center
for the facility, in case the incorporeals *had* taken over inside.

" . . . do know how you feel, Ruth. I'm awfully worried about
David, too."

I jerked my head around, startled as she laid a dainty hand on
my shoulder.

She gave me one of her heart-to-heart looks. "That's why I
think we ought to concentrate, you know, on getting him back.
You're just fretting yourself sick over the rest of it. Best thing
you could do is get some sleep."

Even through my damp skinslicks, the pressure of her hand felt
warm. I shivered again, head drooping tiredly, tempted to give in
to a slow, dark wave of sleep. Sleep. Let the mechmen handle
the first phase. . . .

I blinked and shook my head, irritably shaking off her hand.
"Too much to do." I jerked my head toward the mechmen. "Have
to make contact with the facility." With incoporeals?

"Well, I don't see why we're wasting time with all this equipment. If we could just find Siolis and David, they'd know what
to do about this incorporeal business. And we don't know if those
horrible creatures are even here. Didn't you say your CI contact
was acting kind of funny when he talked about them?"

I gave her a sharp look, but she only smiled, white teeth and
bland blue eyes. Maybe she *was* smarter than she looked. It
wouldn't be the first time CI had played games with me. But if
it wasn't incorporeals this time, what was going on here?

I pushed myself off the rock, picking my way over slippery
stone to the clear stressplex dome where the mechmen were setting
up the communication center. Lilith trailed behind, but the units
trundling along with their loads just altered their courses, ignoring
her unauthorized presence. Rik had done us one service, implementing his camouflage program. I only hoped he hadn't left any
booby traps in the data loops.

I ducked through the dome's entrance, picking a mechman testing part of the interface equipment. "Have you contacted the
facility yet?"

The flat alloy face swiveled, lights flashing. A colorless voice droned, "Preliminary interface established, testing pattern C483 implemented." The face swiveled back.

"What the hell is that supposed to mean?"

The mechman ignored me, its extensors adjusting controls as more lights flashed quick patterns to a high-pitched whine.

"I asked you what—"

Something cold touched the back of my neck. I whirled around, hands jerking up without thought into fighting position. A sharp pain stabbed my left arm before the sling reconfigured to support the heavy cast.

Another mechman was planted there, retracting one of its manipulators. "This unit is your mission liaison. May I help you, Ruth?" The unit CI had upgrade-programmed for me looked identical to all the others, and I was always losing it until it talked. They'd given the tinny voice from its chest speaker a rudimentary intonation.

I snorted. "The first thing you can do is never sneak up behind me like that again! That's an order—CI code RK1. Now, when are you—"

"Acknowledged." The face lights flashed green, returned to attentive blue and red.

I took a deep breath. "When are you going to—"

"Here, Ruth! This'll help." Lilith flounced over from the entrance, pulling loose one of her violet ribbons and trying it in a quick bow around the mechman's neck. "All dressed up, just for you."

I swore under my breath, hoping she hadn't heard my CI mission code. "Shut up, will you?" I motioned her back from the mech, not wanting to push the camouflage programming too far.

"Very well. Deactivating." The mechman's face went dark, expect for the one steady amber ready light.

"Damn." I glared at Lilith, who pouted and plunked herself down on a crate. I turned back to the dormant mech. "Uh... reverse that order. Reactivate."

The face lights sprang on again. "Thank you, Ruth. I am eager to be of assistance." The violet bow bobbed at the mechman's neck, giving it a ridiculously jaunty air.

I sighed. "Okay, Violet. When do we get to talk to the facility?"

The lights blinked, flashed patterns, and steadied. "Communication channel is now open."

An uneasy chill of gooseflesh down my back. Or was I just

coming down with some Cyvriot bug? I shrugged off a recurring ripple of lightheadedness. "What about the facility control systems? Are they intact?"

"Remote testing of system parameters indicates normal configuration."

"Normal power-utilization figures?"

"All parameters within normal limits."

Hmm. "I need to use a console hookup."

"This way, please." Violet extended a polite manipulator.

I stood back just as politely. "You first."

The lights flashed. "There is no need for fear, Ruth. CI benevolence directives remain in full effect."

I wiped damp palms down damp skinslicks and shrugged again. "Where's the console?"

Neck bow bobbing, it led me around a bulky generator, more mechmen at work assembling equipment, and a long bank of data outlets like the ones in the transport. We skirted the dome's central shaft piercing the transport roof. Past a distorting pattern of raindrops, a conglomeration of sensors, rotating sweeps, and antennas sprouted overhead. Catching myself as I tripped over thick cables, I stopped beside Violet, in front of a compact unit with blank screen and attached keyplate.

I touched the plate and a ready configuration blossomed on the screen, pulsing. "Okay, Violet. Make yourself scarce for a while."

Its facelights flickered. "Illogical command. Present mechmen numbers minus one exceed definition of scarcity."

I sighed. "Leave me alone for a few minutes, okay?"

"My operative programs permit me to point out that I would provide better service in close proximity."

"I'll holler if I need you."

"Very well, Ruth, but please do not strain your voice." It waddled off on stiff leg-extensors.

I punched in CI's special code and got to work. I wanted to independently verify what Violet had told me, even though I wasn't being logical. There was supposedly no way the incorporeals, if they'd taken over the facility, could invade a remote system, or affect the mechmen at this distance. Still . . .

I fed in the queries CI had recorded for me, and everything checked out normal. Too normal. The facility was operating exactly as it should have been. All loops responded to capacity and in proper timing. All codes notched into perfect sequence with appropriate response codes. There were no inexplicable power drains to indicate the presence of parasite incorporeals, disembodied intelligences riding the loops and circuits of the cybernet and sucking up its data and energy for their fusion of the one in all. According to CI, even if the incorporeals had taken over the system, they shouldn't have been able to cover their tracks so completely. And the screen concluded the tests by spelling it out: *Facility integrity intact.*

But I wasn't so sure. The uneasy prickle had become a case of the full-blown jitters. I shivered again, fingers flinching from the keyplate as if even that contact could suck me back into the icy fire of the spooks' trap.

One more query, just to be sure. All systems normal. And no record of anomalous signals received or sent.

I shook my head, punching the plate to blank it, backing off to lean against a packing crate. My arm throbbed distractingly in the heavy, dead cast the mechmen hadn't been able to reactivate after the impact in the airlock. I cradled it against me and closed my eyes.

No record of the odd communication that was supposedly the reason CI had sent me here. Were they jerking me around again? Rik had said CI was querying the transport about the signal—but then he could have altered the data for his own reasons. I frowned and shook my head. No, David and Siolis must have picked up something strange enough to send them here. If they *were* here. And were the incorporeals here, lurking invisibly within the facility's energy web, waiting?

I fumbled with my belt pouch, pulling out the flat black plasmeld device CI had given me. It looked like a dopestick case, featureless expect for the inset fingerlocks at one end, coded to my prints. Standard disguise for their little secrets. This one was a powerful null-field generator. Somehow it made charged particles isolate themselves momentarily, breaking bonds. If I opened it up right now, I could disrupt electromagnetic fields within a thirty-meter radius, the capsule of air around me excepted. Or I could concentrate it to a close personal shield, dense enough to scatter laser beams and neutralize high voltage. Or tighten the focus to a directed disabling weapon.

If push came to shove, I could supposedly deactivate the electronic interfaces and energy fields the incorporeals had used before to take over a CI facility. I could stand outside the facility entrance, shut it down, and seal the incorporeals inside. Of course, that would also wipe out the data loops and support systems for the experiments inside. A last resort. I turned the thing over in my hand, a jittery little voice hissing inside me, *Do it now. Before it's too late.*

"May I approach, Ruth?"

I jumped, shoving the device back into my pouch and looking up to see Violet blinking its lights at me from a few meters away. Beyond the mechman, Lilith peered curiously into a rotating holoscope display near the sensor shaft, splashes of changing color playing over her face.

"Blast it." I strode past the blinking mechman, hissing at Lilith, "Will you lay off?"

She straightened with a petulant shrug as Violet's tinny voice followed me with a note of grievance, "I am afraid I do not understand that command, Ruth."

I turned back, swearing under my breath. "Just go on hold for a minute, okay?"

"Very well." The mechanical voice couldn't really have sounded offended. Violet's facelights faded out around a steady amber indicator.

"Lilith, are you trying to get us both in trouble?"

She trailed her fingers over the data outlets, then shrugged. "I'm getting tired of you ordering me around. I'm bored to tears."

"Why don't you go back to the tin can and hook into some entertainment or a game? Or code up a report on me for Helsa. That's what you're along for, isn't it?"

She smirked. "Why, Ruth, what a terrible thing to—"

"One minute elapsed." Violet lurched over to me, a red indicator flashing on its chest. "I have an urgent communication for you, Ruth."

I jerked around. "Go ahead."

"New data from remote sensors indicate unauthorized mobil biological presences within the facility, source incompatible with laboratory experiments. Infrared and subsonic patterns consistent with presence of two viable humans, 17% aberration window within signal-to-noise ratio."

Two. I caught a quick breath. David and Siolis? If they were editing data in the facility's cyber system, that could explain the discrepancies. "Interpret."

"Insufficient data."

"Give me possibles."

"Hypothetical intrusion by native life forms, probability rated extremely low."

So they didn't suspect stowaways. "You mean native humans, don't you?"

Its lights flashed. "I am not programmed to respond to that question, Ruth."

Did CI really think they were going to keep the Cyvriots a secret? I rubbed my eyes. "Are the facility systems still intact? No change in the readings?"

"Facility parameters remain within normal configurations, except for indications of two unauthorized biological presences."

"Ruth! Is it David? We have to go *save* him!" Lilith clutched my wrist, hot fingers pressing insistently against my pulse.

Despite myself I shuddered at her clinging touch, shrugging loose and turning back to the mechman. "Okay, Violet, Phase Two. Round up the gang and let's go take a look."

five

A thin, high-pitched whine shrilled insistently somewhere, setting my teeth on edge. Stark metal walls reflected a merciless wash of light after the gloom outside, and I winced at the mirrored glare shattering off oblivious mechman alloy as the units wheeled smoothly down the corridor.

Violet waited, facelights swiveled back to me, neck bow bobbing in a faint air-filter current. "It is safe to proceed, Ruth. Advance units confirm all facility parameters within normal limits."

I swallowed and tried to unstick my feet from the entrance floor to follow the mechman down the corridor. Despite Violet's assurance, my heart was thudding double-time to the dull throb in my arm. The facility's ceaseless mechanical whine echoed in a jittering hum down my spine, raising my hackles.

"There's something creepy about this place. Like it's alive, watching us." The whisper was close behind me, uncomfortably echoing my own morbid impression. A hot, damp hand clutched mine. "I'm afraid."

I jerked around to see Lilith's face pale and oddly pinched. I found myself squeezing her hand, saying, "Take it easy," my voice falling into the soothing cadences of the cybers' mood music, the maternal tones of Poindros. I pulled my hand free and cleared my throat. "You're sure not like the other Neulanders I've met, Lilith. Didn't think they *had* imaginations."

"Now don't you start on me, too!" She jerked her hands over her face, turning away. Then she gave a little shrug and lowered her arms. "My parents and brother were always after me to be more serious, to build useful things. I just wasn't like them, and I thought I really hated them. Then . . . when they got in trouble for inventing taboo devices, and the cybers took them away . . ." She was staring at the wall, squinting into the glare. "They weren't the same afterward. And I thought when I came to Casino I *could* do something, to show—"

She suddenly turned back to me, putting on the bright smile

64

that somehow looked ghastly in the harsh light. "Well, I guess that's just silly, isn't it?"

I shook my head. "No." I didn't want to feel sorry for Lilith. "Look, we all just do the best we can."

"But *you're* never afraid, Ruth."

"Wanna bet?"

She glanced around, shivering, and edged closer. "Of what, then?" She reached for my hand again.

Her soft little palm clung damply to mine, and I had to force myself not to snatch my hand away. I gave hers a quick squeeze before pulling free. "Just things." I shrugged. "Look, I've got to check things out here. There's no sense making yourself miserable. Why don't you go back and wait at the landing area?"

"*Alone?*" Her voice squeaked upward and broke.

"I'll send a mechman back with you. Their integrated lasers will stop anything likely to crawl out of the ooze after you."

She shook her head, looking quickly around again and shuddering. "I'm sticking close to you." Her eyes glistened bright blue, unreadable, but her fear was almost palpable in the air.

I reluctantly pulled from my belt pouch the small, curved hand laser I'd put away since using it for the first and last time to kill Heinck. I hesitated, then thrust my fingers abruptly through the loops so the locked trigger buttons rested flat against my palm and the firing module rode snug on the back of my hand. Not that it would do much good against incorporeal traps, but what the hell.

Lilith's eyes widened. "That's contraplan, too, isn't it?"

"That's right." I shook off my uneasiness, striding away to catch up to Violet. "What about those 'mobile biological' readings? Can you pinpoint a location now?"

Facelights flashed. "Advance units confirm." A steady blue and amber lit up. "No unauthorized presences are presently detected within the facility. Previous readings were possibly due to remote sensor interference, probability point-five-three."

Again the prickling shiver down my back. My fingers reflexively brushed my belt pouch, feeling the hard, flat shape of the null-field generator inside. I forced my hand away from it. "Okay. Let's take a look at the control center."

"Priority control center or auxiliary control center?"

I'd studied the layout back at the dome. The facility was mostly underground, seismically shielded layers of concentric rings. The upper level had a large loading area and the smaller entrance we'd just come through, leading to the main control room. One level down was a smaller loading area also adjoining the bi-level warehouse space, with sea access for hovercraft. The auxiliary control center was down there, used chiefly for inventory. The lower ring levels were mostly labs connected by a maze of wheel-and-spoke corridors.

I waved Violet on. "Priority center."

"This way, please." The mech's head rotated, and it led down the corridor. Lilith hovered behind, irritatingly close, as I followed.

There were already five or six mechmen in the chamber past the door at the end of the entrance hall, linked in to data outlets in the practically featureless gray console fronts ranked around the circular control room. Facelights flashed colored patterns. Above them, near the ceiling on each console segment, steady amber lights stared down.

Behind me, Lilith gave a high-pitched little giggle. "Is this all there is? It isn't even as fancy as our headquarters!"

"What do you expect? It's not made for human readouts. All the interesting stuff's going on inside." I turned to Violet, tilting my head toward the engaged units. "What are they finding?"

Its facelights skittered and settled on red and blue. "Retesting is proceeding without incident. Control loops remain within normal limits. Laboratory parameters remain within normal limits. Queries regarding anomalous communications solicit negative response, no memory entries. Power consumption figures remain stable. Secondary loop tracers continue to verify."

I paced around the room beneath the unwinking amber ready lights, the back of my neck prickling, still unable to quite convince myself the incorporeals weren't hidden somehow inside the loops, amber eyes watching and waiting. I blew out a long breath and stopped in front of Violet again. "No sign of those unauthorized biological readings you picked up earlier?"

"Negative. According to data loops, no unauthorized intrusions have occurred. Facility integrity remains intact."

"Blast it. . . ." No sign of David and Siolis. No sign of incorporeals, no sign of CI's odd signals. What the hell was going on here? I shook my head, pointing to the seamless gray panels spaced around the room's periphery between consoles. "Can we get through those doors?"

"Affirmative. Corridors lead to equipment maintenance and fabrication stations."

"And the laboratories start two levels down?"

"Affirmative."

"Let's go take a look."

Violet blinked its lights at me. "That is not necessary, Ruth. Mechman units are presently inspecting laboratory chambers."

"So we'll inspect them again." I picked a door at random and strode over to it, half surprised when it whisked obediently up into the ceiling at my approach. Another bright, featureless corridor stretched before me, a "spoke" ending at an intersection with a slightly curving ring hall. I turned in the opening to see Violet wheeling over, Lilith hanging back and biting her lip as she shot a look around the control room. She scurried along as I headed down the corridor, the wall panel snicking shut behind us.

I resisted the urge to look back at the sealed door. My edgy jitters had fused with the constant, shrill whine suffusing the facility. My hand seemed to slip of its own will into my belt pouch to touch the slick plasmeld device inside.

I stopped at the first door, inset into the left wall of the corridor, and waved my hand across a low scanner plate. It whisked aside and I leaned in to glance over an automated repair shop, extensors hanging motionless and sensors inactive. The second door, down the hall on the right, revealed a similar room, this one with a laser slicing a steady flow of mysterious metal circles about the size of my palm. I picked one up, shrugged, and tossed it back on the pile. "All right, let's go downstairs."

"This way, please." Violet rolled down the hall to the intersection and pivoted left, gliding on his locked leg-units to a stop before a wider door panel. There was a sucking whoosh and the door opened to reveal a tubular chamber and the suspended, waiting floor of an anti-grav lift.

I started to follow the mech inside, then halted. "No." The back of my neck was prickling again. Inside the lift, we'd be completely dependent on the facility's control net. "Aren't there emergency access ducts?"

"Affirmative. However, such a route is not recommended. Climbing down the ducts could be hazardous to humans, as well as unnecessarily time consuming."

"That's okay. Take us to the nearest one."

"This unit registers objection." Violet's neck bow bobbed indignantly.

"Fine. Now show us the duct access."

"Ruth." Lilith's fingers clutched the arm of my coverall. "Maybe we should listen. It's programmed to watch out for you."

"I'd just as soon do that myself. Come on."

Violet waited silently beside a chest-high rectangular wall hatch with an inset handle, somehow radiating disapproval. I noted that the mech hadn't politely opened the hatch for me.

"Thanks, Violet." I winked at Lilith and twisted the handle, swinging the hatch open and peering in. I fished my lume rod from a thigh pocket and shone it down, a bottomless dark well swallowing the thin beam. The square duct was about a meter across, lined with horizontal ridges of sure-grip at intervals of about two-thirds of a meter. It was obviously designed for backup use by maintenance mechs, not humans.

Lilith crowded into the opening to peer past me. "You can't be serious, Ruth!"

I nudged her back. "I'll go first. You don't have to come if you don't want to."

"This unit is assigned to accompany you." Violet's facelights flashed.

I shook my head and lowered myself in feet first, groping for the roughened rungs, awkward with my bulky cast. As a ladder, it left a lot to be desired, but once I got used to the long stretches, I made pretty good time to the second hatch down. I braced myself straddling the duct, unlatching its interior handle and swinging it open. Climbing out to a metal corridor identical to the one above, I shined my light up the duct to guide Lilith the rest of the way. Her pale face swung down, tense and blinking, as her foot stretched shakily for the next ridge.

"You're doing fine. A couple more, and you're at the hatch. Okay, step across, that's right, give me your hand. Good."

She gave me a shaky smile and plucked halfheartedly at her tunic, smoothing its fringes. Peering back up the duct, I caught Violet in my beam, still only halfway down, moving in jerky motions as it straddled the duct, extending one leg unit to a lower ridge, retracting the other as an arm extensor anchored it overhead and lengthened to lower the body onto the lower retracting leg, then repeating the awkward process.

I straightened, grinning at Lilith. "Nice to see there's one thing we can do faster than those blasted mechs."

She gave me a blank look, then a subdued giggle.

Violet lurched out of the duct and closed the hatch, rolling past me down the curved hall to another closed door. The high-pitched whine was a faint, visceral presence in this hall, too. I paused, uneasy again, then waved my hand over the sensor.

The door whisked open on a flood of greenish light, rippling eerily through banks of fluid-filled, transparent tubes. I blinked, stepping inside.

Lilith screamed. "Ruth! Oh—" A choking sound.

I whirled around, a shrill hum of alarm exploding through me. Lilith was backed against the corridor wall, face washed to a sickly green hue, hand clapped to her mouth. Her wide eyes were fixed on a meter-high, glistening spider scuttling past her feet.

"It's only a maintenance mech." I shook my head, shaking off the jolt of adrenaline.

Lilith was shaking, too, but now I realized the choking sound was muffled laughter. She caught her breath. "Oh, Ruth, I'm sorry. I thought it was a bioformed monster! But you should have seen the way you jumped." She laughed again, ending in a hiccup.

I took a deep breath, counting more numbers, and turned my back on her to pace slowly past the rows of tall, vertical tubes. They filled the room, mounted on flanged metal bases just about the diameter of those metal circles the laser had been cutting upstairs. Their caps sprouted a tangle of tubing and optic fibers. A deep hum ran counterpoint to the persistent high whine, and the clear fluid in the tubes shivered and rippled, an occasional bubble rising slowly.

I chose an aisle and walked down it, leaning close to peer at one of the dimly green-pulsing tubes. "There's nothing inside."

Violet rolled to a noiseless stop beside me, extruding an extensor to link with the smooth metal base. Facelights blinked. "ID: specimen CLRR634. Microscopic cellular propagation, gonadal excretions of the Danallian giant tesselated tunicate."

"I'll take your word for it." I strolled down a couple more aisles, but all I could see were some tiny blobs floating in a few of the tubes. "So everything's hunky-dory here? This is it?"

"Laboratory 3K status normal."

"Where does that go?" I pointed to a door panel opposite the one where we'd entered.

"Second ring corridor."

It opened for my wave, and I stuck my head out as a light sprang up in another corridor curving slightly back in both directions. Another door faced me, off to the left a bit, and beyond that what looked like an intersection with a spoke hall. I stepped out as a spider mech appeared in the opening of the spoke passage, multiple legs smoothly carrying something in a sealed container past me and around the curve to the right.

"Ruth, look!" Lilith leaned through the doorway, plucking at my arm and pointing back into the lab.

One of the spider mechs had crawled up onto the racks of tubes, detaching one from its base and agilely climbing down with it. The spider carried it, sealed, toward us, and I pulled Lilith out of the way as it bore the tube through the door and headed off around the left curve.

"What's it doing? Let's follow it." I grabbed Lilith's arm and towed her along, whispering, "Keep it down, huh? And don't get lost."

Violet wheeled beside me. "The maintenance unit is transferring a specimen population for sampling and control activation."

"What's that mean?"

"Integrity of Planned faunal species is maintained through cryogenic storage and periodic testing of activated cellular cycles. Occasional extended growth simulations are studied."

"Simulations? You mean they're growing live animals in tubes?" I shook off a reflex shudder.

"That conclusion is vaguely generalized, but essentially correct." Violet rolled ahead, following the spider mech through an opened doorway.

Lilith edged in first. "Ugh!" Then she clapped a guilty hand over her mouth, backing against the wall, eyes wide.

The tubes here had been expanded to cylindrical tanks, pulsing with the same ghastly green light. Livid folds and mounds of raw flesh in blind fetal shapes floated, stirring grotesquely in invisible currents. A long, blue-scaled thing hung limp in another cylinder. Straggling feathers enclosed a bundled mass. The just-recognizable, emerging form of a hairless monkey bobbed with its rudimentary, eyeless face against the clear tube. I swallowed down a surge of nausea.

"Ruth, this is awful," Lilith whispered behind me. "They're growing monsters! I feel sick." She did look pale in the gruesome light, her eyes glittering flat and fixed.

"Why don't you wait in the hall? I'll be right out."

She nodded, gave me a pitiful, apologetic look, and sank down to sit on the corridor floor, leaning against the curved wall. Remembering how imperturbably she'd handled Rik's mangled body, I shook my head and ducked back into the lab.

Violet had rolled over to observe the spider mech transferring a pipette of fluid from the tube to a larger cylindrical tank. I sidled through a narrow aisle between bobbing embryonic shapes, reluctant despite myself to brush the tubes. I stopped beside the mechman, bathed in the sickly green light, surrounded by the hum of machinery, slick lucite curves, slippery viscera and flesh. A large, unfamiliar creature developed to the stage of formed paw pads and fine fur stirring in the tank's current stared blindly over Violet at me.

I dropped my eyes and cleared my throat. "What do the cybers do with them, once they're grown? Don't they suffer, living in those damn tubes?"

Violet flashed its lights. "Grown specimens are processed for dissection and study. Neural development beyond autonomic and reflexive functions is suppressed. There is no awareness."

I glanced again at the furry creature nodding and staring in its cylinder. I turned abruptly away and paced down the aisle. My fingers had slipped into my belt-pouch again, touching the slick plasmeld of the null-field generator. I firmly refused an impulse to race outside the facility and activate the device, wiping the control center to a clean slate, sealing the place and wiping the labs out of existence. Of course, CI would wipe the floor with me if I did. And there had to be some clues here somewhere to David and the rest of it.

I paced on down the room, through the humming whine and the rippling green light. I stopped short, blinking, at the end of the chamber. "Violet, come take a look at this."

Another door panel had whisked open in front of me, revealing an adjoining lab. But the layout here was different. I stepped through into the same rippling light, but the rows of racks held more than just fluid-filled cylinders. There were square tanks beside some tubes, mesh cages beside others. And in the cages, animals crawled, slept, flapped, hopped. . . .

I caught a sharp breath and moved closer to the first row. A long cylinder floated the limp length of a serpent, its coppery scales marked with a striking pattern of crimson zigzags. Beside the tube, a fine-meshed cage held an identical serpent, this one coiled and staring at me with bright amber eyes, its triangular head shifting to follow me. The next tube held the drifting form of a small, furry animal with six stubby legs and a long snout, white pelt decorated with black splotches on the back, two black paws, and a comical black stripe down the snout. The mesh enclosure beside the tube held two more of the creatures, scurrying in quick circuits of the cage and then flinging themselves at the side nearest me. They were both white, with two black paws,

comical black stripes down their snouts, and blotches on their
backs identical to the specimen in the tube.

I leaned closer to stare and one of them swiped a paw through
the mesh. I jerked back and paced quickly down the next row.

More limp floating shapes, some strange, some recognizable.
And beside each one, perfectly identical animals swimming,
climbing, burrowing, fluttering. Doubles. Hissing, growling, war-
bling, mewing. Watching me with wary, curious, indifferent,
aware eyes.

I straightened from a scrutiny of a fish tank and frowned. Doubles. Somewhere that was ringing a bell, but all I could see were
dice tossing, spinning snake eyes. I shook my head. "Violet? Is
this part of the Plan?" It couldn't be, the place reeked of taboos.

No answer from the mech. I turned back to the doorway, but
there was no sign of my attentive sidekick. "Violet?"

No sound but the constant shrill whine and the restless movements of the animals. The nervous hum down my spine intensified,
buzzing in my ears. I glanced hastily around the room, caught a
glimpse in the shadowy far racks of larger cylinders, stirring shapes
on the edge of recognition, something long and pale—

"Ruth?" Lilith's voice in the other lab, hesitant.

"In here. Where's Violet?"

"Ruth!" A sharp scream. "Help! No, stop, you can't—" Another bitten-off scream and the sounds of breaking, crashing.

"Hey!" A hot jolt of adrenaline and I was lunging for the
doorway, fingers unlocking without thought the safety on my hand
laser.

A hissing sound in the other lab and something crashing, splashing. A sob. Scrambling sounds. I hissed, "Lilith," ducking my
head into the opening for a glimpse.

She was crawling through a tangle of tubes, lucite shards, and
mercifully vague wet shapes beneath a blasted gap in one rack.
Behind her, spilling through the corridor doorway, mechmen
rolled toward us, the one in front sporting a violet neck bow and
shooting a quick burst of laser fire to shatter another cylinder and
spray its contents over Lilith's frantic escape.

"Ruth!" She scuttled behind another rack and scrambled toward
me. "The mechmen showed up and all of a sudden went crazy!
They're—"

Another hissing needle of blue-white light and crash of equipment. A mechanical voice blared, "Stop at once. Remain motionless."

"Like hell!" I shot off a quick laser burst and lunged through the doorway, grabbed Lilith's arm, and dragged her back under the cover of the last rack. "It's got to be the incorporeals, somehow hiding in the system, taking them over. I *knew* it, damn it!"

"Humans must stand and present themselves for containment."

"Bloody, blasted . . ." I was squirming backward, supporting my weight awkwardly on my cast, dragging Lilith along through something disgustingly slimy and trying to ignore its smell.

Lilith sobbed and pulled her arm free. "Ruth, we better give up. We can't escape. They have Rules, too, they couldn't really hurt us."

"Don't bet on it if the incorporeals are in charge. If they were worried about it, they'd be using neural darts instead of lasers."

I jerked up above the rack to see the mechs advancing again, and fired off a quick series of bright bursts. There was a squeal of metal against metal and a crash as I ducked down again under return fire. "Come on, we might make it out the upper cargo door if we can get back up through a duct. I've got this little surprise for them." I pulled out the black plasmeld null device.

The blue eyes widened, blank with shock. "What's that?"

"No time. Just get close to me, and we'll stand up and make a run for it. The null-field envelope should be big enough for us both if you keep an arm around me—anyway it shouldn't affect us much for a short haul. It'll cancel out their laser energy-fields." I yanked her closer, crouching. "Count of three. One, two—"

"No!" Her eyes were glazed, uncomprehending, flat as blue glass in the fear-distorted face washed by rippling light and shadow. "No, I don't want to die!" She tore free with panic strength, running straight to the advancing mechmen.

"Lilith, stop!" I jumped to my feet, then ducked as a hissing stab of light burned into the wall behind me.

Past the racks, the mechmen grabbed the screaming, babbling Lilith and held her. Another laser beam sliced past me. "Stand and remain motionless."

"Damn and blast!" My fingers found the concentrated focus and triggered CI's device as I jumped to my feet. I caught a last glimpse of a mechman pressing its hand against Lilith's neck as she sagged with a loose, sedated smile into its cradling arms. There was a sucking, popping sound assaulting my eardrums, then a weird muffled silence as a shimmering distortion sprang up around me. As if through water, I saw another laser bolt spear toward me, then I was enclosed in blackness.

I stumbled and crashed backward through the doorway, blind, bouncing oddly to one side. I deactivated the device with a loud pop and frantically keyed the connecting door shut as another burst of fire flashed through the gap. I fused the lock with my laser and whirled to run. If they caught me there'd be nothing I could do for Lilith or myself. I tore past the racks of cylinders, vaguely registering a wild cacophony of howls and squeals from the cages, my eyes tracking frantically. There. An outer door panel. I was through it, into the ring corridor, as the mechmen burst into the lab behind me.

I fused the exit over a crash and an animal wail. Then I could hear only the thud of my feet and heart as I pounded down the glaring-bright passage, racing around the curve for an emergency hatch. No noise behind me, but mechmen wheels were silent. Gasping, nerves screaming, I raced on, almost passing a dark corridor opening suddenly off the outer ring. It felt like the right direction. I jerked around and tore along it, light springing up ahead of me to light a low, rectangular hatch in one wall. I yanked it open with shaking fingers, tumbling and nearly falling down it before I could catch myself on the sure-grip ridges. Ignoring a lancing pain down my arm in the cast, I braced myself and triggered my laser at the shut handle. The metal latch started to melt, then the beam faltered and fizzled out.

Damn. No way to recharge.

The climb up seemed like forever, my legs shaking and hoarse breaths echoing in the duct. When I finally had the handle of the top hatch in my fingers, I froze, caught in an agony of indecision. Had the mechs taken the anti-grav lift up to wait outside the duct hatches for me? I slipped the null device into the awkward fingers of my left hand and eased the hatch open.

The flood of relief left me almost giddy. The duct opened onto the upper loading area, its gate wide open and not a mechman in sight.

The dark sea hissed and spat at my feet. Clouds lowered over me with their malevolent red glow, reflected in a dull, oily sheen across the water. The sinking sun was a huge, seething crimson mass, melting in a long swath over the sea. I was pressed like the sun between the two massive flat plates of cloud and ocean, squeezed in the narrow space and panting for breath as they closed in on me. I shivered.

Lukewarm drizzle soaked me, damp hair plastered to my face

and neck, a rivulet running down my nose and dripping off it, my hand slippery on the knife hilt as I hacked desperately at the stubborn material of my cast.

With a deep, shaky breath, I straightened, raising from my crouch to glance uneasily over sheltering wet rock toward the landing area. Sitll no sign of pursuing mechmen. Too good to be true. I took another deep breath and gripped my knife tighter, widening the split in the useless cast.

My arm throbbed with a dull ache, a prickling spot on my back anticipating with nagging preciseness the stab of a mechman laser or neural dart. I tried to concentrate on prying and lengthening the split, working the knife carefully, focusing on the perfect workmanship of the blade Jaréd had fashioned for me on Sethar, the smooth curves of the fire-lizard old Anáh had carved on the hilt.

Slow. Breathe deeply, attune heart and mind. Hear the song around you, follow the steps of hunter and hunted. Feel it. Flow.

I could almost hear Jaréd's quiet voice, see his dark face and the quick gleam of teeth in the shadowed jungle. Feel him beside me, the memory at least undying. The jittery buzz in my ears evened out to a smooth hum, my blood pulsing into a deep cycle, senses alert in the balanced readiness of the pre-*timbra* state.

As the knife steadily chewed through the cast, my thoughts finally slowed from a frantic spin.

The mechmen. Why hadn't they come back to the landing area to search for me? Maybe the incorporeals had to tighten their control projections before they could let them out of the facility. The spooks must be still struggling to take over all the backup systems of the facility, or I wouldn't have managed to escape at all, just as the cargo bay doors had triggered shut. Or maybe they were only biding their time, knowing there was nothing I could do out on this wet rock in the middle of all that ocean. I'd tried contacting CI from the field console in the dome, but it was dead. And I'd gotten the hell out before the spooks decided to try reaching me through the remote control system Cl had said would be impermeable.

Again I was tempted to take the null-generator back to the upper entrance and wipe the facility controls, spooks included. But I couldn't seal it off now that Lilith was trapped inside. And the animals. In my present mood, I'd sooner have snuffed Lilith than those other defenseless prisoners. Damn idiot had no business being here at all, losing her head like that. Blowing it.

Double damn. And what about David and Siolis?

The sea kept hurling itself at the rocks, lapping greedily at my feet, impenetrable. They had to be down there somewhere. With the Cyvriots. Maybe the natives would help me find them. I couldn't do anything about the incorporeals without some help.

I shifted the knife and wiped my wet palm, glancing at the net bag of Resistance gear I'd grabbed in a hasty stop at the deserted comfort module. Osmotic breathing apparatus, pressure-compensating suit, and swim fins designed by Helsa's techs for me, just in case. I shuddered.

With a crack, the cast fell apart and dropped from my arm. I flexed my left hand and winced. The arm throbbed angrily, dangling unsupported, but I carefully tried bending and rotating it. The bone ends seemed to have reattached, since it obeyed. But the arm looked like it belonged to someone else, pale and thin, muscles gone slack, damp skin sloughing off like wet paper. As I twisted to examine the back of it, I saw a broad, angry-looking blotch just above the elbow, the whole area puffy and off-color. Another sharp stab of pain, and I spotted the splinter of cast material imbedded in the split, reddened skin.

I plucked it out, catching a sharp breath. The bruised area oozed thick, foul matter. Damn. Must have done it when I broke the cast in the airlock. And I hadn't gotten enough time with the bioelectric fields.

With rummaging, my bag yielded a waterproof pouch holding sealed tubes of nutrient concentrate and a sketchy first aid kit. I wiped down the messy area, wincing again, and smeared some broad-spectrum ointment over it. I quickly taped it and wrapped the whole arm in a thin pressure bandage.

I wiped cold sweat off my face, blinking in the deepening gloom. The arm didn't look so good. Maybe it was only the lurid light. I'd think about it later.

Past the shoreline rocks, the silent equipment dome and landing area still showed no sign of movement. Hastily pulling on the insulated liner and the pressure suit, attaching the skin-cling waste tubes, and sealing the hood, I wiggled my feet into the self-adjusting fins. I stood, grabbed the net bag, and tried to step down over the rocks to the foaming water's edge. I instantly tripped myself and sat hard, arm screaming.

I swore in a furious whisper, longer than strictly necessary, trying to distract myself from the creeping fingers of dark water, the invisibly lurking monsters below, the restless, fathomless presence ready to suck me down into its blind depths.

I shuddered again, fingers shaking as I snapped the thin, contoured stressplex faceplate onto the hood and fused the edges to the suit. I hooked into the osmotic biosupport unit dangling almost weightless down my back, securing it with a cling-tab to my weighted belt. One of the techs had explained how it worked— something about permeable membranes, pressure differential forcing oxygen through, a compact power source driving a fanning movement of the double "wings" to provide continual current, amplified by movement when I was kicking and needed more oxygen. The pressure-compensating suit was copied from one the Valauans used to hand-harvest deepwater pearls. Of course, as the tech said, nobody spent days in the things. Of course.

I'd tried the setup in Siolis' abandoned tank back at headquarters, and it worked. But the tank and this immense, daunting sea were too literally worlds apart.

I took a last breath of the residual air in the faceplate and secured the net bag to my belt, checked my knife in its ankle hilt, felt the flat shape of the null-generator secured in a thigh pocket and wondered whether it would work underwater, pulled on and sealed my gloves. I eased gingerly over the rocks with the awkward fins, sprawling into the surge with a graceless belly flop.

The water lapped over and tumbled me in a rush of blind, choking, threshing panic.

Then air whooshed past my face with a sudden, vivid picture of myself wallowing with my elaborate gear in a meter of water. Hysterical laughter bubbled up, echoing in the faceplate as my fingers found the buoyancy compensators. Whatever kind of demons I was going to meet down below, they couldn't look more outlandish than me.

six

It wasn't cold, but it looked cold. I shivered as the opaque ceiling of water closed over me. The dimness churned, swirling, and grabbed me. Something limp and greenish-black splatted over the faceplate as I flinched and it slid away and I was thrown sideways, rolling against smooth slippery rock. I gasped, caught my breath, flailed futilely for a handhold. The sea heaved and sucked me deeper. I tucked, wincing, borne blindly in the current, fending off the dim shapes of rock looming without warning out of the murk.

Then suddenly I was rolled the other way, pushed back up, spun like a rag doll. I slammed back against something, the flexible breathing wings cushioning the blow, but pain knifing through my arm. Then I was rolling forward again, fighting for air, bits of shredded weeds streaming with me, long straggly plant fingers snatching out of the gloom.

Frantically fending myself off slime-coated boulders, I felt the surge reverse again, rolling me back. But this time I managed to wedge my gloved fingers into a narrow crevice and hunker down over the rock.

The sea pummeled and sucked. I clung until it reversed again, a froth of tiny particles and wriggling shapes boiling past my faceplate. With a deep breath, I launched myself into the flow, kicking this time, the fins driving me desperately through the flood. Another looming mass of rock and I shot down over it, plunging deeper, fleeing the relentless churning. A barely glimpsed slippery something smacked against me, flapping wildly and shooting off in a burst of bubbles.

I recoiled, arms windmilling, dropping deeper. A darker stillness closed around me, a numb place beneath the crashing surge.

My arms and legs went limp. I drifted, ears ringing, heart pounding, gasping for air. My chest burned. I was panting, but couldn't seem to get enough air. The shadows flowed around me, into me, insistent. I was drowning, suffocating, trapped with the dark water pressing in on me and crushing my lungs.

I gasped again, thrashing mindlessly back toward the dim surface but throwing myself instead into an awkward spin, driving myself sideways into open nothingness. I couldn't see a bottom, couldn't tell dimness from dark, for a panicked second didn't know up from down. My arms flailed at my chest, tearing at the confining suit. I couldn't breathe. Red swam in my eyes.

The shrill buzzing in my ears built to a shriek. Something popped. There was a hissing whisper, familiar. . . .

Wait. Listen.

Slippery coils of the Serpent danced head-to-tail forever around me. And the dark, enveloping sea was for a moment the open black stretch of empty space as I flew free among the stars. Floating me, not crushing me. *Feel it. Flow.*

To the deeper, faint ebb and flow beneath the surface surge, my chest shuddered, then fell and rose slowly, drawing in a lungful of air. Slow and steady, deep breaths, like the tech had told me. Again. In and out, easy. My suffocating panic subsided as the buoyancy compensators brought me to a balanced hover, the net supply bag drifting out beside me, still tethered to my belt. Thank Founders I hadn't lost it in my fool scrambling.

I shook my head, still shivering in the wake of adrenaline, back prickling to unseen presences cloaked by the sea. I paddled once in a circle, straining my eyes futilely through the violet-tinged shadows, craning toward the faintly redder surface glow where the sun was being swallowed, too. I kicked around in another tight circle, hearing only the hiss of the air feed and the faint boom of surf overhead, my back feeling utterly naked.

Another deep breath. The gloom around me intensified, even the dim violet leaching away into night. I raised a nervous hand to switch on the lume strip along the top of the faceplate. A flattened cone of light speared ahead of me, lighting up only a sparkling array of suspended particles and a small, finned shape darting quickly out of the beam. Darkness lapped at the edges, intensified by contrast. My back felt even more exposed.

I found myself circling once more, losing my orientation as the beam raked empty sea. I made myself stop, watching the bubbles slowly rise from the exhaust port of my air cycler, trying to convince myself of up and down. I didn't know whether the light made it better or worse, lighting up nothing, sending out a beacon homing in on me.

There were eyes out there, veiled in shadows. Watching, waiting. Fangs and scales and tentacles, monsters out of taboo,

nightmare's sinuous shapes suddenly arrowing from the blackness
at me. . . .

I shook my head sharply, light jerking in dizzy dazzles of reflected particles, and raised the sensor readout imbedded in my
suit's right wrist cuff. My flexed wrist activated it. Figures scrolled
down a tiny backlit screen: DEPTH 9.2 METERS . . . TIME 17.32
STANDARD . . . CUMULATIVE TIME 0.16.47 . . . DIREC-
TIONAL TRACER NOT ENGAGED . . . The screen momentarily
flashed a blue grid with a pulsing red arrow, then scrolled on,
PRESSURE 1.99 STANDARD. . . .

I flexed my wrist quickly twice to reset and start over. DEPTH
10.1 METERS . . .

It seemed like more. I pressed the option switch and the screen
presented another blue grid, this one with a red dot pulsing to the
rhythm of a faint, high-pitched sonar beeping that started up in
the region of the suit's bulky belt. As I drifted, the red dot drew
a line on the graph for the ocean floor below, rising in a jagged
peak and then dropping sharply. Numbers flashed on the bottom
of the screen: 29.4 M . . . 28.5 M . . . 28.1 M . . . 26.3 M . . . 31.2
M . . . 46.7 M . . . 59.0 M. . . .

I shivered at the thought of the depths falling away beneath me.
But that explained why I wasn't seeing anything solid in my beams.
The current must have sucked me over the edge of one of the
deep trenches running between the shallower rock ''plains'' that
made up most of Cyvrus' ocean bottom, according to the sketchy
file data the Resistance techs had coaxed out of taboo cyber loops.
Most of the plant life would be over the shallow areas, along with
most of the smaller sea creatures. The big ones lived in the
trenches, but some of them came up to hunt.

I hastily flicked off the continuing plunge of the graph. The
scrolling figures returned: PRESSURE 2.1 STANDARD . . .
02 CONSUMPTION 1.4 BASE . . . RESERVE AIR 0.09
ALERT. . . .

I checked the back of the cuff and saw the amber warning stud
lit up. I hadn't been under long enough to build up a good air
reserve, so I had to get moving.

Ignoring the insistent mirages of voracious, scaly demons that
kept forming and dissolving in the surrounding darkness, I flexed
my wrist again, putting the readout through its paces. I hit the
stop switch at the directional blurb and cued it to Set mode.
Bending my right arm at a ninety-degree angle and gingerly raising
my left arm straight out, I gripped the elbow to align the sensors

the way the tech had shown me. The tiny blue grid lit up, the red arrow pulsing and floating around until I got myself into the right orientation to position its tail toward my chin. When I'd held it motionless for a couple of seconds, it locked in on the homing signal from the transport landing area.

I went through some more gyrations, flailing awkwardly with the fins to position myself and hover motionless. I set two more points on the faint signals from the two closest of the widely scattered underwater console-station "bubbles" the cybers kept for their mandatory semiannual monitoring of the Cyvriots. My data hadn't said what the natives were monitored for, but even on a taboo world it appeared the cybers wanted to make sure everybody knew standard language and followed the Rules.

The device went through its triangulation and flashed me an ENGAGED message. I eenie-meenied, picking console station number two. The arrow settled into position, pointing off to my left. All I had to do was keep myself aligned so it pointed straight ahead, check it often enough so I didn't swim in circles, and hope my course took me away from the yawning black abyss below.

It would have been easier to aim at some kind of landmark ahead, but all the beam kept finding was its own murky path. And an occasional ripply, vague shadow that melted in and out of being there. Skin crawling, I took another deep breath, reminding myself the suit generated a pressure-stabilizing field. The darkness pressing around me only felt like it was squeezing my lungs.

I kicked steadily into the night sea, trying to shake off a lingering shudder of premonition, keeping my eyes peeled for any sign of Cyvriots. If what I'd pieced together from the sketchy data and my always oblique conversations with Siolis was right, the natives could "read" underwater sound waves even at a distance. Apparently the thick, fatty humps behind their bioformed shoulders acted as receivers, sort of like my sonar depth device. Data indicated that they could even use sonic waves for a primitive kind of communication, pointing out a parallel to the way some underwater creatures on the old historical Earth had contacted each other. Anyway, the natives would eventually realize I was here.

All I had to do was keep swimming and wait for the Cyvriots to find me. Hopefully before something else did.

Right. Left. Right.

97. 98. 99. 100. Start. Over. Left. Right. Left. Kick. 7. 8. 9. Kick.

Cast out into outer darkness forever. . . . Kick. *The blackness of darkness forever*. . . . Kick. Kick. *Beasts full of eyes before and behind . . . and there were stings in their tails*. . . . Left. Right. *Deep calleth unto deep*. . . . 1. 2. 3. Deep. 3. 3. 3.

Deep—what?

A high-pitched, pulsing beep finally snapped me out of it, breaking my fixed stare at the blurred, bobbing red arrow on the blue grid. I blinked, shook my head, lowered my throbbing left arm, and squinted at the flashing alert stud on the back of my right cuff. I flexed my wrist and the readout flared a depth report. Twenty meters. Hypnotized by the seamless blackness, the rhythm of kicking, I'd driven myself blindly down from my ten-meter setpoint. *Deep calleth unto deep*. I shivered and kicked convulsively higher. Gulping down the raw, dry taste of processed air, I shook out my aching arms and readjusted the buoyancy compensators.

I drifted limp for a few minutes, resting and taking a long pull from the water tube connected to the de-sal unit built into the breathing apparatus. Under the suit liner, I could feel the slippery plasmeld of my wild card disc on its chain, sticking to my skin, my heart thudding uncomfortably beneath it. There was a trickle of sweat down my back, and my faceplate was starting to fog up, though the tech had said it wouldn't.

I made myself stay limp, drifting with eyes closed, breathing deeply and slowly, summoning a silent Setharian chant to ease the skitterish race of my pulse. Easy does it. Another deep breath and I opened my eyes to see the faceplate cleared by the slowly circulating air that would eventually absorb the moisture wicked from the suit's liner. But it was best to go slow and easy, not break into a sweat.

I flexed my left arm, wincing, shook it out again, and raised it protesting into position to take another directional fix. Correcting, I kicked slowly along again, resisting the hypnotic reflex to count, muscles screaming down the back of my legs. My eyes blurred again on the red arrow. If I didn't hit some sheltering rocks soon, I'd have to try napping in an open drift. Hovering over the deep. I shuddered again and kicked faster.

My headlight speared ahead, swallowed by emptiness, picking up nothing. I watched the directional arrow, concentrating on kicking steadily and trying to ignore the mirages of form and movement coalescing out of the blackness in my peripheral vision. Though I kept feeling like I was being sucked downward, the readouts said I was maintaining steady depth. I had to rely on the instruments, couldn't trust my own perceptions. I was exhausted, and edgy, and out of my element—and probably running a fever to boot, if my raging thirst was any indication. The persistent back-prickling sensation of presences about to pounce was only imagination or hallucination. There was nothing out there but dark sea. Darkness above and below, more darkness ahead. And behind. Nothing but—

A silver flash of movement. There and gone. Real this time, it had to be. Big.

My heart lurched up into my throat, alarm jolting through me. I jerked around, flailing, light skittering and jabbing through the dark. Nothing—no, there. Popping out of darkness like an apparition. Gleam of scales on a sleek, streamlined fish over a meter long whipping past and down. Wait, two, three of them, the last one darting suddenly close in a flash of teeth.

I jerked reflexively away, thrashing back and rolling unbalanced, sinking into a somersault. And something grabbed me from behind. Long, clinging tentacles.

"Aaah!" My scream echoed harshly through the faceplate. I flailed wildly around, lashing out as a sharp pain shot through my left arm, but the snakelike strands only wrapped me tighter. Arms, legs, and throat snared. I was caught, strangling, panic ripping a hot circuit through me as I squirmed and kicked and the tentacles squeezed. I couldn't see anything, my head forced back by a choking limb and the light raking only stirred-up murk.

No sound from the creature, nothing but a shrill, silent scream inside my head. Finally I had to stop fighting to drag in a breath, gasping and choking. But as I did, the pressure eased up a little. I remembered my knife in its sheath. The thing wasn't moving now, content to hold me trapped. To eat later? My ears were buzzing urgent alarm, but I made myself ease my right arm slowly against the tentacles instead of thrashing. I managed to pull it loose enough to hunker my leg up and reach the knife. Gasping for breath, I eased the point up between the neck of my suit and the arm strangling me.

Tensing myself, I sliced, whipping the knife down to free my legs.

The creature didn't react. The tentacle parted absurdly easily, and there was no renewed attack as I hacked my legs free and hastily backpedaled away, panting. I blinked, bringing the light around and down.

All I saw was a quickly departing swarm of tiny yellow fish and the hacked and drifting pieces of a long, brownish-green, vinelike weed with broad, flat leaves.

I laughed until my faceplate fogged up. Gasping for breath, I drifted, limp with relief, wishing I could wipe my eyes. An odd effect of the faceplate brought a delayed, whispering echo of my laughter. Myself laughing at myself from a distance. I shook my head—I did badly need that sleep—and finned around, focusing the light ahead.

Suddenly sobered, I circled again, carefully. They were all around me now, weaving slightly in eerie silence, looming out of the dark in the moving swath of my light and swallowing the beam in diffused layers of brown-green. I'd drifted into a regular forest of the tall, sinuous plants. They closed in around me, pulsating with an unfelt current, leaves brushing me, long tendrils drifting around my leg.

It jerked instinctively and the loop tightened. Carefully, I eased my leg free and finned slowly upward, parting the long stems, pushing them away. But the plants climbed still higher as I rose, leaves fluttering, stems swaying now to a more pronounced rhythm. I stopped, craning my head back to shine my light upward. The beam flattened against a rippling ceiling overhead. A thick mat of floating, spread leaves and entangled stems. The surface.

Somehow I managed to resist the urge to thrash through to the top and tear off my faceplate for some real air. I could get trapped in the weeds. And anyway I couldn't stay on the surface where the mechmen would be able to spot me from a hovercraft.

I grasped one of the thick stems, staring up hungrily at the barrier between me and the world of air. The faint surge tugged at me, but the stem kept me anchored. I blinked, suddenly realizing the plants were firmly tethered somewhere down below. And that meant the bottom must be fairly close.

Leaving the surface again was like turning my back on a long-lost friend. I reluctantly traced the stem back down, following my little hoard of light into darkness, slippery leaves slapping and sliding over my faceplate. At fourteen meters I could see something in my beam. A shivering carpet of bright green sea grass, rounded dark humps coated with blobs of color. The bottom.

My fins stirred up a lot of floating stuff, blotting out the view, but I hurried down, craning eagerly for another glimpse of something solid. My hand closed over a mass of fibrous roots, then the rock they clung to. Tiny fish shot up past my face, and some spotted, armored little things with lots of legs went skittering away through a thicket of low, lacy weeds. I blew out a long breath and started groping through the blinding silt.

I hovered for a long time, my light shining into a deep crevice in a tumble of rock coated with weeds and pink and orange squishy things. It would have made a good shelter, but I couldn't bring myself to crawl into the tomblike space, even more claustrophobic than the black surrounding sea.

I nested in the slippery weeds against the base of the rock, strapping myself down, my hands clumsy with exhaustion. I was sure I'd never sleep, engulfed in the heavy darkness and defenseless to invisible, lurking eyes. But I had to rest. I made myself grope through the net bag for a nutrient packet, snap it into the bypass shunt to my water tube, and suck down the concentrated goop.

I didn't remember finishing it. Sleep tugged and surged over me, sucking me down into its own black depths.

I drifted in the night sea. A thin stem of seaweed tethered me, floated me in the swaying dance of leaves. Blackness ebbed and flowed. Slippery shapes loomed out of nothingness, brushed me, and melted away. Sinuous weeds swayed hissing in the surge as they closed around me. Tendrils wrapped my body, twisted, tightened. My tether snapped and I was lost, spinning deeper into the dense whispering dark.

All around me, the plants swayed. Cold trailing fingers brushed my face. Helpless, I was spun faster, sucked down a dark whirlpool and spat out floating on a black river.

Shadowed trees and vines swayed to a rhythmic wind, ebbing and flowing to the hiss of serpents. Their coppery, scaly coils wrapped around me, squeezing, strangling. The jungle surged and whispered. Dry laughter. The coils loosened, the scales of my red gold necklace melting from my neck and flowing down over my nakedness.

Listen. Hear the song, flow with it. Dance.

The serpent hissed. The leaves whispered. And Jaréd spoke in a low, rhythmic voice. *Learn the dance of fear. Find it with your flesh.*

He was beside me in the dark swirl of Sethar's dreamsmoke, teeth gleaming in the night, dark eyes on mine, healed scar on his forehead pale against brown skin. I reached for the knife he handed me, felt the fire-lizard carving on the hilt stir to life.

Vines swayed around me in the darkness, serpent tongues hissing. *Feel it. Flow.*

I gripped the hilt tighter, touched the blade to the smooth skin of my cheek, closed my eyes, and pressed down, pulling.

Sharp pain and the bite of smoke, heart pumping the song, hot sting of blood flowing. Electric bolts coursed through me in ecstatic, agonizing shudders. I opened my eyes as I drew the knife slowly down my cheek, and saw with lucid impossibility the slice of an invisible knife appearing down my arm, the skin splitting, crimson blood draining, staining my fingers. Jaréd gripped my wrist as the ceremonial scar on his forehead split open at the same time, crimson staining his face, pulsing to the throb in my arm.

An empty jolt in my belly, and then a hot, sexual rush. We were pressed together, falling through the smoke and whispering vines, rolling, tumbled in the electric pulse locking our bodies and fusing them. Sweat stung my eyes. We grappled, growled, thrashed like animals in the ashes and smoke, the hot fire of him inside me. We were flames—burning, molten, flowing into the dark river.

The serpent hissed its laughter. I opened my eyes to see Jaréd stretched stiff beside me on his deathbed, face gone gray and cold. The laughter swelled around me to a mocking roar, and I looked down to see my arm livid and swollen, bursting into a writhing mass of pale worms. I jerked back in horror, tearing futilely at the putrid flesh. Jaréd slowly rose in a clanking of bones, pale skeletal form gleaming in the shadows, nodding slowly as he pointed to the black river. The empty sockets of his skull watched me, waiting.

The worms swelled to coiling snakes, hissing long poisonous tongues, whispering, "Come with us, Ruth. Leave your rotting flesh. Live forever with us." One voice and many voices blended to the one in all of the incorporeals.

"No!" I scrambled through the dirt, searching for my knife to hack the noxious arm away.

"Ruth. Wait." A calm, familiar voice. Jason stepped quietly from behind a tree, amber cyborg eyes bright in the shadows.

"No!" I scrambled back the other way, but the voices of the incorporeals only laughed, driving me to the edge of the black river where Jaréd's empty eyes waited.

"Ruth, I only want to help." Jason's voice tugged me, and I whirled around to see him standing in the flames, his lean, strong young body untouched. Tawny hair—always a little long and shaggy—fell over his wide cheekbones as he looked down, step-ping toward me. He reached out a big hand—calloused and work-toughened, touching me gently in the moonlit wheat field—touching my face now, softly, on my scarred cheek. The tingling electricity of his fingertips sang through me, whispering intimate promises, and I wanted to sing with it, let it flow and carry me back to him. I jerked away, shaking my head.

Jason only smiled, reached to his left shoulder, and plucked his arm free. "Here, Ruth."

"No!" I backed away from him, but he kept smiling, bringing me his arm, and now I could see it was made of gleaming gold metal, a perfectly wrought mechanism of joints and cables and hidden cogs and wheels. "No."

But he tore the putrid mass of snakes from my shoulder and snapped the golden arm into place. "You'll see, Ruth. It's better this way."

I turned to face the mirror, but it was only a blank oval framed by the coppery loop of the head-to-tail serpent. The serpent laughed and spun then, faster and faster, and I saw myself staring out of the darkness, transformed to gleaming gold planes and angles, cold and beautiful, eyes blazing green jewels.

"No!" The mirror spun over me, sucking me inside, the ser-pent's coils enclosing me. My metal skin squeezed tighter, crush-ing inward, suffocating me. Blackness closed over me, pressing, engulfing—

"NO!"

It echoed in my faceplate. I jerked awake, flailing against my tethers, cracking my head hard against weedy rock. Stars burst and swam. My arm throbbed angrily, and I blinked, panting. "Damn."

I sank back, sucking in air, shaking my head and squinting around me as the muck I'd stirred up settled. A faint violet light filtered down through tall, swaying weeds. Two bulging eyes stared through my faceplate at me.

"Ahh!" I startled back against the rock. The creature scuttled sideways on six jointed legs and reared back, fiercely waving one large spotted claw, one small one, and two thin antennae. I might have been worried if it had been bigger than my fist. We stared at each other for a while, then it slipped into a crack between rocks.

I sat up, loosening my tethers and shaking my head. "Bloody double damn." With an almost physical effort, I shoved the nightmare images away—Jaréd's empty, staring skull-eyes; Jason's bright, amber cyborg eyes and his electric touch, opening me to too much. I blinked quickly, looking around me.

In the dim, filtered daylight, the seaweed forest had its own strange sort of beauty. The colors were flattened, muted to shades of rippling blue-violet, but when I snapped on my headlight its beam picked out vivid swaths of pink and orange blobby growths, a flashing cluster of vividly blue-striped fish, the brownish-green sea vines with their translucent green leaves wafting gently overhead. There was a purple thing shaped like a star crawling very slowly across one of my swim fins. On the rounded rock behind me, small black orbs bristled a multitude of sharp spines. Everywhere the contours of the rocky bottom were coated with an undulating mat of long speckled grasses and stuff that looked like bright green, slippery lettuce. Scalloped shells pulsed their own small currents of particle-laden sea, as a spiraled shell lumbered between them on a broad fleshy foot.

And as I sat still, breathing carefully slow and deep, there were fish everywhere. An amazing variety of colors, shapes, and sizes—fat, skinny, striped, spotted, glistening silver, plumed, streamlined—darted curiously about me and whisked gracefully off through the weeds. The smaller fish seemed to travel in gangs. One cluster of finger-sized, bright yellow ones swarmed in front of me, moving uncannily like the flocks of birds I'd watched on Andura, swerving and diving in a single multiplied motion, then hovering together to nibble along the weeds.

I wondered what alien form of communication kept them in such synchronization. Were there whispers I couldn't hear, lapping and hissing around me as I slept in the dark sea? One in all, like the web of the incorporeals, secret spook voices invading—

Without warning, a black wash of dizziness dropped over me in a jolting dislocation. I lost all sense of place, or I was in two places, like transparent images sliding across each other to form strange new shapes. I was looking at myself from a great distance—no, not looking, but adding up and sorting my pieces in abstracted patterns of flesh and blood, beating heart and firing nerves. What did the puzzle pieces form? Incoherence, confusion. Distress? Threat? With a shock I recognized the intruder in this sea world, the invader, her very thoughts and feelings alien as the machines she wore on her body—

With a wrenching jolt, I was jerked up and back to slam my head against the rock. Stars exploded. I blinked, gawking confused around me, vague remnants of nightmare muffling my mind, an odd sensation of things repeating as I focused on the muted violet daylight and the swarm of bright yellow fish feeding close. Long vines swayed around me, shivering dark serpentine echoes of threat. I blinked in confusion.

Suddenly a long, narrow-snouted, steel-gray fish over a meter long materialized with a ghostly glimmer out of the shadows. Sharp teeth glinted. The smaller fish, electrified, clotted together in a writhing mass and shot directly at me, breaking over and around me like shattered gold. They melted into a dark rock crevice. The larger fish flashed once and was gone.

I blew out a long breath, shaking my head, back prickling again with the sensation of unseen eyes watching. If there were predators about, there was no way I could match the speed and reflexes of the sea creatures. I could only hope nobody decided I looked like breakfast.

Reluctantly pushing off from my sheltered cranny, still fuzzy in the aftermath of the dream, I drifted past the deep crevice I'd examined the night before. Darkness gathered inside, almost palpable, swallowing my thin light. I knew the Cyvriots lived in groups around something called a *bathylabra*, but where did they sleep? Among the weeds, in the rock caves, or simply drifting? They had to be somewhere near. I was stupidly half convinced I could feel them, watching me. I probed the opaque darkness of the cave once more with my light, shuddered, and pushed back to fin hastily away.

The weaving weeds closed around me, and I could almost hear them hissing, whispering sibilant laughter as they wound their nightmare coils around me and squeezed. My heart was beating too fast again, chest tight. I took a deep breath and kicked slowly and steadily, easing my way deeper into the swaying sea jungle, but I couldn't seem to stop craning from side to side, straining through the opaque surrounding murk. Purple shadows hovered, flowed, and reformed, following.

seven

The earth was without form, and void; And darkness lay upon the face of the deep. . . . Darkness suspended me above the blind abyss. The midnight ocean engulfed me, sucked me down into its shadowy embrace. *Deep calleth unto deep.*

I kicked convulsively faster, breath rasping in my dry throat, chasing my pitiful cone of light across the black gap of another yawning trench. Behind me, beneath me, closing in on the narrow, wavering beam, invisible demon presences lurked. Undulating shapes of purple-black shadow coiled and uncoiled just beyond seeing. Distant, muffled thuds and watery groans echoed faintly in my ears, directionless. But they brought weird, feverish sensations—voiceless whispers buzzing up my spine, cold fingers touching and probing my viscera, squeezing my thoughts themselves into strange forms, erratic swings of half-recognized emotions.

My arm throbbed painfully, the infection spreading, and I knew I needed to rest, but I had to find the console-station or at least some solid rock. It was hard to focus on the red guiding arrow when odd images kept forming behind my eyes. Flares of vivid color too quick to seize. Shifting strange places—the seabed shaking and splitting as molten rock fountained under the boiling sea and the waves churned in elemental frenzy, a dreamy bright ocean garden dancing in sparkling clear water, an ominous underwater maze of deep blue glowing rock pulsing with discordant music. And the monstrous creatures.

There. Beneath me. I was suddenly convinced that a huge, writhing shape of bulbous flesh and tentacles was right beneath me, spewing black water as it rose. I could see it, its grotesque bulk swarming up at me. But when I brought my light around once more in a jolt of alarm, there was nothing there.

I was panting, cold sweat breaking out on my back. I couldn't seem to pull in enough air. My skin crawled with awareness of the abyss below, haunting me since I'd been caught by nightfall over another open trench. *Deep calleth unto deep.*

Part of me was a screaming, gibbering, mindless panic thrashing blindly toward the surface, and air, flailing at any cost through the shallow schooling fish and the big, fast ones in their night feeding. Somehow I managed to keep that part separate from the part that could fix on the hazy red arrow and stay at a still black depth, kicking steadily. I could focus only on the blind search for shelter. All the reasons for being here in this nightmare—David, the incorporeals, damn fool Lilith, the cybers and their apocryphal signal—were as remote as Siolis in his murky tank back in Casino.

Siolis. No, he was here. With the other Cyvriots? That was why I was here. Looking for Cyvriots. Swimming for Cyvriots. Seeking the Cyvriots—

Another nauseating wrench, and I was displaced, looking through a blurred lens at watery images splayed and distorted. A monstrous, gangly shape kicking awkwardly past, my companions slithering comfortingly around me, cool scales slippery, smooth focus humming, presences echoing.

I shuddered and closed my eyes, forcing myself to go limp, to shut out the disorienting sensations. My passive helplessness galled. I took careful, slow breaths, groping for balance, finding the silent words to a Setharian chant. Deep breaths, that was it, smooth and cycling through me. Humming an eternal song. I was only a note in the song, a mote swept in the ebb and flow of endless space, bottomless seas. . . .

But the vertigo only intensified, swamping me as I felt cold fingers pry open my skull and the black ocean rush in. Sibilant whispers, down my spine. The song was a shattering racket, exploding inside me.

I gasped and doubled up, gut clenching, eyes popping open as my light beam swerved. Shapes loomed out of darkness. Two, no three in the slippery shadows. Bulky smooth tapered bodies, undulating tails, splayed finlike hands, pulsing gill slits, big staring eyes. The stares pinned me.

I recoiled, thrashing back from the monstrous figures as the light beam skittered wildly. A shadowed glimpse of Siolis in his weedy tank flashed through me. My light caught a last sinuous shape darting and dissolving into the surrounding night.

"No!" I stupidly yelled into the faceplate. "Come back! Please. Help me. . . ." Nothing there but darkness.

Violet light seeped down from above, slowly seeping into my awareness. I blinked groggily, bobbing against my tether, yawning and fighting off the urge to close my eyes again. Wishing I could splash my face with the water pressing around the faceplate, I checked my readouts and discovered I'd slept away most of the morning. Power supply was still fine, but air reserve was down to a couple hours' worth, so it was time to get moving again.

Unhooking the cords tethering me to the first solid rock I'd finally found the night before, I eased my left arm out of its cramped position, biting back a hiss as I straightened it. The arm felt tight and stiff, throbbing to an insistent beat. I considered shunting some pain medication in with the antibiotics I'd added to my nutrient slop, but decided against it. Had to stay as alert as possible.

I sucked down the nutrients, craning up through dimness. I was looking up a tall, jagged black rock wall, coated with swaying weeds, monochrome blotches, lacy black fans, and weirdly shaped spongy growths. The wall melted beneath me into darkness.

I put my readouts through their paces again. Bottom thirty meters below, and falling away steeply. The red directional arrow said I should be going on straight through the rock wall toward the console-station, so the only route was up and over.

Unless it was into the mouth of a dark crevice opening before me as I finned slowly upward. I grasped a slippery handhold of rock and switched on my headlight, bright colors of orange slimes, green moss, blue translucent clustered tubes springing out of flat monochrome in the beam. The light cone swung around into the crevice, followed a rock curve, was swallowed by blackness.

I ignored the red arrow, finning quickly past the yawning dark mouth of the cave. It wasn't the only one. The broad wall seemed to be pitted with crevices and crannies, oozing shadows.

Moving ones. I jerked back as a swarm of tiny silvery fish burst out of a narrow tunnel, flowing around me and reforming. They didn't seem worried by me, nibbling on the plentiful plant life coating the rock face. I drifted slowly up through them, light sparking from their scales to enclose me in living gems. The reddish-blue, wavering sunlight grew a little brighter, and I thought I could see the crest of the wall above. More fish, gangs of small ones and scattered larger ones, busied themselves among the waving weeds and rock crevices. I stopped to watch a tiny, bright blue fingerling dart repeatedly through the undulating, fleshy orange fringes of one of the round, lumpy-looking plants or animals that were stuck all over the wall. A few long, yellow-striped fish hovered off to my right, ignoring a tiny white-and-red banded creature with a lot of legs that hopped comically from one fish to another, scraping its pincers over their scales like a miniature barber giving a shave.

My back prickled suddenly with that unnerving sense of a presence, and I kicked around to peer through the murky purple shadows. They moved just beyond focus. A bulky shape? There. A glimpse of big staring eyes. Gone. No, a smooth shape was coming at me, finning slowly out of the dimness.

I opened my mouth to call out, then snapped it shut. It was a big, green-freckled fish, broad as I was, with thick lips and a heavy jaw, moving ponderously toward me. I shrank back against the wall, holding my breath. Its glassy eyes stared incuriously for a moment, then it turned with the slow dignity of an overweight Poindran hearth-matron, gathering up its fins to glide along the rock face. A couple of small, black-and-white striped fingerlings darted busily over the oblivious massive fish, mouths nibbling along its scales. The matron and her grooming attendants. I let out my breath, smiling as she passed.

Then another form shot without warning from a narrow crack in the rock beside me. The long, sinuous shadow uncoiled into the shape of a huge, toothy serpent.

I jerked back in an explosion of startled little fish. The dark-glinting serpent moved almost too fast to see, attacking the big freckled fish as it belatedly finned to escape. The long coils wrapped around the fish and suddenly the sea jolted with a crackling hiss, more felt than heard. The writhing green fish jerked in spasms to the boiling, electric crackle.

I recoiled, groping away blinded through the swarm of panicked smaller fish. I kicked past them, fleeing into the open, finally slowing as I found myself at the mouth of a sort of narrow canyon sloping upward between high rocky walls. I turned to follow it up toward the top of the plateau. Then I saw them.

They didn't notice me, or they were too busy swimming back and forth across the narrow cleft to care. Were they searching for something? The bluish-violet light was clearer now, and I could see there were three of them. The same ones that had fled the night before? I hovered at the mouth of the canyon, not wanting to startle them again, swallowing down an instinctive shudder at the grotesque reshaping of the human form.

There were two larger ones, though maybe not quite as big as Siolis, and a smaller one, probably an adolescent. I could make out the glint of big, staring dark eyes and wide slash of mouth in the flattened face of the closest adult. The head was joined almost neckless to the smooth, pale bluish tapered body, the upper trunk thick with the rounded hump behind the head that made the tiny thin arms set low over the chest look so deformed. And the fingers were disproportionately long, translucent webs shining between them. I swallowed again, tracing the slippery narrowing taper of the body below the pulsing double gills, the truncated lower fins instead of legs, the long, flattened, whipping tail.

I took a deep breath, skin crawling, repeating to myself that they were human. They moved closer in their sweeps down the slope of the canyon, a few blue-tinged plumy fish about a half-meter long whipping in circles around them, like the fish Siolis had kept in his tank in Casino. The Cyvriots still didn't see me, intent on—

My stomach made a sickening lurch as I realized what they were doing. Lipless mouths gaping wide, they swept back and forth through a glinting cloud of almost-invisible tiny fish, scooping up mouthfuls. I glimpsed a long, snakelike black tongue dart out and rake back a wriggling mouthful as the mouth closed and water gushed out the flapping gills. I recoiled in the water, and the native whipped around, staring eyes fixing on me.

For a second, I could vividly taste slimy raw fish flailing on my tongue as a surge of bile rose in my throat. I choked, gagging.

The three of them hovered close together, the smaller one in the middle and below, staring down the rocky cleft at me with opaque purple eyes. I swallowed and held my empty hands out slowly. "Please don't go. I need to talk to you." I didn't know how they talked underwater, but maybe they could hear my voice through the faceplate.

Suddenly they were moving, the quick whips of their tails propelling them almost too fast to follow. They swooped toward me in an odd looping surge of synchronized passing and crossing sweeps, so close together I didn't know how they didn't collide with each other or the plumed fish, flushed violet now, swarming along with them. They stopped abruptly in perfect unison four or five meters away, the eddy of their momentum washing over me. I noted mechanically a couple of the black-and-white striped fingerlings moving with nibbling mouths over one of the oblivious adults. The three Cyvriots hovered motionless, flat purple eyes staring at me.

I swallowed, throat dry. Again I spread my gloved hands. "Hello. I mean you no harm. I'm looking for Siolis."

No response, no blinking of the huge purple eyes. But two of the violet plumed fish shot out at me, whipping around me with their delicate fins wafting. One of them brushed me, and the odd, tingling dislocation washed through me again with a prickling shock, the natives going out of the focus for a second as a vague sense of alarm or disturbance shivered down my spine, almost an electric crackle of warning. I shook my head sharply, pushing back the dizziness, and glimpsed out of the corner of my eye a darting movement.

I jerked back in the water, kicking around to see the long shape uncoiling from the rock beside me at the entrance to the canyon. It was the sea serpent, or one like the serpent that had attacked the fish with jolting current, shooting now in a black arrow past me, straight for the younger native, who had drifted slightly away from the other two.

"Watch out!" My hand was already grabbing the null device from its pocket, reflexively triggering a stunning beam at the serpent. There was a dull roaring pop in my ears, then a heavy, silent blow. The beam snapped off as the serpent writhed in a twitching knot of coils and sank into the darkness down the steep rock wall. The sea shimmered oddly, floating a hazy suspension of glinting particles condensing out of the water and slowly raining down through it.

My ears were ringing wildly. A sleek shape whipped past in a frenzy of churning water. I fell back, startled as the young native shot away into the open sea, two of the plumy little fish, bright scarlet now, darting in sharp, disjointed surges after him.

"Hey, it's all right, I got the thing." I kicked around to see the two adults thrashing back from me in agitation, the rest of the little plumy fish clustered close, whipping their fins and tails in violent spasms and swimming erratic circles. "Wait, come back." I reached out toward them, forgetting the deactivated null device still in my hand.

Like I'd run into a wall, something slammed me back into blind darkness, the dizzy whirling disorientation splitting me open and spinning me down. Pain. Terror. Confusion. Taboo.

I doubled over in agony, wrenched with nausea again, seeing from a great distance my hand thrusting the black plasmeld device away from me. Then my split perceptions jolted back together. I blinked, shaken, glimpsing the Cyvriots fleeing into the deep open sea. I gasped in a lungful of air as the prickling pain subsided, blinking again and catching a last glint of shiny black as the null device sank spinning out of sight.

Sacred Founders . . . I shot down after it, just managing to grab it, kicking back up with legs shaking. I paused by the deserted mouth of the canyon, paddling in a bewildered circle and peering out into the sea. Only vague shadows and emptiness. I shuddered, then shook my head, crammed the device back into its pocket, and finned hastily toward the shallows above.

Translucent leaves danced through a scattering of thin, reddish sunbeams. The light angle was shifting lower, casting a melting montage of shadow and diffuse halos, mesmerizing.

I had to fight off the heavy lassitude whispering through me, a depressing conviction that I would be swimming through these endless shadowy seas forever, kicking to the same hypnotic beat. I pulled myself up short to stretch and shake out my aching legs and arms, hooking my short tether to the base of one of the tall, sinuous weeds I'd been swimming through for the last couple of hours. I rested limp in the dip and sway of the shallow current, resisting and then tiredly surrendering to the graceful rhythm of the undulating weed forests, drifting to their slow water caress.

I drifted, holding up and bemusedly admiring an iridescent shell I'd picked up earlier, shimmering smoothness wrapped in a hollow, involuted coil. Whatever had lived at the heart of it was gone now, leaving behind its beautiful empty chambers. I tucked the little shell into one of the sealed pockets on my suit's thighs, in with the crystal dice I'd brought along on impulse.

Rousing myself to suck down a bland dose of nutrients, I tried to convince myself it was time to launch across yet another deep trench falling away just beyond the shallow weeds. I didn't know how much farther the console-station was. I didn't know if the natives would come back. But my third day out was fading fast, and something had to give soon. I hoped it wouldn't be me.

I sighed and finished the goop, reached for the shunt to flush it out, and winced. My left arm throbbed, hot and tight in its bandage, so stiff now I could hardly bend it. As I twisted awkwardly around, rolling against the taut tether, it jerked across the injured arm. I bit back a scream, red swimming in my eyes. Sweat broke out on my forehead as the faceplate started to fog.

I took some deep breaths, then checked my readouts and the gear stowed in the mesh bag hooked to my belt. My fingertips brushed the hard shape of the null device in its pocket, and I frowned. Why had the natives seemed so terrified of it? Had they really thought I would use it on them, after I'd used it to defend the young one? Or were they only upset about my presence, breaking their taboos? Upset was putting it mildly, though. If I could trust my own impressions. I didn't know what was happening to me, if the frightening fits of vertigo and hallucination meant I'd been submerged too long in this alien sea, or my fever was worse than I thought, or the natives were somehow sonically blasting my nervous system into incoherence. Maybe my imagination was just plain running amuck.

I shook off the visceral memory of that gaping mouthful of wriggling slimy fish. Since my time in the trees with the peaceful, vegetarian Andurans—and Heinck's bloody invasion—I'd lost my stomach for animal flesh. Which was easy enough with Casino's synth proteins, so I supposed if I was hungry enough the Sethar hunter would revive in me. Anyway, I couldn't believe my killing of the sea serpent could have violated a primary taboo here, since the natives clearly fed on live fish.

Peering through the filtered, wavering light of the weed forest as I unhooked my tether, I wished I'd asked Siolis more about his strange world. Alien life swarmed all around me, thick along the shallow seabed.

Dozens of the round, blobby, fringed things I'd decided were animals clung to the weed-furred rocks, undulating their fat tentacles, trapping tiny swimming fish and insectile creatures, slowly collapsing inward with their prey. Scuttling things with flat armored backs tore with their claws at the pulpy flesh of something dead. Tiny silver swarming fish darted above, snapping up drifting fragments. Larger fish, yellow-striped and black-spotted, flashed out of the dimness to whip through the silvery cluster, jaws whipping through them in thin trails of blood. Even the rough, conical shells encrusting the rocks reached out miniature feathery fingers to rake the water for prey invisible to my eyes.

It was nothing but kill and eat. Survival. War?

I kicked hastily past the feeding frenzy, sickened. The hot flush of dizziness lapped through me again with the throb of my swollen arm, and I was filled with a sudden cynical distaste for the whole bloody, pointless, endless cycle of spawning and dying. I despised myself, despised the swarming fish and the hungry sea serpent and the spongy blobs sucking on the rocks, despised life itself. Nothing but the blind urge to exist at the expense of anything else. No creature could be trusted, no matter how gentle, not with that violent imperative to eat or be eaten slumbering deep inside, like

some alien force ready to invade, wiping out will and blindly
engulfing, hissing whispers of secret needs.

My arm throbbed its painful beat, insistent, pulsing to an overwhelming rhythm now as the black vertigo of dislocation swept
through me once more, scattering logic. All I could grasp was a
jolt of fury, the loathing of my own festering body. I wanted to
rip at the offending limb, tear it off, fling it from me. Escape, as
the incorporeals tempted, the insistent demands of flesh and blood.
Escape the invisible life inside me, even my own swarming cells,
each proliferating madly with its own blind obsession to live, eat,
expand.

Darkness swirled and spun me down, cold invisible fingers
touching me again, probing, tugging with a sharp, painful popping
in my ears. A cascade of crazy sensations and images tumbled up
through me from somewhere deep inside, like I'd opened a door
I didn't know was there.

Anger-disdain-violation. Jason's sun-brown skin, no, plasmeld
melting away to reveal the workings of the machine inside. Smooth
black tube of the laser strapped to Heinck's thigh in the whispering
forest as he sneered and raised the weapon to rake the helpless
Andurans. War-murder-taboo. Babbling voices in my skull, the
spooks invading, taunting, tempting. *Flying, falling like the terrible bright angel of retribution*—my fingers pressed the firing
stud as hate finally exploded and I blasted Heinck out of existence.
Taboo. Violation. A pale, lovely face crowned in coppery braids,
murmuring gently, "You know the meaning of love, daughter.
You'll find the Way. . . ." Purple eyes, staring. *The disruptor*.
Spiral vortex sucking me down, no up into the endless coils of
the serpent, bright snake eyes glinting like stars in space. Coldly
blue-sparking seas whirling me through a dark, twisting labyrinth
of rock. Slippery tapered, finned shapes watching me with huge
purple eyes.

I flailed, choking, suffocating in the blind pounding seas, sinking into the abyss. "No! Stop. . . ."

Another chilling gust of otherness—distress/disruption/incom-
prehension/revulsion/outrage, and then a sharp, alien, but unmistakable command—and I was thrust up and out of it. A sudden
uprush of pressure beneath me, a huge unfelt hand shoving me
up. Then something broad and slippery grazed me, spinning me
to one side.

I gasped, eyes snapping open to see a huge, black, broad shape
disappearing beneath me into the murky depths of an open sea

trench. I flailed wildly around, still disoriented, spotting the faint contours of the receding rocky plateau I'd drifted away from. I kicked frantically against the current, toward the refuge. An invisible wave caught me, forcing me back in its surge. I choked, grappling the water, kicking around to see an enormous dark creature whip past and away. No hallucination this time. It was there—no, gone. I kicked in a panicky circle, raking my eyes through shadows.

It sprang out of darkness, melted up and over me, cutting off the dim light. A black silhouette, demon image out of Poindran hell, hovering over me with wings of night and curving horns, a long whipping tail. The wings flapped, undulating with horrible slowness. The demon thing dove down at me.

I screamed into the faceplate, diving down, kicking panicked into the depths. But the creature flew down past me. Then up, trapping me, forcing me upward atop its slippery back. Between its curving black horns, two glinting eyes fixed on me.

I kicked away from it in terror, thrashing backward.

The black wings swooped and the creature brushed me again, pushing me up and forward, coming around and beneath me and floating me on its back, moving me along on its sinuous glide. Again I tried to escape. It blocked me. I tried once more. It forced me atop it again, wings curving to corral me as it dipped and then rose, thin tail whipping.

Numb and exhausted, I vaguely realized the animal could easily have hurt me with its huge wings. It hadn't. We were out far over the abyss now, and the creature was diving, its rippling wings nudging me along.

The buzzing panic in my ears fell abruptly away into an odd silence. My hand seemed to move of its own will to find a grip on one smooth, rounded horn of flesh. The reflexive movement stirred echoes of strangeness and impossible familiarity, at once terrifying and crazily reassuring.

The creature bobbed, gathered its wings, and plunged faster, towing me through the sea. Flying blind.

eight

I was past surprise when the creature soared finally out of the murky abyss. It swept me along through a lightheaded unreality, and I didn't know if the things we'd sailed past in the trench—ponderous behemoths with huge flat tails, giant tentacled creatures, big daunting fish whipping past like streamlined killing machines, and bizarre amalgamations of saucer eyes, oversized jaws bristling too many teeth, and dangling luminescent filaments—had been there or not. It could have been hours or minutes before the winged black animal swooped me up to hover before a looming rock wall, beside another gaping black tunnel mouth.

I shook my head stupidly. The creature undulated its wings and waited. The rock crevice oozed shadow, somehow inevitable.

Prying my cramped hand free of the animal's curved horn and flexing stiff fingers, I gathered myself for a lunge upward and away from that bottomless dark well. The creature must have felt me tense. It suddenly tilted, funneling its wings to spill me into the entrance of the tunnel.

"No!" I flailed, clawing my way around to escape the enclosing darkness.

The creature still hovered, blocking the entrance, dim light raying behind the black demon shape of wings, horns, tail. I turned slowly, numbly knowing it wasn't going to move. I had to go in. Down the black, jagged tunnel, deeper into the rock.

I shuddered. My ears were ringing, the darkness pulsing to a distant, muffled drumbeat. Shadow ebbed and flowed, seeping into me with a chilly, half-familiar probing. Dull pain throbbed to the penetrating beat, and the rock walls themselves seemed to expand and contract, the artery of a giant, labyrinthine being pumping the darkness and closing in on me.

My hand jerked up to snap on my headlight, its beam raking a suspended glimmer of particles and nervous sweeps of rough rock. Blocking the jagged entrance, the huge, flat-winged demon fish still hovered, dark eyes glinting in the light. I jerked around again, bumping back against stone, light dancing crazily through stirred sediment as I rebounded deeper into the well.

I took a deep breath. Then another, refusing the blind, drowning panic of claustrophobia, the dense masses of rock and water crushing in on me. Another breath and I finned slowly forward, around a rough curve and down. Back crawling, I resisted turning my head to see the darkness closing in, following. I kicked faster, narrow light beam playing over folded black rock and the bright glint of crystalline deposits. Vibrations through the water shivered over me. The silent, thrumming beat intensified, its tangible presence pounding in my head. The rhythm drove me on, my will suspended in feverish unreality, the buzzing alarm of *timbra* screaming its warning through me even as a strange but familiar force pulled me irresistibly forward.

A tight corner, then rock walls curving around again, down. Up? The walls swooped dizzily around me, curving inward in a great spiral maze, and I no longer knew which way was out, which up, which down.

The hum of *timbra* was a wild roar, demanding escape, but the dull, insistent beat was stronger, pulsing and pulling me in. My feet kicked faster and I was hurtling down the twisting stone tunnel. The deepening beat hammered at some wall inside me, breaking into the place that futilely screamed its shrill alarm. The tunnel widened, black rock and a cluster of thick crystals glinting where another branching path joined the passage. A surge of turbulent dark water caught me at its mouth, spun me and flung me against rough stone. My faceplate hit with a painful crack and my light flickered and died. Darkness swallowed me.

I flailed, opening my mouth to scream as the black current grabbed me and sucked me down, up—

Stillness poured through me. Cool dark waters upwelling inside. Strange, familiar. I blinked, staring.

The tunnel wasn't dark. The rough black rock glowed with patches of cold blue luminescence, reflected in scattered angled facets, a dimly ethereal light sparking in the current carrying me slowly now through the passage. I brushed against a wall and pushed off numbly in swaths of icy blue fire as my arms swept the water. I was swept into a dreamlike trance, things seen before but never seen, mind blank but at the same time filled with impossible images somehow recognized. The distant rhythm pulsed, echoing a multiplying chorus, ebb and surge doubled and redoubled as blue luminescence swirled me through darkness.

A dark, submerged labyrinth. Cold blue light. Dimly seen

streamlined shapes with bottomless purple eyes. Deep watery lair.
Bathylabra . . .

I blinked, mind smothered under a heavy black weight and
feebly pushing toward some vague recognition. But my feet kept
kicking reflexively to that pervasive, compelling rhythm. The passage suddenly twisted and spilled me out into a huge watery chamber. Rock walls studded with irregular masses of jagged crystals
soared up, swept down into darkness. Dark sea, trapped but shivering, hummed in the giant bowl—a cacophony of sound and
sensation thrumming, hammering, pounding madly inside my
head. Eerie blue luminescence pulsed through black water.

Eyes reflected it. Bottomless wells, those glinting eyes turned
to me, mirroring the cold violet-blue, surrounding me.

Dim shapes, all around me, closed in—hairless heads, huge
glassy eyes, lipless slits of mouths gaping open like black wells.
Tapering monstrous forms, head joined neckless to bulbous trunk
and tiny, grotesque arms flapping flat, finned hands. Small darting
shapes wove around them in impossible precise patterns, wafting
ghostly plumes. The big sleek forms whipped through the blue-
sparked blackness, gleaming, eyes pools of blind midnight sucking
me down.

The pounding rhythms hammered at me, flashing bits of sharp
crystalline colors whirling out of the drowning dark to slash at
my nerves. The patterns spun into an excruciating pitch, bits of
sensation, sound, tint flung into the center and sprouting into a
bewildering lattice of too many dimensions, aching behind my
eyes. No, my ears. It was a song, a howling chorus, too many
voices in a screaming pitch of discordance rending my spine and
shattering up into my skull.

I clutched my head, screaming and writhing. One last focused
glimpse wrenched into place of the Cyvriots swarming, long sinuous serpent tails coiling the sea, coiling around me as slippery
plumes brushed me with an electric jolt, pain pulsing, gill slits
pulsing to the insane hammering, surging, echoing drum in my
head and my head was a bell, ringing, clanging, crashing. Cracking.

Blackness poured in.

Someone had split my head open with a crow-hammer. They
were prying it wider, pouring fire into me, invading me with
whispers, with sharp sparks of burning energy. The incorporeals,
the spooks, coming after me again—

"Nnnn . . ." Someone far away was groaning, scrabbling against a hard wet surface in the dark, mumbling, coughing, groping.

Pain stabbed my skull and I gasped, air burning into my chest, arms pushing feebly at a flat surface. I coughed, dragged in more air, bumped my head in the blind dark. Prying my eyes open, I numbly registered a dim red light glowing somewhere, a wet floor beneath my face and spread-eagled body. Solidity. No watery drifting. And air. I dragged in another greedy breath, wheezing.

"Oohhh . . ." I rolled slowly over, flinching as my arm dragged, huddling it against my chest and rocking as dizziness slowly subsided.

I blinked, raised a hand to my hot forehead, and craned around in confusion. Dim red and amber lights glowed in a tiny, domed chamber. The narrow shelf of hard floor ended at a raised lip, opening half the bottom to a shivering, agitated surface of dark water. Sea hissed, echoing murmurs, washing over me like the nightmare flood of images, sounds, demon presences whispering through my mind.

I jerked around as the faint pinpricks of light danced suddenly, colors shifting. Indicator lights, blue and red, flickered over the plasmeld face of a cyber console.

Alarm jolted. Those invading presences—the incorporeals. Had they found me through the panel sensors?

I was up on my feet, head bashing against the sloping side of the dome, feet slipping on wet flooring, the smooth, hard shape of the null device clutched in my hand. I pointed it at the console, frantically setting controls, triggering a directed field. There was a painful popping, loud or merely felt, a flash of light, and the console died. Darkness threw its seamless blanket over me.

I jerked back and slipped again in the dark, sitting down hard and skidding against the floor's lip. The sea hissed, louder now, ringing like a bell in the black dome. "Bloody double damn . . ."

I groped over the narrow wet floor to the console, pulling myself up against it, finding my knife still in its ankle sheath. Wild rage poured through me to the shrill buzzing in my ears. My arm hacked blindly at the control surface, over and over until sweat stung my eyes.

"Damn you! Damn you. . . ."

Gasping, I finally stopped. I hunched panting over the console, gingerly feeling out the shredded plasmeld surface and broken screen. The wild ringing in my ears was gone. I took one more deep breath then and did the sensible thing—found the back of the console and disconnected its cable.

:I slid to the floor and sat until I stopped shaking. Then I felt around me for my gear, finally realizing that someone had put me here and taken off my faceplate. And my fins. My fingers found one of them, then the mesh bag. I groped some more and found my backup lume rod inside.

The narrow spear of white light flashed over the wrecked console, the floor and my other fin near the raised lip, the restless dark water lapping against the dome wall. Beside the console was some sort of apparatus with a low, wide ring extending out over the water. Overhead, only a seamless curve.

I took another deep breath. The air wasn't as humid as I'd have expected. Another sweep of the light and I found the recirc grille, behind the console, still wafting a faint current.

Lucky I hadn't knocked out the whole system, going berserk on the com-console. I didn't even know if the spooks had penetrated the cybers' remote systems yet, if the crawling whispers inside my head had been anything more than my own stripped nerves, or fever, or something else. But somehow I felt better. I shook my head, adjusted the lume to a diffused wide-angle, and propped it on my bag. The whole dome glowed dimly yellow now. I was hunched inside a candled egg, waiting to hatch.

First I shed my wings, detaching the connections of the deactivated breathing gear and easing out of the straps. The lightweight, flexible membranes seemed to have come through the rough treatment in the tunnels pretty well. I unfused closures and peeled off the pressure suit, folding it carefully. Next, the liner, and the cheap thrill of plucking free the skin-cling waste tubes. My skin could breathe again. I draped the liner over the console to air out and stretched, rubbing my legs.

Lightheaded, I sat and took a deep breath. Drums were throbbing again, in my arm. I leaned closer over the lume to take a look. Not good. The skin was puffy and discolored, swelling around the edges of the pressure bandage. A fingertip touch sent stars leaping behind my eyes. I gritted my teeth and unwound the bandage.

The smell hit me first. I gagged and swallowed a surge of bile as cold sweat sprang out on my forehead and back. Red welts from the bandage dented what looked like a rotten sausage, a gross mass inflating the skin of my upper arm, twice its normal size.

The skin was discolored, tight and shiny. Cracks oozed foul matter.

I clenched my teeth against a surge of sick dizziness, eased over to the lip of the floor, and carefully lowered my arm into the restless water. I bit back a shrill scream as the salt burned, but I made myself dangle the obscene thing attached to my shoulder in the wash of the sea for as long as I could take it. Shaking, I rolled back onto the wet floor, forcing my fists to unclench, waiting for the pounding waves of pain to recede.

There was a splash beside me.

I jerked upright to see eyes staring back. Slick, dimly blue hairless heads bobbed on the dark water—four, five of them. Oversize purple-black eyes stared from their odd angles between open double lids, glinting fathomless gazes boring through me.

I flinched back, then caught myself and took a quick breath. "Hello."

No response.

I cleared my throat, groping for a remembered phrase. "Uh . . . long has been the sighting."

The dark eyes stared, unblinking. Then the clear inner membranes slid down over them and the heads started to sink back into darkness.

"No, wait! We've got to talk. I'm in trouble—we're *all* in trouble! You're going to need my help, too " I lunged awkwardly toward the water as they sank, brushing my hip against the forgotten null device and sending it spinning across the hard floor. "You've got to help me find Siolis!"

There was a sudden high-pitched burst of sound, echoing painfully in the dome. The heads surged up again in unison, higher this time so I could see the flat, closed nose flaps, the gaping lipless mouths, the monstrous humps swelling behind neckless heads, the gill slits pulsing moistly next to me. I couldn't help recoiling. The clear inner eyelids snapped open and the dark irises flared, then shrank to pinpoints as their eyes locked onto the broken console, then swept simultaneously to the floor and the black plasmeld null device.

Another shrill burst of sound, and another, echoing through the dome, doubled and redoubled in a barrage assaulting my ears, pounding furiously through my skull. I fell back, clutching my head. Feverish shapes and colors exploded behind my eyes.

A last dizzy glimpse of the fixed purple eyes, the monstrous faces and gaping black mouths somehow exuding outrage, drifting away on a tide of lancing pain as another demon shape rose out of the murk, an impossible thing with long, suckered tentacles and shapeless bulbous body reaching over the floor with a snake-like appendage. The cold tentacle brushed me, swayed with a slow nightmare grace, and suddenly shot out to grasp the black plasmeld instrument that the Cyvriots were stabbing with their furious gazes. Clutching it in a coiled arm, the creature plunged away into the murky sea.

"No . . ." The black tide washed over me and whirled me down a labyrinth, a cacophony of voiceless words echoing out of nightmare. An impossible chorus of Poindran Elders, twinned Casino cyberserfs, Siolis, Helsa, the incorporeals, black swimming demons with horns and tail, all shrieked and pointed, accusing me. *Sickness. Contamination. Sin. Disruption.*

Drenched in cold sweat, I pried my eyes open. The Cyvriots were gone. So was the null device.

nine

No hallucination. They'd taken the null device.

I groaned and rubbed my face, shaking with cold chills though my forehead felt like it was on fire. Groping in the mesh bag, I located the first-aid packet, did some quick calculations, and chugged a doubled dose of antibiotics, thirstily draining my water reservoir and forcing down a nutrient packet. Finally I popped the seal on the pain meds and swallowed some. My head pounded to an insistent nagging beat—David. Siolis. The spooks. Lilith. The null device. The Cyvriots. David . . .

Knocked out by the meds, I fell into a heavy, dreamless sleep. I felt better when I woke up, so I decided not to ruin the effect by unwrapping my arm for another look.

Instead, I dragged my osmotic gear over to the dropoff and tried to figure out how to get the de-sal unit functioning when I wasn't in the suit. Switching tube shunts, I activated the wings and lowered them into the dark water, using my tether to strap the gear onto the odd, ringlike apparatus stretching out over the water from the side of the dome. With some adjustments, it held nicely as the wings slowly fanned.

I leaned out to tie another half-hitch. "Ah!" I jerked back, bashing against the console.

A slick blue head had bobbed up inside the plasmeld ring inches from my face, streaming water, huge eyes flicking open double lids to stare glassily into mine. The Cyvriot's black pupils flared and shrank to pinpoints, the eyes deep purple wells drawing me down. Ghostly waves lapped through me, silent whispers and unseen pictures, eerily both strange and familiar. I jerked my gaze away and cleared my throat.

A low hum vibrated the dome. The plasmeld ring extruded an inflating tube, swelling below and inside the rim. Like the gasket ring of Siolis' biosupport unit in Casino, it enclosed the native below the head, sealing along the shoulder hump to enclose his gills. The hum intensified to a whisper of circulating water within the puffy sealing cuff. The ring, floating on the inflated tube, rose, bringing the native's face higher.

Flattened spiral ears fanned forward as the slick, pale blue face bobbed before me. Skin flaps opened with a moist sucking noise to reveal two slits on the vague swelling where a normal nose would have been. The lipless, toothless mouth hung open, dripping water. The face spasmed, air whistling in through the nasal slits and whooshing out through the mouth.

I swallowed, trying to ignore the queasy flip-flop in my stomach. "Long . . . long has been the sighting."

He blinked and kept staring, another gust of air whooshing from his mouth. The black water shivered as one of the ubiquitous plumed fish broke the surface, its blue scales mottled with a spreading violet tinge, then shot down and behind the Cyvriot. The ring-tube finished inflating, and I could see the vague outline of the Cyvriot's smooth, elongated body beneath the water, the shadow of a stirring tail, and tiny arms wafting their splayed, webbed hands.

I stomped down the impulse to look away from him—no, her. Now I could see the slight swelling of breasts below the flotation tube, and the wrinkled ridges of oddly shaped nipples, like a set of barely curved parentheses on her lower chest. I would never have thought of asking Siolis about his physiology, but I realized now that both sexes must have had concealed genitals, retracted within the folded sort of pocket between their truncated lower fins. I met the woman's eyes, feeling even more uncomfortable.

A last whoosh of air, and the slack mouth twitched, pursed together, twisted loosely. The black tip of her snakelike tongue darted out for a second. "Vlllasshunsss."

I startled at the burst of hissing sounds, wrenching my gaze from the writhing mouth back to her eyes.

Deep purple pinned me angrily. Again the hiss of air. "Vllla-sshunsss."

I frowned, shaking my head, tenuous images flickering through my consciousness. Pointing fingers, voices condemning, barely recognized hostile faces . . . I had to shake off an almost physical return to Poindros and my guilty youthful Waywardness. "Violations?"

"Yesss."

"I know I had to break your Rules, coming here. But I had to warn—"

"Vllasshunsss. Llanderss disssrupt."

I could feel the shattered console at my back. "I am sorry about the console." I spoke slowly, understanding now the reason for the floating ring apparatus—the natives' mandatory conformance sessions, talking to the cybers via console. I hadn't realized how hard Siolis must have worked on his speaking skills. "But we're all in danger. That's what I came to tell you. Your world has been invaded by—"

"Lllandersss invade. Vllashunss. Ssicknesss." The purple eyes drilled mine.

"No, you don't understand." How could I explain the galactic system, the true nature of the guardian cybers, the incorporeal invaders to this sheltered native of an isolated, taboo world? I continued gently, "I don't know what the cybers have told you about themselves and your world, but there are a lot of other worlds out there, with humans on them. We're all humans, like . . . like you, even though we don't look the same. We don't intend you harm."

The woman only stared, motionless.

I didn't know if she understood or not, but I kept trying. "I'm a friend of Siolis, one of your Cyvriots, who . . . learned from the consoles how to travel to meet us on another world. Do you know him? Do you know he's returned? He came back because he . . ." I bit my lip, trying to simplify. "He learned that your world had been invaded. Invaded by invisible creatures who live in the cyber matrix. They're like false cybers, and they . . . make the consoles lie to you. They'll hurt you. That's why I had to destroy your console here, why I have to find Siolis—"

"Sssiolliss!" She finally reacted, spitting the name furiously.

A fleeting quirk of memory shivered through me—Siolis' slippery shape whipping into the reddish shadow of swaying water weeds in his tank. I shook off another ripple of lightheadedness.

"Ssiolliss. Ressstansss. Ssicknesss."

"Ress . . ." I wiped a beading of sweat from my face, blinking in surprise. "You know about the Resistance? Then you understand!"

"Llandersss not undsssstand." Palpable waves of scorn rolled off her. "Llanderss invade, dessstroy, dissrupt. Ressstansss vllasshun."

"No, we're trying to help people, help *you*, after what the cybers did to—" I bit my lip, forcing myself not to flinch away from those intense purple eyes set at their discomfiting angle, the expressionless bioformed features somehow clearly communicating outrage and disbelief. "Look, nobody *has* to join the Resistance—

we're not trying to take choices away from you. But the invaders—the incorporeals—will, if they're not stopped.''

No response.

"If you won't help me, at least give me back the null device—the small black case that creature of yours took. The cybers gave it to me, to use against the invaders, the false cybers.''

"Llandersss fallsse! Cyberss protect Cyvrusss from ssickness of monsstrousss othersss, weak and jeallousss, ssick with lliess and ssecretsss. Llandersss bring dissruptor. Chaoss. Sswimmersss bllinded!" As close to a shout as her straining throat and mouth could produce.

"Wait, please—''

"Bllindnesss! Deafnesss! Llandersss musst llleave.''

"All right, I'll go. But your people should stay away from your consoles until—''

"Cybersss not lllless. Conssssll sspeaking Way. Way fllowss seass, sswimsss bathyllabra, swimmersss sseeing, touching, hearing. Othersss bllindnesss, deafnesss, mutenesss. Llander alllone. Ssicknesss. Healll.''

Sliding shadows and whispers brushed me, images twisting in fire and smoke. Helen's flame-colored hair whipping in a hot wind as she turned her face away, the Village Elder pointing her staff of office at me to pronounce atonement, rabid faces crowding in behind her to condemn me to Healing. Darkness and demons closing around me.

I blinked, sweat drenching my back, dizzy. The Cyvriot was sinking into the shadowed water to the hiss of the deflating tube.

"Wait! The Healing's no answer. Even if you sent me for the Steps, the invaders would still be here. You've got to see that!''

A faint splash. Two quick, darting fish wafted purple-red plumes and dove. The dark surface glinted only agitated reflections of the dim lume.

"Bloody double damn and blast!" I pounded my fist against the side of the console. I grabbed up my pressure suit. "Well, if you think I'm sitting here and just waiting for it, you've got another—''

The snakelike thing shot without warning out of the water, wrapping its pinkish tentacle around one ankle. Before I could yell, another twining limb, and another, whipped around me, fleshy discs sucking onto my skin, pulling me toward the floor's lip.

I thrashed, pounded the rubbery flesh flushing now to an angry crimson, groped for my knife and missed as the thing dragged me. I grabbed for the console, slipped, clutched a hold on the suspended plasmeld ring. The creature squeezed tighter around my legs and waist, ripping me loose from my hold and dragging me naked and screaming into the roiling sea.

Salt water closed over me and I gasped in a mouthful, choking, flailing blindly against the tentacles. Lungs burning, red swimming in my eyes, I pawed futilely toward the air as the creature held me under. Blackness lapped at the edges of vision. I finally opened my mouth to suck in water.

I was thrust up into air. Gasping and coughing, I floated limp in the grip of the cold tentacles. They relaxed slightly, holding me submerged except for my head. I blinked the salt sting from my eyes and glimpsed a bulbous body beneath me, tiny dark eyes in the midst of rubbery flesh and too many arms.

I sucked in a deep, shuddery breath, heart hammering. The water swirled around me, wavelets slapping my face. Something slippery and cold brushed my leg. Gone. Then again, more, a horde of little black-and-white striped fish swarming over me. Shivers prickled my skin. No, mouths nibbling. Sucking onto me. Biting.

Panic jolted me. I screamed and thrashed, but the tentacles holding me only tightened, squeezing painfully until I had to stop. Thin, pliant tips of the creature's limbs tugged at my injured arm, plucking off the bandage. The little fish swarmed, clustered, moved higher over my body as my skin crawled with revulsion. They were a thick blanket now, covering the infected arm.

An electric bolt exploded through me as they pierced the swollen skin. Tiny mouths nibbled, devouring rotten flesh, teeth chewing into me.

"Sacred bloody Founder . . ."

The fish, oblivious, kept feeding.

Lapping dark water hissed echoes through the dome. I was only vaguely aware of the tentacled creature finally lifting and rolling me back onto the hard wet floor. I lay there a while, numb, listening to the soothing rhythm luring me into soft black depths.

I jerked bolt upright, looking down. The outside of my upper arm was raw meat, slowly oozing blood and clear fluid. The discolored skin and swelling had been ripped away, along with Founder knew how much else. My stomach heaved as my mind finally pierced the haze of shock, recalling too vividly the tiny mouths nibbling away at the foul infection, chewing into muscle and sinew. I was dizzy again, couldn't examine the ragged tissues. Dragging myself over to the first-aid kit, I sprayed the arm with a foam that made me gasp before it started numbing, then packed it and bandaged the whole mess with the last of the tape. I lay back, sweating, taking deep breaths.

Enough. Time for business. The natives had made it clear they wanted nothing to do with me, and I wasn't sticking around to let them take me back to the cyber facility for Healing. Time to get out.

Retrieve the osmotic gear and the fresh water reservoir. Long swallows of cool water, nutrients, antibiotics. Rub down, and back into the dry liner, fitting the waste tubes, pulling on the pressure suit. I had to rest before reconnecting to the osmotic unit, but I was starting to feel better. Maybe it was the food and water. Maybe it was the thought of getting the hell out of the drowning rock maze.

I strapped my knife sheath carefully to my calf, cursing myself for letting them take the null device. I shook my head. Get out first, then worry about what was next.

I had to be fairly close to the surface, since the suit's cuff readout wasn't indicating much more than normal ambient pressure. If the dome had been located deep inside the rock caverns, the circulating air would have had to be higher pressure to hold the water out.

Still, that didn't necessarily mean there was a quick and easy shortcut to the surface. I eased legs and fins over the floor lip, dangling them and dreading those deep, sunken chambers of dark sea, the twisting black passages with their eerie blue luminescence. But a way in meant a way out. I'd just have to find it.

My breaths echoed fast and shallow in the faceplate. I firmly refused a surge of choking claustrophobia as the dark water closed over me again, resisted the impulse to spin around looking for swarming hordes of hungry fish, long sinuous tentacles whipping out of the shadows. The faceplate started fogging again, but other than the broken lume strip, everything seemed to be working fine. I took slow, deep breaths, finding the rhythm again.

I flicked on the hand-held lume and shined it around. Circular walls surrounded me, topped by the nervous shimmer of surface within the dome. I followed the walls down, emerging into a rough chamber of jagged black rock and glinting crystalline deposits. There were three round openings spaced with odd symmetry around the chamber's perimeter. They were too narrow for my shoulders, but when I shined my light into them, the tunnels ran perfectly straight and horizontal as far as the beam traveled, obviously machine or laser-bored.

One thing I knew was that the Cyvriots had strict taboos against mechanical devices of any sort, and of course they had no need for them, except the conformance sessions with the cyber consoles. The native woman's reaction to Siolis' name only confirmed my belated recognition that the cybernetics expert was an odd duck on his homeworld, too. I looked into the last tunnel again and shrugged, following the only other way out, an irregular rock shaft plunging down.

As I eased through the twisting rock tunnel, I kept my mind carefully blank, sealed off from recollections of floating nightmares. But this time there was only empty darkness and deep silence. No disorienting waves lapping at my fragile balance. No hovering, shadowy images of demons, no silent voices hissing whispers inside me, no slippery cold fingers on the back of my neck. I let out a long, slow breath of relief.

Then I came to the first branching.

The lume painted its thin trail of particle-sparkling light over a folded mass of pocked stone protruding into the passage. Past it on either side, the light was lost in darkness. I hovered, torn between wider straight down and narrower angling up, but tapering rapidly. Regretfully, I followed the main passage deeper.

After exploring a couple of dead ends, I dropped suddenly into empty blackness, the walls of rock falling away on either side. I flailed around, fighting dislocation, the lume finally following my air bubbles up to a cracked ceiling overhead. I traced it down, making a circuit of rough black walls studded with bizarre conglomerations of jagged crystals like the work of a deranged interior decorator. The chamber was big, but not huge like the one where all the natives had swarmed around me. There were three openings leading out.

On impulse, I flicked off the light. Hovering darkness sprang over me, and my fingers clutched the lume tighter. I waited, blinking. There—a faint blue glow, only a dim suggestion of a lessening of blackness. I fixed my stare on it and flicked the lume back on. I was looking at the middle branch, a tall, narrow crack opening off the wide chamber.

I finned over to it, pulled myself around a long finger of broken rock, eased through a narrow spot, and followed the widening tunnel.

It didn't take me long to lose track of the twists and turns and branchings. The dim blue luminescence was all around me now, glowing down the rough passages and reflecting from scattered facets and glinting veins in the walls of the tortuous rock maze. It was empty, deserted. The silence, the black sea and unearthly blue ripples of cold light, the endless weight of rock and water pressed down on me, thicker and heavier the farther I pushed. Shadowed stone tunnels pulsed to the throbbing ache in my arm as the numbing agent wore off. I dragged in air but couldn't seem to get enough. Time was an endless snarl, taking me around and around its loops forever.

I had almost gotten to the point of babbling to myself—and I could hear voices now, tiny whispers in my skull painting pictures I couldn't understand, but all I had to do was answer them, if I could only solve the puzzle, unsnarl the black tangle—when something quick and slippery brushed me.

I jerked out of my daze, bumping myself back against a rock wall. The lume sliced out crazy angles as shadowy plumes whisked across my faceplate and the silent babble briefly intensified, then ebbed. An irrelevant memory flitted like the plumed fins—Elder Rebecca shushing a rowdy classroom—and was gone.

I shook my head, taking a deep breath and groping for the calming rhythm of a Setharian chant. Slow and easy, pulse cycling, thoughts like smooth river sand. Balance.

Like the snapping of a switch, the internal babble was back, a cacophony of voices shrilling inside my head. Bewildering images poured through me. Plumy-finned violet-flushed fish, each the same but each different, thick drifting horde of minute insectlike sea creatures, deep purple eyes, enormous creature swimming like a moving house, shadowy visceral movements within a vague human outline. And sensations flashing through me like numbers spun on a gaming wheel. I was hungry, laughing, afraid, hot, cranky, gleeful, abashed. Lost in the whirl.

Alarm blasted the images into chaos. I groped for up and down, straining my eyes through the dark, forcing coherency. More of the violet fish flitted around me and away, fins wafting. I finned myself around and froze.

They were only children, huge eyes staring, caught in the beam of the lume. A gaggle of them, milling in a tight knot to the agitated whipping of the bright-flushed fish.

I instinctively snapped off the light. The cool blue luminescence swelled, playing over the small, streamlined shapes now moving—undulating sleekly in quick sweeps of tails over, around, beneath each other as the fish darted in and out between them. A living, flowing knot. There was some sort of complex pattern to it. A game.

I hovered, bemused. The small shapes were a warped parody of human, but somehow in that watery blue luminescence comfortably familiar, fitting. The grotesque glimpses—tapered whipping tails, frail awkward arms, pulsing gill slits, webbed fins—suddenly shifted like colored bits in a kaleidoscope to form a new picture. It was oddly soothing.

Another ripple in the blue patterns, and the children were spilling toward me, the knot of slippery intertwining flesh opening to encompass me as I gaped and the lithe shadows whipped and whirled around me in tight near-collisions, circular eddies tugging me and gauzy plumes of their companion fish—the term popped suddenly into my mind—brushing me, electric chatter jittering down my spine like high-pitched laughter.

I blinked and the children had fallen back, hovering around me, big eyes gleaming out of the dimness. Their mouths hung slack, but I could feel the grins.

I smiled behind the faceplate. The bubbly sensation along my nerves changed to a hum. Waiting. They were waiting for me to do something. I didn't know what. But if somehow I could sense their feelings, then maybe they could sense mine. I tried to recapture in my mind the exuberant whirl of their play, the dancing pattern of blue glinting on sleek twining forms and whipping plumes.

The hum inside me deepened and intensified.

I tried to hold it, not knowing how, reaching slowly into my thigh pocket with gloved fingers as I remembered my first encounter with the frightened Anduran child, Li-Nahi. I fished out the slippery crystal dice, tossing them up into the water and flicking on my lume to light up dazzling sparkles from their fiery hearts.

There was a jolt, water boiling around me as the children thrashed around and back from me. Dizzying sensations poured through me again, and I started to flounder, but then somehow I could separate alarm, excitement, and finally faint curiosity. They were human children after all. As I awkwardly caught and tossed the dice slowly spinning in the beam once more, they drew closer again.

I held my breath, trying to radiate harmlessness and encour-
agement, very slowly reaching out to the nearest child with the
dice lying on my palm. "Take them." I tilted my hand to spill
the crystals toward the child's drifting webbed fingers.

There was more startled movement, confusion boiling through
the water, through me. I thought they were going to let the dice
sink, then one of them darted out to pluck a spinning crystal from
the water, and a bigger one grabbed the second cube. They tumbled
into another silently laughing mad scramble, the glint of the tossed
dice part of the knot now with the weaving forms and darting little
fish, as the hum down my spine burst into an effervescent shower
of sparkling sensations.

I grinned, watching them, and suddenly one of the companion
fish darted out to wriggle around me, fins trailing in a quick tingle
as the flashing kaleidoscope bits shook and settled into a brief,
clear pattern. I was filled with an absurdly buoyant glee. Pure
unsullied joy.

I blinked, tears stinging my eyes, and it was gone. The children
whirled in a synchronized unity and shot off down the dark rock
passage.

"Wait!"

My lume speared a froth of churned water and glinting sedi-
ments. The flicker of trailing violet fins. I hovered dazed for a
moment, empty hand outstretched, aching with surprising intensity
for something I hadn't realized I'd lost long ago. I gathered myself
and kicked hastily after them.

Maybe it was only blind luck, but somehow I followed the kids'
trail. More twists and turns, not knowing if the stirred-up sediment
and agitated luminescent patches were only my own feverish hurry.
They led me to a skinny, sharp-angled passage that looked like a
dead end, then dropped abruptly to a well blocked by broken rock.
But around the edges of the rock, dim light wavered.

It was a tight fit with the breathing wings, but I thrust myself
into it, pushed and squeezed, bit back a cry as my bandaged arm
jammed against the rock. I suddenly popped out. After the black
rock tunnels, the filtered red-blue sealight looked bright, and the
murky ocean before me flowed into a wonderful open stretch.

I finned in a circle, taking deep breaths like I'd just burst up
into air. Beside me, another steep cliff fringed with weeds, colored
growths, and lacy fans climbed toward the surface. Assorted fish
and the striped armored creatures darted busily over the wall. I

had no idea whether I'd come out on the same side of the sea-mount I'd gone in on, or kliks away. I didn't care. I headed up toward the light and the top of the plateau.

Something swooped past me. A broad, demon-shaped shadow with horns and trailing tail, cutting off the light.

I lurched sideways in alarm, kicking reflexively toward the wall, where I gripped and hunkered behind a wafting bush of seaweed. The shadow dropped over me in a dazzle of rayed light, swooping past. Now I could see this demon-fish was smaller than the one that had forced me into the rock maze. On its back, one of the native kids rode, clutching the creature's horns with those elon-gated webbed fingers.

They soared down out of sight in the deepening murk, then suddenly burst back up as another of the winged creatures flapped out of the open dimness before me, this one with two smaller children clinging to its back. The first creature swerved and flew at the second. The larger kid launched himself with a whip of his tail onto the second demon-fish, grappling with one of the smaller chil-dren. The two tumbled off the creature's back, dropping into the deeper sea, rolling around each other, writhing and darting and slapping with their tails, in what looked like an underwater wres-tling match.

As the demon-fish slewed around to avoid a collision, the re-maining child was propelled from its wing, hurtling toward the cliff face in a scrambling tumble.

"Watch out!" I kicked off the wall, launching myself between the rocky wall and the child. Before I could reach it, the other demon-fish soared up past me to scoop the child in its wings and glide off.

I gasped as something slippery brushed over my legs, curling around me for a moment and tugging. A tapered, pale blue tail whisked away, the touch pulling me off-balance. I sank, flailing with my arm and backpedaling with my fins, as three larger kids darted down at me, swimming around me in a quick, lithe circle. Companion fish, bright-flushed, swooped with them in a crackle of laughing energy, bubbles frothing the sea as they spun me with their tails and the bright heart of a sunburst-crystal cube flashed.

A webbed hand caught the die, and the children spilled away from me on a flood of silent laughter, joining the swoop of dark, rippling wings.

More of the demon-fish drifted out of the violet haze, some with kids on back, some gently herding swimming children. They swam past me and around the curving cliff as I hovered beside the wall. A last straggler stopped to stare at me with big violet eyes. A returning swoop of undulating wings, and a big demon-fish fluttered up from underneath. It neatly captured the last child, then veered to float me onto its back, too.

I was about to leap off as the creature swam us slowly after the others. Then I caught my breath as the native child grasped a hold on the creature's curved horn and settled beside me with only a faint emanation of confusion and curiosity. I clutched a handhold myself and wondered if the demon-fish that had brought me to the bathylabra had also mistaken me for a lost kid and had been "taking care" of me by bringing me to the cave. Was there some way I could get it to take me on a search for Siolis? But how could I direct it?

The creature towed us slowly around the curving cliff face, swimming back and forth in leisurely sweeps, and I couldn't seem to get my thoughts to focus. The water was suddenly thicker, resisting me, lapping in waves through my head with a silent, familiar drumbeat echoing to the throb of my wounded arm. A dizzy rush of sensations swirled.

Then, just as suddenly, I snapped out of it, as the demon-fish turned away from the wall in another sweeping glide. My thoughts spun. Was it something in the seawater? No, it had to be the natives doing it, sending the rush of sensations. But only in certain spots? I shook my head as the demon-fish swooped again, bearing me through another dislocating wash of reverberating images.

I drifted out into focus again, as the demon-fish swooped us up and around in a wide, banked curve. And then I could see we were heading out over another deep trench, where the dim shapes of the children waited in the purplish gloom at the fringes of a big group of adults.

In the murky open waters, the adults darted and wove with their companion fish, a slippery boil of undulating shapes. Like a version of the children's play, like my feverish glimpses inside the bathylabra as they surrounded me.

I released my handhold, jerking back in alarm and trying to launch myself off the creature's back. It blocked me with its big wings, rising beneath me to keep me on its back. And then I was plunged again into the disorienting waves of bombardment.

Somehow this time in desperation I managed, as the transition tugged at me—strange slippery sensations of cool scales and soft plumes, distorted images of sun-bright sea and brilliant green weeds, rich salt taste of tiny swarming crustaceans, all mixed in with the deep purple wells of Siolis' eyes drawing me in, ghosts whispering through me, the crystal dice spinning out of dark space to wink mocking snake eyes—I managed to make some turning within myself and find a door. Was it familiar? Had it once sealed me away from the incorporeals? All I knew was I could push against it, almost shutting out the dizzying surges.

I clenched inwardly, my arm throbbing as I pushed physically now, thrusting myself away from the demon-fish. But it wouldn't let me escape. While the adult Cyvriots were absorbed in their dance or whatever the hell it was, I had to get away. But how? The silent waves pounded, insistent, tugging at my flimsy shield as I hunkered, my mind slipping.

Then an oily, mocking little voice in me whispered a suggestion. I had one of their children right beside me. If I pretended to threaten it with my knife, maybe they'd send me to Siolis. . . .

It was Heinck's voice inside me, sneering and gloating, reminding me of the way he'd threatened little Li-Nahi to make me help him. He'd been right when he said we'd swim in hate together. Somewhere there was a piece of him in me that I couldn't deny, couldn't kill. I pressed my eyes tightly shut, but I couldn't close out the vivid image I hadn't let myself see at the time. Just as my finger had pressed the laser's firing stud to finally put an end to him, he'd met my eyes and given me his insinuating leer, claiming that last intimate knowledge. Hate boiled through me again as my hand dropped with the reflexes of the hunter to my knife in its sheath.

There was a startled jerk beside me as I snapped open my eyes and saw the Cyvriot child flailing back in agitated whips of its tail. A concentrated blast of raw terror hit me.

"No, wait!" My hand jerked away from the knife sheath. "I didn't mean that. I wouldn't—"

Then I was screaming, flung into a whirling black well as sharp shards sliced me—the Cyvriots, surging up from their dance to surround me, flinging their anger. I groped through the brutal dislocation, futilely searching out a door to hide behind, but their presences bombarded me, bursting my flimsy walls. No, I was outside myself, tasting? hearing? the sendings of the disruptor lander female with her noxious devices. Rejected, like the traitor Siolis. I could see him swimming away through the shimmering clear violet seas. No, I was touching him. No, I *was* Siolis, swimming, striking out alone—alone, how horrible, unthinkable—away from the bathylabra, sealing myself away from the kindred . . . . And I was the kindred, swimming in the tight interwoven knot of the listening, of the sharing. No! I, not those overwhelming others. Ripping into me like the furious incorporeals. Searing pain. I was losing. Fury, horror, outrage stabbed me, invaded me with the alien voices tearing away at my self.

Trapped inside, I screamed, silently this time, the torment exploding out from me.

Somehow through the agony I felt, saw, heard them falling back from me then, recoiling with their own pain, shrieking a wild chorus to the electrified whip of bright crimson companion fish flailing me with their stinging plumes. The pain echoed back from them, doubled and redoubled from me to them and my head was a ringing bell, a hammer pounding it over and over.

Through the boiling agony, purple eyes fixed on me. *Violation. The Steps of Healing.* A massive black weight gathered and whirled down, slamming me into oblivion.

ten

I was hurtling through darkness, soaring outstretched into black emptiness. Open space. There were no directions, no up or down. I could feel only the pressure of great speed. I didn't know how I'd come to be back in my vacuum suit, outside CI's transport. Something must have happened to cloud my helmet, or my eyes. My head pounded like a prize hangover. I couldn't see the stars.

Loops of a taut cord had tangled around me, dragging me through black space. My safety tether? I blinked, trying to focus blurry numeric readouts floating before my eyes.

Pain throbbed in a dull rhythm, pumping outward from my constricted left arm. Vague, incoherent images swirled and buffeted with the emptiness rushing over me. Chaotic pictures and sensations turning me inside out—the Shift? Was I still trapped inside warped space?

I shook my head in confusion and felt my faceplate sliding against something smooth and resilient. Ahead, above, a faint suggestion of formless light seeped into the blackness. I was suddenly tilted, swooping toward it, dragging heavily in the loops of my tether.

Something sailed ponderously between that faint light and me. A huge, black shape, blunt-nosed and tapering. The transport ship? I soared closer, banking around it. I could feel the immense bulk, somehow almost hear in my bones the slow waves of space it displaced. It loomed beside me now, but I couldn't see any running lights, no hatch indicators.

A huge eye flicked open in the dark bulk, staring at me.

Everything spun and turned upside-down. The immense lifeless bulk drifting in space was suddenly an impossibly huge, living creature floating in the deep sea, black skin wrinkling around that glinting eye fixed on me.

Probing me. The pressure of its being there pressed over and through me in lapping waves. Silent reverberations ran the circuit of bones, vessels, muscles, organs. The eye didn't blink. The creature heaved through the darkness, rolling slowly in thrusts of

an enormous fluked tail. The depths parted for it. Black sea rushed
in to fill the gap.

I blinked, feeling myself towed higher toward the slow purple
light, turning my head with difficulty against the slippery surface
and realizing that I was once more being carried by a big demon-
fish, strapped on its back with tough weed vines. I took a deep
breath and tried to shake off the disorienting buzz of presence
echoing in my bones and guts, a visceral awareness of the gar-
gantuan sea creature cleaving the depths below. But the unheard
buzz wouldn't go away. And there was another echo, a shadow
hovering behind me in the murky sea. Distant, but following. Thin
tendrils touched me, groping tenuously, swelled into a pulsing
knot inside. Strange but familiar. Alien sensations lapping outward
through me—

I recoiled, jerking against the tight vines. Invasion, violation
of my self. The whispering shape inside me was gone like a door
slamming.

Then I remembered. The Cyvriots closing in on me, ripping
into me with their anger. They were sending me back to the facility
for the Steps of Healing. They wouldn't believe the incorporeals
were there, ready to snatch me up.

I struggled futilely against the tight cords, trying to reach my
knife, trying to pull free. The demon-fish shook in agitation, in-
creasing the painful pressure on my swollen arm. Drenched in
sweat, I went limp on the slippery, undulating back.

The demon-fish glided surely through the gloom, rippling its
broad black wings, bearing me on. The huge wings curved, veering
us in a sweeping upward turn as the creature soared faster in a
burst of speed. The dim light swelled to a flat violet haze. Movement glinted through the water ahead, shimmering. We hurtled
closer, and the shimmering focused into glinting scales of a tight
cluster of small fish. There was a tug on the vines binding my
arms. Now I could see the weedy cord, looped under and between
the creature's fleshy horns. Another tug, and the horns slowly
expanded. Unfurled.

What had looked like solid horns were actually tightly rolled
flaps of flesh. As they unrolled, they converged downward to form
a scoop. The demon-fish swooped onto the milling fish, funneling
long swaths of them into its mouth. Then it turned again, gliding
once more on its way.

A vivid image flashed through me of the Cyvriots herding tiny
fish, raking them through gaping mouths. The feel of slippery,

wriggling scales on my tongue, sharp delicious taste of salt and raw fish—

I shuddered as the sensation lapped through me with the pressure of a presence probing, groping past me. . . . I slammed my doors again. The demon-fish swam on, bearing me quickly through the murky ocean. Toward the facility.

Abruptly, it faltered, wings fluttering in agitation as we plowed to a stop in a backwash of eddies. Another whisper of intangible pressure lapped past me, and the demon-fish shuddered, then rippled its wings and turned in a tight circle to head back in the opposite direction. As I craned my head, straining to see through the surrounding shadows, I thought I glimpsed for a second a bulky tapered form, faintly bluish, beckoning. No, I wasn't seeing it, only recognizing it. I blinked and it was gone, the demon-fish surging smoothly beneath me, bearing me into the swelling red-blue shallows.

Quick shapes flitted past the mesmerizing ripple of dark wings as the demon-fish carried me helpless to its mysterious destination. Dark-striped fish the length of my arm, a horde of smaller ones, the uncoiling shadow of a sea snake whipping away. We soared around a weaving thicket of vines reaching their broad leaves toward the light. Ahead, a mass of darkness loomed out of foggy obscurity to become the sloping wall of another rock plateau, this one much smaller than the immense bathylabra. I could see it curving around, more like a spire climbing close to the surface. The rough stone was covered with the familiar assortment of weeds, spongy colored growths, fans, encrusted shells and tubes.

Somehow I wasn't surprised when the demon-fish slowed and hovered before a narrow dark crack half-hidden by wafting plant fronds.

I took a deep breath and tugged again at the stems, trying to work them free over the creature's tight-rolled horns. My arm twisted, red swimming in my eyes as the big fish shuddered and came back to its patient hover. I tried again, but couldn't free myself. Three or four little spotted fish darted curiously around my head. I couldn't move it back far enough to shake them off. I blew out a long breath, stretching flatter on the smooth creature and trying to work my leg high enough to get my knife out.

Something grabbed my ankle. I kicked, jerking helplessly in my bonds. My leg was pinched.

I wrenched my head around and down. Staring into my faceplate

were dark eyes magnified by lenses in bulbous goggles. Chapped
lips stretched into a cocky, watery grin.

"David!" It echoed in my faceplate. I blinked, not trusting the
apparition, stupidly repeating, "David?"

The grin broadened. He gave me a thumbs-up, then drifted back
from my range of sight. My knife was tugged from its sheath. A
release of pressure as the tight vines fell away. His hand pulled
me back as the demon-fish dropped slowly down from me, fluttered
its wings, and flew off into dimness. I finned around, grabbing
David by the shoulders and dimly registering a suit somewhat like
mine ending in one broad, fused foot-fin, some sort of streamlined
device strapped around his waist, the rounded goggles bobbing
ridiculous rubber bulbs on each side, and the self-satisfied grin.

"Damn cocky kid." I hugged him fiercely.

His arms tightened briefly around me, then he shrugged free,
beckoning me toward the shadowed crack in the wall. He swam
by somehow rippling his whole body, the one large fin encasing
his feet and propelling him along. For a disorienting second, the
gangly kid who moved his height so awkwardly on land was
transformed to a sea creature, a Cyvriot swimming, undulating
his long body and flattened tail. I shuddered, shaking my head.
Then I realized he had no breathing pack on his back.

And no helmet or faceplate to feed air. He had to be out of
breath. "Hey!" I ignored my fogging faceplate, kicking quickly
to grab his arm and drag him toward the surface. It wasn't far,
we could make it. I kicked harder.

David twisted and struggled, breaking free, shaking his head
and glaring at me.

Lack of oxygen had to be clouding his mind. I grabbed him
again, kicking higher, my own released air bubbling up around
us.

A high-pitched sound shrilled in my ears. David jerked free
again, this time grabbing my gloved hand. He was shaking his
head. The high-pitched sound broke off and he grinned again,
pointing at my air bubbles, pointing to himself, and shaking his
head. He jabbed his finger repeatedly toward the device strapped
to his waist.

No air bubbles escaped his mouth. His long nose was pinched
closed with a curved bit of plasmeld.

I stared, shaking my head.

He laughed soundlessly, gave me the thumbs-up again, and
beckoned me back down. I finally shrugged and followed his

strangely graceful, undulating body, kicking my fins laboriously and quickly falling behind. He was waiting at the opening in the rocky wall.

Back into a maze of rock tunnels filled with sluggishly stirring black water. I shuddered in the claustrophobic dark, fumbling in my mesh bag for the lume rod. David's hand on my wrist stopped me. He tapped my faceplate, still squeezing my wrist with the other hand. Starting to shake him off, I realized the faint blue luminescence had intensified.

Cold blue sparks along the tunnel walls pulsed with a faint ebb and flow of channeled ocean. I took a deep breath, reflexively falling into the sea's rhythm. Then I felt something behind me, pushing its own ripples, moving in fast.

I kicked around, knocking back against David, to see a bobbing orange speck zooming toward me. I flinched, but the glowing blob veered and circled. Somehow its light radiated coolness, too. Squinting, I could make out the vague form of a truncated fish, its flat face dangling the luminescent orange appendage. It finned around David, flicked the dangler, and swam off down the dim tunnel. David tugged on my wrist, following. I blew out another long breath and kicked along.

The rock formation had only a small cavern at its heart, with a rough, crystal-studded shaft running up, murmuring with the unheard echoes I'd stopped trying to shut out of my head and body. They hummed incoherently through me as I drifted up after David, locking my legs and imitating his serpentine wriggle, noting mechanically the three circular openings off the shaft, just like the tunnels beneath the bathylabra's console dome. I broke through a shimmering surface, bobbing.

This dome was just like the one the natives had put me in, except the half-floor was crammed with dimly lit shapes of tools and electronic parts. I floated on the shimmering dark surface as David threw his long fin into the shadows and scrambled out into skinny awkwardness once more.

"Here. Watch out for this wavelength modulator." His voice was muffled through my hood as he hunkered down to pull me over, grabbing my shoulder.

I bit off a shriek as he grasped my infected arm.

"Easillly, David. She iss wounded."

I jerked around, water splashing over my faceplate, bobbing up again to see the shadowed blue head suspended within the inflated flotation ring next to the console. Indicator lights played across the panel, throwing slippery splashes of color over the slick, flattened head, the wide, lipless mouth, the big purple-black eyes watching me.

They caught me, drew me down their spiraling dark wells, and I could feel his silent voice whispering through me and swelling to take familiar shape inside. A disorienting ripple of warmly lit dome, sticky feel of the sealing ring and its pumped water cycling through my double gills, clear shimmering sea, weariness and dizzy pain echoing from outside, and my own pale face behind fogging stressplex, green eyes staring—

I shook myself, jerked around and fumbled at the slippery lip of flooring, finally let David take my good arm and pull me out. I ripped off the faceplate and hood, leaning forward over my bent knees and taking deep breaths as the dizziness settled. Clamping down a tight lid, I raised my face.

"Lllong hass been the sssighting, Ruth." Siolis' lipless mouth twisted into the ironic smile that sat so oddly on his almost reptilian face. Back in Casino, before I'd seen the other Cyvriots, I hadn't realized how much work he must have put into the expression.

I nodded tiredly. "Long has been the sighting." Avoiding those fathomless eyes, I fumbled at the straps of my bulky breathing pack. I took a deep breath. "So just what in hell do you two think you're doing, running off to a taboo world like it's a big joke on the rest of us? Bloody Founders, Siolis! You want me to trust you, and then you pull something like this. Do you have any idea what I've been going through trying to—"

"Yesss."

"Shit, Ruth! Look at this shit." David tugged at my breathing wings.

"Can't you think of anything else to say, kid?"

"Okay." He shrugged, giving me a sly grin. "Metamorphic schist."

"What's that supposed to mean?"

"Who cares? I'm collecting old words from taboo loops. Sounds great, huh?"

"Lovely." I grimaced, unhooking the tubes and easing out of the apparatus.

David pulled it off me. "Who designed this . . . gear for you, anyway? Wait, don't tell me—Deirdra and Thom, right? Between them they've got half a brain maybe. We'll get you set up with a blood-oxy exchanger like mine, I've got a spare, it's stupid to lug all this junk around, and look at those fins. Worthless. See, why bother breathing when you can just—''

"David, slow down a sec." I laid a hand on his arm. "You all right here? Really?" My voice cracked. I cleared my throat, blinking quickly. "If you ever pull a damn fool stunt like this again, I'll . . ." I gritted my teeth and smacked his thigh with the fin I'd pulled off.

"Hey, watch it! You'll hit my exchanger!" He shrugged away, loosening the clasp of the waist device and peeling it slowly back. Reaching to each side, he twisted something, then snapped the apparatus free and put it carefully into a plasmeld box. Protruding through his skin-tight suit above each hipbone was a blunt plasmeld tip with a sealed valve.

"See, all it takes are the two vein and artery taps, and they stay in. Doesn't really hurt or anything, anyway. Unit's got a double-action pump to drive the osmotic exchanger, then the molecular converter breaks the CO_2 bonds—Siolis and I got the size way down—and of course there's a pressure regulator, and O_2 reservoir just in case. Keeps the blood O_2 balance way better than breathing, anyway, you don't get all gaspy when you gotta go for it, pump just kicks into high gear."

He ripped open a cling-strip and wriggled out of the suit, leaning against the console in rumpled skivvies, his skinny legs gleaming white in the dimness. "*I* thought of that part." He grinned. "Anyway, the nifty part is you don't have to get all cluttered up with helmet and hood and all, and sealed off in a pressure-field suit. Gas level's controlled, so depth pressure's no problem with most of your body incompressible water in the first place."

He crossed his arms with a self-satisfied air, pursing up his lips unattractively. "We've got the gear to get you hooked up the same way, and it'll be way easier swimming, you'll feel like you belong down—''

"No." I shook my head, eyes fixed on the valves protruding from the narrow flanks above his sagging skivvies. And the sleek black curve of his cybernetic interface device, sealed onto his upper back with its own nerve connections. "What next, David? Maybe you want to trade your legs for a motor, huh? Why not just go for a cyborg body like Heinck's or—'' Damn it.

"Jason's?" He straightened, grin fading into a scowl.

"David, don't—''

"Yeah, well maybe I wouldn't mind being like Jason. You're always putting him down, you just can't admit you're too chicken,

Auntie Ruth. I don't blame him for staying on Andura, it's all your fault, you just never gave him a break. Why'd you wanna leave Poindros in the first place? You're just as bad as Joshua and Aaron and . . . and Mother, not wanting anything new or better. Blazes, here I am just trying to help you out, and you have to go all—''

"David, plleassse." A faint splashing, echoing through the dome. "Ruth iss illl. She hass gone through much for your ssake. She musst ressst.''

A faint pressure lapped inside me, soothing sleep beckoning with shadow fingers. I slammed that nebulous door again, shaking my head. "I want some explanations first. What the hell are you up to, Siolis? Why did your people give me such a hard time? Why didn't you warn them they're in danger from the incorporeals?''

A hissing sigh. "Allwayss is it not difficulllt to hear a sstrange meaning? My people, llike yourss, bellieve theirss isss the ssuperior Way. Unlllike yourss, they know they llive a sspecialll pattern in the Pllan. The cybersss, in wisdom, guard them sssafe from foolish lllanderss and abusse of meaningss. Llanderss are children who are bllind and deaf, chilldren who would hurt themsellvess and otherss. Cyberss alllow the one fllowing. Illnesss bringss dissruption, outssiderss bring illlnesss.''

He made an odd movement, the ghost of a shrug somehow brushing my own shoulders. "Ssea ebbss, ssea fllowsss.''

"Damn it, Siolis, don't give me your riddles! You don't believe in that 'what will be' stuff any more than I do. We've got to do something. Don't you realize the incorporeals have taken over CI's bio lab?''

The indicators on the console reconfigured above him, flickering red and amber through the dimness. I shivered, jabbing a finger. "They could be in there now, listening.''

"Hang onto your petticoats, we've got that thing plastered with security shunts. Spooks don't even know we're on the planet. After we borrowed a hovercraft to bring our gear out here, we sent it back to trigger a retroactive memory erase of the facility loops." David moved protectively closer to the console.

"Well, they know I'm here." I turned back to Siolis. "Were you just counting on me following David, or what?''

David interrupted, "Hey, Siolis, I left her a message, like you said to.''

"Great. Some message. Anyway, after I deciphered your cute

little puzzle"—I scowled at David's smirk and turned back to Siolis—"Helsa decided to send Rik and Lilith along with me. Rik tried to wipe me out and got killed. The mechmen CI sent along got taken over by the incorporeals at the lab, and they're holding Lilith—"

"Lilith! But how come . . . Dammit, Ruth, how could you leave her in there? What if they—"

"For your information, kid, that idiot was the one who—"

"Pleasse!" The hiss echoed through the dome, jittering down my backbone. "There iss no time for recriminationsss. Ruth, I am aware of much that hass occurred. I could not lleave our work here to sseek you in the sssea. It wass necesssary to shielld our pressence from the kindred, but I llearned you were sseeking uss. The ssendingss did not sspeak the . . . nature of your illlnesss."

"Thanks a lot for the help! Do you have any idea what I was going through—"

"Fire and thorns, Ruth, he went out there to find you and call that manta back when it was taking you to the facility, didn't he?"

"Manta? You mean the demon-fish?"

"You musst ressst now, Ruth. And David," the quietly hissing voice continued, "you musst not fear for Lilllith. There iss no need."

"Frigging Founders, Siolis!" David leaned over the floating ring, clenching his fists. "You *knew* the spooks had her, and you didn't even tell me! You wiped the console entry, didn't you? I can't believe you'd pull that on *me*."

"You know, David, how vitall thiss messsage may be. Fulll concentration wass necesssary."

"Message, sendings, signals, anomalies!" I shook my head in frustration. "You and the cybers. What's this mysterious blasted message all about, anyway? And what gives you the right to decide what's important for everybody?"

"Ssome emergenciess take precedence, Ruth, as welll you should know. Have you not on your homeworlld done ssimilarlly?"

I opened my mouth, then snapped it furiously shut.

David stepped between Siolis and the console, crossing his arms defiantly. "Well, I'm not doing anything else until I find out if Lilith's okay."

A hissing sigh. "Very welll. I willl make data ssearchess. But firsst, find the medicall suppliess. Ruth, more than Lilllith, needss your hellp."

"Oh. Yeah." David hunkered awkwardly next to me, not meeting my eyes. "Hey, sorry."

I blew out a long breath and put my arm around his shoulders. "Me too, kid."

"Me thirdlly." In the dimness, Siolis' glistening face twisted into a brief smile. "But ssoon we willl be hearing voice of 'gllad tidingss.' The ssignalll yet untranssllated, Ruth, comess to usss from unknown oness in a far galllaxy."

An odd dream. Silence, echoing spaces within the lofty curve of gleaming pearl walls. Or was it the rim of a tubular floor? I was moving slowly over faint horizontal striations within the translucent surface, and the wall/floor kept curving higher, sweeping farther above me, twisting into unseen dimensions, drawing me on. In. Around.

I was suspended, but walking. No, crawling like an insect over the endless slippery surface, unable to find a grip. I wasn't breathing, but air surged and ebbed through me in unheard music.

It was a golden light, pulsing through the hard, thin walls, soft and suffused, enveloping me. I was sliding now, drifting, moving through the circular spiral of a great whorled shell, around and in, but at the same time higher.

I could see . . . hear? touch? it now, whatever it was drawing me on. A pure shaft of humming energy, coursing through the center. The center of the shell, the center of me. A deep, smooth, unutterably beautiful tone, blended like white light from the harmony of a multitude of ringing notes, vibrant, silently echoing through the immense whorled spirals and humming in my bones.

I no longer needed to grapple with legs, arms, pain, fear. An invisible, shapeless something whispered around me, enfolded me in its gentle susurration, and floated me. A soothing murmur. I slept, swaddled like a babe.

"Hmmm . . . what? Who—" I jerked awake, jolting up and blinking in confusion.

Lenses flashed a dark glint of light. David. He crouched in front of me, twisting to grab up a metal rod rolling away from him and crunching against a plasmeld box. "Sorry, Siolis wanted you to sleep." He plucked up the dropped part or tool and turned back to hunker over the lume spreading a diffused yellow light through the dome.

"Here, eat this and take the rest of this medicine." Twisting back to squat next to me in the narrow space cleared among the litter of electronics gear, he handed me sealed packets. "Hey, you look like something that just crawled out of one of the deep trenches." He tilted his head toward the light-jittering water, putting on a grin, his eyes behind the spectacles worried.

I took a deep breath, rubbed my face, and ran a hand through my matted hair. "Some hotel you run here, kid. Great cuisine." I eyed the nutrient packet, stomach rolling with nausea, but popped the seal to please him. "What did you do, slip me a mickey in those antibiotics?"

"Who, me?" The grin for real this time. "Come on, take your dose. Siolis says you should sleep some more."

I started to stretch, cut it short with the twinge in my arm, and glanced down at the new bandage wrapping my arm from shoulder to wrist. "Good job, David." I pretended not to notice that the hand was starting to swell now, a faint duskiness flushing it. "You're missing your calling."

"No thanks! About lost my cookies, it was so . . ." Hastily, "But it's really not that bad, I mean it just looks that way. It'll heal up okay, so don't worry, you just need to rest. Damn it, what's keeping Siolis, I wanted to show you what we're doing with— Hey, about time, guy!"

There was a faint splash, reflected lights shattering, a blue-tinged companion fish wafting its plumes past the slippery blunt head emerging within the suspended ring. A hiss, and the tube began inflating. Siolis' head floated higher, streaming water as his clear inner eyelids flickered and slid open. The dark pupils flared and shrank to pinpoints, purple eyes staring blindly.

"Oh, sorry." David bent quickly to dim the lume to a glow barely brighter than the colored console indicators.

"Thank you, David." The oversized eyes focused on me. "Did you resst welll, Ruth?" A faint, echoing hum, unfelt arms rocking my sleep.

I cleared my throat, face uncomfortably hot, looking away from the liquid depths of his eyes. "I'm fine." I ignored a wash of dizziness and swallowed some watered-down nutrient.

"It would be besst if you should ssllleep again."

I wiped my mouth with the back of my hand, shaking my head. "First, some answers."

A faint, hissing sigh. "Very welll. David, willl you try a new configuration? I have found an alternate pattern for the fourth and sseventh rangesss. Frequency shifts sstarting with . . ." He recited

a long list of parameters as the flotation ring finished expanding.
Beneath the dim surface, his long webbed fingers wafted back and
forth, spreading and clutching as if plucking invisible bits from
the restless sea.

David crouched for once intently still, then nodded, stood, and
moved over to the console, the black interface device sealed to
his upper back flaring its crimson activation spark. He sank to the
floor, leaning against the console, face going slack as his eyes
closed. His hands, lying at his sides, twitched spasmodically.

I swallowed, looking away to be trapped by Siolis' purple eyes.
"I hate it when he does that."

He didn't bother responding. "More questionss, Ruth? I musst
sssoon return to our work."

"Just what is so all-fired urgent about this alien message, that
it can't wait until we deal with the incorporeals? You and David
sit here with your noses stuck in a console and think all the
problems will go away. I'm telling you we've got to get out of
here and shut the spooks down before it's too late."

"I am monitoring incorporealss at the lllab. Their matrix iss
occupied with transslating and tracing the allien ssignalll, in both
eagernesss and fear. It iss their way. They musst capture or des-
stroy."

"Hold on! Capture or destroy *what*? You don't even know what
the signal means yet, so how do you know there's anybody—
anything—out there to get all excited about? And if it's that far
away . . ."

"There iss intellligence there. Usse of random doublle-worm-
hole variant of sspace-shift, even cyberss would not know how.
The incorporealls have echoed a ssignall to shifting ssourcess, and
a different pattern hass returned."

"So what makes you think you and David can work it out faster
than the spooks can with their high-powered one in all matrix?"

"They do not resside in sssea."

I blew out a breath and stared at him, frowning. His eyes seemed
to swell even bigger, dilating to dark wells, drawing me down a
deep spiral. The ceaseless murmur of the sea enveloped me, lapping through me with the brush of soft fins and echoing its voices
down my bones, at once strange and familiar. Then something
else, crackling through the coils of the bathylabra, shattering the
comforting, cycling rhythms. Exploding in a silent cacophony of
disruption. Voices howled through a splintering lattice, discordant

chorus shrieking alarm, frantic questions, pain, outrage, and rejection, the pounding torrent invading me—

"No, Siolis! I can't—wait! Stop it!" I leaned forward, pressing my throbbing head with my fingers, fighting off another wave of sick dizziness. This time it was worse, wouldn't go away as the floor seemed to heave beneath me. The entire dome shivered, vibrating a jarring buzz up my spine.

"Hey, what's going on?" I jerked upright, grabbing my lume rod as it tilted over and started to roll away, David's tools skittering across the slippery floor. It wasn't just me. The trapped water boiled in the dome, slapping up against the sides as the trembling slowly subsided.

"Do not fear." Siolis still floated in his ring as the ripples smoothed around him. "We have many ssmalll quakess, releassing tensionss of active worlld core, but not sserious. Did you not feelll one earlier in ssea?"

"Siolis, I've been so mixed up what with one thing and another, I don't know *what* I've been feeling. These 'sendings' of yours, now . . ." I shook my head.

"I willl try once more to expllain." His eyes dilated to dark purple, darkness lapping at my vision.

"No! No more of that. Just *tell* me what you mean."

A faint splashing, vaguely soothing. "Our ssea isss rich in nutrientss, Ruth, upwelllling from molllten core with mineralls and ellectrolytéss, carried on warm currentsss, allwayss flllowing. The ssea sussstains uss, shelterss uss, buillds with new rock the bathyllabras, feedss uss, bindsss uss in itss harmony and ceasellesss cycless. We are one."

His voice had fallen into a slow, hypnotic rhythm, somehow both sad and mocking. I closed my eyes, taking a deep breath as my dizziness ebbed and his words whispered through the dome. "The voicess of the ssea, the ssendings bind uss together, bind uss to changellessnesss. We feell alll, know alll, tasste alll. We fear not, hope not. . . .

"Untilll ssea sspeaks with a new voice, voice of unknown message. Sspeaking through ssallt ssea, fllowing through bathyllabras."

I blinked and raised my face, a new wave of dizziness washing over me. I tried to ignore the faint, sickening-sweet smell not quite masked by my bandages, the cold sweat breaking out on my back. "You mean your sea alters the alien signal somehow, and only the Cyvriots can understand it? I don't get it."

"The natives don't either." David's voice broke in on us, startling me. "All's they know is it's breaking up their own sendings, and they don't even *want* to figure it out."

The kid scrambled up from his slouch against the console, all awkward pale arms and legs as he emerged from his link with the interface. "But that's what Siolis and I are working on, what he's trying to tell you. See, we've got part of it figured, that's why we're taking quantified measurements, testing different patterns with Siolis down below in the cavern transmitter chamber. We've even managed to get some data with him in there when one of those signals came through. So we know it's operating on the same principle as the Cyvriot sendings, a modified acoustic directed-energy pulse train, but of course if there's a meaning to these alien-triggered ones, nobody can read them. So you see why we've got to keep at it."

"Whoa, slow down. I don't see anything." I rubbed my temples, pushing back the lightheadedness. "What do you mean, transmitter chamber, and what are these acoustic pulse engines or whatever?"

"Trains. Modified acoustic directed-energy pulse trains. Call them Adepts." David hunkered down beside me, excited. "It's fantastic, Ruth! See, most all electromagnetic or acoustic waves, even lasers, dissipate as they travel, but I found in the cybers' taboo technical loops they've got some applications for these Adepts, where the ultrasonic pulses don't diffract, even through water. It's possible with electromag waves, too, in theory, but here we're talking acoustics. It's a major ordeal making them, using an array of electronically driven crystals vibrating at different ultrasonic frequencies, and getting them all to interact just right to combine into a skinny Adept. So guess what? The Cyvriots are making their own, right in the bathylabras, they can even generate them in these smaller caverns under console stations."

"What?" I frowned, shivering as memory lapped through me— swimming the drowning rock maze in the eerie blue pulse of luminescence and pounding sensations, water rippling over glinting sharp facets. I blinked. "Crystals. You mean the natives make these . . . Adepts with the crystalline deposits in the caverns?"

"Thiss isss great ssimpllification, Ruth. The ssendings are more than that, travelling far through sseas to touch other kindred. We . . . sspeak in different wayss for cllosser contacts, hear many varied voicess of ssea."

David lifted his hands impatiently. "Well, of course, that's what I was saying. I mean, we don't even know yet how the natural modified Adepts are triggered, maybe it's some interaction with piezoelectricity from the pressure waves with the acoustic bursts, or a combination of forces. But anyway, we do know the natives generate Adepts when they all get together to do a sending, and the pulse trains travel out those horizontal tunnels underneath the console domes. Funny, according to data, the cybers bored those tunnels for structural stress release from all the natural seismic disturbances. We don't know if they even know the Cyvriots are communicating on such a broad scale."

I took a deep breath. "Then somehow do you hear these sendings in the bathylabras, too, Siolis?"

"No, Ruth. The . . . llisstening, the sharing may be anywhere in ssea on pathss of different ssendingss." His eyes were still on mine, and a vague image of the native adults weaving their slippery interwoven dance above the murky abyss rippled through me.

I shivered and pulled my eyes from Siolis' to turn to David. "Have you heard the sendings, too? I didn't realize they'd be so—"

"Offworlders can kind of feel the sonic waves, and the natives can sound us for emotional configurations close up, but of course we can't participate. Use your head, Ruth. Soon as I quantify all the factors, though, I ought to be able to rig some kind of portable receiver-translator. Hey, you know it might just . . . " David frowned with concentration, turning abruptly away to crouch beside one of his instruments and tweak the controls. The red activation light of his interface device flared on his back, and he went still.

I pressed my throbbing forehead again, pushing away the memory of shadows probing me, of lapping images. "Siolis, what's going on? I'm not just losing my mind, am I? You're one of them, can't you tell me how it works?"

"There iss much David and I cannot define, much I mysself cannot explain of our 'primitive' communication."

Ouch. "All right, Siolis, but I still—"

"Cyvriotss llive in unity of kindred, of sensess, of thought. They calll me monsster llike you for llearning sseparatenesss. . . ." A hissing sigh as the water stirred around him. "Sstilll I have fellt the allien messsage as they do, and do not undersstand. Yet there iss . . . bellief . . . conviction that ssendersss expect we can find the way to answer. It iss important, Ruth. We musst lllearn the key before the Incorporeallsss or CI act in error."

"CI," I groaned. "We've got to answer to them eventually. I still don't see why we shouldn't shut the spooks down first and figure out the rest later."

"How, Ruth?" The dark water shivered restlessly around Siolis, vague shape of serpentine tail sweeping beneath the surface and the plumed companion fish darting away. "They do hold Lilllith."

"Lilith." I dredged up an elaborate Setharian curse.

Again the fleeting, twisting smile. "Lilith hass met no harm. There iss no need to feel shame for not feelling more concern for her."

Damn. "Should've been a Poindran, Siolis. You've got guilt down cold." I shook my head, then regretted it as the nausea I'd been holding at bay surged through me. I swallowed. "Okay, so we figure out how to get her out, *then* we close down the lab."

"We would have difficullty without the nulll device. Whille you sslept, I began ssearchesss."

"But how did you know—well, blast it, it was your . . . kindred out there who took it away! I wouldn't have hurt them with it."

"It wass violation of Way. Ssillence maker. Dissruptor like alien ssignall. They bllame alll the dissruption on llanderss."

"Great." I rubbed my face again. "Can't you just explain to them, Siolis? They wouldn't listen to me."

Another hissing sigh. "I am outcasst here, as you on Poindross. Remember."

I closed my eyes, hearing again the Cyvriot woman in the other dome furiously spit his name. Hearing, feeling the chaos of sensations and images as Siolis/I swam from the group, rejecting and rejected. Again the awareness of an alien presence swelling inside me to crowd out my perceptions with its own. My stomach rolled, cold sweat on my face.

"You musst take your medicationss and ressst." An echoing splash. "Plleasse."

I shook my head. There were questions he wasn't answering, but I was having trouble grasping them. I rested my head on my knees, settling the dizziness. "You're stalling me, Siolis. Tell me the rest."

More agitated splashing. "We musst not act in hasste, Ruth. It iss firsst time to heall you." Again a whisper running the circuit of my innards. "The ssicknesss in arm iss grave, but medicationss may halt the sspread."

"I know," muffled. The undeniable smell I remembered from Sethar's humid jungle. "The arm's starting to rot. But don't tell

David." I took a deep breath. "That's another reason to get back to the facility, Siolis, let the mechmen do what they can. Amputate if they have to." I tried to suppress a shudder, the cold sinking inside. One thing the cybers couldn't do was give me a new flesh and blood arm. "But no way am I letting them use the full Healing field. They'd 'heal' my mind, too."

Another splash. "Danger at facility. We musst wait sstill brieflly, Ruth. Hellp iss coming."

"What?" I jerked my face up and met his eyes, that intangible door inside me swinging open as if pushed by a hand.

His eyes held mine. A soothing whisper through me, translucent spiraling walls enclosing me in a deep, silent hum. A presence unfolding gentle wings to embrace the hurts and fears held fist-tight inside, touching me in places no one knew. No one but Jason. No, I wouldn't let myself think about him. But that touch— different, the same. Unconditional caring.

Face burning, I jerked my gaze from Siolis' eyes, unable to return what he offered, too weak to refuse it. His comfort rocked me and I leaned into it.

"Yess, Ruth. It will be welll." His whisper echoed softly through the dome. "Jason comess to share our triallsss."

eleven

The dome was too quiet, the enclosed sea a dark sheet shivering with a barely audible background hiss. In the echoing hush, I could almost hear my heart beating fast against my ribs. My rasping breaths sounded loud inside the curved walls.

I jabbed harder at the frozen valve on my osmotic gear, the screwdriver slipping and nicking my hand. "Blast it." Even adding some polysyllabic Vendavian curses could only keep the silence at bay for a minute. I rubbed my eyes. Siolis had insisted I immobilize my arm and leave the repair work for David. But it wouldn't make any difference at this point. I could still move my darkened, puffy fingers, though I couldn't bend the arm. I kept at it until I got the valve freed and lubricated.

Sweat beading my forehead, I twisted around to set the gear aside and found myself face to face with David. He was back in his motionless slouch against the console, linked into the interface and staring blankly through me. I couldn't help putting my hand over his chest to recheck the faint, slowed beat of his heart and feel the slight expansion of his breathing. His skin was cool. I found his discarded shirt and draped it over his bony shoulders, reaching up to gently close his eyelids. He didn't stir.

I sighed and turned down the lume to a faint glow, glancing over my shoulder as the console indicators suddenly flashed a change of configuration. Red and blue glinted off the leads running from the panel to electrode patches below Siolis' opened ear flaps. He floated motionless in the ring, double eyelids closed, the flat, expressionless face alien and malevolent-looking in the gloom.

I leaned back, closing my eyes, too tired to resist the soft shush of the sea. Siolis had tactfully withdrawn into his matrix work after dropping the bombshell about Jason. Damn. Of course David, emerging from his cybernetic trance, had been delighted—"Hell on wheels!"—and then back into his link, "So we can crack this thing and really have something to show old Jason."

And what did I have to show him? Exhaustion, frustration, and putrefying flesh—everything his perfect body was exempt from. I wasn't ready to face those bright brown-gold eyes and see pity there, be bathed in his compassion. Feel the gentle, healing touch Siolis had echoed, doubling another disturbing echo of memory. Helen's loving hand on my brow. Peace and the Way and the guardian cybers, Healing us of our human pain. Why did I have to insist on it?

And I was facing it only as a cowering mass of fear. I didn't want to die. Didn't want to lose my arm. Maybe David was right— why fight the cybernetic enhancements? What was so precious about weak, jealous, violent, greedy, mortal flesh-and-blood humanity, to cling so blindly to it?

I groaned, then startled upright at a touch on my brow.

"Hey, you don't look so good." David awkwardly shifted his bare feet, pulling his hand back self-consciously. "You better be taking your medicine! I never saw a body so all-fired cantakerous." He folded his arms in a typical Poindran gesture and gave me a ridiculously stern look.

A deep belly laugh broke out of me, surprising both of us. I gasped, "David, you look exactly like Sam!" How the skinny kid with his spectacles and matted, wiry dark hair managed to look like my barrel-chested, grizzled truefather I had no idea, but I could see Sam giving me what-for for climbing out a second-story window.

"Well, I can see why you drove 'em all nuts back home!" But David looked obscurely pleased. He turned toward a sudden splashing behind him as one of Siolis' companion fish jumped, spreading purple-tinged plumes and scattering drops. It splashed under again, stirring overlapping ripples. "Hey, Siolis, make her take her medicine."

Beneath the surface, the long tail swept and coiled, then swept again. Siolis blinked his inner eyelids, and once more I felt an interior sounding. "Do not worry, David. It will be welll." He was watching me as he spoke to the kid. "We musst eat now and return to work."

"Yeah, Ruth, I think we've about got it! It's some wild kind of multilevel permutation, but we're homing in on probables." He rummaged in a mesh bag and ripped open a nutrient packet.

"I willl return ssoon." There was a hiss of air from the deflating ring.

"Wait a minute." The ring stopped deflating. "David needs some rest. You're wearing him out."

"No way, I'm really cruising in the matrix!"

"Time pressess, Ruth. We mussst find the key."

"Yeah, we gotta be ready to move when Jason gets here."

I gave David an exasperated look and turned back to Siolis. "When does he arrive, then? How's he getting here?"

"I do not know."

"Siolis."

"He promised to arrive sssoon, but I cannot know more. In transsit he musst maintain communication ssilllence, for fear of incorporeall or CI interception of messsages."

"Then how do you know he's coming at all?"

"Yeah, how?" David turned to him, too.

A hissing sigh. "I contacted Andura from the transsport on our way, David, then erassing alll trace."

"Damn it, there you go again—"

"Flaming Founders! Why didn't you *tell* me?" David glared at him. "Just like with Lilith! Everybody treats me like a kid, like they have to have all these stupid secrets."

"He's right, Siolis. What are you trying to pull on us? If you've got some secret plan, you better fill us in now, otherwise I'm moving on my own. What about you, kid? Are you going to keep working on that signal without knowing what he's up to?"

David nervously chewed his peeling lower lip, looking from me to Siolis, then casting a longing glance at the console. "Well . . . yeah, Ruth's right. Cough it up, Siolis. What's gonna happen when we crack the code?"

Dark water swirled in agitation, long tail whipping and the two purple-flushed fish darting in quick circles. "Ssea ebbs, ssea flowsss. Alll have a pllace." His long black tongue flickered in the gash of laboring mouth. "There iss no ssecret pllan, Ruth, onlly unfollding time, onlly unfollding pllace for earss to open, for bllindnesss to falll away."

"So all the rest of us are too stupid to understand your little secrets, is that it? You're a real Cyvriot, all right!"

"Yesss, I am Cyvruss, as you Poindrosss. Yet onlly llone sswimmer in cycle of sseas. It iss hard to explllain, Ruth. Llet me show . . ." The slippery shadow fingers probed inside me, questing, swelling.

"No!" I clenched, closing myself from the invasive touch. "None of that sneaky stuff. Give me a straight answer. You never intended to help me shut down the spooks, did you?"

He closed his double eyelids for a moment. "Fear can bllind you, Ruth. Fear of sspooksss, fear of Cyvriot ssendingsss, of Jasson, of alllien invasion of ssself. Allwayss you insisst on lllonelinesss . . . ." A faint, echoing sigh. "Cyvriotss do share much llike one in alll of incorporeall matrix, many smalll thoughtss and memoriess merging to share great work of ssendings and ssinging of the Way. There iss sstrength in joining, yet llimitationss allsso. Yess, I ressisted kindred to lleave and llearn new wayss to ssee and think ssinglly, to use cybernet and data lloopsss as hollder of different meaningss. There are many wayss, Ruth, and we can llearn from alll."

I closed my eyes, shaking my head. "It's too dangerous, Siolis. You know what the incorporeals have done before. Once you give them a foothold, they take over. We've got to stop them before they make us into monsters like them. We're humans, damn it, not bits of energy in a logic matrix."

"Yess, jusst sso. And my human pllace iss to llearn, with David, new messsage here. The resst is yoursss in fulllnesss of time. You and my peoplle can llearn from each other."

My eyes snapped open. "No way. I just want to stop the spooks and get out of here. Your Cyvriots don't want my 'disruption' any more than I want them messing with my head."

"Sstilll you feell guillt of bringing change to Andura? But you cannot keep turning and sso quicklly run. Iss not Poindran ssaying, 'Hasste makes wasste'?"

"Don't get cute with me, Siolis!" I struck out angrily, smarting at the reminder of Andura. "What you're really saying is you won't come back with me and try to stop the spooks. 'Sea ebbs, sea flows,' right? If that's the way you feel, why did you bother joining the Resistance in the first place?"

David broke in, "You know what the cybers did to the Cyvriots, Ruth!"

"Wait a minute, that was human tinkering, wasn't it? A pre-Plan commercial bioforming project . . ." Damn it, he had me there. Humans to blame for that one. I met Siolis' purple eyes, my chin still thrust out defiantly. "So is that why you Cyvriots hate the rest of us?"

"No hate, Ruth. Onlly llack of trusst." The deep eyes captured mine, but this time there was no pushing inside me, only his expressionless face, waiting.

I looked away. "Damn it, Siolis. You're asking too much!"

An odd, breathy laugh. "Yess, it is sso. Allwayss. That iss why I llearned from the conssolle what we were not meant to know, why I lleft Cyvruss to join otherss in Casssino who worked for freedom. There are cossts, Ruth, as welll you know. There are wayss and wayss, yet Cyberss alllow onlly one. The Cyberss were they who imposed bioforming taboo, who ended our com-pllete transsformation to ssomething they judged not human. Sso we sstay hallf-human, musst twisst our tonguess to sspeak with conssolles, using voice we do not need. Sso we llive in issollation, a bllot on Pllan, fllowing alwayss in ssame cyclle, changellesss as the speciess tissue ssamples monitored in CI lllab.'' His voice was a labored rasp. ''Llanderss ssee onlly monsterss. For we are 'fearfullly and wonderfullly made.' ''

I looked up at the hissing phrase from my homeworld's Book of Words, meeting the vivid purple eyes with their darker pupils shrunken to pinpoints. I took a deep breath. ''I'm sorry, Siolis. I didn't know all that.''

''Schist, Ruth, all you had to do was ask him.''

I nodded, still caught by those strange eyes, his silent waiting presence. I hadn't asked Siolis about himself or his world. I hadn't wanted to know. He was right, I'd been just as smugly Poindran as the others I'd always scorned for their closed minds, their fear of anything strange or taboo. I took another deep breath and closed my eyes, groping inside, nudging that hidden door open a crack. *What is your true voice then, Siolis? How do I find those ''mean-ings?''*

A silent gust swept open the door and tumbled me down a dark well. The sea lapped through me, flickering dark to crystal light and dark again. Voices boomed and squealed, distant and close, overlapping babble. The touch of slippery plumes whisking over me with a crackling dislocation. Surge tossing, rolling, sucking me down and drowning me—

Trapped inside, I flailed in panic, clawing for the surface.

A soft touch, and fluid wings enclosed me, soothing, shutting out the pounding cacophony to a gentle background hiss. A weird sliding sensation, like tuning readouts, and one humming tone filled me. It opened up a spilling montage of images, tastes, sen-sations. I was whipping effortlessly through the clear seas, my body streamlined and graceful, strong tail propelling me as the rich, sustaining water pumped through my gills. Companion fish darted over me, brushing with trailing fins and a tingle of energy, melting through rainbow colors that weren't really colors but a spectrum of emotions and tastes. Puzzle pieces of scent, structure, ripples and crackling charges shifted and rearranged the config-uration of meanings. Waves of silent sound lapped through me, echoing from the hollow buoyancy of my back, doubled and re-

doubled in the ringing chambers of the bathylabra as sea and others/
one and companions merged and flowed. Ebb and flow, hypnotic,
ebb and flow . . .

Choking, clawing my way out of the enveloping sea, I gasped
air into my burning lungs. "Wait. I can't—" I dragged in more
air, pressing my hand to my pounding temples, blinking through
the dizzy jumble of meanings. I could almost grasp those elusive
puzzle pieces, crackling at my fingertips—

"Ruth!" David was shaking me by the shoulders. "You okay?
What's wrong with her, Siolis?"

The dome spun dizzily around me. I blinked, taking a deep
breath. "It's all right." I eased his hands from me. "Okay. Can't
say I'm not trying, Siolis."

"You have done welll. Not alll can llearn. Thank you." Soft
splashing. "You ssee I have not wordss for alll meaningss, have
not meaningss for alll wordss. Willl you trusst a short time llonger?
The incorporeallss have sllept llong on Cyvruss. They wake
ssllow."

I shook my head, still disoriented. "What do you mean, they've
slept here a long time?"

"Hell's hubcaps, you two!" David threw out his hands in ex-
asperation. "If you'd stop babbling and look in the blasted files
I got together, Ruth, you'd see the old Poindros Founder and his
buddies back before the Plan were the ones doing the bioforming.
It was like he was trying for some kind of sea-matrix like he made
later with pure energy for the incorporeals. Only his buddies got
caught in the sweep when the cybers took over as guardians, and
he didn't. So he hid out as the first incorporeal in the Poindran
Local System, but he kept Cyvrus for a backup in his takeover
plan. Siolis'n me, we just found out that part. The Founder was
gonna use doubles to penetrate planet clearances, just like he
used—"

He broke off as changing light patterns flashed on the console,
turning with a listening look, his interface contraption glinting its
crimson indicator.

"Like he tried to use Jason on Poindros?" I shook my head.
"So they're building more cyborgs here?"

But David was turning excitedly to Siolis. "All right! The new
configuration's ready. Let's get back to it." He cleared his throat.
"Okay, Ruth?"

"A short time llonger, Ruth? You will resst?"

"Okay, okay!" I flapped my hands irritably at them. "Do your thing." I sighed. "Good luck."

But they were already absorbed in the console matrix. Easing my throbbing arm into position, I leaned back against the lumpy supply bags, blew out a long breath, and thought about Cyvriots and incorporeals. And Jason.

Thinking only took me around and around the same futile loops. If Siolis was keeping any more secrets, there was no forcing his hand. And pretty clearly no convincing the other natives to help stop the spooks. Without the null device, I couldn't shut down the bio lab. Weak as I was, I'd never make it back under my own steam, anyway. I could only wait for Siolis' "fullness of time," wait for Jason to show up. Damn it. I felt like the ball on a spinning gamer's wheel.

I smiled ruefully. I'd wanted chance and risk, hadn't I? At least that was a victory of sorts over the guardian cybers.

Shaking my head, I turned up the lume and pulled my rumpled pressure suit onto my lap to replace a couple of crushed generating junctions I'd noticed. The suit was designed with a lot of local, overlapping repulsion fields, so it could take some abuse and still function, but it had gotten pretty rough treatment in the bathylabra. Activating the suit at low level, I pressed my open palm against the resistance and ran it along the widely spaced row of imbedded lumps down one leg. It felt like pushing your hand against a soft balloon, only you couldn't feel the balloon.

Halfway down the leg, the pressure wavered. Pushing through it, I could feel the shape of the crushed junction. Turning off the field, I turned the leg inside-out and slit open the inner lining to replace the flat disc with a spare. I heat-sealed the liner and worked my way back up the leg.

There was another weak spot on the back of the suit. I frowned, running my hand back and forth. There was a definite dip, but it didn't make sense. The spot had been protected by the osmotic gear.

I shrugged and turned the suit inside-out again. I froze.

The liner had already been slit and resealed over the junction. The shape felt a little different from the others, not as flat. I grabbed my knife and cut it open. It wasn't a junction disc. I stared at the dull silver button that looked exactly like the controlled radiation-emitting tracking devices the Resistance techs had developed for agents where a rescue pickup might be needed.

I was that gaming ball again, spinning on the wheel. Who'd put the tracer there? Rik, as another little surprise? Helsa, as a backup? But she'd have told me. . . . Unless it was for Lilith to keep tabs on me. Bloody double—

If it was Lilith's tracer, she would have babbled the whole thing to the incorporeals by now.

I ripped the tracer free, jumped to my feet, thought about it and checked the rest of suit, but didn't find any more. I grabbed David by the shoulders, shaking him.

He resisted feebly, eyes twitching behind closed lids as his head lolled forward. The red interface indicator stared at me from his upper back like a baleful eye.

"David! Snap out of it. Come on!" I shook him again, repeating it in his ear.

He groaned, swatted blindly at me, then finally blinked and focused. "Friggin' Founders, Ruth! I was right in the middle of sequencing—"

"No time for that, David. We've got to get out of here right now."

"What?" He scowled, still collecting himself.

I turned to stare down at Siolis floating obliviously in his ring, then jabbed a finger at the leads and console. "Do whatever you do to connect with him, David. I've got to talk to him."

He opened his mouth to protest, but I cut him off. "Do it!"

He gave me a furious look and closed his eyes, face going blank for a second.

There was a splashing sound behind me. "Yesss? There iss need?"

I jerked around, thrusting the tracer down toward him. "Look. Recognize it? I was tracked here." A rising buzz of alarm jittered down my spine. "Siolis, the incorporeals know I'm here. We've got to get out. *Now*."

I grabbed my suit liner and yanked it over my legs. "David, get your suit on. Gather up your stuff."

"You're crazy! We've almost got the key. We're all set up here."

"You can set up at another console-station. Move it." I turned back to Siolis. "Can you call one of those creatures with all the arms to take this away? Maybe we can put them on a false scent."

"Yess, I willl ssend. One llivesss near in cave." His eyes went out of focus, staring through me. His long tail swept beneath the surface, stirring agitated ripples and a glimpse of reddened plumes darting around him. He blinked his inner eyelids. "But it iss llikely fallse allarm. I willl ssee if the facillity matrix hollds ssuch data." He closed his eyes, and lights on the console danced.

"Damn it, there's no time for that." Siolis didn't respond. I turned back to David, who stood sulkily over his monitoring equipment. "Look, if they're tracking me, then they know what console you're using and they can put up their own camouflage, right? He's wasting his time. Tell him, Da—"

I gasped as something cold and clammy touched my hand. Whirling around, I saw one of the large, bulbous sea creatures bobbing on the dark surface, its glinting eye fixed on me. Two of its long, sinuous tentacles groped over the floor, a third one twining loosely around my wrist.

"Uhn!" I jerked back, then hastily dropped the tracer and shoved it toward the floor lip with my toe. A squirming tentacle closed over it, coiled snakelike, and snatched it up. The tentacles oozed back into the water and the creature was gone.

I shook off a shudder and turned back to David. "You'd better save what information you need and wipe the console memory. Get through to Siolis. I'll pack your stuff."

He gave me a disgusted look, shrugged, and escaped into his matrix link. I let myself sag against the console then, fighting the weak lightheadedness. I blinked, wiped cold sweat from my face with my suit-liner sleeve, and finished sealing the open front seam. Rigging up a makeshift sling to take the weight off my arm, I crouched by David's waterproof cases and started packing equipment, trying to ignore a pre-*timbra* alarm state hissing warning signals down my spine.

It took forever to get all the gear packed. I finally sat back, shaking my head. Siolis was probably right—if the incorporeals' mechmen hadn't tracked me by now, they probably weren't following the tracer. But it was safer to move to a different console anyway. . . .

Then it hit me. Maybe the spooks knew exactly what David and Siolis were doing, and now that they knew which console was being used, they were just waiting for the two to decode the alien signal for them. And if I could figure that out, Siolis sure as hell could, too. He just didn't care. Or he was already working with them. . . .

"That double-crossing monster!" Full *timbra* was screaming through me now. *Run. Fight.* I slammed the last case closed and shook David. "Come on, kid. Now!"

This time he emerged almost before I touched him, blinking and startled as the console lights danced a crazy tattoo behind him. In the water, Siolis splashed, tail churning the water. The companion fish, flushed bright crimson, leaped and flashed down into darkness.

"David, get your suit on. Help me get the cases in this net and into the water." I was struggling into my own gear. "Damn you, Siolis, we're moving out!"

"Yesss, Ruth, the incorporeallsss . . ." The rest was lost in the hiss of air escaping his flotation ring. I was hit by a confusing jumble of sensations, images, data bits, swelling with the rush of *timbra* into an almost unbearable pitch of tension.

Urgency buzzing in my ears, I wrestled the heavy, laden net to the lip of the floor. Then everything went crazy.

David, wriggling into his suit and snapping his oxygen exchanger into place, calling, "Hey, wait a—"

Siolis lunging from his ring in a violent thrashing of water and an explosion of painful stars behind my eyes.

Myself staggering back, blinded, then dazzled by light—from inside or out? A whirling glimpse of the console flickering fast colors, then steady crimson. And a popping in my ears, a sucking pressure, and then a gush of fresh salt air.

I yanked reflexively against the drag of the equipment bundle, slipped, fell against David, and landed squinting upward. A dazzle of light poured down a wide, open tube where the top of the dome had been. At its end, high clouds and daylight. And a mechman dropping down on a thin cable.

"David, run! Get out!" I rolled and grabbed him and flung him toward the water, throwing his swimming fin after him. David fell with an awkward splash, clutching the fin and thrashing against Siolis. I scrambled for my faceplate, falling against my arm in a burst of pain. "Don't wait for me! Get out—"

But it was too late. The dome was somehow full of mechmen moving too fast to follow.

I went sprawling, muscles turned to jelly by a nerve inhibiter. I couldn't turn my head, but as something plucked me upward and my eyelids drooped heavily, I glimpsed a net closing around the passively floating Siolis and David. The dripping mesh rose and tightened, tumbling the gawky limbs of the boy together with the streamlined Cyvriot tail and pathetically tiny, limp arms with their webbed hands. Beneath them, the water churned as the bright crimsoned companion fish leaped and hurled themselves frantically at the rising net, then fell back into the sea in a flutter of agitated plumes.

twelve

A wrench, tugging upward as my arms and legs dangled uselessly. I brushed numbly against the inside of the tube piercing the dome. Then I was plucked up and out, my lungs laboring to pull in the sharp, moist tang of salt air. Cloud-filtered sunlight was somehow too bright, the flat sea surface too open and shivering with glancing dazzles of light invading the narrow slit between my eyelids. But I couldn't blink.

I winced inwardly at the sharp reflections off mechman alloy and the bright flanks of the open-decked anti-grav flitter hovering over the sea.

Then the cloud cover must have shifted, blinding alloys going dull, the fretful sea going gray and subdued. Mechman arms deposited me against a large container of some sort, where I sagged limply. I could only stare furiously at the narrow slit of vision I couldn't shift or shut out—a pair of feet that didn't feel attached to me and a featureless gray stretch of deck.

Flat alloy feet crossed it. There was a thump and the thin squeal of metal against metal. Drops splattered my face, a splashing behind and above me. Thin, gawky arms and legs dangled in front of me, then were dropped to sprawl against me, David's damp head lolling forward to rest on my thighs. I couldn't feel the weight, but now I had something different to stare at.

A long time went by like that, light changing from dim gray to reddish, back to gray, and then dark. Humming sound of the anti-grav units and whoosh of thrusters. Clunk of mechman feet over the deck. Faint hiss of wind. I gradually became aware of prickling tingles throughout my body, then general aching and cold, then the insistent throb in my arm. The good news was my eyelids regained function first, so at least I could blink. The bad news was it felt like dragging sandpaper across my eyes.

Finally there was a strangled groan, weight shifting over me. David rolled off me onto his back. I flexed my fingers, managed to raise my face and tilt my crinked neck into another position. Rain spattered softly over my face, glinting reflections of amber lights in David's snarled wet hair.

"Mmmta . . . mmmph . . ." After a couple of tries, he pushed himself into a sitting position, leaning beside me. "Mmmt . . ." Then slowly and distinctly, "Metamorphic schist."

I nodded weakly, gingerly stretching my prickling legs and arms. "Okay?"

Before he could answer, a mechman was standing over us, gleaming alloy reflections of the hovercraft's muted running lights. Its wrist swiveled to reveal the neural dart portals.

"Hey, cllloo . . . cool it with that!" David struggled to rise.

I put out a strangely heavy hand to pull him down. "We're . . . not going anywhere. Don't want to harm us, right?" My tongue was finally loosening up.

The mechman flashed its facelights, the voice speaker producing a monotone, "You may rise and walk slowly to restore muscle function. Do not make sudden movements. It is futile to attempt resistance."

I slowly gathered my legs and stood up, feeling like eighty years old.

David stood pale, but glaring. "Where's Siolis? If you hurt him—"

"The Cyvriot rests safely inside this tank." The mechman indicated the large container we'd been resting against.

"Siolis! You okay?" He tapped fingers on the opaque tank, leaning his ear against it, then straightened, looking relieved. "He's moving in there."

I took a deep breath and turned back to the mechman. "You are violating orders. CI code RK1."

"CI programming has been superceded." Indicator lights flashed, but the unit remained motionless.

"What are you doing with us, then?"

"Information will be provided. Do not attempt to resist."

"When? Where? What are the incorporeals up to?"

The mechman stood silent, facelights steady.

I swore and paced across the dim deck. The unit's head swiveled to follow my route. There were more of them positioned at each end of the open deck, sensors glinting blue and red in the dimness of running lights. I leaned over the rail to peer into the thick night, but couldn't separate the sea from the featureless dark sky. I could see only the faint, pale crests of wind-ruffled swell a couple meters below us. A hard alloy hand grasped my uninjured arm and pulled me away from the rail.

"We will disembark soon." The mechman hauled me back

beside the big tank, where another unit held David's wrist. The
kid yanked his arm against immovable alloy, then made a face
and shrugged.

I peered around the mechmen, squinting into the rainy dark.
There was nothing to see, but now I could hear a faint, distant
booming beneath the hum of the craft. The next minute I wasn't
sure I'd heard it. But I could feel it, echoing in my bones. The
voice of the sea, pummeling and ringing through hollow stone
corridors, pounding amplified back at me. Vague, distorted shapes
rippled behind my eyes, a cold touch slipping beneath my skin
and raising gooseflesh.

I shook my head and frowned, peering. Now I *could* hear it,
the sea crashing and pounding against rock. There was a denser
black, bulking jaggedly against the night sky. The sea hissed and
echoed as dark rock swelled over us and swallowed the craft.

We moved slowly into the cave, the flitter dropping lower over
swirling water. A faint glow drew us on. Rounding a tight turn,
the craft settled onto the calmer surface and glided under a low
overhang to bump up against a platform suspended over the water
and running back to the stone floor of a dimly lit cavern. Against
the dark rock walls dim shapes of equipment and stacked metal
crates rose into the shadows.

A line of mechmen waited motionless on the other side of the
platform, amber ready lights glinting on their identical, featureless
faces. One of them still had a bedraggled violet ribbon tied around
its neck.

"Where's Lilith? What'd you do to her?" David wrenched free
of our guards, scrambling awkwardly over the rail and across the
platform to shout, fists clenched, at the other motionless units.
"Where is she?"

"The biological-core unit Andress:P328XS69:Lilith is intact
and approaching—"

"David!" There was a stir in the shadows at the far end of the
cavern. "They wouldn't let me come until I had a fit and convinced
them I'd hurt myself." Lilith scurried across the leveled stone
floor, followed by two more mechmen. "They took away my
pretty outfit and made me pick out one of *these* awful things."
Flushed pink and panting slightly, she paused at the line of mechmen to gesture helplessly at her too-tight drab coverall molding
each curve like an overstuffed sausage, then gave the nearest unit
a shove that parted the alloy lineup. She laughed breathily and

pushed the tumble of honey-blond curls back from her face. "You poor boy, they haven't hurt you, have they?"

She surged forward and flung her arms around him, engulfing the thin kid in her overripe embrace. David, beet-red and grinning like an idiot, raised a hand to gingerly pat her back.

A disgusted sound escaped me as I turned away. A loaded net was being raised from the tank on deck. A splash, flung drops, and Siolis' sprawled form was suspended above me, the bluish stretch of coiled tail, the smooth hump of back, the thin little arms and webbed fingers, the flattened amphibious face trapped by the web in air. The shape that had seemed monstrous and intimidating in the shadowy sea was suddenly naked and frail. Double lids popped open and I was staring into his deep purple eyes.

Despite myself, an intangible current flowed between us, from me to him this time and back. An almost tender, maternal something that caught me dismayingly off guard.

I jerked around and snapped at the mechmen. "Well, what are you waiting for? Hurry! Get him back in the water, can't you see how weak he is from being thrown around in that damn tank?"

The mechmen, facelights flickering, bustled around me, shifting Siolis on some kind of suspended track I could barely see in the dark overhead, lowering his net into a submerged mesh enclosure at the edge of the platform. As the empty net was pulled up again, I pushed past the mechmen to hook my fingers into the metal-mesh walls rising above the surface of the water.

"You okay in there?" Only a vague stirring below me. "Siolis!"

A faint touch, like a thin, frail green plant runner, uncurled inside me. I pushed past my instinctive recoil and let the tendril grope toward that undefined internal gate, nudging open the door. There. I found it again, willed it wider, took a deep breath and poured comfort, sustenance down the coiling path he'd traced. I could feel him vaguely now, a shadowy shape taking on more substance, but still thin and translucent. Barely sensed, meaningless echoes shivered through me.

I frowned, concentrating, but I couldn't see or feel a clear contact, not the way I had before. Not those flickering sensations, colors, tastes, sounds focusing. . . .

Sliding into focus like finding the right band on a tuner. The companion fish and their changing bright plumes, fluttering around Siolis with a crackle of vitality. Around the kids in the bathylabra, around the adults beside the sea-mount. That last image as the mechmen's cable tugged me out of the dome—Siolis' crimsoned companions leaping frantically and falling back into the sea.

"Siolis, your—"

"No." A splash at my feet, and his slippery blue head emerged, dilated eyes fixed on me. He surged upward, lipless mouth working, a gasping, "No. Sspooksss," and a vague shaking of his head as he slid back beneath the dark water.

I glanced quickly around, mind racing. The mechmen remained beside David and Lilith, oblivious. The companion fish. Siolis needed them to "send" properly. So whatever the incorporeals were planning, they wouldn't be able to use him for a full communication link with the "sea meanings," to decipher the alien signal. And Siolis was telling me the spooks didn't know that. He hadn't joined them.

Movement overhead. I jerked back from the mesh as bulky equipment lowered over the open top of the cage, sealing it. A speaking-ring, like the ones in the sea domes, extended down over the water in one corner of the wide enclosure.

Ripples and a dimly glimpsed swirling tail, and Siolis' face emerged within the ring. Air hissed as the ring inflated and brought him higher, a spray mist bathing his head.

"Siolis, you okay, man?" It was David, leaning past me against the mesh, blinking anxiously through the spattered lenses of his spectacles.

Lilith, trailing behind him, let go her clutch on his hand. "Ruth! I'm glad you're all right. I was worried, you know, even though the mechmen told me they wouldn't hurt any of us. They've been treating me pretty nice, even if I'm about bored to death, so I hope you didn't worry too much about me all this time." There was just the hint of an edge to her words, the wide blue eyes catching a sharp glint of cold light from a passing mechman.

I shook my head wearily, biting back a sarcastic retort.

"I'm truly sorry about the tracer, Ruth, but the incorporeals made me tell them." The bright glint in her eyes turned to welling tears, spilling over. "They didn't hurt me, but I couldn't help it, they got me to tell them everything. All about Helsa, too, how she made me keep tabs on you in the first place. I don't think they mean us any harm, Ruth, they just need some help, and *they* want to help *us*. They knew you were awfully sick, too, and that's another reason they wanted to get you back here just as soon as they could."

Maybe she didn't know that was a lie. The spooks could have picked me up me whenever they'd wanted.

She was turning back to David, tugging on his sleeve. "Tell her, David. I couldn't help it."

But he was moving away, toward the bank of equipment against one wall that I'd noticed before. They were modified consoles, lighting up now in the dimness, flickering fast light patterns. It had to be the auxiliary control center for the facility. Lilith shot me a last pleading look and trailed after David.

I blew out a long breath and looked down at Siolis. His face inside the ring was blank and reptilian, eyes staring, out of focus, after David and Lilith. He blinked then and focused on me, mouth twisting into the fleeting sideways smile. "It iss welll, then?"

"Sure, until the spooks start in on us. And it'd be a whole sight better without her." I jerked my head after Lilith, then sighed. "All right, don't say it. I know she pushes all my wrong buttons because she reminds me of those damn officious Poindran matrons hovering with their so-sweet smiles. But it's more than that. She gives me the creeps."

A hissing sigh echoing mine, and a weak, "Llearn to hear yourssellf, Ruth." A faint probing inside, a shape pushing to expand, then faltering.

"Okay, okay, don't rub it in. Why don't you rest and save your energy?"

His eyes fixed on mine, pupils flaring as his mouth twisted in effort. The groping ephemeral touch nudged harder, pushing against a closed gate of recognition. I hesitated, then tried to grasp the handle and ease it open.

A sudden fast dance of colored lights in the corner of my eye, and I barely had time to catch a startled breath as prickling heat buzzed down my nerves. From nowhere, an insubstantial but somehow hard and glittering hand shoved through me, pounding at my doors. Energy crackled at its fingertips, questing, prying for that loosened gate in me. A silent voice/voices issued a too-familiar imperative. *Open. Let us in.* I stumbled back, whirling around to see the console bank blazing with amber and crimson lights. The hot buzz swelled inside me to a fiery current. The spooks.

"No!" I slammed that internal door, frantically battened the hatches, pulled darkness over it, turned to run inwardly down coiling corridors, spinning, tumbling blindly through black seas and losing it even to myself. The hot, sparking circuit faded to a jittery hum down my spine, the insistent hiss of *timbra* alarm.

"Do not fear, Ruth, we mean you no harm. We are only trying to establish contact." The gentle, disembodied female voice was outside me now, sourceless, echoes filling the rock cavern. "We can work together for our mutual benefit."

"I've heard that before." I gritted my teeth, rehearsing a silent Setharian chant, letting its repetitions loop a defensive wall around me.

"David, we offer you limitless resources." The voice was now several voices in one, smooth and rhythmic, humming through the throat of the cavern. "We will not force you, yet together we will all be stronger. We ask your help in learning to answer the alien message."

David chewed his lip, glancing at me and then staring at the floor.

"Siolis," the enveloping voice continued, "you and the boy will not succeed without us. Join us and let us help you. We seek alike to learn new Ways."

"We sseek, yet not allike." Siolis' hissing voice sounded frail and tenuous after the rich, seductive tones of the incorporeal energy fields. "You ssee messsage onlly as threat, or as chance for conquesst."

"You misunderstand us, Siolis." The voice/voices were gentle, reasonable. "It is the cybers who have closed human minds, the cybers who fear the strange new signal from outside their sphere of control, the cybers who shut out all new contact. Even now, Central Interlock sends alarms to all cyber nets, fearing the anomalous signals come from gathering forces of mobile cyborgs readying for penetration of planetary systems. It is amusing, is it not? The cybers are limited by their directives, bounded by their programmed conception of their perfect, static galaxy, and these parameters do not allow them to recognize that the signals emanate from outside their sphere of control."

The voice laughed softly, confidingly. "Whereas you, David and Siolis, have recognized with us that the signals are true anomalies within the Plan. We know they merely seem to originate within this star system, from shifting points in space. And that is what is so exciting, is it not? Have you explained to Ruth what it means?"

The voice lapped against me with a faint energy field, soothing and tingling at the same time. "The aliens use a sophisticated shifting of double-wormhole space warp to channel their signals, Ruth, but they have discovered how to do so without a pre-set receiving point. They take advantage of singularities they find in the target area, so that the signals seem to come from all directions. We don't know how they can do this, but they make no attempt to conceal the mechanism. They simply wait for us to decode the transmissions. Can they be so technically sophisticated, yet trusting? Or are they setting a dangerous trap for humankind? You see, Ruth, it is very important that we learn their secrets, so that we may defend ourselves if necessary. We must cooperate in this.''

"No. Not with you."

"Ruth, you must remember we were—are—human awareness, too. We are the new evolution of humanity, and we welcome this challenging contact. What is different, in your quest for knowledge, from our desire to add new dimensions to our matrix?''

Their energy presence hadn't tried to push inside me again, but I could almost feel them out there, waiting to invade the way they had that first time on Poindros, when their silent force had lifted and tumbled me into a chaos of alien image and sensation. The memories—of soaring and plunging after prey as a blue-feathered bird, of leaping through tall wheat as a sleek pardil, of crawling by extending oozing pods of fluid self as some sort of slime creature—were still vivid.

I shook my head. "What's wrong, you're bored playing with humans and the animals here in the lab? The awarenesses you suck in stay interesting only so long before they fade into your mixed gray? I suppose you spooks would get a real thrill out of something alien to add to your stew."

"Ruth, you are ill and agitated, suffering your body's weaknesses and speaking from remembered fear. Listen, and you will understand that—''

"No, *you* listen! Maybe you ought to try being afraid, too. What if you do make contact with these aliens? What if they're stronger than you, and they take *you* over?"

Near the lighted consoles, David straightened, one hand reaching out as if for balance. He turned slowly toward me, blinking as his spectacles caught a glint of reflected light, and I saw the activated crimson indicator on his interface device, glowing through his thin suit.

"David, don't link with them!"

"Ruth, they're not trying to take me over, they're just sending me information. And they've got a point. If the aliens *are* that advanced, I wouldn't mind merging with them."

"David, you can't be serious. They're tricking you again. Siolis, tell him."

"We will not force you to cooperate. Only willing joining avoids the trauma of a forced linking, as you know, Ruth. And now, you must go with the mechmen to be Healed, as the pain and weakness of your defective body cloud your judgment." Two nearby mechmen turned and rolled on locked leg-units toward me.

"No! You're not putting me in a Healing field." I'd have no defenses against them if I submitted to the field. "I'll die first. You know I can do it now, I can escape from you that way." All I had to do was open that inner door the other way, escape into the black nothingness where I'd hidden from the incorporeals before. Where Jason had found me just in time, snatched me back from the cold clasp of death. But this time Jason wasn't here, and it would be forever.

"Very well. According to our sensors, tissue necrosis has advanced to a degree which would reduce the efficacy of a Healing field to a negligible impact. The mechmen must, however, amputate your infected arm."

I nodded numbly as the mechmen moved to flank me.

"Hey, just wait a blasted minute!" David jerked toward me, but Lilith put out a hand to hold him, shaking her head.

"Do not fear for her, David." The voice was a deep hum in the chamber. "We must act to preserve her awareness within the defective corpus until an intact replacement body can be prepared."

A chill went through me as I remembered the cyborg body Heinck and the incorporeals had prepared for me on Andura. A body that would make me their mechanized servant. "No way! David, they're just the same as the others. Don't trust them!"

I jerked around at the cold touch of alloy. "No, don't—" The mechmen grasped me, picked me up, and carried me kicking toward a shadowed doorway.

David yelled and broke away from Lilith, running after me, but another mechman stopped him. "Ruth!"

"Your fears are irrational. We only wish to help you."

I ignored the voice, twisting to shout back at David, "Don't let them suck you in, kid! Remember Andura."

The door snicked shut behind me, and I was carried through the dark with dizzying speed, vaguely sensing twisting turns and what seemed to be a fast ride down an anti-grav chute. I'd stopped fighting, hanging limp in the grasp of mechanical hands. I took deep breaths, summoning back a silent chant, trying to ready myself for that final black door, if I needed it.

A different door suddenly sucked open before me, blinding me with a dazzle of white light. Doubled reflections shattered across stark polished walls, racks holding fluid-filled tubes of grotesque floating specimens, a gleaming metal table, a suspended precision laser, and rows of small, sharp, glinting instruments.

It was dark. There was a black tunnel, spinning downward in a swirl of sharp red sparks. Flames leaped and burned outside the tunnel. Someone was groaning. Me. Pain burned down my side. My arm. There was a pop, then hissing. The groans stopped. The black tunnel grew wider and wider and it was everything.

Nothing. A long time. No time. A dark tunnel, spinning, spewing me out.

I floated, spread-eagled, black space pouring its stars around me. They glinted cold blue sparks of luminescence as I flew, scattering them in the ebb and surge of space. I soared toward a colored glint of light. It was a crystal cat's-eye, a pale green and turquoise sphere rolling over a black velvet gaming table. What odds for a Home strike? I fell and it plunged up at me, swelling into a world.

I drifted down out of the hot blue sky, floating on the translucent pearl wings of a windtower, to land in head-high, whispering wheat. Coppery stems swayed in a dry wind, singing, hissing in overlapping voices. The deep earth tremor, channeled and evened by the tower rods, sang through me from my feet up.

I took a deep breath of the dry, grass-scented air, and turned.

They were gathered in the field, watching, waiting. Helen, radiant in her pearl-cloth robe catching subtle rainbow gleams, her unbound hair a tumbling copper flame and eyes the green of spring and deep rivers, lips curved in a gentle smile as she held out her pale hands in welcome. Sam grinning, eyes bunched in a net of sun-etched lines beneath grizzled brows, battered old hands holding the contraplan family photograph. Elder pateros Isaac, glimpsed at a distance, shimmering in and out of focus, standing like a silver-haired prophet in his worn coveralls among the wheat. Joshua, the twin so unlike me, sturdy and freckled and dependable, standing with his arms around Marda and the little twins, and lanky Thomas there too, with David's wiry bush of hair, but where was David? Heat shimmered over the field, and now my family watched me with wary, disappointed eyes.

I turned away and there was Aaron, rising from the ashes of the fire that had finally consumed him, legs planted stiffly in the scorched field, dark eyes still smoldering righteous anger, lifting a pointing finger to condemn my trespasses, my sins against the Way.

I gathered my long skirts, turning to run, always running, but a hand parted the hissing wheat and caught my wrist, stopping me. Jason stood over me with his grave, tawny face, sun sparking in the gold-amber eyes.

"Wait, Ruth." Jason's voice echoed in the soft whisper of the wheat. *Wait.*

He turned me back and the faces from home were whirling on a great wheel, the wings of the windtower spinning around our still center, faster and faster as they aged before our eyes. Isaac gone in a flicker, Aaron crumbling back into ashes. Sam wrinkling, shrinking, fading. Helen's voice lifting in sweet melody, then sighing, dying to a thin whisper of wind:

> *Scarcely are you planted, scarcely sown,*
> *Scarcely has your stem taken root in the earth,*
> *When the wind blows upon you and you wither,*
> *And the tempest carries you off like stubble . . .*

Pain poured through me, cold darkness blotting out the sun, and I screamed as the mechmen swarmed around, slicing away my arm with their laser blades. They closed in, metal faces leering to a mad dance of indicator lights as they raised their instruments to slice the rest of my body open and steal my soul, trap me in the incorporeal web.

I screamed again, but Jason touched me and crackling warmth flowed from his hands. A familiar, electric jolt of being and joy connected me to his vital current. He smiled then, in a still place at the center of whirling white light, stepped back from me and pulled the skin from his shoulder. There was no blood as he peeled strips of tawny skin down his arms and ripped it from his chest, revealing the twisted cords, the metal joints, the intricate plasmeld shapes and tubes, the artificially pumping heart, the circuit connections, chips, and power source. His amber eyes held mine as he raised the finely wrought mechanisms of his fingers to strip away the mask of false skin from his face. His skull was a trans-

parent bowl for the only flesh remaining, the wrinkled mass of
brain pulsing in its container, floating on the stem of nerves running
down the spine of the machine.

I was frozen, repulsed yet drawn to the thing that was Jason.
The brain seethed, beating to a rhythm echoed by hissing voices,
invisible pounding drums. White light pulsed from it, filling me.
Electric sparks raced along my nerves, pulsing in time, flooding
me with warmth and ecstatic energy.

The parts of the machine enfolded me, penetrated me, bringing
the source of the light, the fleshy core of Jason's being, closer. I
closed my eyes and the light and I were one, flowing together to
the overwhelming rhythm. Heat poured up and down my spine,
gathering in my head and loins to burst in an explosion of shared
images, sounds, sensations, tastes, wordless songs. Timeless
being.

One in all. A multitude of eyes, surrounding, watching. Amber
eyes. The incorporeals' devouring energy invaded, pounding, tearing at my head, and I couldn't breathe as I spun spread-eagled
into the shimmering white matrix of their nonbeing nonplace—

No.

I thought I'd yelled it, but all I'd gotten out was a groan.
Dizziness surged and slowly settled. I was lying flat on my back,
a dim light pulsing beyond my eyelids. A faint hum overhead.
Beyond a slowly ebbing wall of numbness, pain flickered and
throbbed in my arm.

It was still there, then. They hadn't operated yet. What were
they waiting for? How long had I been here?

I tried to swallow a dry, sandpaper rasp. My eyelids were heavy,
glued together. I finally pried them open, wincing at the dim light
from a bank of instruments overhead. A confused glimpse of a
steady red signal, oddly penetrating green light pulsing in time to
a faint, enveloping hum, a tube running into my right arm. I tried
to lift it and the red light started blinking, triggering a beeping
noise. I let the arm fall, closing my eyes except for a crack and
sinking back into the slow, careful cycle of heartbeat and breath.
The red light went back to steady and the beeping stopped.

I rested for a minute, bathed in the hum and pulsing green light.
The glowing grid bathed my naked body with its waves of green-
ness, somehow sending a vague, humming sense of well-being
through me. The heavy darkness below tempted me back into it,
but something else nagged, prodding. I turned my head by mil-

limeters, very slowly to keep the red indicator pacified, looking left.

Pain throbbed angrily up my arm. Except there was nothing below the shoulder but a stub sealed in bandages.

The room spun around me and the red light and beeper went crazy. A door whooshed open and a mechman rolled in, pushing me gently back down onto the soft table. Another pop and hiss and the black tunnel spun me down.

The next thing I knew I was floating slowly up from dark seas, drifting weed stems parting for me, purple dimness giving way to a green, springtime light. My arm still throbbed vaguely, but I couldn't let myself start wondering how it could hurt when it wasn't there. I felt strangely light and unfettered, charged with energy and ready to leap up.

The beeping started. I took a slow breath and eased my quickened heartbeat back into a slow, smooth rhythm. The beeping stopped.

I cracked an eyelid and discovered the pulsing green light was less intense now. The gentle hum still enfolded me, and there was still a tube in my right arm, but I didn't think I needed it. The bulky bandage had been changed for a close-fitting cap of some sort over the stump of my upper arm. A quick stab of pain, more than physical, a cold sinking in my belly. No, I'd think about it later. A vague urgency made it easier. It was time to get out.

Somehow I had to get around the red-lit sensor. But if I moved, I'd trigger it.

The door hissed open and I sagged back with my eyes nearly closed, summoning the semi-trance state Anáh, the Setharian woodcarver, had first taught me. I could hear the mechman roll over to me. Its hand crossed my sliver of vision, holding a thin disc pinched between alloy fingers. The mechman's ID breast badge.

The disc slipped into a slot in the face of the monitor overhead. The red indicator and the green light went out. I forced myself to keep breathing evenly. The mechman replaced the clear packet draining into the tube in my arm. Alloy fingers pressed a button on the monitor, and indicators flashed a repeating pattern of blue, blue, amber, white. Then the red indicator came on again, and the pulsing green light, and the mechman's disc was spat out into its hand. I closed my eyes as it rolled out the door.

What the hell. With the new buoyancy bubbling up in me, I

had nothing to lose. Taking a quick breath, I yanked loose my chest tether and jerked upright, stars dancing. The red light started dancing too, to the quick *beep beep* from the monitor. I deactivated the skin-cling of my IDisc and plucked loose the wild card disc attached to it, jamming it into the slot of the monitor. The lights died and the beeping stopped.

I held my breath, but the door stayed closed.

Leaning forward to loosen a second strap across my thighs, I found myself reaching for the fastener with my missing left hand. There was another twinge of pain where there couldn't be. I closed my eyes, forcing back a looming cloud of realizations. Later. With my teeth, I awkwardly plucked the needle and tube from my right arm. Another deep breath. I really felt fine, the strongest I'd felt since planetfall. Spooks must have dosed me with something powerful.

It took a while to figure out the system on the portable monitor. I activated the repeating pattern the mechman had produced, thanking Founders the recorder didn't appear to be integrated into the facility data banks. Finally I hit the right combination of commands, and the pattern wrote itself onto an endless loop. The red indicator stayed steady and the green light kept pulsing away when the slot ejected my blank disc.

After a quick scan of the empty little room, I gave up on finding my suit. The door whisked open when I got close, and I shivered in a cool draft of darkness from the corridor. I stuck my head out for a quick look and sucked in a startled breath as I found myself staring into a mechman's face, dimly illuminated by the intermittent green light through the doorway. I jerked back, but the mechman didn't come after me. I looked out again and realized its face was blank, indicator lights off. Apparently it was only triggered by a summons from my monitor. The heat in the cubicle and the pulsing green light—some sort of low-level bioelectric stim field like the one the cybers had used for my broken arm?— were probably bad for its circuits.

I took another deep breath and headed down the empty dark corridor that didn't light up in front of me like before. I could hardly hold down the bubbling urge to giggle over the picture I had to make, if anybody could see me, creeping around the facility stark naked. Somehow my mere fleshiness in the midst of the smooth bare walls and hard, gleaming mechman alloy struck me as hilarious. I took a deep breath and strode openly down the corridor, my right hand following the wall, chuckling silently, carried along by a giddy who-gives-a-damn feeling. Somewhere in the recesses of my mind, I wondered what the spooks had put in the IV fluid. Or maybe it was that pulsing green light field. But I didn't feel fuzzy—just the opposite. Charged. Energized.

I had to find David and Siolis, though, make sure they didn't give in to the slippery spook arguments. I wasn't sure how we were going to get out of the facility, but there had to be a way. Security, anyway, wasn't very tight. I hustled along, checking doors for the anti-grav chute up, but didn't encounter any more mechmen. Only dim rooms of the creepily familiar green-lit specimen tubes.

I was feeling a little more sober by the time I poked my head through the door to yet another lab. I turned away, then stopped short, slipping through the closing doorway, drawn by a vague recognition.

The eerie green light washed over me, rippling through fluid-filled tubes and gently stirring fleshy shapes. I swallowed nervously, glancing around. At the far end, an empty rack. It was the room where the mechmen had attacked Lilith and me. Curious despite a growing uneasiness, I moved slowly toward the connecting door to the next lab.

A flurry of animal sound and movement greeted me. The black and white furry little creatures were still in the cage beside their motionless replica suspended in the fluid-filled tube. A snake hissed beside its double, a catlike animal sprang against mesh, a bat rustled leathery wings as I edged past their cages. At the back of the room, wavering green light bathed long fleshy shapes I suddenly remembered glimpsing in my earlier flight.

I shivered, my heart slamming in the pre-*timbra* warning state. I took a deep breath, reflexively channeling my pulse into a calmer rhythm. My feet, moving of their own will, took me steadily around the room. Passing the last row of bulky cages, vaguely registering more restless animals, I stopped dead in my tracks.

Suspended in a row of tall vatlike tubes of rippling fluid were perfectly formed, naked human bodies. A cloud of long blond hair drifted back from the dreaming face of a voluptuous and unmistakable young woman. Lilith. Cold sweat broke out on my face as I swallowed down a surge of bile. Farther down the row, a tall, lean young man's body dangled in the fluid, arms stirring in a grotesque semblance of life. Jason's blind face bobbed against the tube.

thirteen

The blank face nodded in stirring fluid as I stared, repelled yet fascinated. I mechanically found the ID imprint stamped in the metal base of the tube. Haverson:P376XC48:Jason, Clone A.

The treatment's charged well-being drained away as I slumped to the floor and rested my head against my updrawn knees. My dull wits were finally getting the message. That odd taboo word, *clone*. The animal twins here meant the incorporeals were using contraplan technology to reanimate doubles grown from the animal tissue samples the "Violet" mechman had told me about. And now from human tissue. I wondered if Lilith knew what they'd grown here in the lab. Human doubles. That must have been what David had meant back in the dome, when he'd mentioned the spooks' backup takeover plan and I'd thought he was talking about more cyborgs.

Cyborgs . . .

Despite myself, my eyes were drawn back to the tube containing the suspended Jason look-alike. My face burned with peculiar shame as I stared at the lean young figure drifting naked and vulnerable. Actual flesh and blood this time, no mechanized construct. But no awareness, no memories. Was this the "real" Jason?

The dreaming face with its untouched, pale skin and wide cheekbones hovered over me, lips carved like smooth marble into what looked impossibly like the start of a private smile. The double waited silently, chin fuzzed with the silky start of a beard, drifting hair longer and a little darker than Jason's sun-streaked mane, but the eyes were lowered in a look of gentle patience that twisted something inside me with a familiar pang.

I shook my head wearily, and across the glinting curve of the lucite container I could see my own warped reflection faintly overlying the pristine form floating within it. A worn, battered woman with a matted tangle of dark reddish hair, pale face tracked by a vivid scar, huddled around the sealed stump of her missing arm. A disfigured cripple.

The blind face nodded in its fluid, withholding judgment, waiting.

"Damn your eyes!" The tight knot of suppressed pain, despair, fury suddenly ripped loose. "You know that's what he'd see. He—you . . . bloody double damn!" I rocked myself as the old turmoil and the new shook me, hot tears stinging my eyes. "There's no way—I tried to tell you . . . then you told me—it can't work, Jason! Look at yourself, and look at me. And it's worse inside. Too many scars."

The perfect, virginal shape of Jason only drifted silently as I scrubbed furiously at my wet face. And Jason, the ageless cyborg, was even more remote and untouchable than the inanimate flesh here in the tube. Always would be.

I closed my eyes and rested my head against my knees again, rage fading into grief. There, where no one but his blind double could see, I let myself mourn my losses—the delusion of human love that was Jason, the arrogant assumptions of youth and strength that had been stripped from me along with my arm, the comforts of the old Ways and beliefs. I could almost hear the soft whisper of harp strings stirring inside me, the melody of a soothing lullaby. A hand softly touching my brow. Finally in my weakness I conjured my mother's gently smiling face, radiant with her mysterious sureties. "You know the meaning of love, Ruth, of right and wrong. Things will come straight for you."

I shook my head. Even Helen would hardly say that now. Would she recognize her daughter at all?

No answer but a barely audible hum suddenly crackling around me. I jerked my face up to see the figures in their tubes grotesquely twitching, limbs galvanized by some sort of current. Startled, I jumped to my feet and stumbled back from them.

The Lilith double arched, muscles tightening in arms and legs as they splayed against the sides of the tube. I shuddered at the parody of human movement, even as I noted irrelevantly that though the . . . clone was softly rounded, it wasn't as overly lush in its curves as the original. I turned away to be confronted by the Jason replica's face contorted into a grinning rictus as its body spasmed and then went lax again. It bumped against the tube, drifting back with one big hand beckoning languidly in the stirring fluid, smooth face nodding.

I shuddered, jerking away to pace down the aisle. I scrubbed my face again with my hand, pushing back the hovering cloud of despair and self-pity. Time enough for that when I could indulge in the luxury. I took deep breaths to calm the surge of my heartbeat. I *was* stronger. The incorporeals had cured my infection, at least.

So what was their agenda? I turned to pace back down the room in the wavering green light, past the curious and restless and sleeping animals in their cages beside their inanimate twins in the tubes. How had the incorporeals duplicated Jason, anyway? Had the Poindros Founder dispatched tissue samples from the discarded bodies of his cyborg recruits to be stored here? I supposed it really didn't matter. What I needed to find out was what the spooks intended to do with the replicas. If they could somehow program and control these—I couldn't quite call them people—these clones, the doubles could obviously penetrate planet clearances even easier than the cyborgs with their still-organic brains.

I stopped again at the row of silent, floating figures. I bit my lip, gaze skittering around the lab in search of a heavy tool as I was seized with an impulse to break open the tubes, spill the fluid, and end the monstrous experiment. I strode over to the cabinets along the side of the room and pulled them open, rifling through an assortment of equipment and chemical canisters. I caught my breath as my fingers closed around the glinting alloy tube of a laser blade. I turned back to the vats, *timbra* readiness gearing up into a hot buzz. I paused, eyes tracing the tubing overhead, branching with convenient valves into each narrow vat.

I stepped closer to the Lilith double, making myself observe each detail of the too-familiar features, the half-parted soft lips and fair lashes lying over pale cheeks. My hand clenched tighter around the laser housing as I turned to stare helplessly at the Jason replica. They were only accumulations of tissue, no life in them. But what if the mechman was wrong, and they *were* alive? I couldn't do it. They were defenseless, and I was too guilty already. Maybe I'd be sorry, but I couldn't do it. CI would have to be warned, though, and to hell with the repercussions.

But Siolis had known, apparently, and he hadn't sent a warning. The nagging doubts harangued me again. Did Jason know? Was he really on his way?

Whatever Siolis was up to, I had to get David out of here before the spooks could suck him into their matrix again. Then we could try to reach CI from the remote communication center at the landing site. With his interface device, we ought to be able to cut through the incorporeal dampers. If we could get free of the mech-men. . . .

I took a deep breath, refusing another wave of despair. The sea cavern had to be the best way out, if David was still there. I might be able to take a mechman guard by surprise and deactivate it with the laser blade. They didn't know I was up and about, and didn't seem to be bothering with much security. I didn't know what else to try.

The exit door whisked open before me, but I hesitated in the opening, greenish light spilling past me into the dark corridor. Refusing the impulse to look back at the Jason double, I plunged through.

It was too easy. There were no mechmen to challenge me as I crept through the dark halls, searching for a way up. I located by touch one of the rectangular hatches to the ribbed utility ducts, gripped the alloy laser tube between my teeth, and started climbing. I didn't know how many levels down I'd been, but I passed two hatches going up. A faint air flow wafted over me as I negotiated the intersection with a narrower, horizontal shaft. Peering down it, I saw dim light glowing through a grating at the end. Wriggling along it, bare skin scraping over metal ridges, I pried open the grate to emerge in a shadowed storage area crammed with stacked containers. The lower warehouse space. I threaded my way between dim piles, stopping short as I emerged into the open, high-ceilinged cavern.

I pulled back into the shelter of the stacks, clutching the laser blade and peering out. No mechmen, no flitter at the dock. Only the faint, echoing hiss of the sea and colored lights playing over the console bank on the other side of the cavern, casting a dim illumination over the stone floor. The light glinted off a single, tubular lucite vat—like the ones in the cloning lab—mounted in a tangle of hoses and equipment near the water's edge. A pale, thin shape floated in its wavering greenish glow.

I went cold. "No . . ." Stealth forgotten, I was across the floor and beside the vat.

David's eyes were closed, his face blank and dreaming as he drifted in the fluid. He was naked, his long arms and legs looking even thinner, wrenchingly pitiful, through the distortion of the curved vat. There were tubes connected to the osmotic valves protruding from his hips, running up into the bristling equipment capping the vat. Insulated wires descended from it to a thin mesh of some sort that was pressed tightly over his head, dark coils of hair sticking through it in matted tufts.

Lights danced across the slick surface as the glittering reflection of console indicators changed configuration. I turned frantically to the tangle of equipment, ready to grab the connecting tubes and yank them loose, rip the cap off, and drag David from the incorporeals' test tube. I closed my eyes, gripping the unactivated laser blade in frustration.

They'd gotten him. If I tried to cut him loose from their links—more than physical ones—I'd only injure him, possibly kill him.

I took a deep breath and edged gingerly around the conglomeration of electronics and tubes, unable to figure out what most of it was even for, let alone how to deactivate it. I didn't know why this incorporeal matrix was using neural links to connect with David, instead of the invisible force fields they'd used on Poindros and Andura. I shook my head, turning toward the shadowed water, then flinching back as I brushed against the top of the mesh cage submerged next to the lip of the floor. The tubes and wiring ran from David's vat to another cluster of equipment capping the mesh. I leaned forward, peering inside it, making out a dim, floating bulk motionless in the dark water. Siolis. More tubes and wires snaked down toward his drifting form.

I closed my eyes, fighting off the cloud of despair closing in again as a silent, desperate cry swelled and broke loose inside me. But there was no response, no touch of even the faintest sending from Siolis.

"Blast it, Siolis, this is your fault!" I shook the mesh cage furiously, stirring nothing but lapping ripples.

"Do not attempt to interfere. You will only cause harm to the Cyvriot." The toneless voice was close behind me, jolting me back from the cage.

I bashed into a mechman that had rolled silently across the floor behind me. Gasping, I wrenched away as its extensor reached for me. Swinging around and ducking close into range beneath the extended limb, I triggered the laser blade and raked it across the mech's face sensors. There was a crackling flare of sparks, and its indicators went dark, the upper extensors waving wildly and triggering a random burst of neural darts. I ducked again as it lurched around unsteadily.

"Stop! Do not resist." Another mech sped across the floor toward me, extensor upraised with neural ports open.

I ducked behind the disabled mech as it clunked to a crooked halt and the second unit's dart pinged against its alloy housing. I ducked out again, lower, firing the laser blade as the second mech rolled into my limited range.

The needle of blue-white light hissed over the mech's midsection where the power pak was, flaring off polished alloy in blinding reflections.

"Damn!" I jerked back behind the disabled mech, rolling to the side for another shot, when hard claws grabbed my arm and wrenched me upward, plucking the laser tube from my hand.

"No! Let me go!"

The unit telescoped its extensor, holding me at arm's length as I kicked at it. "Do not resist. You must return to the recovery room to complete your recuperation."

"Like hell I will! And maybe when I get back, David will be gone. What are you doing with them?" I twisted in the mechman's hold, still kicking.

"You will injure yourself. Desist." The second mechman rolled over and clutched my legs, holding me up. Still another rolled in through the cavern door, holding out a dermal patch.

"I don't need your drugs! You'll make me sick with that stuff, and you're not supposed to harm me. Just tell me what you've done with David and Siolis. Damn you spooks, I know you're in there somewhere!"

The advancing mechman came up short, arm still extended, facelights flashing. A slurry of sourceless, blended incorporeal voices suddenly filled the cavern. "Ruth, you are being very foolish again. We have assured you that we're only trying to help you. We did cure your illness, did we not?"

"Right, thanks a bunch. Just so you could get me out of the way and snare David."

"Your nephew and Siolis have joined with us of their own free will. David wishes us to assure you that he is"—the voices switched to an echoing imitation of David's—"hunky-dory, Auntie."

"Stop it!" I clenched my fist. "You expect me to fall for that?"

"As you wish, Ruth. However, we must insist you return to the treatment room for full recuperation and restoration of function."

"No way!" I writhed and kicked as the mechmen started rolling for the exit door. I wrenched against the alloy grip, knocking the bandaged stump of my arm against the mechman holding my shoulders. Sharp stars flared in my eyes and I gasped. "No, I'm fine now. You're hurting me. Just let me stay here with the kid."

The mechmen stopped as the blended voices echoed again, "You should avoid these violent outbreaks, Ruth, since they only weaken you. As we are occupied with other matters at present, we will allow you to remain here at rest until we can complete your rehabilitation. Perhaps you will be less agitated here. We will restrain you for your own welfare.''

The mechmen silently reversed their wheels, carrying me toward the empty docking area. Another unit rolled out a foam pad and what looked like storage drop cloths. They laid me solicitously on top of the nest, held me down when I tried to stand up, and dressed me like patient nannies in a drab coverall, giving me a supply of what looked like emergency rations. They snapped flexible bands around my wrist and one ankle, heat-sealing them and securing them with fused cords to metal rings set in the floor.

''You will remain here temporarily.'' Two of them rolled off through the exit, carrying the damaged unit. One remained squatting by the consoles, its facelights burning amber standby.

Just to check all options, I tested the tethers for give—none—and range. I could squirm to the edge of the dock but not over the edge. So much for drama.

I lay face down by the hissing sea, flushed and weakly lightheaded again, my free foot dangling over the edge to touch the welcome coolness. The incorporeals were holding all the cards. Again. Damn the fool kid, and Siolis for leading him on. How could they have fallen for the incorporeal tricks? Or had it been Siolis, working with the spooks all along, luring him in?

I sagged wearily against the stone floor. There was something rotten here, beneath the new, sugar-coated incorporeal courtesy, only I didn't know exactly what. I should have used the null transmitter when I'd had the chance, should have looked beyond the personal, as Helsa was always urging me, and considered all the other humans who could be herded up by the incorporeals to have their brains sucked dry.

If only the Cyvriots hadn't taken the device. Damn. I could almost feel it in my hand, as I'd hesitated too long. I'd screwed up again. Thinking in my arrogance I could just reach out to the natives and they'd fall all over themselves to help me break their taboos. Just because I'd happened to get along with the Andurans, I'd assumed the same thing would happen here. I'd wised up a little too late.

If only I could wipe out the whole damn mess and start over. But it didn't work that way, I didn't get to call out to Mommy or the great guardian cybers to make it all better. Maybe humans *didn't* have any business taking matters into our own hands, maybe we did need our keepers. We always messed up.

I closed my eyes, sprawling limp halfway off my padded nest, swallowed by dark despair. Drowning in it. Black cold seas poured through me, the obliterating depths sucking me down. And I didn't care—no, I welcomed oblivion, flinging open the gates to let my emptiness be filled by the cold water lapping up through my toes. I let myself be pulled and tumbled by the surge until I didn't know up from down. In the beckoning deeps, dimly glimpsed shapes drifted by, huge monstrous beings with enormous eyes glinting out of the blackness. I could feel their pulses echoing in my bones, shivering through the water filling me. A muted cacophony of distant grunts, squeals, tremolo wailing washed over and into me. Cold shapes slithered across my skin, tentacles wrapping around me, tugging me deeper, squeezing—

I gasped, jerking upright against my tethers on the stone floor of the cavern as the cold, slippery touch squeezed around my ankle and tugged me toward the water. A tentacle, violet-tinged, coiled tighter around my calf.

I wrenched against it, opening my mouth to yell, when another suckered tentacle snaked up from the water and the creature's bulbous body partly surfaced, a glinting eye fixing on mine. A formless urgency silenced me. Another tentacle squirmed over the stone floor, the flexible tip coiled around something wet and glistening.

I stared as the slippery flesh uncoiled and dropped what it carried into my lap. Caught by the glinting eye fixed on me, I couldn't seem to look down as my fingers reflexively closed over slick plasmeld.

"Alert. Intruder. Threat."

I jerked my head around to see the mechman speeding toward me, facelights flashing blue and crimson, extensor raising to reveal an open laser port. An almost-heard hiss, and a thin blue needle of light lanced through the dimness to skim one coiling tentacle.

The creature flared painful crimson with the sizzle of burning flesh, lurching in spasms, its limbs writhing back toward the water. As the mechman shot closer, I flattened and rolled, gripping the null device the creature had returned to me. Pressing it against my chest as I fumbled to set the controls one-handed and aim it, I held my breath and triggered a narrow burst.

A popping pressure, and the mechman lurched to a halt like running into a brick wall, its lights gone dark.

I let out a long, shaky breath and stared down at the device in my hand. I hadn't yet quite grasped the fact that I had it back.

Had I somehow summoned the tentacled creature, as Siolis had directed the demon-fish? Squirming around in my tangle of tethers, I peered down into the dark water, but there was no movement. I turned back to stare at the frozen mechman, the null device, the serenely winking indicators on the bank of consoles. My hand tightened on the device. All right. I had that second chance. It was time to do it, wipe out the spooks and shut down the facility.

I bit my lip, gaze drawn slowly to the wavering green illumination of the vat where David's limp form drifted in its tangle of connections. I couldn't break my tethers to pull him out even if he did survive a shutdown while linked with the matrix. We'd all die. I closed my eyes, gripping the null generator, sweat breaking out on my face and back. But I had to do it now, before the spooks found a way to stop me. Had to—

Something brushed against my back. Before I could react, the null device was plucked out of my grip.

"No! No!" I whirled around, frantically grabbing. "No, you can't. . . . You—" I sucked in a sharp breath.

It was Jason. Dripping seawater, he held the device in one big hand, reaching down with the other to effortlessly snap my tethers with the cyborg fingers that looked human. The grave, tawny face with its wide cheekbones turned to mine. He slowly smiled, crouching down beside me and gently brushing the tangled hair back from my face. "It's all right, Ruth. Let's see if there's something else we can do instead."

"Jason." I stared blankly. "You really came." I shook myself, starting to reach out without thinking.

"I'm sorry I took so long." His gaze flicked over my empty, dangling sleeve and back to my face, his gentle smile never altering, the bright gold-brown of his eyes steady on mine. Reading me like a book. And what was in his eyes? Revulsion? Pity?

I shrugged abruptly away from him. "Good thing you came when you did, I guess." I forced a brittle laugh. "Siolis said you were on your way, but it didn't look like it was true."

"I tried to hurry, but I had to do some planet-hopping, traveling under Heinck's ID. . . ." His eyes flickered over me as I stiffened, remembering how Jason had altered the cybernetic data to fill in the gap of Heinck's death and give himself a cover. He continued with barely a pause, ". . . so I could connect with a freighter passing near this star. Then I had to fake transport reception of a priority cargo demand and get myself shuttled down here with the goods. When the cybers get around to straightening out the data snarl, I don't know what the mechs here are going to do with eighty crates of Biindavi incense.'' He shrugged and the lazy smile split into a quick white grin.

I looked blankly past him to the water, taking a deep breath. "I didn't know if I could believe Siolis. He's had something up his sleeve all along, keeping secrets, and now he's got us in a real mess.'' I jerked my chin toward David's vat and Siolis' mesh cage as Jason's smile faded. ''The spooks here are using a different setup than the ones on Andura. I don't know if I could reach them in the matrix like I did before with David. But I guess we'll have to give it a shot.'' Not meeting his eyes, I gathered my legs to rise.

''Ruth, wait.'' His hand touched my shoulder—the uninjured one, of course. Always so thoughtful, just like the cybers. ''There's no hurry now. Why don't you rest, get your strength back?'' A warm, soothing tingle crept through me from his hand, stirring buried memories of the spicy smell of his skin in the hot moonlight of Poindros, the surprising sensitivity of his work-roughened fingers, his crackling aura joining mine as our love-making in the Anduran forest connected us more than physically.

''Don't—'' I jerked away from the warm link. I didn't need his cyberneticized compassion. ''I'm fine. We need to do something before more mechmen come or the spooks start wondering what's going on here.'' I rose to my feet, finally meeting his eyes, my face set.

He dropped his hand. ''All right, Ruth.'' The planes of his face had gone neutral, eyes sparking a glint of amber. ''But I've already made preliminary contact with the facility system from the communication center at the landing field. The incorporeals didn't have time to build a sophisticated interface in the cavern here, so they receive ambient data transmissions through the mechmen sensors. With this unit deactivated, they aren't eavesdropping on us now.''

He strode brusquely past me, and I followed him across the floor to the console bank. He touched controls on one console, moved to another and adjusted a wavering linear display. He stood motionless a moment, eyes flaring bright amber lights, then turned abruptly back to me. ''I've confirmed for them my arrival on the shuttle.'' His voice had dropped to an almost toneless level. ''Their matrix here was first activated before you and CI uprooted the Founder's major incorporeal network on Poindros, and they've been acting independently since then, possessing only sketchy data about ensuing events. They now believe I am acting as a free agent for the Founder's takeover plan, as are other cyborgs who left Poindros before the purge.''

I carefully watched the console indicators. "Then CI's right, in a way. There *are* other cyborgs still out there.''

"Yes."

"Jason, you—" I cleared my throat. "You know what they're doing here, don't you? They're growing flesh and blood human doubles this time, for their takeover plan. I saw them in a lab upstairs." I turned to face him again. "They've got one of you." Despite myself, my voice shook.

His eyes were human brown-gold again. "Ruth, I—" Then sharp amber glinted from his expressionless face. "Flesh and blood duplicates. I know. Clones to be instilled with programmed memory and priorities. I have to go up to the facility main control center and stabilize the new data entries, to give us some time to work on cracking the system. If you're to be useful, you should get some sleep while I'm gone.''

I nodded, relieved at his practical tone. "All right.''

"Don't worry about David. The incorporeals are keeping his body healthy in that vat—in fact, according to the data here he was suffering from exhaustion and poor nutrition, and they're correcting the imbalances.''

I nodded again.

He handed me the null device. "Keep this, Ruth. But don't tell anyone else you have it.''

I slid the flat plasmeld into one of my coverall pockets. "Who else—"

"Lilith is still in the facility. I'll bring her back with me.''

"Oh. Right." I'd managed to forget all about Lilith. "Jason, they're growing a clone of her, too.''

"I know." He turned briskly toward the exit. "They've started clones of you and David, too, from tissue samples they obtained when they brought you back here.''

"Oh." I looked at David's still form in the vat and suddenly felt sick. I clenched my fist. "I'm going with you. I think we should shut down that lab right away." I strode after him, trying to ignore another wash of lightheaded weakness.

"Ruth, you stubborn . . ." Jason was beside me as I stumbled, picking me up and laying me gently on the foam pad, covering me with the drop cloths. He looked down on me, shaking his head. "How about trusting me to manage for a couple hours? Eat those rations they gave you and get some sleep." His voice had regained its intonations, quietly firm.

I made a face. "Yes, Pateros." I ripped open a nutrient packet with my teeth and wolfed it down, suddenly realizing I was ravenous.

I thought I saw his lips twitch, but I must have been mistaken. The tawny face with its wide cheekbones was completely, mechanically blank as he turned away to the exit.

Jason was right, of course. I woke up feeling better. I polished off another couple of nutri-packs, refusing to acknowledge the persistent signals of pain and presence from my missing arm, the looming weight of despair ready to smash my shaky defenses. I carefully splashed my face with drinking water and smoothed down my rumpled coveralls. I was sitting cross-legged on my mattress and trying to rake fingers through the hopeless tangle of my hair when the door at the end of the console bank whooshed open. A mechman rolled through.

I jerked back on the mattress, hand dropping toward the null device hidden in my pocket.

"Ruth, it's all right." Jason followed the mech in from the shadows. "I've selective-programmed it, like the camouflage loop you used earlier, so it can feed the data we choose down here to the incorporeals." He glanced down at me. "Good. You're feeling better."

"Me? Oh, better, thank you!"

He ignored the sarcasm, turning back toward the door. "Here she is, Lilith. Maybe you'd better—"

"Ruth, you poor thing! Let me give you a *hand*."

Jason winced, but Lilith, oblivious, hustled past him in her skin-tight coveralls to plunk down beside me and scoop my hair back from my face.

"Don't bother, I'm fine. Just—"

"Now don't be silly, you can't have this mane hanging in your face like that! It'll just take me a second." Somehow the knots fell away in her hands as she briskly combed, straightened, and secured the mess into a tidy braid down my back.

I shook my head, testing the braid and edging away from Lilith's hot palm resting itchily on my shoulder. "Thanks." I looked up at Jason, keeping my voice resolutely cheery. "So how's it going? Getting anywhere with the system?"

He nodded, face neutral. "Lilith has something to tell you."

I turned back to her, uneasily remembering her blank double floating in its tube upstairs somewhere. Did she know? "Uh, you okay, Lilith? What did the mechmen do, lock you up again?"

"Well . . . not really, you see I was afraid to come down and . . ." She squirmed on the mattress beside me.

Nervous? Lilith? I didn't think she *had* nerves.

"Ruth, I hope you'll try to understand, you see I really wouldn't hurt David or you for the world. . . ."

Jason, standing motionless, interrupted in a nearly toneless voice. "It's not necessary to prepare an elaborate emotive cushion, Lilith. Ruth has enough experience. Simply tell her."

Lilith looked up at him, face gone oddly blank. It could only have been for a second that their gazes locked, eyes strangely flat, but I could almost hear the wheels clicking, falling into place. Gooseflesh prickled my back, my ears buzzing with the onset of *timbra* alarm as I scrambled back from her and jumped to my feet. "You . . . you can't—"

"Ruth, wait, please listen." Lilith reached up to me, pleading, blue eyes bright with brimming tears—only an ordinary, not-too-bright, overfed, spoiled young woman who'd gotten into matters too deep for her. Only that wasn't what she was.

I shook my head, backing away. "Suvving Founder . . ." I could hear Siolis' hissing smug damn voice. "*Llearn to hear yoursself, Ruth.*" He'd known. Those hot little hands of hers, always trying to touch David and me. It wasn't just because she reminded me of overbearing Poindran femininity that she'd gotten on my nerves. There was more than one reason she'd kept slyly conjuring memories of Poindros—she had to have come originally from my homeworld. Like the other cyborgs.

I closed my eyes and fought off a plummeting sensation. "Damn it, Jason, she's one of the Founder's cyborgs! And you're letting her run around loose. Can't you see?" I turned furiously back to Lilith still playing her abject role on the mattress. "It was you all along, wasn't it? You infiltrated the Resistance, you sabotaged my Matrix game trying to get me out of the way so you'd have a free shot at David, you tried to kill me again on the transport and pinned it all on Rik when you got him instead!" Everything was flashing back at me, only now with a new clarity. And her panic in the lab when I'd pulled out the null device—of course, it would have wiped her circuits. My fingers fumbled with the pocket that hid the device.

"Ruth, wait." Jason moved quietly beside me, touching my arm and gripping it in an unbreakable hold.

I looked up into the blank, machined mask of his face and panic ripped through me. I yanked, but his grip wouldn't give. "You've gone back to the spooks, too! You're both—"

"Hush, Ruth." He allowed his face some expression then, the gentle brown-gold eyes meeting mine. He looked sad, and somehow tired. "You know that's not true. Can't you trust me yet?"

I opened my mouth, ready to voice the old arguments and doubts, but we'd been around that wheel too many times. I shut my mouth and finally nodded.

He released my arm. "Lilith has been subjected to the same trauma of dislocation in a cyborg body, the same conditioning and manipulation from the incorporeals that I underwent back on Poindros. You know what they're capable of. Please listen to what she has to say."

The cyborg in the tight coveralls rose smoothly from the mattress, standing stiff and motionless with a blank face, almost unrecognizable as the coy and bubbly Lilith. I watched her with a face as blank as hers.

Her voice kept a moderate intonation, but sounded flat compared to her former lilting tone. "You have just cause to hate me, Ruth. I can only say I'm sorry. But not everything you saw of me was false. I was more foolish, more impressionable than Jason, and it took me longer to start questioning the conditioning of the Founder and the directives of the incorporeals when they sent me out from Poindros to start infiltrating the system. It was only when I penetrated the Resistance and met David that I began to care in a human way again, that my old emotions were awakened and began to weaken the hold of the incorporeal conditioning."

She paused, giving my inferior synapses time to absorb her information. "Of course, I was still obeying their directives when we arrived on Cyvrus. I contacted the matrix here, which ordered me to allow you to pursue your own attempts to locate David and Siolis. They wanted to learn through your experiences in the sea, and allow David and Siolis to gather more data about the alien signal. As I worked with them, I realized that this incorporeal matrix is structured somewhat differently from the Founder's matrix back on Poindros. Perhaps it was these differences, coupled with my reawakening emotional responses, which further weakened the incorporeal control over me. I was struggling to emerge, struggling with dislocation and guilt, when Jason helped me find the right channels to reclaim independent function.

"I have not yet stabilized my own neural directives. Jason is far ahead of me in understanding his own condition, and I am very grateful for his promise of further help. I know nothing can change the deaths, Ruth, and I take full responsibility for them. I hope to make some amends by helping Jason reclaim control of the facility system. Please forgive me." She waited silently, at least having the sense not to try any more shaped-emotive appeals.

I blew out a long breath. It was all very reasonable. But the warning *timbra* was still ringing in my ears, and I didn't trust her any more than I would a snake.

I turned to Jason. "Fine story, but how do I know it's true? She'd say the same thing even if she was still working for the spooks. You can... link with her, right?" I shrugged uncomfortably. "Could she be lying to you?"

Jason shook his head slightly. "I have linked through our circuit-to-neural interfaces, helping guide her in her response restructuring. I can verify that there was trauma of the same sort I suffered. But Ruth, you've never understood this—I can't 'read' her mind any more than I can read yours. I can only transmit and receive nerve impulses and interpret them with a fair degree of accuracy with the help of my enhanced processors. Lilith could conceivably be lying to me."

"Then we can't just blindly trust her! There's too much at stake."

"You'd deny her, then, the same human rights you're trying to reclaim from the cybers?"

"Damn it, Jason, don't start philosophizing with me! If you could see what's right in front of your face—"

"All right, something concrete then. Lilith knew things about you and the Resistance she hasn't told the incorporeals. She also knew about me, and she hasn't revealed that, either. There is no logical reason for her to withhold information from the matrix at this point, unless she's no longer with them." He paused. "And, on a practical level, I could use her help penetrating the control loops here."

"But..." I sighed and raised my hands in resignation, forgetting I only had one. The stump of my arm still insisted on acting like it was attached to something. I bit my lip, yanking back the trailing, empty sleeve that only underlined what Jason had left unsaid. From this point, I was pretty much useless here.

I irritably wadded the excess material and stuffed it inside-out into a high knot, raising my face defiantly to Jason. Just bloody well let him say anything soothing or comforting. . . .

He didn't. He turned briskly to Lilith. "I think Ruth might be interested in what you had to tell me about the incorporeal matrix here, Lilith."

"All right." She nodded, loosening somewhat from her stiffness, but not lapsing back into the old "Lilith" manner. So damn thoughtful of them to go to all the bother of saying things aloud for my benefit.

"Ruth," her voice was quiet, tinged again with a faint overtone of apology, "Jason's talking about what I was saying before, about this matrix being different from the one on Poindros, and from what I conclude, the one reawakened on Andura when you were there. The basic directives are the same, of course, since they were also generated by the Poindros Founder, but here they've been implemented in a less extreme manner. The Founder established the core of this system before he created the Poindran matrix and invested it with his own awareness, even though this system was only activated much more recently. Jason and I feel that the Founder's slide into psychosis was only starting when he formulated his plan here and left this matrix structure for a backup. The incorporeals aren't evil, Ruth—of course you know that— but only twisted by the parameters of the sick perceptions and directives of their system."

Jason broke in, "It's true, Ruth. Look at the way the matrix reacted to the alien signal. Trapped in the paranoid mindset of the Founder, the incorporeals can only interpret an alien presence as a threat or an opportunity for extending their control. Now, if we could reach the level of directives, we might be able to preserve the complex awareness here and help it shed its voracious aspects."

I shook my head. "Are you crazy? Is that what you two are up to? It can't work, Jason! We've been trying all this time to reach the directive level of the cybers, and haven't succeeded, so what makes you think you'd succeed here? The spooks would take you over, just like they've got David and Siolis right now. It's too dangerous. We ought to just shut them down now, while we still can."

"But Ruth, we can't do that." Lilith shook her head. "Anyway, it would be murder—destroying an awareness just because it's different from yours." Her voice had picked up more inflection. "And what about darling David? Are you totally inhuman, considering killing your own nephew?" Shocked mood intonations quivered in her voice.

"Don't try your manipulative games on me, you pig! You don't even know what human is anymore. What's stopping you, why don't you go ahead with your 'evolution,' get rid of that machine body and merge with the spooks if you think they're so wonderful? I've seen what they can do, what you did for them, and you can stand there and tell me how I should be like the cybers and Heal everyone into peace and light! You make me sick."

Lilith stepped back from me, face swiveling toward Jason, her eyes going flat and sparking a glint of amber through the blue glass.

"She's only upset, Lilith. She's been through a lot."

"I'll get to work. Perhaps she'll be more rational if I'm not present." Lilith pivoted and paced smoothly out the door.

"Damn her! So now I'm only a poor, irrational human, huh?"

Jason's face remained remote and noncommittal. "Give her a chance, Ruth. What she's saying makes sense."

"So you're on her side. Why bother even discussing it with me?"

"I returned the null transmitter to you, Ruth. I trust you to know when and if to use it. Now come." He turned toward the exit. "We have something else to do."

I stared after him with my jaw hanging open as the impact of what he'd left in my hands hit me. I snapped it shut and followed him, shaking my head.

He didn't speak as we rode down the anti-grav chute and threaded a maze of corridors, circles of light springing up before us and dying behind at his remote command, I supposed, illuminating his seamlessly expressionless face. He turned suddenly to the left, a door whisking open before him as greenish light spilled over his shoulders.

"There's someone I want you to meet. He'll help us get the work done here." He moved jerkily through the opening and stood back against the wall of the lab, stiff and blank-faced, eyes glinting sharp sparks of amber.

"Jason, what—?"

"Ruth?"

I whirled around at the familiar voice behind me, a cold sinking in my belly as my gaze flashed over the empty cloning tube. The slender man walking a little unsteadily toward me in loose coveralls had a pale, freshly shaven, baby-smooth face and long hair.

But he had Jason's wide cheekbones and gold-flecked brown eyes.

"Ruth, it's me, Jason. Really me. I remember everything—Poindros and Andura—but I'm a little confused about getting here. I hope it's not a terrible shock for you, but I'm happy it's happened. Founders, I've missed you." He hesitated before me, holding out one big hand.

I looked behind me at the blank, tawny-tinted construct of Jason's face with its unblinking amber cyborg eyes. I looked back at the pale stranger holding out his hand in appeal—at the new face whose every contour and expression I knew better than my own—and sat abruptly on the floor, shaking my head.

fourteen

The sea hissed and shushed through the rock cavern, a monotonous accompaniment to the blinking console lights and the pale wash of green illuminating David's vat. I wished my thoughts could empty into that smooth, rhythmic ebb and flow, but they insisted on spinning futile loops of worry, weariness, wariness. I closed my eyes for a second, then ducked my head away from the kid's pathetic shape dangling in its fluid. I reached into the close-woven net where the mechmen had crammed David's gear from the dome.

Footsteps approached from the console bank, coveralled legs planting themselves in front of me. "Why don't you let me help with that?" Voice low and unemphatic.

I still had to steel myself to look at him. I raised my eyes to see the Jason clone giving me a too-familiar, wry little smile. "All right."

He squatted beside me with Jason's usual economy of motion, brushing his long hair behind his ears. He reached into the netting to extract a storage carton, opening it and laying out the jumble of tools and parts beside the others I was sorting on the spread drop cloths, more for something to do than anything else. He mercifully didn't try to make conversation, simply working beside me with a quietly absorbed expression on his smooth, pale face. I looked away from the big, familiar hands capably testing and grouping electronic gauges, the skin of the strong fingers jarringly baby-soft and uncalloused.

"This probably needs to be lubed and adjusted." He reached past me to grasp a squat signal converter, fumbling as he pulled the heavy box toward him and dropped it. "Ouch! Damn." He shook off drops of blood swelling from his nicked thumb, then sat back on his heels and looked down at the cut with mild surprise.

I stared at the welling blood, ridiculously disturbed. Of course he'd bleed and hurt. Even Jason, playing his role of pateros back on the farm, had faked bleeding from his head "wound" when Aaron had pushed him from the windtower.

Beside me, the clone sucked his cut and shrugged. "My reflexes

182

and muscle tone are still a little off, I guess.'' He reached carefully for the box again, hefted it with a little grunt, and sat back to remove its casing. ''Pass me that silicone spray?''

I passed it over, then returned to untangling a snarl of clipped leads.

''You know, David's gotten into some pretty high-powered work with Siolis. I can't follow some of the data loops he recorded, but I'm proud of him.''

I couldn't help glancing once more at David's vat, before meeting the clone's eyes. ''Lot of good it's done him. Maybe I should have left him on Andura with Ja—''

He flinched, lowering his eyes and retreating into an expressionless reserve that wrenchingly recalled my homecoming family photograph.

I swore under my breath. ''I'm sorry. I know you've got his memories, that you feel like you're Jason, but I just can't call you that.'' Jason, Clone A. ''All right if I call you Jay?''

''All right.'' He shrugged. ''I guess we both need time to get used to me. I keep running into gaps, data I should have access to that aren't there anymore. Without the cybernetic processors . . . .'' He shook his head. ''Maybe I'm feeling a little inadequate here.'' He made an offhand gesture toward the console bank, but his face betrayed him, flushing painful red as he ducked his head over his work. The same awkward flush Jason, my reluctant new pateros, had suffered.

''Hell,'' I muttered, jerking to my feet and pacing across the floor and back. ''This is impossible, he should never—'' I broke off, stopping beside him to gingerly touch his shoulder. ''Jay, look, I'm sorry. But I can't just . . .''

He nodded quickly without looking up. ''I know.'' Voice carefully neutral.

I opened my mouth, closed it, turned with relief as the entrance door suddenly slid open. ''Jason. Did you get anywhere?''

He and Lilith strode with uncannily synchronized smoothness into the cavern. Lilith gave me a look, face blank, and moved over to the console bank, its indicators reconfiguring as she stood there.

Jason stopped stiffly before me. ''I'm afraid we've been unable to accomplish much. The matrix is guarded by an independent security system in the main control center, and it has begun to query data and time-lapse inconsistencies, quite minimal at this point, but which might lead to recognition of our data manipulations. The security is tightening and mechman activity accelerating. Lilith and I agree it's too risky to remain within the facility. There are different approaches we could implement from the remote center at the landing field. Gather anything you want to take." His voice and face betrayed no emotion as he turned to join Lilith at the consoles.

"But we can't leave David here!"

No response.

The clone—Jay—strode past me to grasp Jason's arm. "Before we go, I've found some interesting data entries among David's shunting recorders. I can't analyze them. I think you should take a look."

"Bring them along." Jason turned from the console, and the two identical faces—one tawny and blank-featured, the other pale and tense—confronted each other.

I shuddered. "Damn it, Jason, you can't just—"

"Ruth?"

"Ruth?"

They turned together with the same inquiring tilt to their heads.

I turned hastily away to jab my hand toward David's drifting form. "Blast it, Jason, don't you care what they're doing to him?"

Slow footsteps passed behind me as Jay, avoiding my eyes, moved back to gather up David's equipment and repack it. I turned around to glare at Jason.

His eyes flared amber. "We are doing all we can for David and for everyone else. There is nothing you can do here to help him. Please get ready to leave immediately."

I took a step closer. "Would you drop that bloody mechman act for a minute? *Talk* to me, Jason."

Not a glimmer in the inhumanly bright eyes. "There is no time for idle discussions. Lilith and I must prepare a receptor channel before we leave the facility."

Lilith turned toward him from the console, her eyes flaring their own amber sparks. They faded back to blue as she glanced at me before rejoining him in front of the dancing bank of indicators. Somehow her glass eyes and flawless blank face managed to look infuriatingly smug.

It was drizzling. It made a nice break from rain. The glistening landing field reflected the flat gray canopy of cloud swallowing the tips of two shuttles now. Dull, sourceless daylight merged at the horizon with a sea just as flat and gray, fretting listlessly at wet black rock.

I shook myself out of a blank stare and took in a deep breath of the heavy, metallic air, turning to plod back toward the equipment dome.

Jay, stripped down to his skivvies, was doing pushups in the drizzle outside the shelter entrance. He was a little thinner than Jason's strong lankiness, but the electric stim in the vat had produced a decent, lean musculature. I noticed that even Cyvrus' minimal daylight seemed to have touched his virgin-pale skin with a hint of color. He sprang to his feet, face flushed, strands of his long, light brown hair escaping from a band to plaster wet against his face. The strands were darker than Jason's perpetually "sun-streaked" hair.

He stretched, breathing hard and shaking off raindrops. "A ways to go before I'm in shape again. Ready to get back at it?"

"Sure." I shrugged. "Guess busy work's better than nothing."

His lips quirked into a brief, teasing smile, almost not catching me off guard. "Bound and determined, hmm?" He brushed a dangling strand back from his face and wiped his forehead with the back of his arm.

I ignored the jab. "Want me to cut your hair for you?"

He shook his head. "I kind of like it long, something new for me. And my beard's really coming in now—must've been the last thing to develop in the vat. Maybe I'll let it grow." His eyes held mine as he deliberately rubbed the shadow of stubble on his chin.

I brushed past him into the dome, trying to ignore an unsettling pang as my nostrils caught the spicy tang of his sweat—almost, but not quite, the same as Jason's synthesized scent. I strode blindly past a row of consoles toward the half-assembled parts of communication interfaces we were assembling.

His hand on my arm stopped me. "I'm sorry. I don't have any business making it harder on you." He shrugged awkwardly, wiping his face with a towel. "Guess I just wanted to get some kind of rise out of you. Can't go on sealing yourself off, hurting and not admitting it. Can't we at least be friends? *I* could use one. And I can't pretend we're strangers." He raised his hands and then dropped them, waiting.

I bit my lip, then nodded. "You've got a deal." I stuck out my hand for the hokey old Poindran shake.

He looked surprised, then flashed a quick grin. "Okay." He

gave my hand a firm squeeze, brown eyes steady on mine.

"Okay, well, let's get to it." I turned hastily, almost tripping over Lilith's feet. I jerked back and Jay reached out to steady me.

"She's still . . . sleeping?" I looked down at Lilith, stiff and motionless on a stool, staring straight ahead. Back on Andura, Jason had explained that cyborgs needed dreamtime just like other humans, to keep their organic brains and nerve stems healthy. A couple hours a day was enough for them, though. I looked away from Lilith's blank glass eyes. "You'd think she could at least close her eyes, for Founder's sake."

Jay shrugged and stepped past me. "I don't think Jason's taken any rest since he's arrived. He's pushing himself too hard, but he just gave me the cold shoulder when I tried to tell him." He plucked his coverall off some cartons and pulled it on, sitting on the floor and picking up the component he'd been assembling.

I started to sit down among my scatter of parts for cleaning and lubrication, then turned and marched over to the flickering lights splashing over the shelter's curved wall. Jason stood motionless, eyes blazing amber to match the indicators dancing over the console he was linked to.

I grabbed his arm and shook it. "Jason, snap out of it! We've got to talk. Jason!"

The console lights flashed again, then dimmed to a steady blue pulse. Jason's eyes faded to gold-flecked brown and he slowly turned to face me. "What is it, Ruth? Has something happened?"

"Nothing's happened, and nothing's going to happen if you don't give yourself a break. You know you need some down-time. I don't know what in hell you're trying to prove, but it's not going to help anybody if you collapse on us. Go wake up that lazy pillow-hog Lilith and make her take over so you can get some shut-eye."

His lips twitched, some kind of expression flickering across his face before it went neutral again. His voice had some inflection when he said after a pause, "Eminently logical, Ruth. I wouldn't dare try to argue." He nudged me gently aside and headed over toward Lilith as I stood staring after him, deflated into silence, which was no doubt what he intended.

There was a low chuckle behind me. I spun around to see Jay covering his mouth with his hand. Glaring at him, I plunked myself down beside the scattered parts and the vise I'd rigged to hold pieces for working. He studiously resumed his work, keeping a straight face.

I gritted my teeth and grabbed up a hopelessly corroded, warped gear from the pile, smashing it flat in the vise and attacking it with vicious strokes of a wire brush.

The rebuilt signal interfaces with one-way stepdown transformers were ready, and Jay and I were testing them when Jason emerged from another of his trancelike links with the consoles. He stepped past Lilith's absorption in the flickering indicators and stood watching as we finished activating one unit.

"They're operable? They should help us increase our probe intensity while avoiding a return query strong enough to challenge our system."

I sat back on my heels and rubbed my hand grittily over my face. "You're welcome."

He only gave me his blank mechman look. Jay snapped off his test meter and stood, watching Jason with an odd expression— one like maybe you'd get if you looked into a mirror and saw somebody you didn't recognize.

And he was right, this wasn't Jason. What was going on behind that blank mask? I stood and said quietly, "Jason, I haven't had a chance to ask you about Andura. How's Li-Nahi?"

His face swiveled to mine, eyes dimming to brown-gold, then flaring back to amber. "It would save time if you'd ask—"

"He's fine, Ruth." Jay turned with the same movement. "He wanted me to tell you—" He broke off, the painful red burning his face as he ducked it and squatted quickly before his meters.

Damn. I turned angrily to Jason, but he was already moving away with a wooden, "Please finish your testing. I will assist Lilith in current loop closure, so that we can install the units."

I bit back a furious outburst, putting my back to him to crouch beside Jay. "I wasn't thinking, Jay. I would like to know about the kid, and Raul and the others. Are the we-Children actually taking to the Resistance?"

Jay finished activating sensors on the second unit before meeting my eyes. Then he gave me his slow smile. "Not without their own peculiar notions of 'taking action,' I can tell you. But they really rallied around the new Mother Tree and replanting the forest area Heinck had destroyed. And they're quick with the cybernetics—very logical. Maybe it's their binary orientation, I guess it shouldn't have surprised me. Ki-Linat's been a big help. So's Raul, especially with bringing around the borderline members of Heinck's band."

"That's good."

He triggered a final test sequence. "Raul said, 'Be telling tika she sharp wench, but that wild card slippery play.'"

I shook my head. "Knowing Raul, that's not all he said."

"Oh, and he said—" Jay broke off, then shrugged. "Well, you can imagine it was colorful."

"I can imagine." I laughed, though tears prickled my eyes.

"Li-Nahi said you should come back, and something about it not being good to go too long without seeing from the high branch."

The tears brimmed, and I wiped them quickly as he made another instrument calibration. "He's growing up fast, then."

Jay pivoted back toward me on his heels. "Well, not too fast." Voice dry. "He gave me a message for David, too—reckon it had something to do with his performance tree-climbing with the native kids. 'Buzz-brain still loses lunch?'"

I laughed, losing my balance on my heels and sitting back on the floor, laughing harder.

Jay's smile split into a broad grin. Just like Jason's, only Jay's crooked teeth hadn't been corrected into the perfect cyborg smile.

My laughter went flat.

The grin faded, shading into disappointment as his eyes searched my face and then dropped. He turned quickly back to the instruments. "Well, that's it, I guess."

I gathered myself off the floor, touching his shoulder. "Thanks for telling me, Jay."

He nodded, carefully detaching the instrument leads. "Better tell them the units are ready."

I straightened, wincing as another phantom pain lanced upward from my missing arm. There wouldn't be any more tree-climbing with Li-Nahi. I rubbed my shoulder above the stump as the hot prickling subsided, heading around the storage cartons to get Jason and Lilith. Jason stood alone beside the console, its indicators on steady standby.

"Your interfaces are ready."

"You can help us install them, then." His voice was still toneless. "But first, Lilith has something for you."

Lilith moved smoothly out from the dimness behind the console bank, carrying some sort of alloy equipment. "I've put this together for you, Ruth. Of course it's crude, only a spare mechman part I've modified, but with this remote activator you can wear like David's portable interface, you'll be able to trigger several functions.''

She stepped past Jason, bringing what she was carrying into the light. Reflections of the colored console indicators glinted across the polished alloy mech arm with its four jointed digits.

She smiled, eyes gentle blue, stepping closer and holding it out. "Please take it. A peace offering?" Her voice was softly lilting. "It's silly to keep making do without, Ruth. Of course, it's only until you can get a decent prosthesis and proper nerve grafting, but at least you'll be functional.''

She held up a curved gray device in her other hand. "This is the activator, it will pick up some command signals strapped to your shoulder. Here, I'll show you what the arm can do." Her eyes flared amber and the mechanical arm bent in her grasp, alloy fingers spreading and plucking the air, wrist swiveling in a complete circle. "It's got a superior grip strength to your natural one." She smiled gently. "Shall I attach it for you?''

I backed up a step, shaking my head, staring with fascinated revulsion at the still wriggling jointed fingers.

"Why, Ruth, I believe you're actually afraid of it! Don't be silly, dear, once you get the hang of it you'll see—''

"That's enough, Lilith." Jason, face still blank, took the device from her hand and it stopped moving. He held it up. "Do you want it, Ruth?''

I shook my head dumbly, nightmare images tumbling over me— Jason stepping from the flames to rip away my rotted flesh and snap his gleaming alloy arm onto my shoulder as I turned to stare into the mirror at my cold, metallic image. I took another step back, clearing my throat. "Put it away. I don't want it.''

Jason turned woodenly to set it on top of the crates.

"But, Ruth, it's for your own good!" Lilith pressed closer to me, eyes glinting.

"Lay off. I said I don't want it." I forced a brusque, "Thanks anyway." For my own good, just like the cybers and the incorporeals always said. And did she really think I'd accept a limb she could remotely control? I shook my head. Anyway, that was a good enough reason to refuse it.

Jason stepped up beside her. "Ruth, it's here if you change your mind. We must install the interfaces now, so Lilith and I can make another matrix penetration attempt.''

Lilith stepped back from me to face him, their eyes fixing on each other's and sparking amber in their interface. Their eyes faded to brown and blue again, and Lilith gave me another of her thinly masked smug looks.

Jay moved up behind me, clearing his throat. "Before we go any farther, I think Ruth and I are entitled to know what's going on. Are you making any progress toward breaking through?"

Lilith answered shortly, "We're doing the best we can, but naturally the facility can sustain a more concentrated array than we can. Their security has multiple intersecting loops, constantly transmuting to randomly generated variables, which must be continually matched and recalculated as we make our penetration attempts."

Jason interpreted, "We're encountering problems. The security is very sophisticated, at times almost anticipating our attempts on different data gates, although what we've retrieved indicates we've succeeded in preventing the incorporeals from being alerted so far to our attempts. We have to move very carefully. We're going to try a new approach now, attempting to reach Siolis or David through their mutual linkage to the physical interfaces the incorporeals are using."

"Do you think it'll work?"

"The probability figures wouldn't tell you much, Ruth. There is a fair chance we will succeed."

"Jason, since things are getting a little iffy, don't you think it's time we sent some kind of warning to CI?"

"That would needlessly jeopardize your position and that of the other Resistance members. Open signal channels from the shuttles are always available, in fact I've already issued Central Interlock an innocuous 'report' from you. It's much too early to fall back on last resorts, Ruth."

Did I imagine an emphasis on those last words, reminding me I still had the null generator? Or reminding me that he and Lilith with their souped-up data processors were above my ignorant dithering? His blank face gave me no clue.

"Well, if you're trying to reach Siolis, it might help if you knew what happened between the Cyvriots and me. I think I finally started to understand their communication system a little, and—"

"I have all the pertinent data, Ruth. Your experiences in the sea environment aren't relevant to the current situation, as Siolis is now linked neurally with the matrix. We need to install the signal interfaces now. Priorities."

He brushed rudely past Jay as his clone shook his head in disbelief.

"Blast it, Jason, will you get real?" I yelled after him. "All right, you don't have to pretend you're so low as to have human feelings, but at least you could keep an open bloody mind!"

Lilith swept past me as if I didn't exist, following Jason. Moving in their smooth synchronization, they plucked up the heavy communication units and carried them past us to the consoles, their seamless blank faces apparently oblivious to anything but their own damnable "priorities."

The sea snarled and foamed over the rocks, wind stirring up a chop and flinging spray to join the driving rain stinging my face. I welcomed the lowering dark and the violent storm, leaning into the lashing gusts, striding and scrambling among the tumbled stone. I closed my eyes and let the drops pelt me, yearning for the clean, honed essence of the rocks as they faced the onslaught of wind and sea with simple solidity.

I shook my head sharply. I wanted my anger, needed its hot spur now.

"Ruth!" The voice was faint, almost swallowed by the gusts.

I turned, scraping whipping wet strands from my face, to see Jay waving an arm through the dimness. I waved back, picking my way toward the shelter, pushed by the drenching wind.

He squinted into the drops, shouting as I approached. "You can't stay out here all night! Come on."

I stopped beside him, catching my breath and raising my voice. "Are they still at it?"

He took my arm and turned me back toward the light burning at the dome entrance. "Still linked into the consoles."

"Good. I don't want them trying to stop me."

He groaned. "Ruth, what are you up to this time? Come on, let's get inside where we can talk." He tugged my arm.

"No, wait. Even if they're linked in, they still might be monitoring us. We've got to talk out here."

"At least get in here, then." He turned his back to the wind and opened his rain poncho, pulling it up to tent over his head and drawing me under its cover, tucking me under his arm as he wrapped it around us. "You'll make yourself sick, drenched like that."

I suppressed a qualm, leaning against his dry warmth. "Thanks. Look, Jay, I don't know what's going on with those two. I don't trust Lilith as far as I could throw her. I don't know what's gotten into Jason, but it's starting to make me nervous."

I couldn't see his face in our dim huddle, but I could almost feel his calm, considering look. "It's bothering me, too. I can't understand why he'd start acting this way, it's not like him—me—us." He shook his head in frustration. "He's under pressure, of course, and maybe he just doesn't want to worry us with the details. I can't say what he's feeling now—he only gave me his memories up to the point of leaving Andura to come here. Maybe something happened on the way. I don't know. But I know if all this is as hard on him as it is on me, he's not having the easiest time of it." His voice had picked up a rough edge.

I closed my eyes, inhaling his warm scent, wishing I could give in to the urge to nestle into his arms, give him the comfort and intimacy we both craved. But I couldn't. It wouldn't be fair. We were both too mixed up.

I cleared my throat, keeping my voice matter-of-fact. "I'm afraid Lilith might be influencing him through their damn interfaces. Maybe she's stronger than he thought. Or maybe they're both just carried away with their superiority, and who knows what they're really planning?"

"It's that old serpent rearing its head, Ruth?" Jay sounded tired, and too much like the old Jason in the dark. "You've never gotten over fearing the cyborg part of me, have you?"

I ignored the pronoun. "But isn't it at least partly true? He told me on Andura that sometimes he wondered if he was still human, he could move on such different levels. What if they've gotten to the point where normal humans *do* seem petty and irrelevant?"

He sighed. "I don't have any easy answers, Ruth. I just know we—he wouldn't betray you."

"But he could be making mistakes, like anybody else! I don't know about you, but I'm not going to just sit here and wait it out. If push comes to shove, I'll shut down the facility and the spooks. But I'm going to try one more time to reach Siolis and David in the matrix. I think I can get through to the natives now. Maybe if they really understood, they'd help me contact Siolis. I'm sure they could do it."

"But . . . how do you think you could shut down the facility, when Lilith said she couldn't? Am I missing something?" Then with a painfully wry note, "I guess I'm a little slow, compared with what you're used to. You'll have to explain."

Double damn. "Jay, I can't tell you. . . ."

"I see," his voice flat. His arm stiffened across my shoulder.

I chewed on my lip, then took a deep breath. Hell, what was one more gamble? "All right. Lilith doesn't know I got it back, but I have a null-field transmitter that could wipe out the matrix. The only problem is, we've got to get David and Siolis out first. That's why I'm going back underwater, to try to get in touch with the natives. You'll have to be my backup here, cover for me, and not let Lilith know. Or Jason."

Silence for a minute. Then, unsteadily, "Thanks for trusting me, Ruth." He cleared his throat, then continued briskly. " I'll go with you. David had two sets of those osmotic pumps, right?"

I shook my head against his shoulder. "No. No sense you going out on a limb, too."

"I'm going. No use arguing. Now let's get the gear together before they come out of it." His arm quickly tightened around me, then he swept open the poncho to a gust of damp coolness. "Look, wind's dying down. That's a good sign." His big hand closed over mine and we were sprinting for the dome and the diving gear.

fifteen

The wind and driving rain had subsided, clouds dropping lower to wrap the night in thick darkness. Our headlamps cut narrow, dancing swaths through drizzle pockmarking the low swells rolling in to hiss over the rocky shore.

Ahead of me, Jay's dim bulk, blacker against the dark sea, waited. Slipping on the shifting cobble, I caught myself against a wet boulder and paused for a deep breath. One of my last for a while. I touched the osmotic pump strapped around my waist and couldn't help shuddering at the visceral memory of Jay inserting the vein and artery valves at my hips. But of course David was right, it was a much more manageable setup than my awkward breathing wings had been. I suppressed my qualms and moved carefully toward the water, my beam catching Jay in David's insulation suit stretched to the skintight maximum.

He squinted against the light, and I tilted it to take the glare off him. "All set?"

He tied the cords of our mesh supply bag around his waist, fumbling with shaking hands. "Sure." He looked out over the swirling dark sea and cleared his throat. "Think maybe we should go over those hand signals again first?"

"Sure," I said gently. We quickly reviewed the simple signals we'd agreed on.

He nodded, taking a deep breath. "All right, guess we better get to it." His voice was still unsteady.

"Take it easy, don't try to push too hard until you get used to it." I touched his arm, hesitated, then pulled the null generator from my thigh pocket and showed him how to set the controls. "You'd better keep it, you've got two hands to use it if you have to." When he started to protest, I cut him off. "You'll be my backup, Jay, in case the sendings are too strong for me. Sometimes they can knock me out. Here, can you help me get this fin on? I'll go in first and wait for you."

He nodded wordlessly, slipping the null device into his sealed pocket, the whites of his eyes glinting in the dimness. I squeezed his arm and sat at the edge of the sucking waves, steadying myself

194

against a rock as he worked the single large fin over my feet and adjusted it for me. I gave him the thumbs-up and scooted backward into the slap of the swell, grateful the chop had died down. A last deep breath, and I found the nose clip on its cord around my neck, snapping it on to tightly seal my nostrils. Undulating my legs together, I kicked out between and over submerged rocks, bobbing in the swell to beckon Jay after me.

My light caught his grim face as he sat to slip on his fin. He placed his nose clip, took a deep breath, and launched himself after me.

Clamping my lips and jaw until they hurt, dreading the return to the dark sea, lungs already screaming David's contraption couldn't work, I submerged. Catching Jay's arm as he flailed past, I kicked down and tugged him after me. The waves closed around us, surge catching and sweeping us back toward the rocks. Jay tumbled against me, hands grabbing out of the darkness. I blindly grasped his arm, kicking and driving us deeper, out of the currents. Vague shapes rushed past in the glittering spill of our light beams, a pale fish darting away, slippery weeds splatting over my face and gone. We dropped deeper, into dense black and stillness.

I started to loosen my grip on Jay's arm, and he flailed around, clutching me, kicking convulsively for the surface. My light caught him as he started to open his mouth, air bubbles escaping. I slapped my hand over his mouth, holding it closed as he thrashed against me, eyes wide with the horror of suffocation. And I felt I was drowning, too, my lungs crushed with the pressure of depth and burning for air.

Only they weren't, I realized with a sudden jolt. There was a low hum of the pump at my waist, kicked up into high gear with my exertions, but I really didn't need the breath my reflexes were clamoring to suck in. Fighting the stubborn habit to gasp air into my lungs, I wrapped my legs around Jay and clung as he thrashed his way to his own realization.

Finally he blinked into my light, still dazed but calmer, his hands no longer clawing the black water. They slowly eased my hand from his mouth. He shook his head, blinked again, and made an apologetic motion with his arms that sent him into another drifting tumble. This time he managed to right himself and fin awkwardly back to me.

I gripped his shoulder and smiled into the dazzle of his headlight, nodding approval. When I held up my hand in our *OK?* signal, he answered it *OK*, kicking around in the same nervous circle I'd

first made in the sea, his narrow beam swallowed by the engulfing
darkness.

I took his hand and drew him with me, out farther and deeper,
away from shore, getting the knack of the undulating movement
with the single fin. He picked it up quickly, driving himself ahead
with a sudden thrust of his long legs, our linked hands catching
him up short. His grip remained locked on mine.

As we dropped deeper, my goggles began to cut painfully into
the skin around my eyes. Making a high-pitched sound in my
throat, I finally caught Jay's attention, and he reluctantly released
my hand, hovering close.

I raised my hand to one of the silly-looking rubber bulbs built
into each side of the diving goggles, finally realizing what they
were for. A couple of squeezes, and air pressure equalized inside
the goggles.

After Jay had followed suit, I checked our gear and gauges.
Everything seemed to be working fine. I made sure the tiny backup
air cylinders were still secure on our belts, for use in case the
compressed air in our lungs accidentally escaped and couldn't
reinflate our lungs on surfacing. It still felt fundamentally wrong
to be floating deep in the sea and not breathing, but the reflexive
urge to gasp had faded.

Jay activated the instrument cuff I'd transferred to his suit, going
through the same awkward directional calibration I'd first learned.
We'd decided to head toward the closest bathylabra and hope to
make contact with natives once we'd put some distance between
us and the facility island. I steadied him as he drifted, peering
over his shoulder as he gripped the elbow of his outstretched arm
and the red arrow locked onto target.

We kicked out into the blackness over a deep trench, our big
single fins driving us in a smooth, hypnotic rhythm. An occasional
shadow darted into and out of our narrow light beams, distant
mutterings and groans echoing faintly out of the deeps to lap over
and through me. I didn't have to look at Jay's red arrow to follow
a vague pull onward. *Deep calleth unto deep*.

I pulled up short, giving myself a shake and tugging Jay's fin
as he kicked on. He drifted back to me, shaking out his arms in
the swerve of my beam and lifting his shoulders in question. I
held up my hand in a "wait" motion, closed my eyes and started
to take a deep breath, checked myself, then made myself go limp,
listening to the sea.

Diffuse moans, clicks, and watery squeals ebbed and flowed

around me, deeper sounds past hearing shivering through my bones. I groped inwardly, pushing past reluctance, past fear, nudging open a crack in that elusive gate. I tried to let unseen images, unheard voices, unfelt touches flow in, but there was only vague incoherency. I tried to send out a plea, a warning, but there was no response.

I blinked and shook my head. We'd have to get closer. As I gestured toward Jay's instrument cuff, my lume caught his pale, apprehensive face glancing down into the abyss swallowing his light. His shrug was more a shudder as he raised his arms again and kicked on with the red arrow. The familiar, claustrophobic dread closed around me, too, as I followed him, back prickling. I gritted my teeth and forced my defenses open to the sea and its lapping presences.

The hypnotic beat drew me on, pulse pounding in my ears. Undulating strokes of legs and torso flowed into its rhythm. Dark shapes swaying, ghost fingers beckoning, tapping inside the drum of my skin, ringing its beat in my head, colors dancing in the blackness—

I caught myself up short again, fighting the urge to gasp, to recoil from the path of the sending pulsing through the sea, surging through my bones and nerves and tumbling me in its flow. I slowly unclenched my fist, closing my eyes and forcing my doors open to the pounding waves.

Vague shapes slithered into being, dim bulky forms—no, clear now, natives swimming a tight weaving mesh through the cool blue glint of a bathylabra, rolling closer, violet-plumed fish darting, huge dark eyes and blue slippery flesh, long tails whipping, closing looping coils around me. I jolted back, and the images shattered into a sickening plummet of chaotic sensation—musky tastes, shrill noise, hot and cold, pain—as I started to flail in alarm. Something caught me, a solidity inside me, and I grasped it, hauling myself inside-out through an odd turning. . . .

And I could see/feel/hear now, through a vague murkiness, the kindred gathering. I could sense their unease, an unfamiliar worry, a jarring vibrato in the smooth harmony of the Way. Abrupt flashing image of a cyber console dancing reflected lights in a watery dome. Confusion, distress, commands striking up ripples breaking the smooth pulse of the cycling ebb and flow. A dizzy echoing image of myself seen from a wavering distance, vision wrenched outward and turned back in, the form alien. The landers being thrust away from the sea, from the world—rolling vision of metal needles launching them away. The console again, lights pulsing, flashing insistently, unintelligible voices shrilling from it with impossible questions, Rules, changing voices, changing truths, no, something else—

I couldn't grasp it, the waves pummeling me with disjointed sensation and flashing colors, spinning shapes, but then another clear moment when I was filled with a quivering agony of unfamiliar doubt, confusion, questioning. Disruption, disruption.

Then it was gone, snapped off like a switch as I drifted and the dark sea swept through me with cool blankness. I was blinking, peering around me in the night for Jay, when a wave of light surged out of nowhere, crashing over me in a spill of brightness to spin me in its boiling plunge.

Again I scrambled for balance, but the river of sparkling colors lifted me in its rippling flow, and suddenly I didn't have to fight it. This was different from the sendings, but I didn't know how. Its waters bubbled with wild vitality, tossing me, spinning me in the effervescence as laughter tingled through my veins in instant giddy drunkenness. A flicker of alarm—*disruption, invasion, violation*—was swept away. The torrent whirled me in a dizzy dance and spat me out into the dark sea.

I drifted, numb, blinking, lifting my hand into the beam of my lume to be sure I was solid. I was still shaking. Then I realized that Jay was shaking me, grasping my shoulder and peering down with a dazzle of light into my face.

I pushed him feebly back, shaking my head slowly. Disruption. It had to have been the alien signal, breaking up the native sending with its own . . . Adept. And the natives were upset. About the signal? But it hadn't seemed so awful to me, just overwhelming, like the giddy whirl of the windtower wings when you rode them, or a wild race through the Matrix game. My heart surged in deep, strong beats, blood singing. A truly alien contact, Siolis was right, it was extraordinary, offering the excitement of change and challenge we'd blindly groped for with our Resistance. And somehow I was filled with an obscure conviction that we could understand the message if we could learn to ride that wild tumble of energy, drink in the giddy effervescence. . . .

I blinked again, shaking my head sharply this time. It throbbed like an instant hangover. I frowned, pressing my fingers against the pulsing ache, grimacing as the wild fantasies faded into confusion. The alien signal—the Adept—had to somehow act on the nervous system. I felt like the morning after a liter of champagne,

only I'd been hit over the head with the bottle instead of drinking
it.

I winced as Jay flashed his lume close over his hand making
the *OK?* query. I nodded, repeating the query to him. He shrugged
and made a face, pointing at his ear. I didn't know if he'd felt
the same thing I had. But we had to get to a bathylabra and find
the natives. I was sure the turmoil I'd felt in their sending had to
do with more than the alien signal. Those images of the console—
were the incorporeals spreading out through the network already?

Finning back farther from the place where I thought we'd in-
tersected the sending beam, I again motioned Jay to wait. We had
to get some help. And now I knew I could call it.

Once more I closed my eyes, letting the cool darkness flow
over and inside me, listening to the deep mutters shivering through
me. The wash of half-heard sounds began to sift into separate
sources and distances, different sensations and presences reaching
thin fingers to grope along my nerves, the touch of deep swimming
awarenesses almost as alien as the signal from another galaxy.
My bones hummed with silent echoes.

I groped inwardly for a nebulous key. Slowly, painfully, it
unlocked one by one the shackles of safety, privacy, ingrained
revulsion, fear. As each layer peeled away, the humming core of
me opened and expanded, flowing outward to join the vast ebb
and surge of the night sea. When I was one with it, absorbed and
absorbing, I let my pain and confusion, the old and the new, mine
and the Cyvriots from their sending, pour out. I was the image,
the sending, of a child lost. Crying for rejoining in the dark sea.

Time was suspended with me. It could have been immediately
or hours later that I felt something cold and slippery brush me and
recede, leaving a swirl of water in its wake. I jerked back, flailing
off balance.

My eyes flew open on a dazzle of disorienting light. Without
thought, my hand shot out and snapped off Jay's headlamp. I
propelled myself around, catching a glimpse of his anxious face
and the sweep of huge, undulating black wings dipping down on
us. I snapped off my own light and groped for Jay's hand, squeezing it as I felt him shiver.

Poor Jay. I'd tried to prepare him, but he was getting all the
shocks of this strange environment in one fell swoop.

He gripped my hand painfully in the darkness, but didn't try to
switch his lamp back on. I couldn't see the return of the huge
demon-fish, yet somehow I could sense its shape. It swept over-

head, then came up from below to hover beneath us. My grip tightened on Jay's hand, pulling him closer to the creature. He started to pull back, then shuddered and followed me, grasping as I guided his hand to one of the thick, rolled "horns." I groped for the other one, fingers fumbling over slippery, rubbery flesh as the demon-fish launched slowly forward. It picked up speed, plunging with us into the depths as Jay's arm came around me and anchored me firmly beside him.

A vague purple dawn seeped down from the surface as the demon-fish finally soared out of the depths. It swept us in a long curve past the dim bulk of a rock plateau, slowing in the open waters of another trench. The rippling wings brought us closer to a dim, moving mass in the violet murk ten to twenty meters below the surface.

Jay's arm tightened around my shoulders as I squinted over the creature's horns, making out what looked like a twisting ball of shadow, a coil of writhing snakes. We veered to one side, and a shiver of sendings lapped through me—rippling blue light, the kindred, disruption, alarm—and faded as the demon-fish swooped out of the path of the Adept and brought us around to a scatter of idly swimming Cyvriot children. Beyond them, the dimly heaving shape resolved into a tight knot of adults swimming their inter-woven dance of listening.

Big wings undulated in a hover as the children darted over to curiously circle us, the tickling pressure of their soundings—like the Adept sendings, but not like them—humming through me. Jay's eyes behind the goggles were even bigger than the magni-fication of the curved lenses could account for. I squeezed his shoulder and eased out from under his arm, absently patting the rubbery back of the demon-fish as I finned away from it, moving cautiously closer to the adults.

A small, tapered form shot past me—one of the children, launching herself—how did I know she was a girl? but I did—at the churning froth of sea, Cyvriots, and red-violet-flushed com-panion fish. The living knot unraveled and exploded toward me.

They stopped at a couple arms' length, boiling around me with whipping tails and agitated red plumes, waves of surprise, outrage, and contradiction washing over me, confusion and disbelief at my presence. I thrust awkwardly past the disorienting barrage, closing my eyes and groping. I focused all my energy on a picture of Siolis, trapped in the cage, trapped in the matrix of the incorporeals. I visualized the "false cybers" invading the system and the dome-consoles, echoing my disjointed glimpse from the sending. I shaped as best I could a plea for help, of reaching out to Siolis and helping him emerge.

I could only hold off the waves of pressure with my concentration for a moment. I blinked, drained, as their soundings buffeted me in a blurry confusion of colors and shrill tones. I shook my head, trying to gather myself for another attempt, when two of the bright-plumed fish shot out from the others and whipped around me in a crackling, slippery brush.

The tumbling sensations jolted, slid, and coalesced to a clear image of the alien, the lander female with her monstrous emanations and devices, her illness of self-lies and other-lies and concealments, swimming impossibly here when the cybers said she was gone, Healed and sent away with the horrible machines. Disruption. Disruption.

The Cyvriots fled in a whirl of agitated eddies.

No, wait! You've got to listen—They were gone into the purple depths.

I took another metaphorical deep breath, gathering the frayed strands of determination, then kicked around to find Jay and go after them. They had to see the truth, if only I could show it to them. I pulled up short.

Jay drifted a few shadowy meters away, a strange look mixed of wonder, confusion, and slowly dawning delight on his face as he held his empty hands out toward the Cyvriot girl hovering before him, two violet-tinged fish darting in quick circling passes between them.

And then I realized I wasn't seeing the expression so much as feeling it flow between them. With a tingling shiver, the sensation lapped through me as I saw/felt the two plumed fish that had darted out of the dancing mass still wafting their lacy fins around me, knowing in a flash of a sense I couldn't define that they were Siolis' lost companion fish, that the girl was the one in the bathylabra who had caught the second of my tumbling sunburst-crystal dice, that there were three familiarly configured adults who had turned back in the murk beyond my seeing, circling around and warily watching. And then the logical connections of recognition were scattered in a bright burst of bubbling light as the remembered silent laughter of the children, the girl's delight as I drifted closer to Jay and her, the exuberant effervescence of the alien Adept-

sending swirled in the glittering tumble of crystal dice and floated us up.

I blinked, head throbbing, and saw Jay swimming toward the surface, beckoning the girl after him. I followed, vaguely aware of the three adults following me, and I tried to reach out a reassuring contact, but I couldn't separate any sense now from the nebulous mumblings of sound and touch.

The sea shimmered, clearer blue as I rose and the waters surged, and then I was breaking the ruffled surface, blinking in cloud-filtered reddish daylight. I gasped, coughing as my lungs expelled their stored air in a painful spasm and dragged in a fresh breath, wavelets breaking against my face.

Jay was paddling with his arms, bobbing as he craned around at the slippery bluish surge of the native girl surfacing and plunging back down in a splashing circle around us. "Ruth," he spluttered as spray slapped his face, "it's incredible! I could feel her, opening up to me—or maybe opening me up to her, I don't know. It's all a blur, but you could feel the joy, couldn't you? What a wonderful Way they have here. We have to try to help them. I don't know how, but I knew she'd try to talk to us at the surface, since I can't talk to her down below."

He beamed as the girl broke surface again, rolling smoothly onto her back and floating, wide mouth gaping open and dark pupils narrowed to slits in the huge purple eyes. With a flick of her long tail, the girl slid under again.

"Jay—" I broke off as a prickling buzz swept around me with the flutter of slippery fins and a warning—no, alerting, noticing?—whispered through me. The girl splashed through the surface again, followed by three slippery blue heads, expressionless faces watching us.

"Long—long has been the sighting." Did I recognize one of the adults? There were two men and a woman, their faces all looking the same to me, but I could feel differences in their sea echoes the darting companion fish somehow amplified or focused in erratic snatches. I took a deep breath, undulating my foot-fin to stay afloat. "Thank you for coming back, for listening—"

Jay, bobbing beside me, broke in, "We want to help you, but your Way is being threatened. We want to work *with* you, if you'll let us—"

"We sssee. . . ." The closest adult's mouth twisted on a laboring gush of air. "Hear lllanderssss. Cybersssss telll—"

"Conssolllesss sspeaking." Another of the adults struggled with a hissing whisper, long black tongue flicking. "Lllanderss llleave. Dissruptionsss sssending sstill."

"But's that not us—"

"Wait, Jay. I think they know that." I turned back to the Cyvriots, trying to pick out which one had just spoken, but they were restlessly circling us now, stirring the water to an agitated froth as the little violet fish darted quickly into view and then down. I cleared my throat. "I think I understood a little of the sending down below. Are the consoles telling you something new, something not right?"

"Cybersss sspeaking—"

"—sstrange wayss. Calllling ssome to facilllity."

"Taboo. Taboo."

"Cybersss truth. Cybersss lllies. Taking—"

"—llandersss from ssea, from Cyvrusss. Ssent away. Not sssent."

"Wait." I blinked, dizzy from trying to turn in the water to see who was speaking as they circled and interrupted each other, the laboring whispers blending into a fluid hiss. "You mean the consoles said they had sent us—the landers—away in the shuttles? I thought I saw in the sending—"

"Yesss. Thisss one ssees—"

"—hearsss part, telllss ssome truth. Cybersss can no liesss."

"Conssolllles callll to facilllity, calll to return ssilllence maker to dessstroy. Llanderss gone, taboo gone—"

"—yet llanderss here, taboo here." Ghost fingers rippled over me.

"You're saying the consoles told you to bring the null device— the silence maker—to the facility? It's taboo for you to go there?"

"Yesss, taboo. SSilllence maker ssent to facilllity. Cybersss sstill calll."

"If you sent that creature with all the arms to take the device there, he gave it to me."

"Taboo here." Another ghostly shiver ran through me, heavy with fear, loathing, the barely contained impulse to flee.

"Ruth, I think—"

"Wait, Jay." I turned back to the last speaker. "It's true the real cybers gave it to me, to use against the false cybers that have invaded your world and are talking to you now through the consoles. We won't use it, except against the false cybers. You can feel me. You know I'm telling you the truth."

"Other-truth."

"Ssellf-sssecretss, confusion—"

"Cyberss. Falllsse cyberss. Llandersss illnesss—"

"Falllsse cybersss illlnesss, disssruption. Conssolles ssay new ssendingss sspeak new Way for Cyvrusss. Kindred musst llisten and share with cyberss at facillity."

"Taboo. Dissruption."

"Wait. The signal—the new sending—isn't from the false cybers. They want you to tell them what it means."

"Dissruption. Illnesss."

"Heallll." Another wave of outrage, revulsion swept through me, but this time I didn't think it was directed so much at me as at the false cybers.

"Yes." Jay was still paddling around, trying to face one of them. "Let us help you heal the system of the false cybers. But you have to help us reach Siolis, in their web at the facility."

"Kindred mussst hear—"

"—sssee—"

"—sssing—"

"—ssendingsss of llanderss. Folllow to bathyllabra." The slippery expressionless faces and huge purple eyes circled once more.

"Wait! I can't—" I lunged around, but they were sinking out of sight. "Damn!"

There was a surging splash, and the young girl burst up from below, splatting her tail in a wild spray and whipping around Jay to pass close by me. Siolis' companion fish darted around the others, then flashed back to brush me with a jittery rush of urgency, excitement, a hesitant sensation of opening or invitation. I closed my eyes, groping to sort through disorienting babble. I could sense the girl below, waiting to show us the way.

Yes, all right, I'll try. I opened my eyes to see Jay watching me with a puzzled look. "All right, then, let's follow her."

"Follow her? Who?" Jay shook off a splash of foam. "Ruth, what's going on? I'm all mixed up."

"You may be feeling that from their soundings."

"All I can see is they don't like us." He hesitated, a smile playing over his lips. "Except for the girl, she'd like some new friends—but how did I know that?" He shook his head. "Ruth, you're not telling me you can really communicate with them underwater, are you?"

"I don't know, Jay. Maybe a little, if I try to let them in." I shivered as the sea lapped against me. "We've got to go down and try to convince them. The others aren't going to be as open-minded as these ones were, but maybe they're getting shook up enough by now to listen. Just stick by me and pull me out of there if things get too sticky, all right?''

He took a deep breath, then nodded and followed me down.

The girl swam quickly ahead of us, fading into the purplish shadows and then looping back to surge out of the gloom, circle, and tease us on. She was gone again from sight, and I groped for her soundings, letting the faint sensation of eagerness and laughter fizz through my veins. Her darting presence coalesced somehow into the equivalent of fluid sunlit golds and coppers, so I called her Bright Girl to myself as I followed her over the dark abyss.

There was a sudden return pressure pulsing back to the ripple of the blue-violet fins of Siolis' companion fish, an acknowledgment, and I knew without formulating it that the natives had a lot of names that weren't really words, along with the word names they only needed for the cybers. I wondered what other names Siolis had.

Bright Girl flashed past again in a swirl of fins and tail, then shot toward the dark looming mass of the plateau the demon-fish had brought us past. Another bathylabra.

Jay and I followed with our slower undulations of body and foot-fins, but the girl was swallowed in the gloom of the rock walls towering over us. I closed my eyes and groped for her presence, or any sign of the three adults who'd talked to us, who'd pushed bravely past their taboos to listen, but there was only a vague, generalized shiver of energy from the bathylabra itself. I traced it closer.

The usual pale-colored blobs and fronds and streamers encrusted the wall, beckoning in the wavering purple light. A cloud of tiny, silver-glinting fish shot from a crevice and swarmed over us. Jay jerked around, startled, bumping against the rock and fighting his way through a tangle of drifting weeds. I anchored my fin against the wall and snagged his ankle as he tumbled off-balance, arms windmilling.

He righted himself, making an abashed face, then gestured around to indicate surprise, craning his neck to watch three larger, striped fish fin gracefully past.

I snapped on my headlight, colors springing up in its beam, and pointed out one of my favorite little red-armored creatures waving its antennae busily as it scurried over a pink spongy growth. Jay smiled. I smiled back, then sighed, glancing up at the distant shimmer of the surface, and beckoned Jay toward the jagged slice of darkness behind a fringe of slippery green fronds. The cave entrance pulsed slow waves of unheard sound.

A spotted sea-serpent darted its head out of a crack in the rock portal, then as quickly retreated. Directing my light in cautious sweeps, I finned slowly inside, Jay following apprehensively.

I swam into the dark twists of the bathylabra in an odd dissociation, part of me turning back to reassure Jay, to guide him through the tortuous tunnels that looked familiar and strange at the same time, to point out the first glow of blue luminescence reflecting in scattered facets along the rough black walls. The other part swam against the pressure of more than depth and dense rock closing in on me, breasting the unheard waves of a drumbeat revving up with the pound of my pulse.

With an effort, I gave up resisting the rhythm, let it fill me and beat through my bones with its silent, urgent summons. Blind panic grabbed for a moment as I flailed inwardly to escape the alien energy penetrating me. But I forced myself to let go my reflex defenses as I'd let go the urge to breathe. A silent humming intensified to a taut, vibrating wire, pulling me along the glowing tunnel.

I looked back one more time to see Jay rubbing his ear as if at a minor irritation and shrugging, shooting me a confused and anxious look. The pounding, swelling sendings were deafening me now, shaking me, swirling around me and hurtling me along as my fingers numbly switched off my lamp and I raced into the throbbing blue glow, oblivious to Jay's wavering beam fading behind me. There was only the maze of dark water and stone, the cool, mesmerizing blue in the sharp glint of crystals, and the echoing sendings sucking me inward.

I shot out suddenly into a great open dimness, the cavern at the heart of the bathylabra. The natives were there, dancing their sending song, weaving their writhing slippery knot of sound, image, sensation, emotion.

I saw it with my eyes, skin, tongue, ears, bones. The cavern was a ringing cacophony of echoing sendings, blasting through me with chaotic intensity, indecipherable fragments. An impossibly complex dissonance, clanging, muttering, sliding into instantaneous flashes of the illusion of coherence and then as suddenly into a wild clashing flail of noise and pain.

I screamed silently, spinning dizzily inward down a spiraling tunnel, ripping at the violent dark with my fingers for any handhold to anchor me. Nothing. The random whirl of dark space. The pulsing vortex of the incorporeal matrix, swallowing me. I writhed in terror to escape.

No. Not the energy web of the spooks, but somehow like it. I forced myself to stop fighting, to swim in the mad spinning plunge, and then I could glimpse flashing shards of light, hear ringing tones spinning with me. Like the bright sparks of experience in the matrix, whirling in a convoluted, multidimensional lattice in the blackness. I was spun near one, and I touched it, vibrant colors blossoming over me in a cool plunge of blue sea, murmuring voiceless whispers, rippling black wings of the demon-fish and a sharp salt taste, Jay's long hair drifting around his bewildered face, the harsh depthless contours of the monstrous device in his pocket. The vignette whirled away, and I was plunging upward with the roaring whirlpool torrent, with the unfolding lattice as it doubled and redoubled echoes of a black rock maze, funneling intensity to flicker through a thousand faceted angles and reflections. The torrent, the lattice split and reformed, shattered and coalesced as the world spun upside down, stretched, and snapped into the pure form of a ringing, humming, pulsing harmonic, pumping outward from the heart of the bathylabra.

The vibrant hum suddenly blossomed into enfolding presences, a multitude of voices of every conceivable tone, range, and distance melding like blended white light to form symmetry. And a stray memory of Poindros tumbled up through me—the Gathering Hall of our farming village, all the faithful raising their voices in a swelling chorus of harmony.

The picture slipped, slid in a jarring dischord. With a slippery crackle, darkness rolled outward to reveal the Cyvriots whipping out from their slippery lattice to gather around me in a floating phalanx, huge eyes glinting reflections of cold blue. A hammer of furious soundings pounded me.

Biting back another scream, I rolled with the impact, falling back down that spinning black tunnel, letting go the anchors of vision and place. At the bottom was a closed door. But I couldn't find the handle, the chaos was battering me and the door kept spinning, too, refusing to stay in place, floating insanely upward to become a black velvet gaming table.

With the mad logic of nightmare, I knew what I needed. My lucky sunburst-crystal dice. They were somehow in my hand, only my hands were somewhere else, but I was shaking them, the sparkling effervescence of the children's laughter and the alien

signal bubbling up as I concentrated on snake eyes. I could see
them, the head-to-tail serpent rolling his laughing, hissing loop
around me as I shook the dice and rolled. They tumbled over the
gaming table and snake eyes blazed out of the dark. The door
sprang open.

A wrenching sense of dissolving and refocusing, slippery
plumes sliding me into the light. I could hear the Cyvriots' voices
now. *Lander. Outrage. Impossibility. Cybers. Truth. Lies. Confusion.*

I seized the last sounding, opening it up with a new clarity to
reveal all the pictures it contained, thrusting it back at them.
Images of the lab facility, the incorporeals and their warped experiments, the danger to the Cyvriots. Siolis without his companion fish, trapped in the mesh cage, trapped in the matrix. David,
helpless in the spooks' web. I opened myself, letting them travel
my circuits and see.

Images echoed back from them, reverberating meanings now
clear to me. Shock, anger, slowly dawning comprehension. Outrage at the broken taboos and the deceptions of the false cybers.
And, still, a visceral abhorrence of the invading landers and their
monstrous ways. Cyvrus to be purged of contamination.

The chamber roared, a whirling vortex crackling with a furious
summons. Sendings to the ponderous beasts of the deep. A call
to gather and destroy the facility.

I couldn't take any more. The slippery door slammed violently
shut over me as I curled into myself in pain, battered by silent
hammering furies. Unsorted glimpses—the Cyvriots closing in
with lashing tails and fixed eyes, glinting blue spinning around
me, flames leaping up in the Poindran hell of broken taboos, a
hard hand clutching my arm and wrenching me up and away.

I fought weakly, but the hand had me, wouldn't let go as it
dragged me up and through twisting corridors. Running—no,
swimming, dark water pouring over me with welcome coolness.
And then a final wrench and heaving, a hard floor and the touch
of air, chest convulsing in agony as lungs labored and finally
inflated, water gushing from mouth and nose. Someone was
screaming, clawing at bleeding ears.

I was shaken hard. My hand was pulled away from my ear.
My eyes snapped open to see Jay gripping my shoulders, frantically shaking me, lips forming words I couldn't hear because of
the pain and ringing in my ears. I blinked, said something, took
another deep breath, finally nodded.

His grip loosened, arm going around my shoulders to support me. ". . . thought I was too late."

The ringing subsided to a background hum. I focused blurrily on my discarded fin on the damp half-floor opening to dark water, a dim ready light glowing over curved walls from an unactivated console. Jay had pulled me out, found the dome.

". . . get through to them, do you think?"

I nodded numbly. "Through." I cleared my throat. "Got through, all right. And I just made everything worse."

sixteen

I'd blown it again. Thinking I'd break through with the natives and show up Jason and Lilith, those superior cyborgs? They were right, I hadn't stopped to think maybe my meddling would only endanger David and Siolis. I was just an ignorant human, a pitiful mass of animal reflexes and hungers absurdly howling at the untouchable stars.

"Snap out of it, Ruth." Jay gently shook my shoulder, his warped shadow looming over the curve of the dome above the diffused lume. "Why don't you get out of that wet suit and get some rest?"

I shrugged away from him. "Maybe the cybers were right, keeping their taboos from us. You know, they've got parts of the original, historical Book of Words locked up in security codes. Like, 'My days are swifter than a weaver's shuttle, and are spent without hope. . . .'"

"Don't forget the rest while you're at it." Voice ironic. "Doesn't it go, 'Man is born unto trouble'?"

I looked up, surprised. But of course he'd had access to all the forbidden data. Or, rather, Jason had.

"So we're reclaiming our birthright from the cybers." He gave me an odd, crooked smile and peeled off his stretchy tight suit, leaning over in his skivvies to lay it out to dry. "It's just part of learning to be free again, isn't it? Making mistakes? Don't be so hard on yourself, you gave it your best shot."

"I guess so." Even if it wasn't enough. I slowly rose and peeled off my own sticky suit. I stretched wearily, thought about shucking my damp microslick, too, then glanced at Jay and decided to keep it on. "But one way or another it's still trouble. We've got to warn Jason the natives are planning to attack the facility."

"All right, but it'll take the natives a while to organize. World's not going to end while you sit down and eat something." He squatted, rummaging in the mesh bag. "And we can't swim back without getting some rest first."

I sat cross-legged, accepting a nutrient pack. "It would take too long to swim back. And I don't know if I could get a demon-fish to take us *away* from the bathylabra.''

He swallowed and looked over his shoulder at the unactivated console. "We could send him a warning."

"And fill in the spooks at the same time? Don't forget what those three natives told us. The incorporeals are spreading through the network to the consoles.'' My eyes skittered uneasily over the steady amber ready light glinting in the dimness. "Maybe we should zap this one. They could be monitoring us now.''

"I don't think so, Ruth, with the interface unactivated. They'd have no reason to know we were here, but if we knocked out the console, they'd probably trace us." He touched the bulge of the null device in the pocket of his suit spread beside him. "If I have to, though, I'll use it."

"I guess you're right." My back still prickled at the thought of the spooks lurking silently in the dome with us. "But back on Poindros they didn't give us any warning, just caught us with that force field they somehow generated from the console.''

"I remember, but that was after they'd ordered me to modify the family console for them. I installed a different interface that could generate the short-range—'' He frowned, then shook his head. "I can't remember the theory. Damn." He shook his head again. "When I broke free of the incorporeal control, I had to restructure some of my cyborg neural interfaces. I decided to store most of my technical data in my integrated cybernetic analyzers, so I could isolate those functions from my organic responses if the situation called for it. So I could stay human in my thought processes . . .'' He trailed off, staring at the dark, shivering water.

"Jay . . .''

He jerked his face back to mine. "Right. Jay. I can't find those memories from . . . Jason, those data entries. But what I was trying to tell you was the incorporeals seem to have a different interface system here than they had on Poindros or Andura. You know, the way they've got David and Siolis linked in—''

"With electrodes and all, right. But in the cavern I swear for a few seconds they were probing me with some kind of energy field like they used before." I shook my head. "I don't get it. Everything's screwy on this world.'' I pointed at the ring apparatus suspended over the water beside the console. "Why do the cybers make the natives go through such an ordeal to talk to them, when they could just use electrode patches like Siolis was using to interface with the console? Why make them learn standard speech when supposedly they'd never have contact with any of the other worlds?" I frowned, a vague recognition or pattern nagging somewhere beyond grasping, or maybe it was just hangover from the pounding nonverbal sendings in the cavern below. My head still throbbed dully.

"Ruth, you know the cybers and how literal they are with the Rules. They have to align Cyvrus as close to the rest of the Plan as they can."

I sighed and rubbed my aching forehead. "I guess so." I took a deep breath and straightened. "Anyway, all this is well and good, but it doesn't get us anywhere. How are we going to warn Jason?"

He chewed his lip. "Just maybe . . ." He frowned, staring at the opaque water again. "I think I could still do it."

"Do what?"

"A code, one only I—he and I would know. I think I've still got enough of it . . ." Then he shook his head. "I forgot. The incorporeals would still be alerted to a message."

"No, wait, it might work." I turned eagerly toward him on the damp floor. "If the system basics are the same here as everywhere else, the central facility would send out a routine maintenance monitoring signal regularly to each console, right?"

"Sure, I guess, but—"

"Well, don't you see? You code your message and send it piggyback on the returning confirm signal. Jason's monitoring the system—he'd pick it up."

He nodded slowly, absently picking at his crooked front tooth with a thumbnail. "He just might. Looks like our best bet." He got to his feet. "Let's see what the rotation schedule's like—basic operating functions shouldn't be too hard to get at. Still got your blank data disc?"

I raised my hand to my necklace and unclipped the wild card from my IDisc. "Think you can do it without triggering any alarms?"

"I reckon I can still handle that much." Again the irony and the tight little smile.

I was through trying to apologize. I followed him over to the console.

"Here, I'll open up the back panel and pretend I'm a repair mech. You cover with the disc, all right? Request simulated voice mode, and we'll hope it works like it did on Poindros."

"You're right about the cybers, they don't change anything

unless they have to. I just tried the same old trick back in Casino, and it worked.''

''Good.''

We got to work. I was no cybernetics whiz like David, and Jay lacked Jason's cyborg skills, but between us we managed to penetrate the rudimentary security on the console functions. We learned that the maintenance signal would go through in a little over two hours.

Jay frowned. ''I could try to record a loop for transmission, but I think it'd be safer to feed it direct.'' He set a timer and we sat down to work out his coded message.

Half an hour later, I raised my face from the crooked code squiggles we'd scratched on the side of the console, rubbing a painful crick in my neck. ''Guess that should do it. Just hope we're doing the right thing this time.'' The ache wouldn't go away. ''Anyway, don't worry about the missing code characters— Jason will figure it out.''

''Right. *He* won't have forgotten any of it.'' Jay scowled and picked at his tooth again.

''Damn it, will you stop that?''

He jerked his head up, dropping his hand.

I sighed. ''I mean, stop comparing yourself to him.''

''Will you, then?'' he snapped back. Then he closed his eyes and blew out a long breath. Still with his eyes closed, he asked quietly, ''Still in love with him, aren't you?''

My shoulders jerked into a shrug and I turned away.

''You know, this may sound crazy, but I'm glad of your loyalty to him.''

I turned back and he was giving me his painful little smile. ''Ruth, you know I'm only here because he—we love you.''

''Don't you think I know that?'' It came out a snarl. ''But you—he didn't have the right to do this to us.''

''Maybe you're right.'' He shook his head. ''But I can't help feeling this life I've got now is a gift. So whatever happens, it's okay by me.''

''You mean you don't care what happens to you?''

He spread his big hands and looked at them. ''Funny, they still look strange to me, too, so soft and pale.'' He met my eyes again. ''Okay, sure I care. I mean, I don't know where I stand, and I'm not sure how I feel about being 'standard' again. I'm excited, but I'm afraid, too. I'd put all that behind me, for better or worse— pain, sickness, aging, being weak and getting mad like I just did.

Panicking like I did when we first went underwater.''

He rubbed the dark stubble of his beard. "Ruth, I don't know for sure who I am now, but I *feel* like I'm the real Jason, if you've got to insist on one. I know I've lost some of what I had as a cyborg, but I've got the memories and the true feelings I've always had for you. Some of what I remember from the other Jason feels like it's behind a veil, and I can't quite grasp it, so I guess I can't really say my feelings are the same, but they're real.''

I couldn't think of anything to say.

"Now I've said my piece, and I'm not trying to make you answer. Let's get a little rest, all right?''

I finally nodded. I ducked my head away, rubbing the insistent crick in my neck.

"Here, let me rub that out for you. Sam used to say my massage was the only thing let him wind down.'' He flashed a quick grin.

I found myself smiling back. "Sam never could manage to relax and take more than three or four naps a day, poor thing.'' I let him sit me down, closing my eyes as his fingers massaged the tight muscles of my neck and shoulders.

He still had the knack for finding the knots. Tension loosened and dissolved as his strong fingers rhythmically kneaded. I leaned back, giving in to tiredness and the sleepy memory of a hot summer night on Poindros, candlelight in the parlor, and Jason massaging the kinks from old Sam's shoulders. I nodded to the lulling rhythm of the massage, almost hearing the harp strings quivering under my fingers as I played soothing glissandos and Jason's big hands began to move in time to my music. Slow warmth spread through me, whispering the old tune, and I found myself humming it under my breath.

Jay's hands abruptly pulled away and he moved back from me. "I better stop.''

I twisted around, blinking sleepily. "Hmmm?''

He turned away gruffly. "I better stop touching you now or I won't be able to stop.''

Damn. And I'd wanted him to go on. I jerked to my feet, the sleepy spell broken. "Jay, look at me! You can't really want this.'' I gestured choppily at the capped stump of my arm, lifting it in a defiant, grotesque movement. "Your body's fresh and brand new, and mine's been around the block too many times. You're strong and perfect, and I'm a scarred-up cripple.''

"That's crazy talk, Ruth!'' He jumped up and caught my wrist. "I'll never forget that first night on Poindros when I finally met you and you touched something inside me even the incorporeals couldn't cut away. But even then you were afraid to let your beauty shine out.''

"Beauty! Don't tell me that, when you had Helen for your wife."

He gripped my wrist tighter. "Yes, I love Helen, but that's not the same feeling. Her beauty's a different thing. It's that fire in you that—"

I yanked against his grip, refusing to look at him. "I don't want yours, or anybody's, pity. Let me go."

He shook me. "Damn it, look at me. Tell me this is pity."

I finally met his eyes, their bright, gold-flecked brown catching a reflected gleam of my own pale, set face. I couldn't look away, and I couldn't pretend his eyes didn't mirror my own need, the fire he'd stirred with his touch.

"Damn . . . "

"Ruth. Do you always have to fight?" He tugged me gently toward him.

I started to resist, then reached up quickly to brush the long hair back from his face, pulling him down to kiss me. The baby-softness of his lips and scratchy abrasion of his stubbly beard were a brief shock, then the familiar, spicy tang of his skin enveloped me and I was pressing hard against him as his arms tightened almost painfully around me.

He finally groaned, pulling back and breathing hard, face flushed as his hands fumbled at the straps of my thin microslick. He tugged me down to the floor with him, on the thin padding of our discarded insulation suits. Neither of us noticed the inadequate bedding. Jay pulled me on top of him, his big hands touching me in all the places Jason knew so well. I caught my breath, raising myself to look in his face and meet Jay's urgent eyes. I ran my hand over his chest and down the lean belly, struck once more with a qualm as I traced the contours of his pale, untouched body. He groaned as I stroked him, suddenly pulling my hand away and rolling us over, pushing me down onto my back.

I blinked in surprise and he panted, "Ruth, I can't wait."

"No need." I pulled him down and he slid into me with an electric jolt that made us both gasp. I started to smile and then it was forgotten as I met his eyes and his intensity caught me up into it. We rolled and writhed over the floor in an animal frenzy, and nothing mattered but clawing our way closer together.

He groaned, gasping, "I can't hold back." And he thrust deeply, crying out.

I clutched him reflexively, my own violent climax catching me off guard as it exploded with his. We shuddered, collapsing together.

We lay motionless a long time, slowly catching our breaths. Gradually we sorted out our tangle of damp limbs and managed to roll back onto the meager padding of our suits. Jay pulled me tightly against him in a sudden fierce squeeze, then lay back and blew out a long breath.

"Ruth, I'm sorry I was so rough. I couldn't seem to control myself."

I squirmed around to face him again, running my hand slowly over his chest. "Did I look like I minded?"

He caught my hand as it wandered lower, raising himself on one elbow to look intently into my eyes. "Next time I'll go slower, give us more time. It caught me off guard, I'm not used to being . . ."

So human. I nodded quickly, tugging my hand free to cover his lips, refusing the insistent comparisons to Jason—that timeless, overwhelming linking of more than bodies. I drew Jay's head down onto my breast, but before he lowered his eyes, I could see as they searched my face that he hadn't found the reassurance he was looking for.

We were slower, more gentle, the second time, in an almost painfully heightened awareness of each other's sensitivities and frailties. I was grateful he'd given me back my confidence. He— I hoped—was finding his balance in what he was. We leisurely built our pleasure in caring little touches and long caresses, and as we climbed together toward release it became more than just that. A hint of . . . what? Maybe only a promise of more to discover.

We seemed to reach a mutual agreement not to examine its fragility too closely as we silently dressed and prepared to tackle the console again.

I reached down to scoop up a nutrient pack and toss it at him. "Here. Maybe the vitamins will make up for that nap we didn't get."

He smiled, then suddenly sobered, his eyes intent on mine. "Ruth—"

He never finished. There was a splash from the dark, enclosed water, and a dripping head started to emerge. My stomach gave an unsettling lurch as I thought for a second one of the Cyvriots had come back to talk. But the head was blond. Lilith vaulted effortlessly over the lip of flooring.

I backed up. "What—"

"Lilith! How did you know—I mean . . ."

She shook back her hair and wrung it out, giving us apologetic looks from expressive, humanlike eyes. She said quietly, with a hint of her former lilt, "I'm sorry to barge in on you two, but Jason and I were terribly worried when you disappeared. Jason thought he ought to stay with the com-links, while I tracked you down."

I shrugged uneasily. "We're fine. You didn't need to—"

She raised a placating hand. "I see that." A glance at Jay and a fleeting smile. "But I realized it was my fault, that I'd driven you away, and I felt I had to apologize. I was still unbalanced, and Jason had his hands full trying to help me adjust my neural interfaces and tackle the system at the same time. But you were right, Ruth, we had no right to exclude you from the planning." She looked down. "We haven't had much luck breaking through the facility control channels. Maybe we ought to all sit down and talk about trying to reach Siolis within the matrix."

Jay stepped forward, putting an arm around me. "It's a good thing you came, Lilith. We were just going to send a message through the console to warn Jason and you—"

"Jay. Slow down a second, okay?" I eased away from his arm, trying to catch his eye.

He misunderstood, flushing his painful red as he dropped his arm away from me.

Did Lilith look amused, or only concerned? "Warn us about what?"

The cat was out of the bag now. Maybe I had misjudged her. "Let's start at the beginning. Jay and I decided we ought to try— well, go ahead, Jay, you tell her." I took his hand and squeezed it, facing Lilith and forcing a smile.

Jay, looking confused, cleared his throat. "We thought Ruth should try contacting the Cyvriots again, thought maybe they could reach Siolis if they understood. . . ."

Lilith nodded when he finished explaining. "We thought maybe that was it." She turned to me, blue eyes reflecting what looked like genuine puzzlement. "Ruth, I don't have to tell you that as a cyborg I have some limitations along with my added skills. From

hints in the memory data Jason has shared with me, I've formulated
a hypothesis. You have some sort of special ability, don't you,
that lets you do more than understand the Cyvriot communication?
If so, you've got to tell me as much about it as you can. We all
need to put our heads together to come up with the means to
contact Siolis.'' She gave me a tentative smile. ''I am sorry we
didn't listen to you before.''

I swung abruptly away from her, pacing across the limited floor
space and back. Damn Jason, telling Lilith the intimate things
between us. I shook my head. ''You're jumping to conclusions.
Why do you think I've been having such a hard time breaking
through with the natives? I can only pick up bits here and there.
And I don't even know if I'm getting through to them at all.'' It
was the truth, on a certain level. I *didn't* know.

The blue eyes were intent on mine. ''But, Ruth, don't you think
even those fragments you can perceive may be related to the way
you escaped the incorporeal matrix before?''

Damn. Was she reading my mind? I forced my hand to remain
unclenched, summoning the silent beat of a Setharian chant to
baffle intangible probes, though I hadn't sensed any from her the
way I'd felt Jason's before. ''Lilith, I don't know what Jason told
you, but maybe he didn't make it clear I didn't escape from the
spook matrix, just found a place inside it where they couldn't
make me do things, where they couldn't force their thoughts on
me. But I would have died in there if he hadn't pulled me out.
Whatever this so-called talent of mine is, it's totally unpredictable
and unreliable.''

Her intent gaze stayed on me for a second more, then she sighed
and lifted her hands. ''I'm afraid you're right then, that won't be
much help to us.'' Did she look ever so slightly gratified? ''Then
the only thing to do is to try to protect the facility from the attack,
and try to persuade the natives to reach Siolis within the matrix.
Perhaps we could contact them through their consoles. Jason and
I could still shield signals in the outlying system from detection
by the control center.''

Jay shook his head. ''The natives wouldn't trust anything from
the consoles now, not with the 'false cybers' speaking from them.''

''You're right, of course.'' She turned back to me. ''Do you
think you could try one more time to contact the natives, Ruth?
The more times they hear it, the better the chances that they might
be convinced.''

I hesitated, then shrugged. ''What do we have to lose?''

"I'll tow you to the facility sea entrance, then, and we should encounter the natives on the way. But I must first alert Jason to the planned attack. I can code a message through the system so the incorporeals won't be alerted." She moved smoothly to the console, her eyes flaring their inhuman bright amber as colored indicators flared into life on the panel, danced briefly, and died.

Jay looked at our tedious code scratches on the console and glanced at me, sighing faintly as Lilith finished and turned quickly back to us.

She gave me a concerned look. "Jason agrees that we should follow the Cyvriots and attempt another contact. But he wonders if you are up to it, Ruth."

"I'm fine. Let's get going." Lilith could at least get us to them faster than we could make it on our own.

Jay looked down into my face. "Are you sure, Ruth? I think you need some rest."

"We can rest later, Jay. Plenty of time later."

seventeen

I could feel them gathering before we got to the facility. Building waves of pressure, thick with a turmoil of energies, crashed over me, and they had nothing to do with the churning current Lilith stirred up in a blur of kicking fins as she towed Jay and me through the sea.

Jay was tethered first on the line attached to her belt, taking the brunt of her wake. I was swept along behind, catching dim glimpses of sea mounts receding, weed forests whipping past, startled schools of fish scattering. And larger shapes like menacing shadows, all bristling teeth and streamlined sinister grace. But they were intent only on moving past us, away from our destination.

My ears rang with the edgy warning of *timbra*. Nebulous dread shivered through me, a jagged bass throb running counterpoint to the swirls of intensifying sendings and soundings. The new element was an explosive, repetitive jarring, stirring deep uneasiness not only within me, but seemingly within the sea itself and the unstable crust beneath it. I blinked behind the goggles, shaking my head.

Then I blinked again. The sea around us was darkening. Some small fish shot frantically past, and then there weren't any more. The lukewarm waters were heating. They frothed around us now, tiny bubbles and particles boiling upward. Beneath us, the ocean floor groaned.

Lilith veered to the left, plunging us away from the now-audible rending. A pulsing glow lit up the dim purple sea from below. A surge of hot, metallic-tasting current hit us, sweeping us faster to the side. Chunks of twisted rock hurtled past as Lilith ducked and dodged, hardly slowed by the water's resistance, Jay and I flung behind her on a delayed whip. As she straightened and fled, I twisted back to glimpse red, molten rock fountaining upward out of the depths, to be cloaked in a cloud of steam and particles billowing toward the surface.

My head ached with the dull assault of intersecting sendings, suddenly clarified as we swept around and past the underwater eruption. Pulses of alarm, righteous anger, incomprehensible commands swept through me, and I realized that the quaking seabed and eruptions were more than Cyvrus' mild regular readjustments of its crust. The upheavals were linked to the uneven, percussive shock waves echoing over me. They drummed louder, closer.

Lilith, without pause, swung back on course for the facility sea entrance and the source of the turmoil. It wasn't only her towline sweeping me along. Caught like a fish on a hook, I was reeled in by an urgent summons.

Time poured into swirling eddies, ebbing and flowing to the pound of waves on a rocky shore, drowning vision in a tumult of boiling images and sounds, then receding to reveal the dim, submerged world framed by my goggles. I was tugged back and forth by the engulfing rhythm, registering only vaguely that Lilith had stopped and Jay was unhooking me from the towline. A glimpse of his anxious eyes peering in through my goggles, and then another surge of dizzying, compelling otherness washed over me, beckoning. Beneath it all, the sharp, exploding shocks of sound.

Another glimpse sliding into focus: Lilith darting away as Jay pressed his hands to his ears and then shook his head, pointing past her. A dim, enormous shape, impossibly broad and long, rose slowly from the black depths, glinting an unblinking eye and ramming its ponderous blunt head against the rising walls of a sea mount. But I didn't have to see it, maybe I wasn't seeing it. There were others, presences of giant creatures summoned out of their basking fathomless trenches to blast the deeper rock enclosing the facility with violent bursts of focused frequency. The echoed blows pounded through me. A last glimpse of Lilith through the shallow water—seen, or reverberated through the soundings?—flitting upward past the enormous, ramming beast, a flicker of intense laser light flaring from her hand, but dispersing in the swirl of water around the creature.

Then other presences swam toward me, familiar echoes, two women and a man sending out hesitant probes to ripple down my bones. I kicked around, blinking through the murk, but couldn't see them. Their soundings doubled back in confusion, conflict, alarm. I tried to shape images of the facility and the leviathans attacking it, urgency to stop the pounding waves of pressure, a plea that they'd listen again, but somehow it got all mixed up with

echoes of Lilith firing her deflecting lasers at the huge creature,
shivers of fear and revulsion, contours of the alloy cyborg monster
and taboo devices. The natives circled and fled into the pulsing
summons of a renewed sending.

Wait. Listen. Come back— The sending swallowed and scattered my frail effort, lapping and tugging me.

Something was shaking me. Jay's hand, gripping my shoulder.
But I couldn't pull free of the suck and swirl of the sendings.
I ripped away from him, racing away from the sea mount after
the trio, into the deeper channel toward the gathering of natives
and other creatures I could feel threshing the sea in a swelling,
writhing knot of swimming presences. Invisible waves clashed
and crashed over me as the natives danced listening to an echoing
sending beam, danced singing of their group response, sent
whirling pulses of soundings to command the creatures of the
deep.

Caught in the deafening, blinding surge, I barely registered
the two crimson-flushed, plumy fish darting from the assembly,
fins brushing me and circling. I stopped fighting the crashing
waves and let them tug open that door inside, tumbling through
into the place where chaos reassembled into complex coherence.

A convoluted structure of image, sensation, taste, emotion expanded with each new voice joining in, but the meanings were
insistent: *Preserve our Way. The intruders must be rejected. The
disruption must be purged and Healed.*

Landers, false cybers, alien sendings—all were inextricably one
to be expunged from the Plan. But words and definitions were
irrelevant. The song of the multitude was clear to me now, and
bewilderingly beautiful. I could explore each vibrant tremolo, each
glittering facet, each pungent taste or pattern of hot and cold
forever in complete contentment. It was the structure that was
important, the being of it. Purpose and outcomes didn't matter,
weren't even desirable. That the song existed at this moment solely
to direct the destruction of the facility was only a vague, fading
concern.

I rode the wavelengths coursing through me, myself coursing
through the countless channels of the sendings. I was pulsing with
it, merging with the complex rhythms, becoming only a pure,
voiceless tone—

Without warning, a jolting charge ripped through the ocean,
tearing the song to shreds and flinging me into a spin. The perfect,
static lattice of the song ripped into a million shards, sparkling

like gems as they whirled down a river of light. The river whirled us all, plunging us into eddies and tossing us up in a spray of frothing laughter. Warmth, excitement, energy bubbled through my veins as the glistening river bore us to the crest of a bottomless cliff and plunged into velvet blackness.

I floated limp in the buoyant darkness, the jubilant swirl of the river slowly ebbing, draining into the sea. I was smiling.

A silent, chuckling echo hummed through me as I slowly regathered my scattered perceptions, reaching out for the bright, gemlike shards of the broken sending lattice. Disconnected words and images sparkled: the alien signal, not just disruption. Siolis' whispered voice, his dark purple eyes drawing me down a spinning black well. The electrolytic sea. The slippery crackle of the companion fish and their wafting plumes, flushing different colors. Sliding over me as image, taste, touch slid into focus. The native sounding songs ringing through dark mazes, through angled facets, doubling back, realigning in impossible complexity with a humming surety. Sunburst-crystal dice spinning over black velvet in winking snake eyes. The cybers' speaking-ring suspended in a console dome.

Suddenly all the bright pieces came together, like the kaleidoscopic images of the sendings sliding into a new picture. The Cyvriots didn't need to destroy the facility to stop the incorporeals. But they didn't realize what they held in their hands.

I blinked, finning around and peering into the murk. Hesitant pulses washed over me—*confusion, outrage, disruption*—as the regathering natives sent out probes, as tentative sendings resumed from a nearby bathylabra. As the dancers, the listeners and singers, reformed their writhing knot to recover the scattered form of their song, I gathered up my own images and joined the facets into a new shape. The Cyvriot song swept through me again, gathering strength, swelling and ringing, expanding outward into its lattice of pure, balanced harmony.

I flung my own oddly faceted sending into the burgeoning structure, knowing it couldn't merge into the pattern, fit with its stubborn sharp angles into the proper congruencies. It tore through the harmonics, blossoming into a wild counterpoint of new melody. Part of it was me, part Siolis, part the alien sending, part themselves seeing new ways to live their Way. And I felt echoes of surprise, a vague groping—

Another disruption exploded, ripping the songs, flinging the

singers into reeling pain. This intrusion was different, though—
a violent, palpable detonation.

Shock waves hit me like a huge hand flinging me into an eruption
of deafening noise. I struggled to right myself in the turmoil of
expanding pressure, the sea around me heaving to a second explosion pounding pain through my ears. I clawed past churning
ripped weeds and stunned fish, opening my mouth to gasp and
only choking on seawater. Two more charges detonated almost
simultaneously, triggering blinding flashes of light and a crashing
roar. The natives and the creatures gathered with them were a
milling confusion of frantic fins and whipping tails, scattering. A
dark cylinder splashed through the surface overhead, tumbling
down and bursting above the fleeing natives.

I flailed backward in the surge of impact, hit something slippery
that wriggled away. A hand grabbed my arm and I tumbled against
Jay.

He pulled me around, eyes alarmed behind his goggles as he
urgently flashed our *OK?* query. I could only nod and tug him
toward the surface as another missile dropped and burst into fire
behind us.

We fought the churning currents, kicking up past desperately
thrashing, disoriented fish through the pounding bombardment
and clamoring inward echoes as painfully wrenching. Finally we
broke into the air, coughing and gasping as our lungs reclaimed
function. The surface heaved with colliding waves, flung spray,
tossed and bobbing shapes of stunned fish and natives. Overhead,
hovering flitters caught the fading light in a dull gleam of alloy,
flying slow patterns as mechmen dropped their deadly cylinders
into the sea.

"Jay! Hurry—" The chop broke over my head, and I gasped
water, thrashed back to the surface spitting and choking, fumbling
at Jay's sealed pocket for the null device.

"Here. I've got it." He pulled out the slippery black plasmeld.

"Wide dispersion, maximum range—" I coughed again, pointing upward.

The mechmen had spotted us. The nearest flitter veered from
its course, bearing down on us.

"Ruth, you've got to unlock it first."

"Damn! I forgot." I pressed the inset fingerlocks and it
clicked, but the device slipped between our fingers, spinning
down into the dimness as something hissed into the water near
my head.

We ducked under, plunging away from the mechman darts. Jay surged ahead, grabbing the sinking device and fumbling at its controls. Another cylinder splashed through the heaving ceiling overhead, tumbling down at us. I jerked Jay's arm around at the cylinder and he triggered the null field. A popping pressure, cloudy sediment swirled by the choppy sea, and the cylinder dropped past, silently tumbling.

Jay shook himself and launched upward.

The first flitter was already crashing down into the waves as I broke the surface after him. It drifted nearer, mechmen only fallen conglomerations of frozen alloy on its deck. Jay was treading water, staring at the device in his hand.

"Watch out!" I tugged him over to the shelter of the disabled flitter as the two others closed in. Another dart ricocheted off the alloy hull as we ducked under its flat bottom and resurfaced on the other side. Jay raised the weapon.

"Wait," I gasped. "Let them get in close range."

The mechmen couldn't have realized what had happened to the flitter, or they wouldn't have brought both the other craft in so close. They swept overhead and Jay neutralized the first one. As it fell from the sky, a laser burst from the last one flared off the hull close to us as the impact of the other crash flung us on its waves. Before the mechmen could try anything else, Jay had caught the last hovercraft in a null field. It smashed nose first into the sea, throwing up a plume as it plummeted, and then popping back up to bob aimlessly in the churning litter and feebly thrashing fish.

I blew out a long breath.

Jay paddled back on the lift of the swells that had separated us. He shook his head and grinned. "Hot damn." He spit seawater. "Got 'em. You okay, Ruth?" He kicked closer.

Another surge splashed over my head. I shook off the spume, gasping, "Jay, I've got to go after the natives again. I think I've finally got it! I don't think the spooks realize yet, but CI must have had some inkling because the Rules here make them speak in the console domes instead of connecting neurally, which might have given them the idea."

"What?" He coughed, bobbing closer.

"The Cyvriots! They don't realize it themselves. For them, the alien signal and the incorporeals and the Resistance are all rolled up into one taboo ball of wax, and they've got to purge the Way of us. But they don't need to destroy the facility." I paddled up and over another choppy swell, fighting my way back toward Jay, who was still holding the unlocked device above the waves. "Jay, if they'd let themselves, I'm sure they could use their sendings to interact with the facility control system. Somehow they can transform their bioelectric energy, focus, and amplify it with the help of their companion fish, but they only use it for communication, to enhance the sonar. I've got to get through to them—"

"No!" Lilith burst through the surface between us, snatching the null device from Jay's startled grip. "Now you've told me what I needed to know, I can stop this fiasco. The Cyvriots are going to stay ignorant animals like you!" She smirked and sank out of sight before we had time to react.

Jay shot me an agonized look and without a word dove after her. Numb, I jackknifed and shot down on his trail. We had to stop Lilith. I'd been right all along about her, should have trusted my instincts. And now she had our last defense.

Jay was well ahead of me, and Lilith only a frothing wake. I kicked harder, undulating my body and driving forward with my single fin. Around me, through me, I could feel the mutter of groping contact, pulsing soundings as the natives stubbornly re-gathered to shape their Way once more. The deep, percussive booms of the leviathans below rumbled upward. The Cyvriot song gained substance, tugging at me.

Ahead, Jay closed the distance between himself and Lilith. I could see her now, coming up short before a small cluster of swimming natives. They radiated palpable waves of shock and contempt as they turned and the echoes of their soundings returned from Lilith's mechanical body and the taboo device in her hand. Among them was the woman who'd talked to Jay and me. I swam harder, seizing on her distinct configuration, shaping a warning to thrust toward her. Only vague rejection echoed back. *Landers. Betrayal.* Two of the bulbous, tentacled creatures shot out of the murk behind the Cyvriots, wrapping their snaky limbs around the cyborg.

There was a blaze of burning light as Lilith fired her integrated lasers point-blank at the sea creatures, their torn bodies convulsing in a swirl of blood. The Cyvriots' horror flooded me as they finned slowly back from her, stunned and disbelieving.

Go! Run! I tried to shape urgency, as Lilith's hand lifted with the null device that could kill on a tight beam. A silent, wrenching scream tore at me. With a reflex jolt, the door in me slammed shut, sealing me off from the agonized group soundings as Lilith raked three of the natives with the deadly disruption of the beam. The fourth somehow escaped.

Soundings roared grief and fury, pounding down my doors again as huge shapes hurtled up from the depths to resume their attack on the facility. There was a wild ringing in my ears, and I surged past Jay's shocked face as Lilith launched, null device outstretched, after the native fleeing to the regathering group. Crazed with the hammering pulses of sound and my own rage, I flung myself onto her back, clawing for the device.

The cyborg shook me off like an irritating insect, flinging me backward as I grappled water to recover. She turned, blond strands drifting in a leisurely kiss across her face. The silky veil parted and the sharp amber lights of her eyes fixed on me as she gave me her pouty little smile and raised her hand, fingertip splitting open to reveal the laser port.

I scrambled back from her as she deliberately fired off a glancing burst, the water-diffused beam sizzling down my right leg, melting the suit and scalding me. I barely felt it, a cold fist clenching inside me as her mechanical pout widened to the same smug smile she'd given me in the facility. She launched toward me, murderous hand outstretched.

Somehow the bare seconds swelled into agonizing, slow suspension as I caught a blur of movement overhead. Jay shot downward, eyes meeting mine in a wrenching echo of Jason's parting gaze from Andura, as I opened my mouth to scream "No!" and it burst out as a silent sending. In the final split second, something flickered in answer in Jay's eyes, and then they flared with pain and shock as he threw himself between me and Lilith's point-blank laser burst.

His eyes went blank. There was a boiling spill of blood, and his torn body fell against me, tumbling lifelessly away.

I could only drift, unable to move, caught between chill horror and the hatred igniting in a searing roar. The monster in the cyborg body raised her hand with the laser port again, the smile turning to a contemptuous sneer as Lilith moved closer.

Her bright eyes intent on their prey, she didn't see the dark shape snaking up from the murky depths below. One of the tentacled creatures, injured and trailing a cloud of dark blood, but still alive. I could only stare as its limbs shot out to seize the null device gripped loosely in Lilith's other hand.

The cyborg whipped around, bringing the laser to bear on the creature. Somewhere there was another deep, roaring echo.

Grief and rage exploded, spinning me down a black tunnel. Were they my eyes focusing a blurred, distorted image of Lilith raising her murderous hand toward me? My own multiple snakelike limbs tightening on the null device, finding the controls and triggering it into Lilith's face? It didn't matter. Killing was easier the second time, the corrosive spill of vengeance pouring into the treacherous human core of the machine.

Lilith's cyborg face went blank, bright amber eyes dying to colored glass. Her limbs splayed and spun heavily into black depths.

A sharp wrench, and I was blinking, staring at the tentacled creature as it slithered back from me, still clutching the null device, toward two natives surging out of the dimness. I reached out with a reflexive, feeble plea, but the huge purple eyes were fixed on me, filled with loathing for a noxious viper. *Murder. Horror. Taboo.* Soundings pulsed like a flat hand shoving me back behind the doors of my self. The wounded creature tightened its tentacle, crushing the null device, then jetted away in a spill of black ink. When the cloudy effusion cleared, the natives were gone, too.

Drifting, staring blankly into the dark sea, I finally shook myself. I searched mechanically, found Jay's drifting, mangled body, and managed to press the lids closed over his vacant eyes before the black waves of the group soundings broke over me.

Numbly towing Jay's body, his limbs drifting in the sea in an eerie semblance of his pre-animate body floating in the facility vat, I kicked wearily toward the sea mount. I vaguely noted that the massive sea creature ramming the shallow rock had been joined by another one. They seemed equally oblivious to my tiny intrusion as I kicked slowly past them, into the crevice funneling upward to the cavern entrance.

I wasn't surprised to see sealed metal gates barring the cavern entrance. Nor surprised at the twisted crack ruptured by the battering at its foundations. It was a task my body seemed to handle of itself, squeezing Jay and me through the narrow gap. I kicked even more slowly, Jay bumping mutely alongside, just beneath the surface of the dark, still water in the cavern.

It wasn't until I reached the dimly wavering light penetrating the water from above, and traced the dark, jutting bulk of the dock, that I registered the two small fish still somehow finning about me. I felt the brush of a slippery plume, a whisper of something stirring an answer inside. The companion fish darted away from me, swimming through the wide mesh of the submerged cage to rejoin the passively drifting Siolis.

eighteen

Jay's body was surprisingly heavy. It took me a long time, panting and heaving, tugging him with my one hand partway up to the quay and then dropping him splashing back, finally wrestling him up again as I grimly wrapped my legs around his sodden limpness and flipped him up and onto me. His arms flopping grotesquely, I rolled us both backward onto the stone floor. I lay gasping in a cold puddle, mercifully numb.

Gradually the chill seeped into me, demanding attention as I shivered violently. I sat up, vaguely registering indicators dancing wildly over the console bank in the dim, silent cavern, the erratic quivering of the stone floor, an insistent amber light flashing. I looked down at Jay's sprawled legs and fought off an insane urge to howl with laughter over our grisly dance.

The shivers shook me again with a dash of icy clarity. Jay's body lay twisted awkwardly beside me, still dripping seawater, the terrible gashes slicing almost through his torso and gaping open on severed spilling shapes. I choked down a surge of bile, blindly pulling his heavy limbs straight and dragging one of the discarded drop cloths over to cover the horrible wounds.

There was very little blood. Most of it had drained away into the sea, leaving his blank face ghastly pale. I fumbled the cover up to his chin, dropped it, and fought past a reluctance to touch his cold cheek.

Without warning, deep sobs wracked me, the bitter salt tears finally pouring out. I hunched beside him, rocking myself, furiously and silently damning myself for his death. It was all my fault. And why hadn't I told him . . . cleared the air, at least . . . explained if nothing else that silly misunderstanding in the dome? His hurt face, he hadn't understood, and Lilith smirking. . . .

I clenched my fist as a boiling surge of hatred shook me. No. I pushed away the detested image, refusing to let her invade again.

Taking a deep breath, I wiped the back of my hand across my face, reached out to stroke the tangled wet hair back from his forehead. Why had I been so damned stubborn, why hadn't I just given him what he wanted? To be loved as Jason.

Now Jay was lying there, mirror image of Jason's body torn by the laser weapons of the Poindros guards as he tried to save me. Damn. It should have been me. Would have been me. What was I supposed to do with these sacrifices? Didn't deserve them. This time he *was* finally dead. The mortal flesh and blood couldn't be resurrected. Not unless I could believe the Book of Words. Heaven or Hell. Nothing but ashes. To be loved as Jason. Only a weak human. But hadn't it been a true Jason act, that last deliberate intervention? Now when it was too late to tell him.

I shook my head furiously. No, even that wasn't fair, he wasn't just a duplicate. It wasn't Jason's death, it was Jay's. Damn it, he deserved at least his own name.

I finally drew the cloth up to cover his face. As I dropped it, someone tapped my shoulder. "Ruth."

I whipped around, stomach jolting. Lilith.

Sacred Founders, even still with a hint of a smile on her murderer's face. The cavern spun crazily as *timbra* roared through me on a hot flood of adrenaline. I leaped to my feet, springing at her with nothing but the unalloyed reflex to kill the monster.

An eye for an eye . . . everything reduced to a simple imperative. My hand was at her throat, grip tightening as she stumbled backward, cringing, arms flailing ineffectually. Then I realized what I was seeing. Lilith's face, grime-streaked but pale and tired-looking, ordinary blue eyes wide as her mouth opened on a thin, choked wail of terror, the figure in the rumpled coveralls rounded but not lushly bursting the seams.

I jerked to a stop, hand dropping heavily to my side. She fell back, stumbling, catching herself, eyes locked on me as her hands with chipped nails came up dramatically to clutch her throat. She swallowed and edged farther from me.

Then, when I didn't move, Lilith's clone took a deep breath and drew herself up, thrusting out her chest and giving me a shaky imitation of the cyborg's smirk. "Well, we were sure right about you meatheads! All you can do is act like animals."

The draining of the violent adrenaline surge left me trembling. I couldn't speak.

Another sideways glance from the blue eyes and she tossed her loose hair back. "When *she* gets back, you'll watch your step! She's going to make me a cyborg, too, so we can really share everything. We'll be the ones in charge around here. So you better think about staying on my right side, Mistress think-you're-so-smart Ruth, if you know what's good for you." She produced the lilting laugh that wasn't as musical as Lilith's. Only grating.

I shook my head, fighting back the impulse to slap her aside like a buzzing insect, let the humming readiness rise again in me and take over with its honed fighting responses. Even with one hand, I could hurt her, kill her. But she wasn't worth it.

I cleared my throat. "You're even more stupid than she was." My voice shook with contempt. "*Was*, get it? She's dead, and there's no magic kingdom for either of you."

"She is not! You're just lying."

"No, I'm not as good at that as you are, little Lilith Number Two. Your Number One's dead, and she was only using you, anyway, like she used everyone else. You must be a spare part so she could make sure she'd keep on with her wonderful self. She—you—you're the center of the universe, right? Well, I've got news. You both just lost out, and probably none of us are going to make it out of here, because the Cyvriots are hammering this place down around us!" I waved my arm at the urgently blinking indicators on the consoles and the insistent alert flasher. Beneath us, a deep tremor shivered through the stone floor. I didn't really care, except that I could see it scared her. "See?"

She shot a frightened look at the consoles and back at me, opening her mouth to gape like a fish.

I pressed closer to her, lowering my voice as she cringed. "Did you actually think Lilith would let you compete with her on equal grounds? Think about that, if it doesn't hurt your head too much. Would *you* have shared?" No answer, but her pale face blanched white. "Get out of here, you make me sick."

I turned toward the consoles, and the pathetic floating form of David, still suspended in the greenish illumination of his vat.

"Ruth, please!" A clammy little hand reached hesitantly to touch mine. She flinched back as I looked down, her eyes nervously flicking back and forth and not meeting mine. "Don't make me go. I'm afraid. Can't we do something?"

I moved past her. "I'm going to try to get David and Siolis out of here. You do what you want with yourself."

"But Ruth, I know where Lilith put Jason. She tricked him, you know, trapped him in a force-field containment down below."

I froze, then slowly shook my head and moved on toward the console and the impossible tangle of equipment connected to David's vat.

"I know the unlocking code," the voice behind me wheedled. "Please, Ruth. I see now I was wrong. She tricked me, too. I'll help you, do anything you say. Only don't let them punish me. Do you want me to go get him?''

The rage was building in me again, colored by disgust. ''I don't give a damn what you do! Just get out of here before I—'' My voice strangled.

''All right. Don't get all upset, I'll just . . .'' She scurried across the floor and the door hissed shut.

I closed my eyes, took a deep breath, and refused to examine the snarl of questions seething for attention. Another tremor shook the floor, and I could almost hear a grinding far below in the rock. First things first. I stepped past the urgently reconfiguring indicators, making a slow circuit of David's vat and tracing strand by strand the complicated web of connections.

My examination told me nothing. I didn't know how to disconnect David without harming him. I turned from my hopeless scrutiny of the kid's empty, bobbing face to stare blankly at the submerged mesh cage where Siolis dimly floated.

I rubbed my aching forehead, trying to focus. The incorporeals here were definitely using a different sort of neural interface from the ones we'd encountered on Poindros and Andura, physical links of electrodes and leads. Maybe they'd suspected, as the cybers must have, that the Cyvriots might have the ability to deflect their energy fields. At least Lilith hadn't had time to tell them what she'd learned. Maybe Siolis could catch them with their defenses down if I could somehow get through to him.

I poked again through the assemblage of instruments and cables and pumps connecting David and Siolis to the matrix and to what was left of their lives. I sat abruptly, gripping a plasmeld case I found tucked among the equipment. We'd missed it before. I'd forgotten about it. David's portable interface device.

I opened the case and stared at the curved black plasmeld instrument with its skin-cling and tiny, needled interface that could link me with the matrix. I was stupidly afraid to touch it. The warning buzz of *timbra* rang in my ears, my hands shaking as I lifted the device out of its case. It stood for everything I'd fought for so long—the cybers and their consoles and their changeless Ways, the incorporeals and the cold calculations of their energy webs, the machines obliterating human perceptions and values. I didn't even know how to use it, but I knew it was the only way. For David, I'd do it.

With a physical effort, I thrust away the buzzing alarm and the

doubts and bone-deep taboos. I loosened the neck of my suit and
slid the device over one shoulder, my skin crawling under the
slippery plasmeld as I pushed it awkwardly toward my upper spine.

"Ruth, wait!" The door whisked back into the cavern wall and
Jason hurried through, the blond clone skulking behind him. She
hovered in the shadows near the wall as he strode over to me.
"Wait. Don't do something crazy. We've got to talk." He plucked
the device from beneath my collar.

"There's nothing to talk about, Jason." I stared woodenly up
into his face.

He was back to "normal," if there could be such a thing, his
face gravely concerned, gold-brown gaze dropping uncomfortably
before mine. "Founders, Ruth, I'm sorry. I was wrong—totally,
stupidly, inexcusably wrong. And I thought I was doing the right
thing. . . ."

If I hadn't known him too well, I'd have thought he was inventing the "emoting" that broke his voice. But he was only
allowing the circuits of his body to reflect his mental state. I was
the one feeling nothing, sitting somewhere above us watching and
analyzing.

He shook his head. "You were right not to trust her. She fooled
me with her tricks. All along she was playing us, trying to decide
which side could offer her more. At the end, I think she believed
you and the Cyvriots had some secret that would let her take
control of the incorporeals and rule the entire system. She—"

"There's no time for that. It doesn't matter now. I don't give
a damn about those arrogant blind Cyvriots or any of the rest of
it. I just need to reach Siolis and David and get them out of the
matrix before the natives bring the place down around our ears."
I reached mechanically for the device in his hand.

"Wait." He pulled it back. "The facility is in danger, but it's
not critical yet. The remaining mechmen are down below, making
repairs to containment ruptures—"

As if to spite him, there was another tremor, more pronounced
this time. He jerked around to face the eerily silent frenzy of
flashing indicators on the console bank as the amber warning
flasher turned to a crimson pulse.

His eyes flared their own bright amber, then faded as he turned
back to me. "All right. I'll disconnect them and we'll hope for
the best. It's all we can do now that—" He broke off as he turned
and saw the sheeted shape on the stone quay.

He strode abruptly past me, over to Jay's body, and pulled back the cover. He stood frozen, holding the cloth, face gone blank.

"Jason, come on," the Lilith clone whispered, sidling over to him in the shadows of the stacked cargo. She tugged at his arm, but he didn't budge. She looked down and gave out a little cry. "He's really *you* lying there, isn't he?" She bit her lip.

"Leave him alone!" I stalked over to them and jerked the sheet out of Jason's fingers, glaring at the blond clone. She scuttled back toward the door as I yanked the cloth back over Jay's blank face, the livid mirror of Jason's. "Don't you dare say it. He wasn't you. *You* weren't there. He was alive, and now he's dead. He earned his own identity, damn you!"

"Ruth, please." He shook himself, shot me an agonized glance that looked too much like Jay, and tried to catch my hand. "I was only trying to give you—"

"What you've given me is another person to mourn. Leave me alone." I jerked away and strode back across the cavern, picking up the interface device he'd dropped. I pressed it hard against my upper back, felt the sting of the needles, and then numbness.

"Ruth, you don't know how to use that! Don't try it, you'll only—"

He broke off, startled, as I screwed up my eyes, found the neural trigger, raced tumbling down a mad slide of connecting circuits, and shot out along a preset channel: *Oh yes, I can!*

Then fiery pain ripped through my head, and a crazy spewing of lights, noise, wrenching sensations that turned me upside-down, spinning me.

Something grabbed me, giving me a center to the wild whirling. Jason's voice was inside me, soothing, almost the same as the few times I'd allowed him a direct neural contact. *Wait. Slow down, I'll help you orient.* And then he was only a solid, safely impersonal presence anchoring me against the black flood of panic as a multitude of data loops and signal triggers and things I didn't understand began presenting themselves, and I started to spin out of control. There was an easing as several gates shut down and my balance settled around me. *You don't need all that. I've left you data processors and channels for direct contact. But please, Ruth, don't try it. You know you barely made it out alive the last time on Andura. And you'll have less defense against the incorporeals this way.*

I took a deep breath in the darkness of the link. *But I'll be able to reach Siolis easier, too. I won't have to go as deep into the matrix to find him as I would David. I can . . .* I realized suddenly

I didn't have to formulate words. I shaped the concept of *sending* and passed it into the channel.

He must have received more than I thought I'd sent, because he stopped trying to talk me out of it. We both knew there was no other choice. Jason didn't have whatever the ability was that had let me enter the spook matrix twice before and resist their tortures and temptations to join them. Neither of us knew whether it would work this time. But I thought, with the companion fish back, that I could reach Siolis. And if he, in turn, could help David emerge, then Jason could shut down the whole facility.

I opened my eyes to see Jason, with a perfectly blank face, checking my osmotic circulation gear. He helped me open the top of Siolis' mesh cage. There was a fleeting whisper of something passing through the channel, a presence, but no message. I didn't want one. I didn't look up at him as I took a last breath and dropped under the surface.

Cool water, dimness, and the slippery bodies of the companion fish wriggling over and around me, their wafting plumes crackling with energy. Siolis was a shadowy bulk of tapering thick body and coiled tail. I eased over to him, closing my eyes and reaching out to actually touch him for the first time.

His hairless skin was smooth, thick, and strangely resilient. I remembered his changeable violet eyes drawing mine, pinning them as I tumbled down spiraling wells. At the bottom, that elusive door. I edged it open, but this time there was no one there. He was far beyond. Caught up in dreams. Or nightmares.

I willed myself out through the nebulous doorway, and it spun away behind me as I floated out into darkness and a dim, distant muttering of sea voices. They were only distractions now, and I shut them out. All but two flickering presences, the two little plumy shapes with their peculiar signature-charges fluctuating, ebbing and flowing through me. In the unbreathing trance, I signaled the channel Jason had shown me.

The matrix answered at once, blackness unfolding outward with bewildering speed into fanning dimensions, welcoming me. Enfolding me.

Vertigo and frightening velocity as I poured through the incorporeal channels, sucked into an irresistible current. Endlessly hurled—or only for a fraction of a second?—and time was left behind, irrelevant. There was a junction, and I divided, flowing outward, inward, back and forth through the tracks of a glowing multidimensional grid that was only an illusion of inside-out space, and I was shunting back and forth, switching charged states and simultaneously plummeting and drifting free.

A popping sensation, something slippery stirring, and I was floating in blood-warm darkness.

Where?
* NO WHERE *
but I
* NO I *
no, you
* NO YOU * NO I * YOUI WEUS * ONE IN ALL *
when . . .
* NO WHEN NO TIME NO NEED *
No—!
* NO * NO NO NO KNOW NO *

No. There was nothing, only the endless flowing into nothing, into a sourceless origin, the nonpresences melding in nonlight. Random sensation, floating sealed bits of a being somewhere else, but not here in this not-ness. No I. No memory. No they. No David or Siolis.

NO! That was it. The purpose. But there was nothing in the not-here. Everything in the here? One in all. Only a dizzy, empty flowing. Fathomless. Forever. Already over. Nothing to rend with a silent nonscream.

But nothing suddenly answered me. A probing touch, sparking a locus of reference, drawing me to it. The incorporeal awarenesses, intangible, but drawing me deeper.

No way, no where to escape. Except . . . A groping awareness of more, somewhere. A different contact, tingling through the convoluted channels lost outside the nothingness, another unfolding dimension guiding me toward a bewildering map of the countless strands of the nonspace.

The web still pulled me inward, deeper into blackness. But now there was something to resist. I pulled against it, sent myself in the opposite direction along an invisible strand. Hot pain coursed down it, sizzling me.

* NO * JOIN MELD ONE IN ALL *

No more answering. I groped again for that flickering connection through the interface somewhere beyond this nonplace. The presence out there—Jason?—showed me another strand of the web and I flailed wildly toward it, a searing trail of torn and crackling charges flaring in my wake. Fire and slashing blades sprang up

around and before me, cutting me off, but I dropped down, through
the flaying whips of the incorporeals, into another unfolding dimension.

Silent, chilling laughter rang around me, melting to a smooth
globe, sealing me off, sealing me inside. I flung myself against
the seamless curves, but there was no escape.

Bodiless voices chimed around me, echoing sourceless. *Cease
this pointless game, Ruth. Join us now. We have so much to offer
you. Your body is damaged, aging in the wink of an eye. With us
you can join forever the ones you love—David, Siolis, and soon
Jason. Haven't you fought your limitations long enough?*

A soft murmur of harp strings shivered through the globe as it
expanded, the walls stretching away into infinity, floating me
upward into a rarified, crisp ether that was air and water and
sustenance all at once, filling me with buoyant elation.

Why cling to mortality, when we offer you transcendence?

I was flying, free at last, into boundless skies, all of experience
and delight opening out before me.

Planets, a flaring sun whirled past, and I was soaring into the
velvet depths of space. The silver light of the stars glinted, beckoning. With incredible speed, I was among their cold fiery spirals,
hearing the crystalline chime of their ethereal songs.

Join us, share the mysteries, learn the secrets. The stars spun,
coiling around me in a flashing vortex sucking me into a chaotic
barrage of sensation as the sharp sparks broke over me in strange
shapes and unknown colors, sounds past hearing, warped dimensions of alien worlds, twisting loops of time turned inside-out, the
blaze of promised power pouring through my veins.

I tumbled, dizzy, flinching from the endless bombardment, the
cold, compelling song of the star shapes. Lost, battered, I was
tempted to grasp one of the glittering shapes as they wanted, to
seize any anchor against the insane whirl.

A vague memory stirred somewhere in the chaos. I seized it
eagerly, summoning the hoarded little chip of sight, sound, and
place I'd grasped in the Anduran incorporeal web to defend myself.
With a bright flash of light the vignette tumbled over me and
expanded, floating me down out of the whirl to land on the solid
floor of a dim room with a pulsing crystalline ceiling. I caught
my breath, lowering the arms I'd thrust out against my fall, and
saw the same oddly configured cyber console set flush along one
wall of the room. I recognized the gray-haired woman dressed in

a plain robe, the quick blue eyes in a lined face turning from the console. The Founder of Andura's worldplan.

Before she could speak, I strode over to her. "Can you help me find David and Siolis? We've got to stop the incorporeals before they do here what they tried on Andura."

She didn't seem to hear, looking through me. "Yes, the unchanging grand Plan originated as much in cybernetic Directives as in the human decisions of the Worlds Council. . . ."

"Precisely."

I jerked around to find the source of the voice intruding in the room. A thin, short man with a pinched face and wispy brown hair, wearing a strange, sharp-angled suit of opaque black, stood behind me. As I stumbled back from him, he gave me a compressed smile and gestured. The suit, enclosing him seamlessly at wrist and neck, reconfigured its odd angles and lifted the man to float closer to me. Silver light raced in cracking flashes across the geometric planes encasing him.

"Know me. I am—"

"The Poindros Founder. I know." I swallowed in a throat gone dry. "Who invited you?"

He laughed drily. "Delightful as ever, Ruth. You will make a fine addition to my matrix. Aren't you convinced yet that we truly represent the new evolution of humanity?"

I edged back, glancing around for a way out, but the room dissolved at its edges into shadowy nothingness. "I'm not convinced of anything, I—"

"There's no place to run, Ruth, so you may as well face it. As my colleague was pointing out"—he gestured to the Anduran Founder, frozen before her console—"it's the cybers who are truly our enemy, who have tried to take our future from us. You know that," he chided.

Another gesture in the disturbingly shifting plates of his sleeve, and a globe sprang out of the shadows. A world of blue sea, cloaked with clouds, spinning slowly through space. "'O brave new world.' Cyvrus, to be plain." The suit brought him around to face me. "My dear, it was a grand experiment, a noble effort. Think of it, a new breed of humans learning to communicate without the need of words, learning to build without the need of gross hands and tools. But then the new cybernetic directives halted the bioforming midstream, leaving the Cyvriots neither fish nor fowl, you might say, turning our genetic laboratories into their facility to 'maintain faunal purity.' Turning it into a monument to static sameness!''

The thin face was flushed now, eyes sparking. ''Of course, you know I was preparing even then a more ambitious project. When my colleagues were apprehended, I managed to send my activated clone on to Poindros and escape into my experimental incorporeal matrix here, concealed in stasis with the other Cyvriot awarenesses until we could be reactivated in the fullness of time. And now nothing will hold us back. When we learn the advanced technologies of the aliens—''

''Hold on! You're not going to learn anything, you can't even decode their signal. And the Cyvriots are battering this place down around you, in case you haven't noticed.''

His pale blue eyes narrowed for a second, then he smiled. ''Minor difficulties of a temporal nature. If you would share the timeless abundance of our fusion with us, Ruth, you would realize how irrelevant—''

''If they're irrelevant, how come you're so anxious to suck me in, to get David and Siolis to help you?''

''We only want to share, Ruth. Share our great knowledge and capacities, share your stimulating individualities—''

''I've heard that before. I know what happens to you awarenesses in there. Maybe you haven't been activated long enough, but the others found out. It all goes gray, doesn't it, or rather white, in your fusion? The interesting little differences in your awarenesses all get fuzzy around the edges until it's that boring, blended one in all.''

He raised his palms. ''I will share the truth with you, Ruth. Yes, we have recognized that tendency already. That is one reason we seek the alien input. But more importantly, why we wish you and some Cyvriots to join us. My children of the sea grew in ways even I had not anticipated. There is an ability you share with them beyond our analysis with the insufficient data we now possess. Is it so much to ask that you share it with us, when we offer you so much?''

His eyes held mine, hovering closer, mesmerizing, so close now I could see only one eye pinning me. It swelled in the darkness into a spinning blue world, drawing me down as the ethereal blended voices of the stars whispered through me with their siren song. *Worlds, universes of knowing and being, sharing and power. Excitement and change. Everything the cybers have denied us. Freedom from shackles, from pain and death.*

They were right. The song flowed through me with inevitable rightness, and I lifted my voice to join in as I plunged up into new constellations.

But somehow a nagging doubt weighed down on me, made me too heavy to fly. An image rolling out of the darkness—Jay's pale, cold face, shackling me to humanity. The memory of something flickering in his eyes just before he died. . . .

Flickering? Crackling. A sensation, far away, almost lost. The faint brush of whisking plumes, touching the body I'd once had and then fading. I flailed in the dark emptiness, groping, plummeting from the rarified heights, grasping after that vanishing contact—and suddenly I was floating in a different kind of darkness, a fluid rippling. A presence nearby, a faint whisper of energy.

Siolis. I could sense him now, muffled, somewhere near. Evanescent, slippery shadows teased me, drew me on. He was closer. I was bobbing now, through a sea of bubbles, a frothing eruption of data, configurations, equations, discoveries fountaining me upward in a cascade of heady excitement. Floating among them, Siolis was a flashing sphere of light, rolling and bouncing in the tide of vitality. Somewhere, farther, David was . . . beyond reach. But I could grope and slither and be gushed upward toward Siolis' glittering sphere.

Bubbling and bursting images jetted me higher. Siolis and his sibilant chuckle as the companion fish leapt about him in a swirl of colored plumes. The eternal Serpent, hissing with laughter, its amber eyes winking. Snake eyes glittering on the sunburst-crystal dice. The bits of memory catapulted me upward to smack against the slippery globe encapsulating Siolis' awareness.

The Cyvriot was still dreaming, eyes closed, floating in the glittering womb as his toothless mouth vaguely smiled. The globe was seamless crystal, flawless as the ocean song of the native sendings. I hammered in desperation, but made no dent in the smooth surface. I clenched my fist to pound again, and opened it in surprise to find I held an odd little gem, made up of rough, awkward facets and angles. It flashed and swelled in my hand, ringing a chiming little tune that was somehow familiar. I swung the graceless thing and its sharp angles pierced the glistening globe, pouring out a flood of jarring melody.

Siolis opened one eye.

And I was tumbling into a dark well again, this time through the rent in the sphere and into drowning purple seas. There was a wild clamoring rage of pursuing incorporeals outside the globe as Siolis pulled me down. His soundings shivered through me in urgent question, and then the sharp little gem of recognition was slicing me open, too, pouring out my own gush of images, one melting into the next.

Siolis, whispering as his huge purple eyes drew me in and his companion fish leapt in a whirl of color-changing fins and crackling charge. His long whipping tail stretching, changing to the coils of the jolting electric sea serpent. Rolling into the endlessly cycling loop of the head-to-tail Serpent, hissing laughter as its bright eyes winked. Becoming the flashing snake eyes of the spinning crystal dice. Growing, burgeoning into the complex, faceted angles of the crystals of the bathylabra, glinting cold blue light. Mirroring an explosion of colors as the bright ecstatic river of the alien sendings frothed around me, tingling. Tingling with the itch of the bioelectric healing cast. Pulsing as waves of more than sound shivered through me with the sea songs. Shivered through Siolis, pulsing outward as the colored indicator lights of a console danced to his tune.

Yesss!

Siolis' voice was stunned, excited, rueful. It rippled through me, silently lapping, as the purple torrent swept us away from the pursuing denizens of the matrix. *Of course, Ruth. I have harbored the self-lies we Cyvriots pride ourselves on escaping within our sharing. Perhaps I fostered it in my solitude. Always the old horror of links with machines was there, the revulsion of taboo nurtured in us by the cybers, lurking secretly within me like the shark in the deep trenches. It kept me from guessing, from trying.*

I flailed, following his lithe plunge deeper into the flood. *Now you know, Siolis. Help me find David and get him out, then you can seal off the incorporeals.*

A burst of fizzing laughter through my veins. *Listen to yourself, Ruth. No more secrets.* He shot ahead, laughter echoing back, leaving me wallowing in a trail of bubbles.

Damn him. Even in the link of the matrix, only giving me riddles. I was lost in his blind seas, out of my element, drowning, the companion fish gone with him. Abandoned. And outside his ocean, the spooks hovered.

I screamed mutely, silent rage crackling through my veins, sparkling at my fingertips, sizzling into the salty dark waters. I stared. Then I pushed, sending the sparks out from me, lighting up the sea and pushing the shrouding darkness back. A deep breath, and the charged air flowed through me, the electrolyte

sea pumped through my vessels, my salt blood sang with a
humming song. I was the bathylabra, the sendings echoing
through my mazes. I was the complex crystalline lattice shimmering with energy.

I threw back my head and laughed then, and bolts of blended
white light shot from my fingertips to pull me through the dark
nonplaces of the matrix as the sea ebbed behind me. I could see
David now, caught in the strands of the incorporeal web, emerging
slowly as Siolis circled him, breaking the glowing bonds, sending
the sharp sparks of furious awarenesses spinning away. David was
blinking, shaking his head in confusion.

I swept closer, circling them both, spinning them away into my
own nonplace as the roar of the pursuing incorporeals echoed at
my back. White light swirled, spun, swelled to the glare of hot
sunlight shimmering over the whirling sapphire-silver sails of a
Poindran windtower. The air roared as the huge wheel bore us
around in its dizzy plunge, coppery wheat fields and burnished
blue sky spinning around us.

"Fire and thorns, Ruth!" David, white-faced, clutched desperately to a climbing rung of the alloy spoke. "Did you have to
bring me here? I'm gonna puke."

"No, you won't. Mind over matter, kid." I grinned into the
fierce rush of wind and color, reaching out to ruffle his snarled
hair. "Thought you wanted to be pure energy?"

"Ha ha." He scowled, then reluctantly grinned. "Pretty fancy,
anyway, Auntie. Where'd Siolis go?" Still gripping the rung, he
craned around.

"Besside you, David." And Siolis was there, somehow transformed into a long, bluish serpent with a sly smile, winking
purple eyes as he wrapped his coils about the spoke. "We sssee
together, Ruth. Did I not ssay we would llllearn?" He laughed,
dry sibilant music blending with the wind and the hiss of the
stirring wheat.

"Damn right, Siolis!" David thrust his face forward eagerly.
"Ruth, I'm learning incredible things in the matrix. Like how to
navigate the energy plasma, I've almost got it, I think, but it's
going to be complicated trying to get to the point of changing
directives. They're somehow part of the entire configuration. Of
course that's putting it dimensionally."

I shook my head. "The main thing is, are you all right? They
didn't hurt you? We're safe in here for now, but we've got to
think about getting out."

"They didn't hurt me at all, Ruth, not like in the Anduran matrix. You know it's true, this matrix is different, it's more open, really dedicated in its directives to exploration and development. They were showing me all kinds of data, but keeping a leash on me, promising more if I'd help them decode the alien signal. I sort of led them on a little, I guess"—he shrugged— "but then they promised me and Siolis they had some information we didn't have, too, and it didn't amount to much. See, they'd got to the point of realizing all the permutations of source and electromagnetic patterns weren't really significant, that it was some transformation in the sea that was crucial. So they wanted to know what data Siolis and I had on sonic reverberations and chemical interactions. I thought, why not, we hadn't got the key that way, either, but that's when Siolis clammed up and the spooks got kind of huffy. So they isolated us in separate sectors. They still gave me data to work on, but there's something missing somewhere."

"What's missing is your mind!" I shouted over the roar of wind and snapping sails. "I can't believe you were actually considering helping them, David. You ought to know by now the kinds of tricks they can pull. We're getting out now, before they figure out what Siolis can do with their control interfaces, and between us I think we can pull out far enough to pick up Jason's homing signals. Get ready now, and don't let them lure you back—".

"Blast it, Ruth, you're just running scared! If Siolis has got the key now, we can do it with the help of the matrix. Encode an answer to the aliens! We're so close to breaking through."

"Ruth iss right, David." Siolis finally broke out of his silence, uncoiling from the rotating spoke and swaying his blunt head to the whip of the wheel. "They are different in ssome waysss, yet not to be trusssted. The ansswer to allien ssignalll willl not be found in matrix. I musst return to sssea." The reptilian face swayed closer to mine, purple eyes questioning.

I nodded. I stretched my arm overhead, gripping the spoke with my knees, riding the windy mad whirl as billowing mylar sails sparkled sapphires and pearls, melted into a dazzling kaleidoscope of jeweled colors, spun faster into a pulse of blinding white light. It was the effervescent energy of the alien sending whirling us now, pulsing its dazzling glints of color between Siolis and me, then whipping David into its torrent.

I laughed, dancing in the turbulence as David was borne around

the whirlpool grinning in surprise, tossing and juggling bright
bits he plucked from the surging currents. Siolis plunged his
coils through the froth, sending up a song echoing the joy of
the alien sendings in the sea, its tones ringing out welcome,
curiosity, change, discovery—everything the Cyvriots were
trained to fear—singing through flesh and bones. We all laughed
as the message rang clear through us, nothing to do with the
complex permutations of signal energies that bore it toward
transformation through electrolyte sea, crystal, sound, and flesh,
but everything to do with reverberations from the heart. An
invitation, waiting for an answer.

The sparkling exuberance spun us upward as Siolis' coils looped
around David and me and we soared out of the whirlpool, up from
the spinning windwheel into the hot blue sky, into the seething
sun, into the velvet darkness of space.

David suddenly struggled, thrashing against the slippery coils.
"No, wait! I can't leave—"

"Now, David." And I plunged with him through the boundary
of my nonplace back into the matrix.

It buzzed furiously, sharp stars swarming, closing in. But this
time I could see the invisible pattern of their multidimensional
maze as we raced down twisting, crackling, inside-out paths to
escape. More blazing sparks sprang up in front of us, cutting us
off as we circled, plunged, fell through darkness and unfolding
levels, a howling rage swelling around us. Voices echoed, pulling
back at us.

Then another voice, a faint presence, lighting up different
paths, flinging out a frail thread. I grabbed it and the thread
tugged through the maze, pulling us backward as the planes and
impossible angles of the matrix folded and unfolded around us.
But the jolt of wrenching space and time was too fast, and I
couldn't catch my breath, pain exploding in my chest. I remembered that I had to warn Siolis about the native attack, but
it was too late. The force had me paralyzed in its hold now,
gripping me by the back of the neck and dragging me through
dizzy channels, flashes of light and images, wavering shrieking
noise, prickling heat and then cold. No air, and the force crushing, suffocating me.

I gasped. Bitter seawater flowed down my throat and into my
lungs, choking me. My heart had stopped. I was drowning, thrashing feebly.

Something long and pliant coiled around me, catching me, pushing me back toward the surface. A dimly purple, staring eye. And a silent voice, hissing through me, laughing with the dancing song of the Serpent whipping its eternal head-to-tail cycle.

My heart lurched into a violent beat and Siolis' tail thrust me up into the air. Jason caught me.

nineteen

Jason's hands plucked me effortlessly out of the sea and efficiently ejected the water from my lungs. Before I had time to gag or blink, his fingertips, with a quick tingle of electricity, urged my heartbeat into a normal rhythm. Then he left me to gasp and cough on the wet stone, turning to the cylindrical vat where David's skinny legs frog-kicked madly against the curved walls. The blank, dreaming face was now grimacing as he waved and pounded on the transparent vessel.

"Hurry!" I choked.

But Jason had already swung open the cap and was somehow up and straddling the top of the tall cylinder, plucking David out. The kid dangled, dripping and still kicking, and then Jason sprang down with him.

David, deathly pale and fragile-looking, clawed at his throat as Jason pried his jaws open and quickly extracted a rubbery plug. His cyborg's hand flattened over David's chest as the bony ribcage shuddered and rose. David gagged and snorted a gout of fluid, then grabbed the tubes still trailing from his arm and plucked them out. "Ruth . . . gotta—" He coughed and staggered over to me, eyes wide and blind-looking without the spectacles. His hand groped over my shoulder and under my collar to rip the interface device free with a sharp sting.

"What—"

"No time." He coughed again, twisting to slap the plasmeld instrument against his own naked upper back. "Made me leave my calculations still cycling. All that data I gathered. Gotta finish—"

"No, David." Jason's eyes flared amber as he caught David by the shoulder.

"Hey, cut it out! Open those channels back up so I can connect with the matrix." David glared myopically, staggering back from Jason's grip.

"You're in no shape to do anything right now. I'll take care of shutting down the facility power, and then we've got to get

247

out." He gestured toward the crimson danger signal still flashing above the dancing console indicators.

"You can't do that. The matrix. You don't see—"

"Wait!" I straightened, holding up my hand. "Be quiet!" I gestured urgently, and David subsided as I screwed up my eyes, concentrating. "Just wait a sec. . . ." I scooted over to the edge of the stone quay, flipping my legs over the lip into the water. I tried to relax, letting the water flow over me. And suddenly the soundings slid into focus.

I nodded, blinking and turning back to Jason, who was frowning slightly. "Siolis says to wait, he's taking care of it without shutting down the whole facility."

"What do you—" Jason broke off, face startled, then blank as his eyes flared amber again. He blinked, eyes fading to brown-gold as he nodded. "You're right. Siolis has somehow interacted with the facility control system. He's separated the incorporeal matrix from the operating programs. I can't explain it—it's not like the stasis CI used to imprison and neutralize the other matrix. The incorporeals are still cognizant, but they can't penetrate to initiate functions with the system, almost as if there's a seamless bubble around their matrix." He shook his head.

I laughed weakly, nodding. "It's the song, Jason, the sending song! I tried to tell the natives. . . ."

David leaned close to peer into my face, then patted my head awkwardly. "Hey, take it easy." He straightened and shrugged at Jason, then burst out, "Man, you should've been in there! When Ruth came in and got Siolis and me back together, we got it all clear. We can break through now on the alien message! But blast it, Ruth, then you had to go and yank us out just when we were getting going. If you would've given me time to—"

"David!" Jason's sharp tone startled me, as the kid broke off gaping at him. "Why don't you try listening for a change? According to Siolis' transmission just now, Ruth was the one who showed him the key. So stop showing off. And if you have any complaints, *I* was the one who finally yanked you out of there by the scruff of your silly neck, you impudent young pup. Now, aren't you forgetting something? Ruth's risked herself again to get you out of hot water, putting your welfare before her own. . . ."

David swung from Jason's stony face to me, giving me a shaky imitation of his usual cocky grin. "Hey, Ruth, tell him to lay off. I was only—'' He caught a sharp breath, squinting fuzzily down at me. "No!" He dropped suddenly to his knees beside me, touching the dangling empty sleeve of my diving suit. "I forgot, Ruth! Sacred Founders . . ." He blinked quickly, biting his lip, whispering hoarsely, "I'm sorry." He cleared his throat.

I nodded dully, the charged visions of the matrix gone, drained away into gray weariness. Blinking through a pounding headache, I focused on David's trembling legs. He was shivering, hunched naked on the cold stone beside me.

"Hey, kid . . ." I threw my arm around his shoulders and drew him against me, glaring across him at Jason. "He's had enough, Jason! Stop being a bully and get me something to wrap around him."

Almost before I finished, Jason was draping one of the drop cloths around both of us. "Now, why don't you get off that cold floor?"

"Wait." I could feel Siolis, still trapped in the mesh cage while the hammering soundings, the pulsing sendings echoed from the sea. "Jason, Siolis needs to get out of that cage. He—" A violent tremor shook the cavern, dark water slapping against the quay and splashing up my legs. I closed my eyes against the insistent red danger signal, groping past jittering alarm. "He says . . . we've got to get out. Open the cage and he'll go try to persuade the natives to stop the attack on the facility." I rubbed my aching forehead again.

David gave me a blank look, then went back to shivering against me, clutching the cloth tighter. Jason strode silently to the cage, jumping in the water and tearing open one mesh side.

A swirl and splash as the companion fish broke the surface and dove. A slippery shape brushed across my bare feet in a vague slurry of comfort, warmth, reassurance, appreciation. Then a focusing, and something about him finding it—me finding it?—inside, what he'd been waiting for. I shook my head and Siolis was gone.

Jason plucked up David and me as one blanketed bundle and hurried through the crimson strobes toward the dim warehouse space as another tremor jarred up from below. A spider mech skittered past us, reversed abruptly, and darted off into the gloom.

"Lily, come on."

"Is it all right, Jason?" She must have been hovering back in

the shadows. Now she scurried after us, eyes wide, hands clutching
and clenching each other.

"Lilith?" David squinted, teeth chattering.

"David, she's not—"

"Please, Ruth?" She shot me a pleading look. "Can't we wait
until later for that?"

Jason didn't pause, bearing us past looming black shapes in the
dark warehouse. A faint grinding echoed beneath us. "I'll take
you all up over these storage stacks and out the cargo bay to the
landing field. Then I'll put together a fail-safe destruct on the
facility, just in case." Did his taut voice actually sound tired?
Alarmed?

I was too exhausted to care. I couldn't summon the energy to
protest when Jason laid David down and carried me up first,
clambering with superhuman agility over a tall, swaying stack of
crates.

Beneath us in the gloom, a faint lilting voice. "Oh, you poor
boy! I was so worried about you. . . ."

I closed my eyes and sighed.

"It's raining again." The clone's voice was relentlessly cheery.

I shook myself out of a blank stare at the grayness outside, the
random pattern of drops sliding down the transparent curve of the
equipment dome.

She shot me an uneasy look as she paused inside the doorway
to shake off drops, then hurried on past deactivated consoles to
the other side of the shelter, where David was linked in again with
the remotes, still trying to penetrate the communication blackout
at the facility. He and Jason had hardly rested in the days since
we'd escaped through the cargo bay, first trying to protect the
facility from the sonic bombardment, then, when the natives had
suddenly stopped the attack, working to break through the ominous
silence and the locked doors and force fields surrounding it. And
stalling urgent queries from CI. Even Lilith had been busy, pre-
empting a little nook among the equipment piles for a "comfort
zone," and bustling around with food, hot water, and clean coveralls, helping David, when he wasn't immersed in his link, sal-
vage some of the corroded equipment Jason had brought back on
a recovered flitter from his fruitless trip around the island to try
the facility's sea entrance.

Surrounded by all the urgent activity, I felt as flat and gray as
the sky pressing over the landing field. And as useless as the

blank-faced mechmen stacked against the side of the dome, waiting for reprogramming.

Beside them rested the canister containing Jay's ashes. I'd insisted Jason make another climb through the warehouse to bring him out of the facility with us, and I'd built a sad imitation of a Poindran pyre for him.

"Still no luck, David?" The Lilith clone's voice echoed across the dome. "Take a break, then, and I'll heat up some of that nutrient stew."

A mumbled reply, ". . . get this mech put back together first."

"Here then, I can hold your tools." A muffled giggle.

David's voice, louder, "Hey, Ruth, got those chips ready yet?"

I slowly picked up the tray of tiny components and data chips I'd indifferently cleaned and sorted. I followed the clone's trail of perfume. "Here."

David looked up from a prone, partially disemboweled mechman, pushing his spectacles back up on his nose. He was still too pale, even his freckles faded away into pasty white from all the time in the vat. "About time." A hint of the Casino drawl was back in his voice. "How come you get to do the easy stuff, and I had to muck through all those corroded gears?"

I shrugged and set down the tray.

His eyes flickered toward the Lilith clone and then back to me, a smile moored haphazardly beneath his big nose. "Well, you're just lucky you didn't mess up my interface, using it like that without even knowing how to operate it." The drawl thickened. "Metamorphic schist, *Auntie*, these things don't exactly grow on trees, you know."

I blinked, realized I was staring at an indicator display without really seeing it. David had stopped talking. "What?" I blinked again.

His eyes behind the lenses looked uneasy. Then he shrugged, elaborately casual. "Nothing. Hey, we're doing fine here, why don't you get some sleep?" He picked up a set of tweezers.

"Keep up the good work, David," I mumbled, turning away from the clone's stare.

Behind me, a barely audible whisper and then a hissing, "Sshh." I didn't bother wondering what they were going on about now. I moved mechanically past an active monitoring console, vaguely reflecting that David didn't seemed bothered in the least by his new helper, Lilith Number Two. "Well, it

wasn't *her* fault, was it?'' And that seemed to cover it. Maybe
it did.

I went through the motions of checking voltage readings and
switching leads from fully recharged power paks to drained ones.
Reaching the end of the row, I found myself staring into amber-
glinting eyes. I blinked and stepped hastily back.

Jason reached unhurriedly to his chest to unplug the power
lead snaking through the unsealed front seam of his coveralls.
''That should hold me for a while. I'd better get back to work.
If we don't hear anything from Siolis pretty soon, we'll have
to try a more aggressive penetration of the facility defenses. I'm
decoding CI data on parameters for that null device they gave
you.''

''I heard that!'' David poked his head up above the consoles
across the dome. ''I told you, Jason, no wiping the system. We've
got to preserve the incorporeal matrix.'' His head popped down
again.

I didn't bother protesting. I'd memorized all his arguments by
now. This incorporeal matrix was different, still open to new
directions. The spooks were alive in their own way, like the cybers
said, they used to be human and had a right to live. They had a
lot to teach us. They could help us learn to navigate the energy
plasma. They could help us communicate with the aliens. They
could possibly be purged of their destructive aspects, the paranoia
of the Poindros Founder, and wasn't it better, like Great-Aunt
Helen always said, to Heal than hate? Maybe the matrix could
teach us how to reorient the cybers' directives. Siolis had said we
didn't have the right to pull the plug. . . . And I'd used that one
on Helsa, back in Casino.

A quick touch on my shoulder. ''Ruth, why don't you get some
rest? This work can wait.'' Jason gestured to the trays of parts to
be cleaned.

I jerked away. ''Right, it's just busy-work. It doesn't matter.''

He sighed. ''That's not what I was saying. At least take a break,
then, and eat some of Lily's stew.''

''I wouldn't touch anything from her hands. That cold-blooded
monster! How you can all just—''

''Ruth, you said Jay wasn't me, and you're right. And Lily's
not Lilith. She's trying to—''

''I don't want to hear it.'' I turned away.

His hand grasped my arm and pulled me around. ''No, you've

got to listen. You can't go on like this. Give yourself a chance to heal.''

I jerked the stump of my arm defensively back.

"I don't mean that, Ruth. I mean the guilt and the blame. You just keep taking on more since Andura, since Poindros, even. You've got to let it go. It's only hurting you to hold onto this hate for Lily, this anger at me. Damn it, I'm sorry about Jay, we all are, but—''

"I should just pretend it didn't happen, like the rest of you?''

"Hear me out, Ruth, and then I'm done and I'll leave you alone. Let me say I'm sorry. Don't you think I've been damning myself for what I did? Trying to give you what I thought you needed—a flesh-and-blood lover, not some alloy excuse for a man—and everything would just add up like a perfect equation. Well, I was wrong, and I hurt you—and Jay. I can blame myself until I'm blue in the face, but it's not going to change things. I don't expect you to forgive me, especially for the way I acted like a superior ass, but I only thought it would help you turn from me to him. . . .''

He broke off, and when he spoke again, his voice had dropped to an even monotone. "Anyway, I made another mistake. In case you haven't noticed, I've made lots of them. I trusted Lilith, wanted to give her a chance. She was so devious, and it just didn't occur to me that she could fake the sort of neural damage I'd suffered in my break from incorporeal control. She was playing both sides of the fence, once she realized the options we could offer her, but all she wanted was more power.''

He shook his head. "I think she had an even more monstrous ego than Heinck's. She was always hungry for more gratification, and she loved the way she was playing with people's lives, both back in the Resistance and here on Cyvrus. She wanted to be able to keep on with it forever, and she actually thought once she'd managed to learn whatever secret she was convinced you and Siolis had, that she could master the matrix and use it to control the entire system. Which I suppose was the ultimate extension of the Founder's original delusion. And after you and Jay left—''

"Hey, that's my story! They're *my* memories.'' The clone— Lily—stalked around the consoles, jerking her chin up in imitation of Lilith's insolent little gesture. "I'll tell her, and maybe she'll get off her high tower!''

She moved in close to me, staring defiantly into my eyes. "I don't care, I'm not ashamed to be part of her, because she was smart and she tricked you all! And she never would have hurt David. But Jason thought he was so smart, and so kind to give the poor girl a chance to re . . . to re—to make it up.'' She frowned and gave her head a little shake. "Anyway, that was when I . . . Well, see, she knew you and Siolis had something she needed. I can't quite remember all the details, but it doesn't matter anyway, all that technical stuff. She tricked Jason, and it was easy, he was *so* nice, and we put him in that force-field containment where he couldn't make a fuss. No, wait, that was before she woke me up. But, anyway, she was going to come back for me, you bitch-face, and you killed her, so don't go trying to tell me how superior and wonderful and all you are, because you're no better than anyone else!'' She was shaking, fists clenched, and she almost got up the nerve to slap and claw me, but couldn't quite do it.

I just stood waiting for her to decide, didn't care much one way or the other.

"Well, anyway. That's what happened, and you can go to hell!'' She hissed it in my face and whipped around to stalk back to the other side of the dome.

And somehow watching her quivering, plump backside disappear around the side of the consoles, I made a decision. Or rather, let it make itself. The slippery images of Lilith and Lily, Jay and Jason, slid and overlapped and tumbled like colored bits in a child's kaleidoscope. The patterns kept changing as the pieces were shaken, and one didn't have any more meaning than another. All at once the hatred deflated and drained away. There was only the flat taste of ashes in my mouth. I should have been getting used to it.

I groped blindly for my stool, sitting slowly.

"I didn't mean for that to happen.'' Voice quiet.

"It's all right, Jason.'' I didn't want to look up and see Jay's eyes.

"Ruth—'' He made a startled movement beside me.

When I did look up, I saw bright amber eyes burning in a blank cyborg face.

Across the room, David gave a whoop. "Hey, I got it, too! All right.''

The sharp lights faded in Jason's eyes as he looked gravely down at me. "It's a message from Siolis, Ruth, coming through the facility channels. He says to tell you, 'No more lies.' The natives want you to join them at a bathylabra to dance with them.

Or sing, that part wasn't quite clear. Then they'll talk to us about the facility."

"I'll go instead, Ruth." David hurried over to us. "If you're not feeling so hot . . ."

I shook my head. "I'll go."

"You'd better stay here with the com-links, David. I'll take her out in the hovercraft."

David started to protest, looked at Jason, and threw up his hands, turning back to his consoles.

"But there's something we have to do on the way." I stepped past Jason, avoiding his eyes, to get the canister with Jay's ashes.

Jason didn't try to make conversation as we skimmed a meter above the sea, leaving behind the flat rocky island that was the only thing breaking the monotonous horizon. He stood at the controls, not touching them, his sober, tawny face turned toward the endless gray swells. I huddled in a poncho beside the canister, hugging my knees in the dying drizzle and trying to think of fitting words for the scattering of ashes, but I couldn't seem to come up with anything.

I just stood there, trying to swallow around the constriction in my throat, when Jason lowered the flitter to rock gently on the dark sea. The rain had stopped.

He came up beside me, quoting quietly, unemphatically, "'Ashes to ashes. Dust to dust.'" His face was rigidly blank as he pulled the canister gently from my grip and removed the cap, handing it back to me.

I closed my eyes, but they were only hot and scratchy. The tears wouldn't spill. Grasping the lip of the canister, I leaned over the rail and slowly poured the fine ash. Jason had made sure the fire burned hot. A faint breeze caught Jay's powdery distillation, spreading it in a cloud to settle over the restless surface. The sea absorbed it.

I turned mutely from the rail, and Jason brought the hovercraft up again, taking us farther over the ocean. High gray clouds, flat gray sea.

There was nothing at the surface to distinguish the place where he finally lowered us onto the swell again. I threw off the poncho, shivering in my diving suit though it wasn't really cold, and snapped the osmotic unit onto the valves Jason had reinserted at my hips. I accepted his silent assistance to adjust the big foot-fin and climb over the rail.

"Ruth." His hand on my shoulder halted me as I was about to push off. "Do you think they'd mind if I came along? It might be too much for you again." He paused. "And I'd like to see if I could communicate with them through my neural channels. It would be wonderful to experience their Way, their community of sharing, like . . ."

"The matrix link?" I finished reluctantly. "It is, in a way." I shivered again. "You miss it, is that it?"

"In a way." His hand lifted away. "The connection to something more than myself."

I shrugged uneasily, watching the opaque surface. "You can try if you want. But I don't think they'll let you in. I'm surprised they want me here."

"You don't have to go, you know—" He broke off as ripples broke the surface beside the boat.

There was a splash, a slippery bluish head surging up, then a tapered body and tail arching and crashing back into the swells. Another splash, flat tail slapping to fling spray up at me. Violet eyes, pupils narrowed to dark slits, fixed on mine, and laughter fizzed through my veins, eagerness, bright buoyancy, an impatient tugging and questioning of my slowness. A flashing glint of bright colors tumbling.

I adjusted my goggles and pushed off, dropping into the cool shiver of sea and soundings. *Bright Girl. Long has been the sighting.*

A swirling crackle of welcome brushed over me with the whisk of slippery colored plumes. She circled and was gone. I broke the surface, paddling in a circle, and four adults burst into the air around me, companion fish darting. I didn't recognize any of them.

"You willll come?"

"You willl ssssing?" Labored hissing as they encircled me.

Dread lapped up from the deeps, from memory of the dark rock maze and pulsing pain. I took a deep breath. "Yes." I glanced up at Jason leaning over the flitter rail, wishing I could send him instead, if he wanted to connect with them so badly. "But first, Jason here wanted to ask you—"

Agitated soundings broke over me. Alarm. Revulsion. Outrage. Rejection. Vague images of the blond cyborg and her killing devices. "No. Monsstrousss."

Jason pulled back from the rail, face gone perfectly blank again. "I see. I'll wait for you, Ruth."

The natives led me down in a surge of urgency and apprehension, uneasiness and—yes—groping curiosity. Violet-flushed plumed fish circled me as I followed through an undulating weed forest, over the edge of a sea mount rippling graceful fronds and lacy fans, through a shimmering school of tiny yellow and blue fish. The purple gloom deepened as we plunged down the rocky wall to the jagged black cave entrance.

Echoes of the sendings rippled ghost fingers down my spine as I followed the natives' frothing wake through the twists of rock corridors. The cold blue luminescence swelled, pulsing, glinting through scattered facets as the summons pounded and tugged, ringing louder through my bones.

I was numb, pulled inward through the maze, directions and time lost in the lapping waves of sound and sensation. I floated out into blue-limned blackness, into the quivering heart of the bathylabra, encircled by swimming shapes, yet alone.

Siolis?

A vague, comforting presence enfolded me, tugged me closer to the swelling knot of writhing, surging shapes weaving the dark echoing sea.

They surrounded me, whipping in their impossibly fast patterns, surge spinning me as slippery plumes brushed my face, crackling. The barrage of their sending song pounded at my head, my ears, but I was numb, sealed inside my echoing shell. I was surrounded, but alone, and Jay wasn't there to pull me out.

Not alone. A familiar shape, touch, taste? poured over me, elusive images glinting out of the dark. The three natives circling Jay and me at the surface, braving their taboos to talk to us, her hissing echoes, one of them, a woman soothing children frightened by sharks, the frenzied tumult of the sea as the leviathans hammered at the facility and sendings pulsed urgently, the same woman watching, feeling, in horror as the Lilith monster murdered her kindred.

A surge of grief flowed through me, echoed from her, from me as I spun down the black tunnel and the sealed doors sprang open to admit the roaring chorus of their harmony, the pounding waves of their sensations, whirling me through the glinting angles of their lattice, as my own song poured out:

> *Scarcely are you planted, scarcely sown,*
> *Scarcely has your stem taken root in the earth,*
> *When the wind blows upon you and you wither,*
> *And the tempest carries you off like stubble . . .*

Our griefs and fears and confusions flowed together in dark
purples and heavy thicknesses, and then I was surging with them
upward through shimmering violet waters, through unfolding images or reenactments of memory, through surprise and disorientation and dawning wonder as the revelation of the alien sending
and the new truths of Siolis and the landers sang through the
lattice. The strengths of the Way rooted it—*joining, sharing, no
other-lies, no self-lies*—and there was still pride and anger, the
anger now like towering waves crashing over cyber consoles, the
voices of secrets and deception, the fetters of imposed blindness
falling away.

As the roaring voices of the chorus and the whirling dance of
the lattice swirled around and through me, I was lofted higher,
up toward a sparkling, odd-shaped glinting. It was the rough,
awkward little gem of sending I'd hurled at them in the sea by
the facility, and Siolis was there, dancing around it. I touched the
prickly angles marring the smooth dimensions of the lattice, and
it burst open in an explosion of colored balloons, a humming flood
of energy racing through my circuits, a wild melody clashing with
the chorus.

Siolis joined my song, teaching me his footless dance, as we
played singleness against and then with the oneness, otherness
with sameness, ringing changes from the deep unchanging Way.
Hesitating voices, shapes, movements rose to join us, shivering
with reverberations of disruption. The disturbance shimmered and
then swirled into an effervescent echo of memory—the alien sendings frothing with delight, discovery, invitation, bearing us onward
in a bright river of joy.

Siolis beside me, I felt myself opening, fear dropping away as
we flew upward on the foaming crest of a rainbow-colored wa-
terspout, singing an answer, sending a welcome. The kindred
joined, one by one, then more as the new chorus built into a surge
that shot us up the funnel of rock to shatter in light through the
facets of a thousand crystals. The colored beams, the waves doubled and redoubled through reflecting angles, and I—we—were
the lineaments of the crystals, reshaped and humming the meaning.
Yes.

There was no time in the taut, vibrant suspension. Sea, rock,
Cyvriot, lander, all one shimmering tone.

An answer finally shattered us into a million scattering shards,
a new alien sending pulsing through the bathylabra in wild eddies.
Confusion, disruption. But now the fragments coalesced into a

flood of delight, exchange, invitation. And a baffling burst of incomprehensible information.

I was jolted out of the sendings, head pounding with the impossible barrage as I flailed in panic through the drowning dark.

Ssllowllly, Ruth. Here. And Siolis was somehow beside me, coiling his tail about me to right me, a shimmer of reassurance and the flickering image of a huge iridescent shell sheltering me in warmth, and then he was guiding me away as the natives slowly regathered their scattered group in the dark cavern.

Disoriented, I let him tug me along the twisting corridors. *They answered us! But it was too much. My head hurts. I don't understand.*

Nor do I, ssinglly. It wasn't quite words he was sending, but I knew the meanings. *Yet the kindred willl remember together, willl ssing the messsage. The ssum greater than partsss. Conssollles willl hellp, now we know new waysss.* He was nudging me gently out the dark entrance into the open sea.

The big purple eyes held mine for a moment, and a complex shimmer of emotions whispered through me as he turned back into the bathylabra. *Rejoice.*

twenty

Shadow was banished from the facility's auxiliary control cavern, lit up now by strings of optic fiber David had had the reprogrammed mechmen drape around the walls. The festooned brightness added a jarringly festive touch to the rough stone chamber with its echoing *hush, hush* of the sea. The bank of consoles no longer pulsed its danger strobe or filtered incorporeal commands, the colored indicators reconfiguring instead to the data inputs of new human controllers.

I stopped in the doorway, Tig and Rig gamboling about my feet, making their sharp whistles and leaping up to be held. I knelt to pet the wriggling balls of white fur with identical black splotches and comical stripes down their snouts, each with two black paws out of six. David had let the cloned twins out of their lab cage, and the little pests insisted on following me everywhere.

"Take it easy, RigTig." Nobody could tell which one was which.

They whistled and rushed to nip at the extensors of a spider mech mincing down the corridor with a lab beaker of steaming fluid, following it past me into the cavern.

"Ruth, I have been seeking you. Mech units require permission to transfer aquatic life-support units for modification in shuttle." Violet rolled down the corridor to me, a faded ribbon still drooping around its mechman neck.

"Fine." I shrugged. "I'll be out later."

"I will relay confirmation." Its facelights flashed. "Further instructions?"

I shook my head. Jason, trying to make me feel useful, had asked me to supervise the mechmen installing cages and tanks for the incorporeals' activated animal clones in the shuttle the mechs were modifying for shift capacity and a long intergalactic flight. The bewildering barrage of the new alien message, once the Cyvriots had imparted their group memory of it to be analyzed by the purged cyber loops, had turned out to be directions and a location. The aliens had only been waiting for a signal of receptiveness from the natives before sending an invitation and a map.

The whole thing was really a laugh at the landers' expense. Once Siolis, David, and Jason had worked out the complicated interplay of their message mediums, it had turned out that the aliens thought the Cyvriots were the only civilized life forms in our system. The Cyvriots had "true communion" while the rest of us were only "organic machines" passing coded symbols back and forth. As far as the aliens were concerned, Cyvrus with its "speaking sea" was the heart and soul of the galactic system implemented by the cybers.

Everyone else was getting a tremendous kick out of it, but I couldn't bring myself to really care. I stood in the doorway, looking in at David and Jason standing in their motionless links with the system. Somehow the young man with his unruly black hair and spectacles and an oddly dignified expression of absorption, and the tall man with the shaggy sun-streaked hair and wide cheekbones, his tawny face gravely expressionless, looked like strangers. I absently rubbed my shoulder as phantom pain throbbed dully up the missing arm.

"Excuse me! Coming through." A cheery voice behind me.

I jerked around to see Lily, in an electric-blue frilly jumpsuit she must have found in Lilith's luggage, carrying a tray of dishes, biscuits, and some kind of seaweed-looking salad.

"Now where did that spider mech go with the soup? You should try some, Ruth, I mixed different nutrient broths—it tastes better than it looks—and Violet said this kelp stuff would be good for us. I'm going to *make* David take a break. Violet, send him a message through the link that it's getting cold." She bustled importantly past me, to the alcove she'd set up with cushions in the warehouse area. I noted irrelevantly that her curves were getting plumper.

I changed my mind about going in, turning back to the corridor.

"Ruth, don't go. Siolis wants to talk to you." Jason was somehow beside me, though I hadn't seen him move.

I flinched. "Damn. I hate it when you do that."

The hint of a smile flickered over his grave face. "Sorry. But I wanted to catch you. We've been having some interesting . . . discussions with the natives through their new system links. They've really jumped on the bandwagon since they've realized how the cybernetic Plan cut them a short piece. The part they can't stand, I think, is that they were deceived, and deceiving themselves. So now they're taking pretty seriously the alien notion that they're the ones in charge. They can control the facility now, and they want to use that to bargain with CI.'' He shook his head. "They're learning fast."

"I guess so." I shrugged. "What does it have to do with me?"

"Ruth . . ." A faint sigh. Or had I really heard it? "Okay, we've already sent your message to CI telling them the anomalous signals originated outside the galaxy, so they've calmed down about the cyborg invasion threat they were afraid of. David and I have been editing memory loops to camouflage our activities here from the cybers, but now the Cyvriots insist on recognition in the system. In return, they'll maintain the world as a communication center, and share what they learn from the aliens with the rest of the system. David and I are trying to persuade them to wait until we can get back to Casino and try implementing some gradual directive changes with the cybers, if we can take what we're learning here about the matrix plasma that far. But they won't go for that. They want everything out in the open. 'No more lliess.'" He gave me a rueful smile.

I looked past him at the flickering console indicators. "Why not?" The dancing lights and the crimson activation signal on David's interface device seemed far away and not quite real. I could almost hear Helsa suggesting maybe change had to be violent. I shrugged. "Like Sam always said, we can't walk the fence forever. Let the chips fall where they may."

"Snap out of it, Ruth!" Jason's voice was surprisingly sharp. "Think it through."

I swung back on him. "Go ahead and think it through for yourself. That's what you're good at, isn't it? I'm just a fifth wheel around here."

"Only if you insist on being one—if you keep refusing to link with us and participate in the conferencing. There's a reason the natives invited you back to help them finally answer the alien message, you know. You've got a special gift, you could be an important link, with Siolis, but you keep denying it, refusing to share. You're throwing away the opportunity to join in a fantastic effort."

My chin thrust out stubbornly. "I have a right to my privacy. My free will. You're just like the cybers, or the spooks, trying to invade my mind."

"You're running again, like you ran from Poindros, ran from Andura—"

"You sent me away from Andura! You're the one who was too good for a mere mortal."

"Stop fooling yourself, Ruth. You know I sent you away because you wouldn't see what I was. You convinced yourself that I wasn't really different, that you could love me like a 'normal' man. I'm not, and I can't accept the limitations you were putting between us, putting on yourself." He stepped closer, grasping my arm. "Can't you see—" His grip tightened, sending through me an electric buzz of frustration, grief, longing, impatience, compassion, and beneath it a terrible loneliness.

I jerked away from the neural jolt. "Don't." Shaken, I stepped back from him, refusing to meet his eyes. "All right, damn it, I'll talk to Siolis." I strode past the consoles toward the dark, hissing water.

The Violet mechman cut me off. "This unit will provide voice-mode communication link through the system."

I pushed past it. "Never mind." Pulling off my boots and coverall, I plunged into the water and swam out from the bright cavern, into the echoing shadows. I dove. *Siolis?*

Welcome, reassurance, approval, excitement lapped through me, and his smooth tail coiled about my legs to buoy my face above water as the companion fish wafted about me. Other, distant, presences lapped echoes from him to me and back. Half-familiar native shapes swimming in and out of recognition. And an even more distant configuration, a vague voice filtered through Siolis to me. *Ruth. Hell on wheels! We're moving in the matrix? lattice?—now. . . .*

The words that weren't really words in a voice like David's faded as I recoiled in alarm. Siolis' soundings lapped comfortably through me. *Wait. They come.*

The other swimming shapes echoed closer, booming around the bends of the cavern entrance, sliding and surging to circle us in a submerged ring. Five adults, and—

Bright Girl. The echo was doubled, a gleaming fizz of excitement and delight, and a far, fading chuckle and grin.

The girl shot away with a last bubble of laughter, and the adults spun their soundings into merging waves lapping through me to take humming shape inside. Images, forming and reforming concepts, the whispering ghost of words, counterpointed by echoed emotions.

They wanted me to help them, help myself and the other landers at the same time. Shivering images of the facility, the labs. They wanted to continue the evolution the cybers had stalled halfway, become truly creatures of their water world and cast off the burden of air-speaking. More genetic bioforming. I shuddered reflexively, the soundings dissolving and then reforming. A question. Would I be lander-kindred? A confusing warped image of Casino, filtered through Siolis' memory. Myself as their liaison with the cybers, with other landers. Teaching. Learning. Landers and Cyvriots alike learning new Ways.

I flailed in disorientation as the images and emotions accelerated, waves cresting and crashing too fast over me. *Siolis. Why me?*

The other natives circled once more and retreated with a fading echo of waiting. I thrashed through tumbling dark images of Poindros and a scorched wheat field, ashes and accusing eyes, Fial-Li's sleek, lovely furred body lying torn beneath the towering Anduran trees, the devastating waves of Cyvriot grief as their kindred died. *No more. I can't.*

No more Iliesss, Ruth. Siolis anchored me, sliding back into focus. *Courage. Be healled.* With a rippling hiss of water, he was gone.

I crawled slowly back onto the quay, a hand reaching down to haul me up. "Hot damn, Ruth!" David's pale face was split by a wide grin. "You're gonna do it, aren't you?"

He circled around me, insistent, as I turned to pull my coveralls back on. "Just think. With me and Jason working on breaking through on directives, and you pushing for the Cyvriots, we're gonna blow the cybers wide open. You know, we're making real progress bringing the spook matrix around to be more cooperative, persuading them maybe we could purge some of the sick directives and still maintain awareness integrity. They're really open to exploration, and I think we can work with them and learn a lot."

He raised a hand as I stared, numb. "I know, I know, you don't trust them, but Siolis and the Cyvs still got a tight rein on 'em. They've already helped us, though, with the recalculations on the new alien data. I mean, we could get some real dialogues going, and that's what it's all about, right? Who knows where we'll go on information-sharing with the aliens? Too bad their double-wormhole communication only works for energy transfer, and it looks like they can't leave their world, so it'll be a real long trip using standard shift connections, but . . ."

He hesitated, pursing his lips, then reached to the back of his neck and pulled his interface device free. "Here." He held it out to me. "Just be careful with it, and you can see for yourself. I've got the data accessed, it'll explain better—"

"David!" Across the floor, Lily crossed her arms in the doorway to the warehouse. "The soup's gone stone cold, but you're just going to eat it anyway. Now hurry on up."

"Just hold onto your petticoats a blessed minute!"

"Well, I would if I had some." She flicked the trailing ends of her sash and made a perky face, turning back to her alcove in a teasing huff.

David gave me an abashed look, still offering the device. "What do you say?"

I shook myself and finally smiled, then pushed the instrument gently back at him. "Thanks. Maybe some other time."

He shrugged. "Okay. You coming for some lunch?"

"In a minute."

He straightened and sauntered after Lily.

I rubbed my face and pushed back my dripping hair, walking slowly across the cavern. Jason was absorbed in his link with the system, eyes a fixed bright amber. I took a deep breath and touched his arm. "Jason."

The amber faded into brown flecked with gold. He turned and waited, face neutral.

Another deep breath. "The arm graft you were trying to talk me into. Would you show me now?"

More expression on his face, cautious enthusiasm. "I'll take you down to the lab and show you the simulation models I worked up. Like I said, it's contraplan, so if you don't make up your mind to have it done here in the labs, the best the cybers would do for you later is a prosthesis with limited neural interfaces. It's worth thinking about."

I nodded and followed him to the anti-grav chute.

The mechmen had moved the tall cylinder into a different lab, one with a wall of electronics equipment and a long counter with a suspended dissection laser and rows of glinting instruments. It took me a few seconds to realize it was the same room where they'd amputated my arm. I stiffened and started to back for the door.

"Wait, Ruth. Nobody's jumping the gun on you, I just needed the equipment here. Give me a minute to bring things on line." Jason eased me forward and started fiddling with readouts on a wall screen.

My feet took over, moving me to the curved lucite container with its pale, suspended body.

My own dreaming face bobbed before me, the hint of a secret smile curving smooth lips. A cloud of red-glinting dark hair swirled in the wafting fluid, veiling then revealing the untouched face drifting in remote serenity. She had my features, but she didn't look a bit like me. Helen, maybe, not me.

Her face and form were a little too full, the arms and legs slender but softly rounded. This body had never known tears and sweat, had never pushed or lifted, groped or run. She just kept smiling her mindless virginal smile.

"See? I've set up a simulation to show you how we could graft the new arm below your shoulder. Ruth?"

Jason eased me around to face the animated graphics on an activated screen. "Using your earlier recovery data, the prediction is for ninety-eight plus percentage on function, maybe slightly less for sensation. It's entirely up to you. You know you'd have to spend a little time suspended in one of the healing vats, the way they had David, to make sure the interfaces formed properly, but it won't affect your awareness. I'd be monitoring to make sure. Or, if you'd rather, Siolis would monitor the system."

He plugged in a set of leads and snaked them over to me. "I want to show you just one thing more. This is what the cybers would pick up on a brain scan from you." He touched the electrodes to my scalp, and the screen blossomed with a complex, pulsing pattern. "Now I'm shunting to readouts on the clone's neural activity." There was a different pattern, a few wavering lines. "Now I'll filter out autonomic functions." The screen went blank.

"Nothing, Ruth. Unless you choose to animate it and duplicate your awareness patterns, it's only a bunch of cells. Like toenail or hair clippings."

He briskly rolled the leads up, moving away to putter among the equipment. I found myself back in front of the tube, staring at the double that looked like the perfect, seamless cyborg duplicate Heinck and the incorporeals had prepared on Andura. Toenail clippings. I shook my head.

"Will it harm it if you open the top?"

Jason turned, surprised. "Not for a short time. Why?"

"I want to touch it."

His face went neutral, but he brought over a cart, climbing onto it and closing valves. He swiveled the cylinder's cap aside and jumped down, lifting me onto the cart before I had a chance to reconsider.

I took a deep breath, suppressing a shudder as the images echoed through me for no logical reason of the Cyvriots' plan to continue their taboo bioforming. I thrust past squeamishness, reaching into the vat. The fluid was blood-warm and slippery. Drifting strands of auburn hair snaked around my hand and wrist as I reached deeper. I shivered, then flattened my palm on the smooth white forehead. Closing my eyes, I fell inward to that hidden door and yanked it open, calling out for a sending, my summons echoing back through me.

But there was nothing else. Nobody home. No spark of answering energy, no flutter of the soul's wings.

I slowly withdrew my hand and climbed down, the blank clone nodding blind against the walls of its tube. I closed my eyes. "All right, Jason. Sharpen your knives."

Somewhere there was a faint, familiar *beep beep*. I frowned, groping toward it through a thick sea of black. I was rising, thickness draining from my head as soothing washes of green pulsed over me. *Beep*.

My eyelids flickered open. Overhead, a suspended monitor chirped as it bathed me with pulses of its healing green light. I slowly turned my head against a receding tide of dizziness. It was the same room where I'd recovered from the amputation.

I jerked upright, choking myself against restraints and falling back, stars dancing. I took a deep breath and slowly turned my head to the left, willing my eyes to reopen.

I was naked on the narrow bench. Attached to my shoulder was a very pale white arm.

Gritting my teeth, I braced myself and thought about wiggling my fingers. They moved. It didn't hurt.

Shaking, I managed to loosen the restraints and sit up. The monitor lit up red, the door whisked open, and Violet rolled through.

"You must remain at rest. Optimal recovery period is not yet—"

"Shut up and go away."

It did. Things were definitely looking up. I blinked as the door shut behind the mechman, swinging my legs over the padded bench and numbly flexing and lowering my arm, making a fist and loosening it. It wasn't until I placed my two arms side by side and saw the difference—the pale, sinewy right arm with the creases at the elbow, and the absolutely white left arm with its baby-fine

skin and rounded soft contours—that I could convince myself I
hadn't dreamed the whole thing.

I jumped to my feet, filled with restless energy, almost tasting
the springy sap of the energizing green rays coursing through my
arteries. I noticed a long locker with door ajar and pulled it open.
The inside of the metal door had been buffed—by whom?—until
it shone mirror-bright. I reached for the clean coveralls hanging
inside and stopped as my reflection caught me.

Leaning closer, I peered into a face pale but not gaunt with
strain, green eyes gleaming with recovered health, cheeks flushed
a faint rose. I lifted my hand quickly to my cheek, fingers tracing
the thin ritual scar that still tracked it. An absurd rush of relief
poured through me.

I shook my head. He'd thought of everything.

I pulled on the clothes in the locker and turned for the door. I
didn't know how long I'd been out of it. There were still a lot of
questions to face. But the heavy weight of numbness had been
lifted from me, as if a physical barrier I'd been unaware of pushing
against was gone.

Even the strong spring in my legs as I strode down the facility
corridors, and the way the circles of light popped into being just
ahead of me, were imbued with a special magic. Even if it was
only the effect of the healing treatment, it felt damn fine just to
be alive.

The upward plunge of the anti-grav chute sent a sensual tickle
through my solar plexus. I hurried on toward the cavern, triggering
the door and calling, "Anybody home around here?"

They were working at the bank of consoles again. Jason turned,
his eyes sparking a quick flash of amber and then going gold-
brown as he smiled.

Colored lights washed over David's pale face as he swung
around. "Hey, Auntie, looking good!" He whistled and grinned.

I smiled back, then blinked. "What happened to your spectacles, Da—"

"Don't need 'em anymore." David's voice came from the other
side of the cavern, behind me. "I figured, well schist if I'm going
for it, might as well get the full treatment with lens implants."

I whirled to face the voice and saw David shrug uneasily. Except
it wasn't David. Or maybe it was, clearing his throat as he shot
a quick glance past me at Jason. Or at David, beside Jason?
Another David.

I backed for the door, shaking my head, the buoyant well-being draining away in a cold flood of denial. "No. I'm going to go out and come back in, and this won't have happened. It's not real."

Jason crossed the floor in quick strides to catch my arm. "I was going to tell you before you came down. We didn't think you'd be up so soon."

I could only stare dismayed at David, then his clone. Or was it the other way around?

One of them chewed his lip and the other one blurted out, "Look, Ruth, it's no big deal. See, Siolis decided he'd accept the alien invitation for contact—why should we just send animals?—and we've already got the shuttle refitted with a purged matrix subsystem. But it's gonna be one real long trip, since we do have to use standard shifts, and I mean a lot of them. Anyway, I knew you'd scream bloody hell if I said I was going, since you kind of need me around, and I didn't want to miss out on going for CI's directives with Jason, and abandon the Resistance and all. Well, I couldn't make up my mind, so—"

"So," the other one cut in, "I said why beat my brains out over it? I'll do both."

They both shrugged. "So no problem." The first one glared at the other one.

I fought an hysterical urge to howl. "David . . . damn it, which of you is the real David?"

"I am."

"I am." Each pointed at himself.

"Jason, they can't be serious . . . ."

He nodded slowly.

"Well, don't get your petticoats all in a bunch, if you'd just stop and think about it—"

"I've gotta go with Siolis. It's an incredible chance for a face-to-face contact, see we're not sure just what kind of critter they are, and—"

"Now wait just a suvving minute!" the other David yelled. "I'm the real one, and I'm the one who's going."

"No way. You wouldn't even be around if it wasn't for me, and I'm going."

The two pale, skinny kids with the wiry snarls of dark hair glared at each other, then started shouting simultaneously.

"Liar!"

"Get me a break, you—"

"If you think I'm gonna—"

"Stop it!" I sprang at the nearest one, yanking his pullover up to reveal pale, untracked belly.

"Hey, hands off!" He batted at me.

"No scar from the pardil attack on Poindros." I pointed. "This one's the clone."

"Wait a blasted minute!" The other one pulled open the front of his baggy coveralls and pointed to smooth, white skin. "See, they healed me in that vat."

"No way! I'm the real one, you ungrateful—" The one in the pullover yanked himself free of me and flung himself on his twin, pummelling.

Jason pried their thrashing limbs apart. "There's one way to settle this." He produced a glittering credit chip from somewhere and tossed it spinning high into the air. "Heads or tails?" He caught it, concealing it in his hands. "Heads goes with Siolis, tails goes with Ruth."

"Sacred bloody Founder . . ." I turned my back on them, stalking away, only to be brought up short by the Lily clone, hurrying out of her alcove in the warehouse.

"Ruth, I'm sure glad you're better. How about letting bygones be bygones?" She smiled, dimpling. "You know, I've decided to go with them. Siolis says it's okay, though those two boys can't stop fighting over which one's going with me. But I think it would be best for everyone, don't you think?"

I could only reel wordlessly past her, over to the edge of the quay, to stare at the dark, light-mirroring water shushing against the rock. I sat abruptly, pulling off my boots to dangle my feet in the soothing sea. I closed my eyes, muttering, "Oh, yes, damn fine. Everything's just fine. . . ."

A slippery plume shivered across my foot. Converging ripples, and Siolis' streaming head surfaced in front of me, his uncomfortably angled purple eyes holding mine. He bobbed higher, hissing, "Iss welll, Ruth."

He rolled slowly under, his long, sinuous tail coiling around my ankles. The door inside me sprang open and I was leaping with him in the waves, swimming free into sparkling, violet-tinged depths.

David musst make his own choicesss now.

I nodded numbly.

Gllad tidingsss, Ruth. Cyberss willl conssider changess to our Pllan. New contingenciess make new Waysss. A liquid, echoing laugh.

It's a start, Siolis. I'm glad.

You willl hellp? Images, sensations of myself mediating with CI, with other landers.

A voiceless sigh, and assent. *Why do I keep feeling like . . .* I formed the image of a rug being pulled out from under me.

Another bubbling chuckle. *Isss Hisstory happening again. We willl pllunge eyess open now?*

Frothing colors bubbling around us as Siolis leapt with me in a bright fantasy sea garden of rock spires and rainbow gems and vivid green plumes, sun sparkling through crystal-clear depths. Dancing the gladness. He leaped higher, deeper.

I floundered in his swift, frothing wake. *But what about you, Siolis? Don't you mind becoming an exile from your world again?*

A warm caress, a knowing, joyful intimacy closer than the flesh had given Jay and me, as the hissing laughter of the amber-eyed Serpent danced its head-to-tail spin around me. *I am ollld man, Ruth, I have found what I wass ssseeking.*

And as I reeled with one more jarring dislocation—Siolis old?—the chuckling flow gently subsided in a last caress. *Good faring, Ruth. Time, for me, for one llassst adventure.*

twenty-one

It was raining. Drops splatted and trailed down the transparent curve of the equipment dome. The amber-lit numerals on one of the consoles melted down the count, oblivious. Seventeen minutes. Sixteen.

I pulled another card from the Knights in Tarot deck, ignoring the lighted console numerals, ignoring the echoing silence of the dome, flipping the card over. A blindfolded woman beside the sea, holding crossed daggers. I sighed and laid it on the solitaire pattern, above the key cards at the center—The Universe, a naked figure dancing within a spiral of stars, and The Twins again, caught on the whirl of fate's gaming wheel. Already aligned on the right were the Magician robed in blue in a shadowy green bower, holding his staff twined with snakes, and the Fool, young innocent in bright colors setting out smiling on a perilous journey. To the left, only the Sun Knight, clad in burnished armor and bending with an oddly gentle smile to pet a fierce creature that looked like a pardil. At the bottom, the forbidding cold stare of the Ebony Knight.

Despite myself, my eyes flickered to the countdown again. Fourteen minutes. I shifted to put it out of my line of sight.

Another card. The Hanged Man, eyes turned inward. My hand tightened on the thick, slippery card, then I laid it on the top row, between the blindfolded woman and the crimson heart pierced by daggers in the rain. My fingers started to grip the next card, then instead I pulled the card at the base of the deck.

I blinked quickly, staring down at the card as it warmed in my hand. I hadn't forgotten the Empress of Flowers, radiantly enthroned in a field of ripe grasses, her lovely heart-shaped face with the enigmatic smile that could have been painted from Helen's, the scepter tipped with a heart sharp as a knife. I slowly smiled and laid it at the base of the pattern, counter to the grim Ebony Knight.

Then I shook my head and started to lean forward to scramble the pattern. There was only one vacancy, beside the Sun Knight, and I was tired of the game. As my pale, baby-soft left hand reached out to rake the cards, it checked and pulled back. Instead, I fanned the deck and plucked a card at random.

The Rogue grinned up at me, slender figure in green posed rakishly with one booted foot on the coils of a winged serpent. The wild card.

Damn. I threw it down, hastily sweeping the pattern aside. Shrill whistles pierced the dome and two squirming balls of black and white fur shot across the floor, leaping onto me in a frenzy of excitement, scattering the cards.

"Rig! Tig! Down." They writhed and shook drops and one jumped up to lick my face, then they were off again out the door. Nine minutes.

I sighed and strode out into the rain, over the slippery rocks to the edge of the featureless gray sea. Jason and David looked up from their wet stones and stood, and we all silently turned to look back. The low ceiling of dark cloud hid the tops of the shuttles. There was a muffled echo as the acceleration tube sealed its clamps around the more distant of the ships, the one modified and outfitted for an extended voyage. Then a shaking hum and a thin, sucking squeal of air as the anti-grav thrusters suddenly flung the narrow shuttle through the clouds.

A vacuum, sensation suspended. And then the delayed clap of shattering sound waves. Ringing echoes slowly subsided into the soft hiss of the swell against the rocks.

David—or the clone?—finally lowered his face, still looking naked without the thick lenses. He gnawed chapped lips, hunching his gangling height in his poncho and shrugging. "Just patched in to the remote com center. All systems go." He cast one more envious look up at the rent in the clouds and moved off down the shore, kicking rocks.

I shivered in the damp, looking after him. "Damn! How is he going to handle this? For that matter, how is *he*?" I jabbed a finger upward. "Whoever's who."

"Does it really matter?" Jason kept his careful distance. "David will do fine, he's got a lot of resilience. All of this is only part of what you and the rest of the Resistance have set in motion, Ruth. Natural change. You can't stop it now."

He didn't say it, but I could almost hear it—I was just another fearful Poindran. I couldn't help snapping, "All right, then tell me where we're going to set the limits. If we don't have something to go by, we'll all end up like Lilith, grabbing whatever we can get. I don't know if David had the right to do this to himself—

his other self—but I know damn well you didn't have the right to experiment with Jay and me! I don't care what you say, all of this *isn't* natural.''

Jason whirled around in a startling blur. ''Damn it, Ruth, how long are you going to keep pounding us both? So what if we're not natural or normal, as long as we love each other? Why do you have to put new Rules on us? Why can't you open up? Tell me that!'' His shout ringing painfully in my ears, he swung around again, flinging his hand in a fist and pounding it furiously against a thick boulder. The stone shattered into pieces, sharp shards flying.

I jerked back, shocked out of my surly gloom.

Jason stood frozen, staring at his hand. The perfectly controlled cybernetic hand that had just struck out in unreasoning anger. The hand that had been unable to harm Heinck, even in defense of Fial-Li or me or himself. He'd told me on Andura that he was no longer capable of those primal animal reflexes.

I shook my head numbly. Leave it to me to drive even a cyborg around the bend.

Suddenly it was too much. I stumbled backward, slipping on the wet rocks and sitting splashing in the shallow surge, howling with laughter.

His hand on my shoulder shook me gently, a faint warm tingle ghosting through me. I looked up and he was shaking his head, bewildered and apologetic. ''Ruth, I . . .'' His troubled eyes found mine. ''I don't know if this is good or bad.'' He looked down at his hand again, flexing it. Then he raised his eyes with his fleeting, self-deprecating grin, tilting his chin toward David and saying quietly, ''Maybe we're *all* 'fearfully and wonderfully made.' ''

I looked over at David scuffling back toward us, then at Jason. I took a deep breath, steeled myself, and reached out a hesitant sending as I'd touched my lifeless clone in the vat. At first, I felt only the bulk of inorganic machinery and cybernetics. But no, there was something else. A close packing of brilliant energy, a strange and daunting shape—a glittering diamond instead of the softly shimmering web around Siolis or David. A person could hurt herself on those sharp edges. But I'd survived worse.

A wave slapped against me, whispering diffuse echoes from a sea-sending, a faint doubling of the images of Siolis and David launching blind and fearless into the abyss. I finally stopped trying to make it all add up.

The shuttle was gone, racing out past the galaxy, rushing into the embrace of distant stars. We were here, in the drizzle between flat gray sky and flat gray sea.

I managed to smile and meet Jason's eyes. "Guess nobody promised it was going to be easy without Rules." I held up my new hand to him.

He pulled me up and wrapped his arms suddenly tightly, almost painfully, around me. I caught a quick breath as the spicy scent of his skin enfolded me, the simulation of his heart beating fast against my ear. I pressed back against him, eyes stinging. The doors flung open in a surge of velvet darkness and fire, silent words tumbling too fast, whirling us past the need of them.

"You two are totally disgusting." The careful Casino drawl, not quite convincing. David swatted half-heartedly as Jason turned to pull him into a hug. "Hey, wait a minute, hands off—"

I dragged him closer as we all three stumbled, laughing, over the slippery rocks, Jason catching us short of a fall and David's arm slipping around me as we pulled him into our little huddle of warmth in the rain.

ABOUT THE AUTHOR

A former nuclear reactor control operator, Sara Stamey has taught Scuba in the Caribbean and Mediterranean. Back in her native Northwest, she is currently teaching writing at Western Washington University, while completing a near-future novel set in the Greek islands.

THE FINEST THE UNIVERSE HAS TO OFFER